No Bars and a Dead Battery

The Summer 2018

Owl Canyon Press
Short Story Hackathon
Contest Winners

No Bars and a Dead Battery

The Summer 2018

Owl Canyon Press
Short Story Hackathon
Contest Winners

Compiled and edited

by GENE HAYWORTH

With an Introduction by Tom Strelich

Owl Canyon Press
Boulder, Colorado 2018

First Edition, 2018

All Rights Reserved

Library of Congress Cataloging-in-Publication Data

No Bars and a Dead Battery —1st ed.

p. cm.

ISBN: 978-0-9985073-5-4

2018911718

Owl Canyon Press

Boulder, Colorado

CONTENTS

CONTENTS (CONT.)

INTRODUCTION

It's official, there are some truly talented, uniquely creative, and simply great writers out there: from quirky space alien abductions that end with a BBQ, to a road trip with three women I can't possibly summarize, to surprise sisters and their epically truth-challenged father, to a strangely self-aware and insightful sex robot, to a parallel universe full of chainsaw slashers in the Berkshires, to a heartbreaking Dystopian odyssey through New Mexico, to a school headmaster hiding in the trunk of a car, and beyond, and *beyond* beyond.

While all of the stories you're about to read are wonderfully singular, and wildly different from one another, you'll notice that all of them begin with the exact same opening paragraph, and that they all end with the exact same closing paragraph. What you'll find simply astounding is that such an explosive variety of short stories could be spawned from the same opening and closing paragraphs. That was the challenge presented by the Owl Canyon Press Short Story Hackathon.

They wanted to provide a first and last paragraph since that's something a writer can actually work with, in contrast to a theme or a topic which generally either causes a writer to freeze up or results in the writer hammering and otherwise contorting an existing short story such that it conforms to the topic or theme. They wanted something more dynamic and fresh that would get the writers' creative juices flowing and get them to create something completely new from scratch.

They wanted the stories to be 50 paragraphs, including the opening and closing paragraphs because they didn't want novellas, and they wanted each paragraph to be at least 40 words because they didn't want flash fiction either: i.e., they wanted short stories.

In the pages that follow, I think that you'll experience 26 examples of wondrous, exhilarating, and moving creativity and that you'll also see proof that the creative spark has not been extinguished by smart phones, IM, and the Internet, but is actually alive and well as evidenced by the great stores that await you.

Tom Strelich
Author, *Dog Logic*

THE BIGGEST SALMON BARBECUE IN THE GALAXY

David Greenson

No coverage, not even one bar, the battery was dead anyway. It was still daytime, but there was an overcast and the sky had a perfectly even dullness, so there was no way to tell what time of day it was, much less which direction was north or south or anything else for that matter. A two-lane blacktop road snaked up into the distance and disappeared into some trees, or a forest if you wanted to get technical about it. It also snaked down toward some lumpy hills and disappeared there as well. What sounded like a two-stroke chainsaw could be heard in the distance, but it was impossible to tell whether it was up in the forest or down in the lumpy hills. This had been happening more often lately. Two different ways to go, with a dead battery and no bars, and nobody left to blame.

Zak had never been inclined to go uphill if he could avoid it, so he started walking toward the lumpy hills. The landscape was boring, so he walked with his eyes downcast, watching his Jordans as they shuffled along the road's shoulder, kicking pebbles and dust as they went.

There was no point in beating himself up about it, he said to himself for the fourth or fifth time. The aliens' last question had stumped him, like most of their questions had, like everything seemed to these days. Where did he want to be dropped off? If he hadn't been overthinking it he would have just given them his address. But the thought of his tiny studio made him feel sad, with its futon sofa that didn't fold up all the way anymore and the chipped Formica coffee table with last week's pizza box on it. He had been tempted to give them Ashley's address on the Upper West Side, but he knew she was still pissed at him and might not let him in, and he didn't think he could deal with that right now. The only other place that had come to mind was his parents' place in West Orange, but he hadn't been back since the funerals and the idea of going there made him shudder. So he'd told them to just drop him wherever. By which he obviously meant anyplace in Manhattan. But that implied preference hadn't been obvious to the aliens, which he should've anticipated after spending a week with them. They were a literal bunch. So they had dropped him here, wherever the fuck this was.

He'd never really gotten comfortable talking to the aliens, but most of that was on him. They'd certainly tried to put him at ease. Assuming the form of Grama Jean, for example, that was a thoughtful gesture. He didn't know how they knew she had been his favorite, but they were super smart about things like that. And they had her appearance down perfectly, from the thin fuzz on her upper lip to the pink housedress. The problem was that Zak never saw an alien alone. There were always at least two of them in the room with him at a time, and sometimes more. No matter how soothing he found Grama Jean's wry smile, five of her smiling at him was just weird. Also, they gave her a bland Midwestern accent, nothing like the nasal Brooklyn twang he remembered. Who knows why.

Still, you had to appreciate the effort, assuming a familiar form, instead of showing up in whatever their whacked-out natural shape must have been, probably a mass of tentacles or spidery legs or something. They customized their look for everyone they'd taken up to the ship. At mealtimes, when the humans were all together, he learned that everyone got someone special. Grandparents were especially popular, as were elementary school teachers, along with a few public figures like Mr. Rogers and Oprah. This one dude kept not wanting to share until he finally admitted he got Olaf, the snowman from Frozen.

He imagined telling the whole story to Ashley, and her laughing and punching him in the arm and saying *"for real?"* Zak found it comforting to conjure up these fantasies of Ashley being into him again, but they never lasted more than a few seconds before her face shifted and was filled with icy rage, just like it had the last time they'd FaceTimed. He'd been telling her that he thought they should see other people and she hadn't liked that. Her eyes had narrowed and her mouth had puckered and she had told him to fuck off. It had been a stupid move, he knew that now. That was pretty much his only takeaway from the whole abduction thing. It had been at least ten days since he'd spoken to Ashley, and it was almost certainly too late to turn things around with her and get her to forgive him or even talk to him again. He wouldn't know for sure until he got a signal and at least a few percent on his battery.

He had been walking for some minutes now—it might have been five, it might have been fifteen, he wasn't really keeping track—and it was clear that the sound of the chainsaw was getting louder. He wasn't sure whether this was a good sign or not. Whoever was handling the chainsaw could tell him where he was and which direction he should be heading in, and they might let him charge his phone. On the other hand, everybody knows that these country backwater places are full of psycho-killers, so they might dice Zak up into little pieces. There would be some relief in that, just being done with it all. He kept walking in the same direction.

Before he reached the first hill, he noticed a streak of deep blue beneath the sky, and realized that he was near a large lake or maybe the ocean. He remembered a driving trip with his parents from when he was a kid, up the coast all the way to Maine. His mom kept pestering him to look around the whole time, but he'd preferred to watch stuff on his tablet. She'd kept poking at him until he'd lifted his head up and looked around—okay, okay, see I'm looking, it's great, beautiful, yay—and then he'd gotten back to what he was watching until the next time. But then there was this one time when he'd finally looked up, irritated and tired, and there was the ocean, vast and churning and alive, and it really had been beautiful. He must have stared at it for a whole minute or maybe two. And when he'd gone back to watching videos, he'd felt this warmth in his chest that had lasted through two or three of them.

After another period of time, about ten minutes he was pretty sure this time, he rounded a corner and came upon a large single-story house with brown siding and a sloped roof. Just beyond it was an acre-sized garden and a red Prius in the driveway. In the front yard of the house was a tall hedge, and in front of that was a man with his back to Zak. He was holding a hedge trimmer. That seemed less intimidating than a chainsaw, but Zak figured you could still do some serious damage to a person with it.

As he got closer, he realized that he recognized the man. It was the old guy from the ship, the one with the bushy beard and the thinning hair. They hadn't talked much. He remembered that the aliens took the form of Barack Obama for this guy. The guy thought this was very funny. He'd tried to joke with his aliens about it, something about how the birthers weren't ambitious enough in alleging Obama was from Kenya when he actually was from another part of the galaxy. Apparently, not one of the aliens got the joke. None of the humans gathered at lunch laughed either.

When Zak was close enough, he called out to the man, who turned around and immediately recognized him too. He gave a little shout of excitement and walked right up to Zak. He went to shake his hand, but he could see Zak eyeing the hedge trimmer, so he put it down on the ground first, and somehow that two second delay allowed even more enthusiasm to bubble up so that instead of just shaking Zak's hand, he pulled him into a hug. And not just a manly slap-on–the-back hug, but a full-on lingering hug, the kind that Ashley used to insist on. When Zak would try to step back, she'd always hold onto him harder, until he had to relax and let it happen. The old guy wasn't so persistent. As soon as he

No Bars and a Dead Battery

felt Zak start to pull away, he let him go. The old guy wanted to know what Zak was doing here. Zak wanted to know where here was. The old guy told him that they were about five miles north of Clovus. Zak wanted to know where the fuck that was. The old guy laughed and told Zak that Clovus was in Mendocino County. Zak just looked at him without expression. The old guy added that San Francisco was about three hours away. Zak realized he was in California. Unbelievable.

The old guy kept laughing and smiling. He told Zak that this was where he lived, gesturing at the brown house. Then he corrected himself: he didn't live there anymore. He was leaving today—for good. He was very excited about it. He asked again what Zak was doing here, shaking his head in disbelief. Zak didn't know how someone who had been through what they'd been through could still be so surprised.

Zak explained what had happened, how he just assumed the aliens would drop him somewhere in the city, which was after all where they had picked him up in the first place. The old guy smiled and shook his head. He told Zak that the aliens weren't good at reading between the lines, as if Zak didn't already know that. The old guy wondered aloud why the aliens had dropped Zak off so close to the old guy's house. Zak thought about it for a moment and was about to say that it was probably to save fuel for their journey home. No point in making a whole separate trip since they thought he didn't care one way or the other. But before he could say anything, the old guy's eyes brightened and he put his hand on Zak's shoulder. It was a sign, the old guy told him. The aliens must have realized that they were supposed to find each other and do something important together.

The old guy was obviously one of the people who believed the aliens were here to help us in some way. Everyone on the ship loved to speculate about what the aliens were up to, why a few hundred human beings had been brought onboard, and so on. It was the most popular topic of conversation at mealtimes. Three dominant theories emerged.

ιe first, popular with the geekier people on board, was that the aliens were simply curious. Maybe they were scientists, and were gathering data about intelligent life all around the galaxy. This was the sanest theory, in Zak's opinion, although he thought all of them were pretty lacking. The second theory, popular with the more paranoid, was that the aliens were malicious. This was an advanced reconnaissance mission, preparing the way for the full-scale invasion to follow. Given the aliens' technological advantage, it didn't seem to Zak that they needed to do any careful preparation to kick our asses. Plus, they just seemed too nice for that to be their ultimate aim. Then again, who knew. Sometimes nice people could turn out to be assholes. The third theory, popular with all the woo-woo types, was that the aliens were here to help us, to give us some new tool or scientific insight so we could reach our full evolutionary potential. These people tended to think that this wasn't the first time the aliens had visited, and that they were probably responsible for the discovery of fire and the building of the pyramids and penicillin and the Internet and pretty much everything impressive that human beings had ever done.

Zak had learned that it was pointless to argue with anyone wedded to a particular theory, but especially the woo-woo people. So he just nodded his head when the old guy said they were fated to meet again. They just stood there for a moment until Zak finally asked if he could charge his phone. The old guy said sure, and he led Zak to the house. The entryway had one of those tall pieces of furniture that had a mirror on it and lots of hooks, similar to the one that Grama Jean used to have. What had she called it? A hall tree. Hang up your coat on the hall tree and stay awhile, Zak baby, she used to say. Beyond the entryway of the old guy's house, Zak could see a living room with a big sofa on it, and beyond that a kitchen with three stools at the counter. Despite the furniture, the house felt empty.

Zak plugged in his phone, but it was so dead that nothing happened. It had been unresponsive for almost week and Zak wasn't sure how long it

No Bars and a Dead Battery

would need to charge before he could start it up. He felt irritated but also relieved. A short delay until he confirmed that Ashley was lost to him forever. He found himself staring at the phone's blank screen because he wasn't sure what else to do. The old guy kept looking at him. The old guy repeated that he was leaving this place. He had an appointment in town, and then was headed south. Zak was welcome to stay in the house, but there wasn't much in the fridge, just some beer and condiments. The old guy told Zak he should come with him instead.

Zak imagined what it would be like to stay on in the house, once he confirmed that he and Ashley were through. Maybe he could grow his own food. His dad had been a big gardener when Zak was growing up, and had tried to get Zak to join him, but Zak had never liked getting his hands dirty. Maybe he wouldn't mind so much now.

The old guy told Zak to think it over, and then walked back outside and fired up the hedge trimmer again. He started shaving the hedge in front of the house. Zak wandered out after him. Now that Zak took a closer look, he could see that the hedge was formed into a crude shape, with what looked like legs and a tail. The old guy was working on the other end now, trying to make some kind of head. After a few final strokes, he shut the machine down. Zak asked the old guy if it was supposed to be a horse. The old guy said a dog. A dog named Jerry. The old guy explained that he had buried him here fifteen years before and planted this bush on top of him. He always wanted to turn it into a sculpture that paid tribute to him, but his ex had protested that it would look stupid. The old guy walked all the way around the hedge and admitted that she had been right. It was a pretty shitty likeness. But it felt wrong to leave without giving it a go.

A crow flew past them and landed on the edge of the roof of the house. They both stood there, watching the crow watching them. After a moment, the old guy began to look around, scanning the sky. Zak wasn't sure what he was looking for, but found himself doing the same. After a few minutes, the guy shook his head. He announced that it was time to get going. He told Zak that he should come, too. This house doesn't have good energy. Whatever, Zak said. He got his phone and followed the man to the Prius.

The old guy backed it down the drive and out onto the road. Zak opened up the center console and found a USB port to plug his phone into. The car's radio was tuned to some country station. A song came on and the old guy got excited and turned it up. He started singing along. Something about the rivers all running dry and the stars falling from the sky. He must have noticed something in the way Zak was looking at him. Didn't he like Hank Williams, the old guy wanted to know. Whatever, Zak said. After they'd been driving for less than a minute, they came out of a turn and there was the ocean, stretching from one end of the horizon to the other. It looked boundless and fierce and cold. But comforting somehow at the same time.

The old guy wanted to talk. About the ship and the aliens and what it had been like to be up there for the last week. He had particularly liked the food. Wasn't it strange that the aliens could be so awkward when it came to conversation, but they could make the best Fettuccine Alfredo he'd ever had? Zak shrugged. He hadn't been as impressed, but then maybe it was because he only tried the gluten-free pasta—Ashley had suggested it might help with his depression—and that had tasted just as shitty on the ship as it did on earth.

The old guy wanted to know what Zak's take was on why the aliens had chosen them, out of all the people on the planet. Zak shrugged that he didn't know, and hoped the old guy would move on to another topic. This was another one of the things that people on the ship had loved to argue about, on and on. The geeks thought that the humans chosen were a random sampling, and each of them was there just by pure chance. The paranoid and woo-woo people both thought the aliens had deliberately picked them out because they were strong and courageous people.

No Bars and a Dead Battery

Because of course those are the ones you want to focus on defeating, if you are going for world domination, or helping, if you are ushering in an age of rebirth. Zak couldn't believe how narcissistic people could be. He kept nodding his head at the old guy, even though he wasn't really listening to him. Finally, he couldn't help it. He told the old guy that they were picked because they were losers. The old guy looked at him with a confused expression. Zak elaborated. Nobody was going to notice they were gone. Nobody was going to listen to them when they got back. The old guy started to argue, but then he got very quiet. After awhile he told Zak that he needed to work on his self esteem. Zak regretted saying anything.

They arrived in the town of Clovus, but town was a bit of an overstatement. It was a post office, one restaurant, and a car repair garage. The old guy seemed to forget about the conversation when they got there, and his eyes sparkled again as he pulled through the outer door of the garage and honked his horn. It was the kind of thing Zak's dad used to do. He loved to honk his horn in every situation other than what it was designed for—when there was danger. He honked hello at people. He honked whenever he went through a tunnel. It had been so annoying.

There was another opening at the back of the garage, which led out to a back lot, and a man emerged through it. He was wearing coveralls and wiping his hands on a rag. He smiled at the old guy and greeted him. He called the old guy Jeremiah. Zak realized that in all that time on the ship he'd never asked the old guy his name. The garage guy and the old guy started haggling over a car the old guy wanted to buy. The garage guy wasn't offering much for the Prius as a trade-in. In the end, the old guy called the garage guy a greedy motherfucker, but he said it with a hint of affection. Then he agreed to the price and shook the garage guy's hand.

The old guy opened up the glove compartment and pulled out a pack of gum, a tire pressure gauge, and a little pad of lined yellow paper. Zak could see a list on it. At the top of the list was "carve Jerry monument" and then "buy car." Then there was something about salmon. Zak didn't have time to see anything else before the old guy had tucked the pad under his arm and climbed out of the car, putting the gum and gauge into his pocket as he stood up. He circled around to the hatch and got out some luggage and then disappeared into the office with the garage guy. Zak figured he should get out of the car.

He found a plug along the wall and started charging his phone again. Maybe once he got the bad news he could get a job working here. He didn't know anything about cars, and it was hard to imagine that the garage guy would be eager to teach him. But he seemed like a no- bullshit kind of guy, somebody that Zak wouldn't mind being around. He stood there for some minutes thinking about it, he wasn't sure how long, maybe ten or fifteen minutes. At some point, the old guy must have come out of the office, because the next thing Zak knew, he was driving a giant powder blue old-timey car through the rear door to the garage, leaning on the horn. It was the loudest car horn Zak had ever heard. The old guy stopped the car inside the garage and got out to put his bags in the trunk. Then he got back into the car and he looked at Zak with a questioning expression. Zak came around to the passenger's side of the car and looked in. The old guy asked him what he was going to do next. Zak admitted he didn't know. Maybe get a bus to San Francisco. Maybe get a bite to eat at the restaurant. The old man shook his head. He told Zak that he didn't want to eat there, that the food was terrible. He told Zak that there was no bus from here. He suggested that Zak could get good food and a bus in Fort Bragg, about thirty miles down the coast. Zak had to admit that this was a better plan. He unplugged his phone and got into the car.

The old guy reached up and yanked on a latch above the windshield on both his side and Zak's side, and then flipped a switch on the dashboard and the top of the car started to pull away and fold up. Once it was settled, he pulled back onto the road and started driving down the coast.

No Bars and a Dead Battery

The Pacific Ocean gleamed and swelled, and the salty air swirled around them. Zak looked for a place to plug in his phone, but couldn't find one. The old guy saw him fumbling around. This is an analog car, the old guy said, chuckling. He thought he was so clever. Fuck, said Zak. The old guy told him not to worry. He said they could pick up a cigarette lighter converter thing from a service station along the way.

Zak asked him why he was so hot on this particular car. Was it considered a sweet ride when he was a kid or something? The old guy gave him a funny look. This is a 1955 Cadillac El Dorado, he told Zak, as if that was some kind of answer. The old guy asked Zak how old he thought he was. Zak said he had no clue. The old guy looked vaguely hurt. He was forty-eight. It was just a classic car, that's all. A thing of beauty. He'd been admiring it for months, ever since the garage guy had restored it. It was still available because the price was crazy. You could get a car like this for less if you looked around. Zak asked why he hadn't looked around then. The old guy grinned and said carpe diem. Then he started to explain what it meant, but Zak told him that he knew what it meant.

In order to change the subject, he asked the old guy what his plan was. Bucket list, the old guy said. What a cliché, Zak thought. But he didn't say anything. The old guy felt the alien abduction was just the kick in the ass he needed. He decided he was going to leave his old life behind, his house and all the things it reminded him of, and he was going to drive down to Peru. He was going to Machu Picchu. He was going to see the Amazon. A lot of the woo-woo people on the ship had talked about doing things like this. Going to more primitive places, connecting with indigenous peoples.

Zak thought such plans were pathetic, but he perked up a little at the mention of South America. He wanted to know whether the old guy was thinking of going through Ecuador. What about the Galapagos, he wanted to know. Zak had read The Origin of Species the summer before.

It was one of the few things he took from his parents' house after they died. He meant to have it as a keepsake, but then one day he had started to read it, and he was shocked by how good it was. He'd read the whole thing over the course of a weekend.

The old guy nodded. The Galapagos were a great idea. Zak listened to the rest of the old guy's plan, which included Brazil and Uruguay and eating a lot of meat. It continued to sound lame for a while, but by the end Zak had to admit it sounded pretty good. Better than his plan at least. Since he didn't really have one.

They passed through a town and there was a Shell station on the edge of it, with a little convenience store just beyond the pumps. Zak reminded the old guy to stop. Inside, there was a young woman behind the counter. She had a silver pyramid jutting out under her nose, some wide gauges in her ears, and ink up to the base of her neck. There was a display of cables and cases and portable chargers at the head of one of the aisles. Zak found a cigarette lighter converter and brought it up to the front. The old guy was trying to talk to the tatted-up girl. Was the venison jerky any good, he wanted to know. There was a jar of it by the register. She just kept looking at him indifferently, barely glancing up from her phone. Finally the old guy gave up. He asked Zak if he wanted any, and Zak shook his head no, so the old guy just bought one stick.

It made sense to fill up while they were stopped, so the old guy pulled the car up to the pump. He chewed on his jerky. They both leaned against the car, waiting for the tank to fill, and looked out at the ocean on the horizon. A crow flew past them and landed on the edge of the roof of the convenience store. They watched it for a moment. Then the old guy started looking around, just like he had at the house. Zak asked him why he did that. What was he looking for? Another crow, the old guy said. Zak wanted to know why it mattered. The old guy explained that one crow was a bad omen. It means bad luck or bad weather or both. But two crows were another story. Two crows might mean a new beginning or a transformation. Zak shook his head. Did the old guy really believe in that kind of superstitious bullshit? The old guy just smiled at him.

They got back on the road. Zak plugged the converter into the cigarette lighter and then his phone cord into the converter. He kept pressing the home button, and nothing happened, and then all of a sudden something did: the battery icon with the tiny sliver of red showed up. Thank God. It wasn't entirely dead. He wasn't sure how long it still needed to charge. He was both eager and full of dread. He set it on the seat between them and tried not to look at it every two minutes.

The old guy wanted to know what Zak was going to do once he got to San Francisco. Was he headed back to New York? Zak shrugged. He wasn't sure he wanted to go back. It had dawned on him that maybe the aliens hadn't misunderstood him, but had actually sensed this reluctance and dropped him off far away on purpose. He didn't tell the old guy any of that. He just kept shaking his head. The old guy wanted to know if Zak had a job in New York. Did he have friends or family there? Zak shook his head. He didn't tell the old guy that he'd been living off the inheritance from his parents for almost a year, not doing anything productive. He didn't tell him that he knew a few people but he wouldn't really call any of them friends. The old guy kept pressing, sure there was something he'd left behind there. Zak shrugged again, but the guy kept asking, until finally Zak told him about Ashley, just because he was too tired to keep resisting him.

As soon as he mentioned her, the old guy perked right up. I knew it, he said. Zak told him it was probably over. He'd know in five minutes once his phone got to a few percent and he got at least one bar. She'd probably found somebody new already. The old guy wanted to know what was special about her. Zak stuck to the generalities. The fact that she was smart and pretty and funny. As soon as he started talking about her, images started flooding his brain, things he was never going to say out loud. It was distracting, trying to carry on a conversation with the old guy while all he could think about was being alone with Ashley in her bed at night, and how fiercely and tenderly she would look down at him, her face lit only by the flickering green of her wireless router. It was like she could see right into his soul or something. He felt his face flush from thinking about it.

The most obvious thing that he didn't want to tell the old guy was how excited Ashley got around the prospect of travel or adventure. She was always talking about taking off, hitchhiking through Europe, going to Indonesia or some such. He knew that the old guy's face was going to light up if he said that, and he was going to tell Zak that the three of them should go to South America together. The old guy was going to say it was *destiny*, and Zak wasn't sure he could keep it together if the old guy said that. But beneath the disgust the truth was he had already started fantasizing about that very thing, although he imagined that Ashley and him would ditch the dude somewhere along the way. The whole idea of her coming out to join him seemed like such a long-shot, so the last thing he wanted was to get the old guy all pumped up about it too.

They crossed a small river and were starting to roll past a few buildings. The old guy announced that they were now in Fort Bragg. It was a bit bigger than Clovus, which wasn't saying much. The architecture was uninspired. A lot of pick-up trucks and white people. A few of them commented on the car whenever they slowed down at a traffic light. Nice wheels, one guy wearing an A's cap said. A middle-aged lady in a tank top whistled. The old guy laughed and nodded. He loved it.

They crossed another small river and then took a few turns, before pulling into the parking lot of a marina. There were hundreds of boats, most of them shiny white sailboats and a few bigger yachts. There were some fishing boats, too. The air was thick with the smell of smoke and salt. The old guy parked the car and told Zak that today was his lucky day. They held the world's biggest salmon barbecue once a year on that very day. The old guy told Zak to come with him and eat.

No Bars and a Dead Battery

Zak told him to go ahead, he was going to wait for his phone to show some signs of life. The old guy told him that a watched pot never boils. That was something Zak's mom used to say, whenever he was eager for whatever was supposed to happen next to just happen already. It had irked him whenever she said it, but he had come to realize that she was usually right, that it was better to stay busy and not just wait for things to happen. The old guy was probably right, too. But he needed to settle the Ashley question for good. Plus he could use a break from the old guy. He told the old guy to go ahead without him. The old guy shrugged and said suit yourself. Zak asked him if he could leave the keys, so he could keep the car on and continue charging. The old guy smiled and told him there was no need. The juice in a classic car like this was always flowing. He walked off in the direction of the crowd.

Zak sat in the car. It started to get hot, so he opened the door to let in a little air. He kept pushing the home button on the phone, but it just kept showing the battery icon with that same slender sliver of red at the bottom. He decided to count to a hundred before he checked again. He made it to thirty-eight. This time, when he touched the home button, the phone sprang to life. He watched the Apple icon appear, and then the line under it that marked its boot progress. His stomach was churning with fear and anticipation and probably hunger. He wasn't sure when he'd last eaten.

Finally, the phone asked him for his passcode, and once he gave it, he was in. It was July 7, a Sunday. He had a few texts waiting for him. He scrolled through to see if any of them were from Ashley, but none of them were. There were also a few Facebook messages, and he glanced at those, too. Same story. He had half a dozen missed calls, but most of them were from his therapist's office. He opened up Facebook and found Ashley's profile. Most of her recent posts were political. He scrolled back to look at earlier that weekend. Someone had tagged her in a group photo at some restaurant. A bunch of her college girlfriends. He double-tapped the screen to zoom in on her face. Did she look happy? It was hard to tell. He backed out and then scrolled through the rest of her weekend. There was certainly no evidence that she had gotten together with anyone new. But of course there wouldn't be, he realized suddenly. She wouldn't post about that. This was stupid, looking for clues in her social media. If he wanted to know where he stood, he was just going to have to ask her.

He went back to his message app and typed in her name. Their last exchange came up, the one just before the FaceTime chat that had ended so badly. Ready when you are, she had written. What kind of an idiot fucks with that, he thought to himself. This idiot, he thought. He started to write to her, a long text, telling her how she was never going to believe what had happened to him, how much he missed her, how bad he felt for their last exchange, begging her to just give him another chance. He read it over. It sounded really pitiful. There was no way she was going to read this whole thing. He deleted it. He typed in *"you there?"* and clicked send.

He watched the screen for what felt like an hour, but it was probably more like a minute. He was waiting for the bubbles. He knew that it was almost certain they weren't going to show up. She probably had blocked him. Except maybe not because she hadn't unfriended him. But that was probably an oversight. In any case, she wasn't going to respond. He knew that. He had to give it a go, like the old guy had said about his stupid dog sculpture.

And then there they were, the bubbles. He felt his heart leap. Of course, she was probably writing to tell him to fuck off. He knew that. He was as ready for that as he could be. If she told him to fuck off he would know that it was hopeless and he could figure out what else to do with the rest of his life. Maybe he'd stay in this hick town. Maybe he'd get a job on one of these fishing boats and spend his days out on the ocean. Then the bubbles stopped. She'd thought better of it, decided no response was the best response. But then they started up again. And then her message popped onto his screen. It said yes.

No Bars and a Dead Battery

Sometime later—maybe ten minutes, maybe twenty—Zak left the phone to finish charging in the car, and went looking for the old guy in the crowd of people at the barbecue. The old guy was standing near a long barbecue grate that hung over a bed of coals. He was halfway through a piece of corn on the cob. There were kernels stuck in his beard. He was trying to talk to one of the salmon chefs, standing on the opposite side of the grate. The old guy was saying something about how they should call this event the biggest salmon barbecue in the galaxy, not just the world. The salmon chef was nodding and smiling nervously, wondering when the old guy was going to stop talking to him. The old guy saw Zak coming and greeted him. He told Zak he had a plate for him. He led him to a spot on the grass. Zak sat down next to him and took the plate. He took the plastic fork the old guy offered, and he took a bite of salmon. It was the most delicious thing he'd ever eaten in his life.

He looked at the old guy. South, huh, he asked. The old guy nodded. South. There was a stage and a band was playing some kind of jazz or blues, Zak wasn't sure. They were all really old, and it was the kind of music that he usually found completely boring, but for some reason today he found himself swaying back and forth to the chunky beat. As they finished their meals, the overcast, which had seemed so impenetrable all day, finally cracked just enough so they could see the sun go down over the ocean.

They made their way through the crowd, and back to the El Dorado. And as they approached it, a crow flew directly over their heads and landed on the hood and then looked at them. They stood some distance away and watched the crow watching them. Another crow flew directly overhead and landed beside it. The first crow squawked and then both flew away. They watched the crows disappear, looked at each other, and then got in the El Dorado. Only one way to go this time, with five bars and full battery.

HALF OF WHAT YOU SEE

Lorain Urban

No coverage, not even one bar, the battery was dead anyway. It was still daytime, but there was an overcast and the sky had a perfectly even dullness, so there was no way to tell what time of day it was, much less which direction was north or south or anything else for that matter. A two-lane blacktop road snaked up into the distance and disappeared into some trees, or a forest if you wanted to get technical about it. It also snaked down toward some lumpy hills and disappeared there as well. What sounded like a two-stroke chainsaw could be heard in the distance, but it was impossible to tell whether it was up in the forest or down in the lumpy hills. This had been happening more often lately. Two different ways to go, with a dead battery and no bars, and nobody left to blame.

Leslie asked Kim if she knew where they were. The bruises ringing Leslie's eyes had begun to yellow; her nose was still swollen and curved left from the bridge. Tufts of yellow hair jutted out from her scalp like exclamation marks. Kim had warned Leslie she'd never cut anyone's hair before, let alone dyed it. Leslie had said to go ahead and do it. She looked like a lemur.

Kim had no idea where they were, didn't know how long they'd been walking, didn't know where they were headed. And the truth is, she didn't much care. She just wanted two things: to charge her phone and to be done with Leslie. No hasta la vista, just adios. She looked up the road toward the forest, then headed down toward the lumpy hills. Leslie followed a few paces behind.

No Bars and a Dead Battery

◆

Leslie had shown up at Kim's door with two black eyes and a dirty white bandage over her nose. It's me, was all she had said. Kim hadn't seen or heard from her for—what had it been?—eight years. As far as Kim was concerned, that wasn't long enough. They'd been close friends, best buds, up until that last semester of college, when life had pulled the rug out from under their friendship. Kim had collected her diploma and left. And that was that. Finito.

Kim had told Leslie to wait on the steps, brought her a glass of water, and pulled out a twenty from her wallet. Leslie took the glass of water, but didn't touch the twenty. Kim started to close the door. I think he's followed me here, Leslie told her, and looked over her shoulder at the street. There was nothing there—no car, no he. It was getting dark, and the neighbors' porch lights were beginning to flick on. Kim let her inside.

Leslie told her she had nowhere else to go—or at least, she couldn't think of anywhere else. She had taken a Greyhound from Albuquerque to Oklahoma City to Kansas City to Des Moines. She'd gotten there around noon, and it had taken the rest of the day to find her way to Kim's doorstep. She couldn't stay, Kim told her. Leslie asked her if she couldn't at least have something to eat.

◆

They'd have to leave the car here. Damn it. Kim had hit the trench in the road head on. She had two flat tires and one spare. A crow flew overhead. *Crow grinned...flying the black flag of himself.* Where was that from? It alighted on road in front of them and pecked at the carcass of a dead animal. Leslie put her hand over her eyes like a visor. Kim grabbed her bag, locked the car, and tried to get her bearings.

Crow crow crow nailed them together. Ted Hughes. That's who it was. Ted Hughes. His poet wife—his genius poet wife—had put her head in an oven, then his lover, Assia, did the same and took their child with her. A second crow joined the roadside feast. How do you get out of bed each morning after that? How do you summon the energy to put one foot in front of the other and go through the motions after that? How do you turn off the lights at night and find sleep in the darkness after that? I guess you write poetry about crows, Kim thought.

◆

Leslie had wolfed down a bowl of Mini-Wheats, put her coat back on, and asked which way to the Y. Kim sighed and told her she could stay the night. She gave her a blanket, pointed at the couch, and went to bed, aborting any conversation other than to let Leslie know that in the morning, she would drive her to the shelter on Mulberry where Leslie could figure out what to do with her life. Leslie had said, okay.

But shortly after 1:00 a.m., Leslie woke Kim, shaking, finger to her lips, and pulled her into the closet. Kim's kitchen window had been shattered. The two of them waited in darkness and silence until, hearing nothing more, Kim lost patience. She gathered up an armful of shoes, knowing her pitching arm was strong and true, and told Leslie to stay put. There was a rock in the middle of her kitchen floor, surrounded by shards of glass reflecting the moonlight. Kim leaned out the kitchen window and yelled that she was going to call the cops on the bastard. Leslie begged her not to. She confessed she had a few issues with the law. This is fucked, Kim had said.

Kim put the rock on the kitchen counter, swept up the glass, and made a pot of coffee. The rock hurler, Leslie told Kim, was Abuser # 3. She had thought he was different. He had promised to take care of her, had promised to love and protect her, and had promised to honor her with all his soul. He held doors for her, did the dishes, and told her she was his sunshine on a rainy day. Until she wasn't. You'd think she'd have learned her lesson, she told Kim. You'd think so, Kim had said. Leslie had tried killing herself, but he'd found her each time and had taken care of things—stomach pumped, wrists bandaged, belt cut from the ceiling fan just in time. There had been no escape—until a few days ago. Kim told her to expect no sympathy here.

◆

The sky lightened as the two of them followed the road through the hills. They walked on the berm until they heard a car approach and then they retreated into the tall grass, tickling their arms as they crouched in its sweetness. Do you think it's him? Leslie would ask. Don't know, Kim would tell her. After it passed, they'd wait awhile and then continue their trek along the road.

Her life had never been the same, you know, Leslie told Kim. Kim kept walking. How were Kim's parents doing, Leslie wanted to know. She rarely spoke to them, she told her. As they started up an incline, they heard another car approach. There was no scrub to hide in here, so they kept walking, heads lowered like pilgrims. The car slowed. Son of bitch, thought Kim, son of a bitch.

The car was old and large, the kind that old people treat like pets. "El Dorado," had been written on a piece of masking tape with a Sharpie and pasted over the car's metal nameplate. The driver, a scrawny woman who gave the impression of having just been set afire—dyed orange hair, bright yellow blouse, gold bracelets jangling on her arms—rolled down the window and asked if they wanted a lift. Kim asked her if she had a phone. The woman said nope. Kim got in the front, Leslie in the back.

The woman didn't bother with preliminaries or fundamentals—no what's your name, where you headed, was that your car way back there—

but started right in on the warp and woof of things. She and Marvin Gaye had the same birthday. The Supreme Court had got it wrong about the Second Amendment. She once got the flu from ice cream. There were no such things as ghosts. She turned on the cassette. Pay attention, she told Kim. You too, she said, leaning back to speak to Leslie. Marvin Gaye sang to them about the grapevine and believing half of what you see.

They approached a roadside stand—a picnic table under a large red and white umbrella—with a hand-lettered sign that listed its inventory. The woman asked if they wanted a cantaloupe. Kim said no, but she could probably use some water and a phone that worked—although at that point, Kim had no idea of who she'd call. The woman docked the car next to the picnic table, where a fat woman in a babushka sat, swatting flies. She doesn't speak English, the woman told Kim and Leslie. They followed her to the table, and Kim pantomimed phone and water, which had no effect. The woman's eyes were milky with cataracts. Their driver picked up a cantaloupe and pressed two quarters into the old woman's hand. They climbed back into the car.

◆

Dropping off Leslie at the shelter on Mulberry hadn't gone as Kim planned. They had no room, they told her. And as far as the intake counselor knew, there were no vacancies at any of the others. That pretty much was the story throughout the state, she told them. Kim knew she shouldn't have come inside with Leslie. The counselor took Leslie's name, gave her some pamphlets with information about civil protection orders and hotlines, and told her to stay with her friend here; she'd call as soon as there was another opening. On the way to the car, Kim told Leslie she'd better figure out a plan, that she could stay with her one more day—two days tops—dropped her back off at the house and went to work.

No Bars and a Dead Battery

When Kim got home that night, her house was on fire. Leslie was standing out front, wrapped in a blanket. The Red Cross said they'd put them up nearby. No thanks, Kim had said and dragged Leslie to her car. She told her to get in, that she was taking her to the bus station, so Leslie could move on to fucking up someone else's life; her quota for Kim's had been met several times over. Leslie, in a voice Kim barely could hear, pointed out that the guy who had torched Kim's house had connected the dots and Kim was now in his sites, too. Maybe Kim should come with her. This guy was very persistent. She was very persistent, too, Kim told Leslie.

They pulled up in front of the Greyhound station. Would you do one last thing, Leslie had asked. She took out a pair of scissors and a box of Lady Clairol Born Blonde. Jesus Christ. Kim parked the car, and they found a restroom. A few women came in, looked at the two of them without comment, went into the stalls, and left. Like "The Fugitive," Leslie had said. Hardly, Kim told her.

The bus terminal wasn't crowded at that time of night. Kim walked to the exit, past a family sitting on a bench—a father, a mother, two small children and a baby. As Kim passed them, one of the children reached over to grab a bag of Fritos and the paterfamilias slapped her in the face. Kim turned and stared, the man stared back, then reached out and gave the girl another smack. The mother kept her head down and looked at her feet. Kim turned around and headed to the ticket counter. Come on, she said to Leslie.

Kim had no destination in mind. She needed to think, to devise a plan—logically, dispassionately, sensibly. The simple truth was she wanted out of her life. There had been plenty of days where she had imagined herself walking out of her office and not looking back, leaving the stack of loan applications stacked on her desk for Stan and Natalie to deal with. She'd pack what could fit in a suitcase and not even lock the door, let the mail pile up in the box, let the electricity, then the gas, then the phone be turned off. Maybe someone from work would file a missing persons report, maybe not. You can't find out where you are unless you lose your way. Or so said Nathan Zuckerman.

After Kim had yanked Leslie from the line at the bus station, she began to have second thoughts. As they drove along, she began to wonder, how'd the hell did that guy figure out Leslie had been staying with her? Kim looked over at Leslie, who was slumped against the door like a boxer on the ropes. Maybe the guy hadn't known. Maybe there was no guy. Kim nudged Leslie and asked her to hand over her phone. Leslie hesitated, then gave it to her. Kim slowed down, rolled down her window, and threw the phone as far as she could. That killed a few birds with one stone.

They drove most of the night without talking, making their way past the outskirts of Des Moines into the dark empty landscape. The irony of the situation was not lost on Kim. Here she was sitting next to Leslie, the person whom, at one time, she had actually told she'd walk through fire for, the person whom she had laid out under the stars with and talked about the power of silence in a friendship, the person whom she'd always thought would rescue her when rescuing was what was needed.

The funny thing about deciding not to talk to someone ever again, is it gets increasingly easier. You begin to forget what it's like to have someone to report into about your day, your thoughts, your ideas. And you reach a point when you don't even miss it for a second. Not a second. Kim looked over at Leslie. She'd really done a number on her hair.

♦

The three of them drove on listening to Marvin Gaye until the woman suddenly pulled old El Dorado over to the berm. Gotta pee, she told them, and squatted next to the car. When she was done, she opened the

No Bars and a Dead Battery

trunk and got out the cantaloupe. She walked over to a grassy spot, raised the cantaloupe over her head, and smashed it to the ground. She opened the gash with her hands and scooped out pieces, flicking the seeds this way and that. Without asking, she dropped a piece in Kim's lap through the open window and then reached around her and handed a piece to Leslie. When all that was left was the rind, she got in the car and said, let's go.

The landscape was empty. If someone told Kim, the woman was deliberately avoiding civilization, she would have believed them. The woman turned to Kim and asked her if she had a story to tell. Kim shook her head. How about you in the back? the woman said to Leslie. Leslie pretended not to hear. The woman raised her voice and said that it looked like Leslie had more than one story to tell. Leslie said she supposed she did. Then let's have it, the woman had said.

Leslie had always been a good storyteller. She knew what details to provide and which ones to embellish. She told them about life in Albuquerque and then as if reciting her resume, gave them the run-down on the three men who had found Leslie to be a serviceable punching bag.

The first guy was older and married. Great catch, Kim thought. He was kind of a Bill Clinton-type, made you feel like you were the most important one in the room. His wife got wind of things, so it ended, just at the point when he was getting rougher and rougher. He had only given her one or two fractures.

She hooked up with the second guy not too long after. He was closer to her age and wrote poetry. Was it any good? the woman wanted to know. She didn't know, she guessed, Leslie told her. There was a lot of sex in it. He liked to act them out. You mean the poems? the woman wanted to know. Yeah, Leslie told her, the poems. Of course he did, Kim thought. There were ropes and chains and red-hot tongs. He told her it was art. When Leslie said she'd rather not, he'd beat her but good. He ended up killing himself, wrapped his motorcycle around a pole.

The last guy was the worst. He just burned down her house, she told the woman, nodding at Kim. She met him while she was bartending at a strip club. How romantic, Kim thought. He was classy and took an interest in her. He had connections and said he could even get her into movies. The woman shook her head. He was the one who did this, Leslie said pointing at her face. Did he do that to your hair, too? the woman wanted to know. No, Leslie told her, she did that, and nodded at Kim.

The woman asked them if they were a couple. What do you mean, Kim had asked. I mean lesbos, the woman had said. Kim told her no. After hearing those stories from the backseat, the woman said she'd understand her not wanting anything to do with a man. And you, the woman told Kim, seem to be smoldering over there. She figured it had to do with Blondie in the backseat.

I killed her brother, Leslie told the woman. The woman said that explained things. Kim looked out the window and watched a murder of crows swirl upward, then land one by one on the telephone wire up ahead. His name was Willie, Kim told the woman. That put an end to story time.

If Willie had been in the car with them, he would have set the record straight. Kim had been no great shakes as a sister—she taken great delight at making fun of his lisp, begging him to say "sweet and sour sauce" over and over for the entertainment of her friends. And he was pretty sure she was the one who had taken Tiger from under his pillow and thrown him in the trash. But she had improved with age. She was smart and loyal, if not always nice.

As for Leslie, Willie would have said it wasn't her fault really. He'd been the one to keep drinking shots to impress his Brothers. It wasn't Leslie's fault that he had poisoned himself with Everclear. She was just one in a crowd of people who hadn't stopped him or called for help after he had passed out and stopped breathing. He'd probably have done the same thing.

No Bars and a Dead Battery

◆

The El Dorado accelerated as they passed fields and barns and insect-like irrigation systems nearing the end of their use for the season. The woman seemed to be all talked out. They approached a town, if you could call it that—a few houses huddled together with their backs turned toward a diner set back from the road apiece. The woman said she was hungry and parked in the gravel lot next to three pick-ups.

The diner smelled like a grandma's kitchen. Not Kim's grandma, but a grandma who wore aprons and baked cloverleaf rolls and did the Jumble each morning. The patrons were what Kim expected—farmers slurping coffee and reading the paper—and the waitress was, too—a tall, sassy thing who barely looked up when the three of them walked in.

The waitress called their driver, Janie, and asked her what she wanted. Janie told her the usual and asked Kim and Leslie what they wanted. The waitress handed them plastic coated menus, and Kim asked her if there was somewhere she could charge her phone. The waitress took Kim's phone and dropped in in her pocket.

The menu had been typed up on a typewriter apparently missing an "o." Kim ordered atmeal, t ast, and c ffee. Leslie wanted a liverwurst sandwich, heavy on the mustard. The waitress narrowed her eyes and asked if Leslie wanted some frozen peas for her face. Leslie told her, no thanks.

Janie started talking mid-flight. El Dorado, she said, that's what she was looking for. She asked Kim and Leslie if they'd ever heard of El Dorado. Leslie said she had seen the movie—the cartoon one, not the one with John Wayne. Man of Gold, Kim said. Leslie looked at her. That's what she was looking for, Janie told them, a Man of Gold, and emptied three packets of sugar into her coffee.

Kim asked her if that's what that masking tape business was about on

41

her car—El Dorado written on its haunch as a declaration. No, actually, Janie told her, she was correcting the damn Cadillac people who had made it one word. *Eldorado*, why they did that, she didn't know. Things like that drove Janie nuts. Destroys the integrity of the language, she told them.

Leslie wanted to know more about this Man of Gold. Janie told them he'd buy her a pool—above ground would be okay, as long as it was close to the house, so she could hop right in without much of a walk. He'd have a Mariachi band play for her on every birthday, and he'd buy her expensive shoes that didn't hurt her bunions. Kim said that Leslie had bunions. Not any more, Leslie told her. Abuser #1 had paid for the surgery right before he went back to his wife. Janie said no one was touching her feet with a knife.

Janie turned to them and asked them who their Men of Gold were. One that didn't make her face look like hamburger would be good, Leslie said, as long as he wasn't boring. That's it? Janie asked her. Pretty much, said Leslie. It would be nice if he had a sweet car, too, she added.

Janie and Leslie looked at Kim. There's no such animal, Kim told them. Come on, they said. Kim wasn't hooked up to a polygraph, Janie said. Kim took a drink of coffee and looked up at the ceiling. He'd want to make her put her head in the oven if he left her, that's what Kim's Man of Gold would be like. And he'd write poetry about crows when she was dead.

The three of them finished eating in silence. Janie took out a vape and lit it. She asked them what their plan was. It was pretty obvious Leslie didn't have one. She turned to Kim and asked her what happened if Abuser # 3 tracked them down. Then what? Kim said she hadn't thought much about that. Maybe you should, Janie told her. Ever read the Book of Samuel? Janie wanted to know. She didn't wait for an answer, told them about the wise woman who had the head of the man Joab was looking for, cut off and thrown over the wall, to save the city from Joab's

No Bars and a Dead Battery

destruction. Leslie began to cry.

What would Janie take for the El Dorado? Kim wanted to know. The waitress overheard her, came out from behind the counter, and sat down at their table. One of the farmers signaled for more coffee. The waitress waved him off. She wanted to hear this.

Let's see, what does a pool go for these days. A deluxe one with the heater would be about a grand, maybe. Mariachi band on every birthday for the next ten years? Say a hundred bucks per, so another grand. Half-dozen pairs of Mephistos. Figure another grand there. So $3,000.00 for Janie's heart's desires. Add another three grand, so Janie could buy herself a ride with the name spelled right—a nice Monte Carlo or Crown Victoria. The waitress told Janie, Ed's kids were asking two grand for his T-Bird. Kim took out a wad of bills from her bag and counted out 60 hundred dollar bills and laid them on the table.

◆

Leslie popped in Marvin Gaye. Janie had said he belonged with El Dorado. The waitress, after handing Kim her phone, had told her there was a gas station about ten miles up the road in Hannaford. One of the farmers shook his head, said it was more like twelve.

Kim pulled into the gas station on Hwy 1, filled up the tank, then drove into the center of town. The road was blocked off. A banner that looked like it was made by a child announced it was Hannaford Day. People had set up card tables on the sidewalk with things for sale—pies, all manner of crocheted scarves and adornments, and things that people had thrown out, which were now passed off as antiques. Kim parked the El Dorado in a dusty lot and got out. Leslie followed her through the crowd of Hannafordians. A few old women clucked when they got a good look at her face.

Kim pawed through the junk on one of the tables. Its purveyor asked if she was looking for something special, he had some additional items in two large buckets under the table. She told him she wanted a map of the United States and a phone charger, the kind that plugged into a cigarette lighter. He picked up the map from under a pile of magazines and fished out the charger from one of the buckets. He said he had some band-aids for her friend if she wanted. No thanks, Kim told him.

They made their way through the crowd, and back to the El Dorado. And as they approached it, a crow flew directly over their heads and landed on the hood and then looked at them. They stood some distance away and watched the crow watching them. Another crow flew directly overhead and landed beside it. The first crow squawked and then both flew away. They watched the crows disappear, looked at each other, and then got in the El Dorado. Only one way to go this time, with five bars and full battery.

BIRDS OF A FEATHER
Julie Hall

No coverage, not even one bar, the battery was dead anyway. It was still daytime, but there was an overcast and the sky had a perfectly even dullness, so there was no way to tell what time of day it was, much less which direction was north or south or anything else for that matter. A two-lane blacktop road snaked up into the distance and disappeared into some trees, or a forest if you wanted to get technical about it. It also snaked down toward some lumpy hills and disappeared there as well. What sounded like a two-stroke chainsaw could be heard in the distance, but it was impossible to tell whether it was up in the forest or down in the lumpy hills. This had been happening more often lately. Two different ways to go, with a dead battery and no bars, and nobody left to blame.

Well that wasn't exactly true. This time, her father was to blame. If not for him and his lousy timing—who went to hospice at the age of sixty-six?—Erin wouldn't be on this road. She would never have turned off the highway, wouldn't have even been *on* that patch of godforsaken highway and she would not have forgot her phone charger in the motel, as if she could afford to stay in a motel. She didn't have that kind of money yet she had managed to scrape up enough to make this trip. Now she would have to eat an even higher ratio of ramen to real food, if that was possible, so she could pay Josie back and also get her mother's silver picture frame out of hock. That would take a while and it wasn't her fault at all and furthermore, Frank Gilmore wasn't even going to appreciate what his daughter had to do in order to see him one last time.

At least it was cool up here for June. Not like Phoenix where her blouse was always sticking to the car's vinyl seatback. Maybe one day she'd have air conditioning. The nose of her crappy Dodge Neon was pointed up the hill. Phoenix didn't have hills but her car still struggled to shuttle her the few miles between her crappy apartment and her crappy jobs. The first eight hours of this trip had been hot but blessedly free of hills. Once she'd turned north at Albuquerque though it seemed she'd been staring at a horizon that was forever rising like the morning sun. The little car kept going but its pace had slowed exponentially and Erin thought it might be mathematically impossible for them to reach their destination. That would be okay. At least she could say she'd tried. But now, within what had to be less than a mile or so to go and with a car that miraculously was still willing to deliver her she knew she'd have to turn around and use time and waste gas and spend money just so she could charge her stupid, crappy phone. She fired up the Neon which muffled the noise of the chainsaw and only then realized how annoying the fly-buzzing drone of its motor had been. Maybe whoever was out there chopping down trees could give her directions. This was such an unlikely spot for a hospice, at least an hour from the closest hospital. Of course, it wasn't like a hospice needed to be near a hospital. She wondered how far to the nearest cemetery. At any rate, someone familiar with the area would probably know which direction to point her. She put her little car in gear and pulled out. One mile, two at the most. She'd drive slowly and maybe get lucky and find it on her own because the idea of wandering into the woods to ask directions from a person wielding a chainsaw was probably a bad one. Erin had seen horror flicks. When you're all alone in the house you do not go into the basement. And when you're all alone on a deserted road and the sky is darkening and your cell phone is dead, you do not go into the woods. You turn your car around and return to the nearest town. And yet, faced with these two different ways to go, Erin was doing what she always did—making the most

No Bars and a Dead Battery

dubious choice.

Yesterday she'd got a late start leaving Phoenix. It wasn't like there was much to pack but there was the money that needed raising and the cat that needed watching and the time off from the paper and the radio station that needed arranging. Erin would have been on the road five minutes sooner if she hadn't gone back for the picture. Until that morning it had trespassed in her mother's silver frame—Frank and Amy Gilmore, just married and squinting into the Vegas sun. The picture had lived on Erin's nightstand since she was a child and she had examined every detail. The color and style of her mother's shoes, the floral pattern of her dress, the ring on her finger, Erin knew her mother only thru this photo. And as she grew she would return to the picture hoping to see at least a little of Amy's visage emerging in her own aspect. Sadly, she was undeniably Frank's daughter. *Birds of a feather* he would say. This always made her cringe. If Frank was a bird, he would be a mynah with that big beak of his constantly squawking. She had avoided his honker of a nose—that would have been a tough one for any girl to grow into—but she had inherited the very brown of him. Eyes, hair, even his complexion, all a dusting of dusky beige compared to the golden shine of Amy. Erin did get her mother's height though. Even after subtracting out the heels you could tell that Amy was taller than Frank. These days she hardly looked at the photo. It hurt too much. Seeing how young her mother was and how not young her father had been made her feel sorry for the girl in the picture. Because that's what she was, a girl who never became a woman. Good God, it was 1989, not '59. Why did she think she had to marry him? For that matter, why did she think she had to go thru with the pregnancy? If she hadn't then Amy would still be alive and Erin would have never existed and maybe that wouldn't have been such a bad a trade-off. Now she wanted her father to see the picture before he died. Maybe he would feel sadness or remorse. Maybe it would make him happy or maybe, most likely, he wouldn't give a hot damn. Erin hoped for the former but expected the latter.

When Janet Whatshername from the hospice had called, she'd let Erin know that there wasn't much time and couldn't she fly in that day? Erin hadn't bothered to look at flights. She would spout wings and fly sooner than she'd be able to get that kind of cash. She would get there as fast as she could she'd told Janet. Hopefully he can hang on another day or two. What she really wanted to say was that Janet should tell him she'd be there right away. She should string him along with continuous lies—*keep your eye on the door Frank, she'll be here any minute now*— and if the old man was anything like his daughter, he'd believe every one of them. But of course she didn't say that. Janet wouldn't understand. And now here she was, so close, creeping along the narrow road, halting and peering down every graveled Jeep track intersection hoping to see what— a flashing neon sign announcing *Hospice Open 24 Hours*? She hadn't even gone a mile yet. This was ridiculous and unless she was going to start turning down those Jeep tracks and exploring the forest in depth she needed to pick up the pace and drive on a little farther before calling it quits, at least until she could charge her phone and print out a map.

Why was she even doing this? She'd been asking herself that question since she got the call on Tuesday. The last time she'd seen her dad was the day she gave him an invitation to her graduation. He'd told her he'd be there and part of her believed him but a bigger part knew he wouldn't so she wasn't very disappointed when he didn't show. She'd left Las Vegas the following day. That was eight years ago and since then they'd spoken on the phone exactly once. A year ago he'd called to tell her that his health wasn't good and he was moving to Colorado. Now here she was in Colorado looking for his hospice. And again, why? She couldn't escape that question and she couldn't answer it though she'd tried for the past eight hundred miles. Well, there was an answer but it made her feel stupid, the way she always felt around Frank. What she wanted from him was an apology. She wanted acknowledgement of how relentlessly,

No Bars and a Dead Battery

insidiously awful he had been. But for that to happen he would have to be aware and that was the thing she had never been sure of. Was he even aware of how full of shit he was? So much of it was little stuff of the sort that when you tried to tell your therapist she just looked at you like you were the crazy one.

What's the best steak you can buy Erin? Chuck steak! Put that ribeye back. In later years hamburger would surpass *chuck* as the best beef. *A Buick, Erin! That's the best damn car on the road. All the luxury of a Caddy but more dependable.* Erin barely heard him above the rattle, tap and wheeze of their '85 LeSabre. *Apartment living is way better than a house Erin. No upkeep and we have a pool.* And a pervy guy who lives across the hall. *Encyclopedias Erin. These will take you all the way thru college.* These were the little, livable things— almost funny in retrospect. The big lies weren't so funny. *We need to get you some new clothes for school, don't we Erin?* That was an annual fib as reliable as Ralph Lauren announcing his fall line. *I know your throat's sore honey. I'll pick you up after school and take you to the doctor.* Her fault for missing the bus home. What a little fool she'd been, waiting on the curb like that. *Lock the doors and windows Erin. I'll be home late tonight.* Erin was nine when she heard that whopper except she didn't know what a whopper it was until two days later when she finally heard his key in the lock.

As far back as she could remember, every word out of her dad's mouth was a lie—EVERY WORD—even when there was no reason for it. If Frank was talking he was lying and she supposed that would mean his apology, if one was coming, would be a lie too. Well she would take it. After all, she had accepted so many other lies so why not that one?

With another mile behind her there was still no hospice or any other structures for that matter. She pulled over, killed the engine and stepped out of the car. The chainsaw had stopped or was blessedly out of range. She listened for signs of life: car doors, voices, death wails. What would you hear near a hospice? Erin didn't know and she wasn't going to find out that night. The cloud cover and the forest canopy had colluded to usher in the evening. She couldn't see more than a few dozen yards into the woods though it occurred to her that they should be lighting up the building by now. It would probably glow in the dark making it easier to spot. She would drive forward a little farther, just a little more.

As she got back into her car, a pair of headlights appeared on the road ahead. A vehicle was approaching though she couldn't tell what kind. Nor could she make out a driver or passenger. All she could see were the lights inching along at a slow and determined pace. Should she take off or should she wait and see if this person could give her directions? Or to rephrase, should she go into the basement or should she make a quick u-turn and beat it back down to the valley? The vehicle must have been moving faster than she'd thought for she could see now that it was a silver pickup truck with a single occupant, a man sporting a red ball cap and a bushy gray beard. He stopped when his window was even with hers. Had she locked her door? She didn't remember. It would look weird if she did it now. Her window was down but she didn't crank it up when he got out of the truck and approached. Again, she didn't want to make things weird.

He stood at her window and she looked up at him, her hand on the key and her mind running over the steps she'd need to take to get the car moving fast. Depress clutch, turn key, press gas, release clutch. Had she left it in gear? Was the emergency brake on? Her heart was racing faster than the Dodge engine would ever run. She waited for the man to decide which way this was going to go. It seemed to take forever as he stood there looking out into the forest. She couldn't clearly see his face from that angle, only belly and tufts of beard. When he finally spoke, she jumped.

It turned out he knew her dad. *Everybody knows Frank. Everybody knows everybody up here.* She wasn't sure, she still couldn't see his face that clearly, but she thought she saw a look of disdain when he'd said her dad's name and that would mean that he knew Frank alright. And he laughed when

No Bars and a Dead Battery

she asked about the hospice. *There ain't no businesses up here. Not unless Frank's got some operation going and I wouldn't put it past him.* He was able to give her directions though. She'd have to turn around and take a right down one of those dusty little side roads but it wasn't far. Before he went back to his truck he leaned down and Erin got a good luck at his full face. His complexion was so ruddy it throbbed even in the dim light of the evening and his eyebrows were almost as bushy as his beard. She thought she might have smelled alcohol but maybe it was just mouthwash. He looked her right in the eye, his face barely a foot away from hers and told her that he didn't *mean no offense* but that Erin would do well to stay out of anything that Frank was up to. She wanted to tell him that her dad was dying but the man was already climbing into his truck and besides, she was starting to get that stupid feeling again.

Somehow she managed to find her dad's house. The dirt road was narrow and rutted and pocked with rocks. It was a miracle that Erin noticed the downed mailbox labelled GI MOR , so intent was she to keep her car from bottoming out in the lane. She turned up the steep driveway and her tires slipped in the gravel but still the Neon managed to advance. No such thing as a quiet approach. She expected that her dad would have come out to see what all the ruckus was about, maybe even brandishing a shotgun. Wasn't that what people did when they lived alone up in the hills? But he hadn't come out and she nervously locked her doors and approached his house.

She had wanted to find a cabin made from logs. The real deal with a stone chimney and the glow from the fireplace blinking out of frosty windows. But that was a Christmas card and not the place that Frank Gilmore would have wound up. She stood on a small concrete pad at the bottom of three narrow wooden steps. The porch light was out but enough light was leaking from the windows for her to tell that her dad lived in a mobile home. There was no skirting around the bottom of the trailer and in the dark it appeared to hover two feet off the ground. Erin wondered what creatures might live under there and she vaulted the stairs in two strides and knocked on the flimsy door. It took a minute and a few more knocks but finally the door was opened.

Four days later, as she navigated the Dodge over the ruts and back to the relative luxury of the black top road she tried to sort her thoughts and feelings into three piles: real, total bullshit and who the fuck knows.

Real. That *was* her dad alright. No denying that she'd spent the last four days with Frank Gilmore. He was older and thinner but besides that, he hadn't changed. Or had he? That was the real question. The answer to that would determine if everything else fell into the *real* or *total bullshit* pile. With Frank there wouldn't be any in-between. For now, the mound of *who the fuck knows* had reached the sky and Erin wasn't sure where to begin.

Frank had been so surprised to see her. He had cried. She tossed that action into the bullshit pile right away but after four days she wasn't sure. To her recollection, Frank had never cried. Not once in the twenty years that she'd lived with him listening to his lies had she seen him cry. Surely he would have trotted that one out before now and the fact that he hadn't made her wonder. Those tears *might* have been real. Then he'd invited her in, grasping her hand and patting her awkwardly on the shoulder before giving her a tentative hug. He felt so slight. She'd never hugged her father, not as an adult. He was no bigger than she and as he hugged her and cried she could only hug him back and wonder. Was this real?

They had talked until late in the night. He'd made dinner for them both, a can of beef stew and some Wonder bread. *This is the best damn bread you can buy, Erin.* He'd asked about her trip, how was the ride, *What are you driving these days?* And she thought he made a sour face when she told him it was a Dodge. *I'm still a Buick man. LaCrosse. But it's in the shop.* He'd promised her that in the morning she'd see how beautiful it was up there in the forest. They'd see deer and blue jays and maybe even some

No Bars and a Dead Battery

wild turkeys and they actually had. That was all real. But the other things, stacked in the pile of *who the fuck knows*, those she might just have to take on faith and she had little of that to spare.

Frank looked sick. He'd told her he was dying. It was *home* hospice and no, he wasn't going to die tomorrow. She must have misunderstood Janet, his home health aide. Bullshit! She knew what Janet had said though *maybe* Janet had misspoke. And just like that, Erin had returned to her youth, doubting her father's words while at the same time trying to mold them into truth.

Frank was so mad at Janet. *She had no right to call you. That's a hippo violation.* Erin didn't bother to correct him. She also didn't see Janet the whole time she was there and she asked about that. *She only comes when I need her, after the chemo.* Frank said he had leukemia and the chemo was the kind that doesn't make your hair fall out. The treatment wasn't working so much anymore and he was going to stop. He'd need Janet more often then. He probably only had a few months left, a year on the outside. Bullshit? Could be. This was one of the first things she'd research when she got back to the land of the internet. But there had been a stack of doctor bills on his bookshelf, many for an oncologist in Colorado Springs. Real? Invoices could be faked though she didn't think her dad had those kinds of skills—he didn't even have a computer— and besides, he'd never gone to any great lengths before to substantiate his lies. Just in case, Erin had copied the oncologist's phone number down. She didn't expect to get much information though, if the number was even valid, what with the *hippo* rules and all.

If he had stopped at the cancer and the year to live, on the outside, Erin probably would have believed Frank. A kindly nurse had violated patient confidentiality to help a father and daughter reconcile which they *had* in a way so call it even and call it done. Be thankful and move on. Frank had apologized to his daughter. *I know I wasn't the greatest dad but...* No, he wasn't but he was sorry. He was really sorry. He loved her and he'd always done whatever he had to do to keep a roof over her head and keep her out of the foster care system. That's what her mother would have wanted and it wasn't easy, being a single parent and all. Why, what did he know about raising a kid, a daughter? Everything he'd done, every sacrifice he'd made had been for her and he'd succeeded because just look at her! A college graduate and wasn't he proud? She stopped herself from mentioning it was a lousy two year degree in journalism from community college and had come with a pile of debt almost as tall as the *who the fuck knows* pile. But there had been an actual apology in all of that and she had accepted it. Her dad was proud of her. He knew he'd been awful but now, as she looked at it through the calcified filter of time, she could make out how hard it must have been for him. He'd traded his wife for a newborn daughter all in the same hour of the same day. Erin *was* lucky not to have ended up in foster care. Her mom had grown up there and left on her eighteenth birthday only to meet Frank Gilmore a week later and the rest was history as they say. No, her dad wasn't awful, not really. He had mostly done the right things even though he'd mostly done them the wrong way.

On the last morning of her visit Erin and her father returned to the trailer. They were coming from the meadow where they walked every day looking for wildlife. Today they'd only seen a couple of crows. Perched in the pines and carrying on like old ladies at a church social the birds were seemingly unaware of Frank and Erin. *You know I always thought you and me were birds of a feather.* These words still made her cringe. It was a long time since she'd thought of ol' Frank, the mynah bird. She almost asked him why. Aside from a physical resemblance what was it that made him think the two of them were alike? They were nothing alike. Erin had sculpted her life not with the idea of who she wanted to be but with the vehement assertion of who she would not be. Words, behaviors, thoughts, anything that slightly reminded her of Frank, she had chinked away like an artist chiseling at a marble statue. And now she wasn't sure exactly who she

No Bars and a Dead Battery

was, who had emerged from that process, but she knew damn good and well who she was not. But would you tell a dying man that you only ever wanted to be his exact opposite? No. Erin wasn't cruel but she couldn't resist a little poking. *Aren't crows a bad omen? They mean death, right? Why do they remind you of us?* She didn't hear how that sounded until the words were flying thru the air right at her dying father's ears and then she felt like crap. But Frank was unscathed. *Oh no, crows aren't bad luck! They symbolize change, like being reborn or getting a second chance.* What the hell was he talking about? It seemed Frank had a neighbor, Mary Two Feathers, who had shared some animal lore with him. Should Erin even bother to look this one up? It was meaningless, insignificant in the realm of Frank and his stories yet it stood out like a red-breasted robin perched atop a dung heap.

Back at the trailer, Frank sat at the little wooden table that was wedged into the tiny kitchen. Erin put a second pot of coffee on and opened a box of store brand powdered donuts. She was rinsing their cups from that morning when she heard her father's sobs. This was twice in four days that he'd cried and she still didn't know in which category it belonged. She turned toward him. He was staring at her with a look that she'd never seen him wear. It was more foreign than the tears and if she'd seen it on any other face she would have named it fear. Remaining at the sink, she asked him what was wrong. They had not arrived at a place in their relationship where she would rush forward to blindly comfort him. Perhaps they never would. Her father answered in a hushed voice, the words evaporating as they hit the air. *You see, the thing of it is Honey...I lied.*

He lied. Did he say he lied? Erin almost laughed. She was waiting for the punch line, expecting her dad to follow up this revelation with something like *you know, those days the sun came up in the morning?* But there was no punch line coming and it slowly began to occur to her that the L word had never crossed his lips before. Even in his apologies over the past few days, he hadn't admitted to lying. He hadn't apologized for any specific behavior. He'd just given a general, blanket apology. And though their reconciliation had been good, *this* was what she'd really come for—Acknowledgment! If that's what it was. She didn't know how to respond. There was more that she wanted him to say. She needed him to elaborate on all the ways he'd lied, the big lies and the little ones. If he needed prompting, she could give him examples. And elaborate he did, but not in the way she ever could have imagined. For the entire eight hundred miles of her drive back to Phoenix the next day, she replayed her father's announcement—the words that came after *You see, the thing of it is Honey...*

Because the thing of it was that he told her that her mother was alive. Erin thought she might pass out, she was breathing so fast. She sat down hard on the worn linoleum floor. *No, wait honey. Let me finish. Your mother was alive after you were born. And she was definitely alive on the day she left us. But she's not alive now, I'm sorry. She died a long time ago.* Frank told her everything he knew.

Frank and Amy and baby make three. They'd had a nice little life for a while. Amy had been there when her daughter turned one. And when Erin mouthed her first words, her mother was there to hear them. *But she got fed up with me I guess. Can't really blame her.* Amy had met another man, fell in love and left her husband and child behind. *She was like a kid leaving her folks and going off to college. She never looked back.* She told Frank that she'd return for Erin. She just needed a little time to sort things out and get settled in her new life. She was moving to California. Frank waited, meanwhile Erin turned two. Amy called him a few months after she'd left and told him she would be out that summer. She was going to take Erin and Frank was going to let her because after all, what did he know about raising a kid, a daughter? And that was it. Frank never heard from her again and he wasn't surprised. *She was young and kind of crazy. Truth is, I knew we were never gonna last. So I told you she was dead. I figured that was better than you growing up thinking she didn't want you.*

Erin wished she didn't know the truth. There were so many other things her father could have stopped lying about but this? This one she wished he had taken to his grave. For all her life she'd embraced the righteous comfort of semi-orphanhood. Now, with just a few tearful words, her father had forced her to trade that in for the shameful loneliness of abandonment. She should hate him but she couldn't. After all, he was the hero, wasn't he? The one who stayed and tried to do the right thing though mostly in the wrong way. She thought of her parents smiling at her from the silver picture frame. The literal and figurative juxtaposition of the photo had always struck her: Amy, young and beautiful and saintly and Frank, older and predatory and fraudulent. There were so many times that she'd wanted to cut that photo in half, removing her father as if without him her mother would still be around. But Erin had been wrong. She had been one hundred and eighty degrees wrong about her parents...*if* Frank was telling the truth.

So many questions were flitting thru her mind but chief among them was *Why tell me this now?* There was nothing to be gained, not for her or for Frank. *Why?* Frank's reply was simple. *Because you have a sister.* Well technically a half-sister but regardless, Erin had a right to know. And no, he hadn't kept it from her. He'd only found out a week or so ago, by accident, when he ran into the guy that Amy had run off with, the father of Erin's half-sister. *Bullshit! Ran into him a week ago? That one was total and absolute bullshit.* But Frank went on. The guy, his name was Scott, told him that Amy *had* died—in childbirth of all things. *Can you believe it? I think they call that irony.* Erin knew irony and that wasn't it. It was tragedy and it was real, she was almost certain he was telling the truth.

By the time her father was through confessing, if you could call it that—rationalizing and explaining was more like it—Erin had completed several one eighties and was still spinning. She had gone from deifying to damning to mourning her mother in a very short span. And her emotions about her father were more confused than ever. She'd figure out those feelings once she got back to civilization and could finish her task of sorting Frank's words into the three piles. But first she would find her sister and armed with information she'd had all along, her mother's maiden name and birth date, it shouldn't be difficult.

When she left, Frank walked her to her car. He'd not said another word about her mother or the past in spite of Erin's repeated questions. Now he wouldn't look at her but instead patted the faded hood of the Dodge. *This thing gonna get you all the way home?* Erin shrugged but her father didn't see it. *You know Honey, one day I hope you can get yourself a Cadillac. Best damn cars ever made.* She smiled at that in spite of her anger and confusion. It was comforting to hear her dad still sounding like her dad though she'd grown up wishing he would sound like anybody else. And then she remembered their cranky old LeSabre. Weren't *Buicks* supposed to be the best? *Aww Erin, you had to know that was bullshit. Everybody knows a Cadillac's the best.* And that *admission* of bullshit may have surprised her more than anything else her father had ever said.

Finding proof of the life of Amy Gilmore, née Erinsson, had been easy. Having access to the resources of the Phoenix Daily Post was helpful but the truth was anyone with an internet connection could have done it. But it had never occurred to Erin to do a search on her mother's maiden name. Frank's tale of Amy, a waif without family, dead at the age of eighteen, had been unquestioningly complete in Erin's mind. It was the lie she was born into, the original lie integrated as deep into her very existence as was the color of her eyes or the color of the sky. She had learned over time to doubt every word her father spoke but she had never doubted the story of her origin. Finding her sister took a little more doing but still it wasn't difficult. Her name was Erica Stephens, daughter of Scott and Amy. Erin located Erica's birth certificate and Amy's obituary during her lunch hour the day after she returned from Colorado. Amy Erinsson. That was the name that appeared on both. A query on Amy Gilmore turned up a single document, Erin's birth certificate. In the age of highly indexed and accessible information—some real, some bullshit and some who the fuck knows—there was nothing to electronically connect Amy Gilmore to Amy Erinsson. There was nothing to suggest that Amy Gilmore had even existed except for a brief moment in a delivery room when the culpability of lineage was officially recorded. Erin felt motherless and that is not to say orphaned. Orphaned happens when a parent leaves you before their time but would have given anything to have stayed. Motherless was the residue left behind by a heedless creature who leaned against a wall for a minute longer than planned.

She would have screamed or thrown something if she hadn't been at work. Instead she walked out of her cubicle robbed of the satisfaction of even being able to slam a door. She was pissed off at the world. Pissed off at the mother who had lingered in her life about as long as a Greyhound bus at a rural stop. Pissed off at the sister whose mother had wanted her enough to at least have shared her true identity. And she was pissed off at Frank Gilmore. Leave it to her father to give what amounted to a death bed confession—*Hippo* be damned, the oncologist confirmed he was dying—that was peppered with lies. She was sure of this, sure that he must have known about her half-sister for a long time unless… Unless the story about running into Scott Stephens was true. Oh *bullshit* and what did it even matter now? She had a sister and regardless of how long Frank had sat on that information, it was her turn to decide what to do with it. There was only one way to go with that one. She would contact Erica of course. There was no way she wouldn't but she cringed at the thought of how ridiculous it would sound. *Hello? You don't know me but I'm your half-sister. Our mom was with my dad two years before she was with your dad.* Erin tried to imagine how she would react if she received that call from a stranger. She'd hang up the phone. Then she realized she actually could receive such a call. Who was to say that Erin didn't have an older sibling out there? Good God, she really could! It would be her luck that in this post-millennial, Brady Bunch scenario that was unfolding, she would be

Jan. She'd deal with this later if there was anything to deal with. For now there was no avoiding that she'd have to contact Erica. And she wanted to, the only question being how. After much deliberating and a few near phone calls, she wrote a letter, by hand, on real stationary and dropped it in the mailbox. *Dear Erica, you don't know me but...*

Days slogged by. There was no word from her sister. When two weeks had passed Erin knew it was time for phase two, electronic contact. She would email Erica and if she didn't get a reply within forty eight hours of hitting the send button, she would call her. And God help her if those attempts failed because then she'd be forced to drive to San Diego, to the address that her sleuthing had turned up, to knock on the door and hope to somehow recognize the person on the other side. After work she picked up some courage from the liquor store and went home to write an email. It started out slow. She was insecure and she chose her words with a painful and conciliatory accent but by the time she'd had her third shot of tequila, she was mad. Email sucked! *Select All* followed by *Delete* was not nearly as satisfying as ripping a letter to shreds or balling it up and hurling it across the room. *Dear Erica, I am your sister whether you want to believe it or not so why don't you grow up and pull your head out of your ass and answer me? Love, Erin.* But she didn't hit send because after all she'd only had three shots, five might have been enough, and besides someone was at the door.

Erin answered it, clear headed mostly except that she normally would have looked thru the peephole first. The late afternoon sun pounced as if it had been pacing, waiting for the Trojan horse of a mailman or a salesman or a recently discovered, long lost sister to let it in. A shadowy figure stood before her eclipsing the bright and jagged light. Erin's pupils adjusted slowly, in a kindly but futile attempt to give her heart and head time of their own to adjust. But that was going to take more than the blink of an eye. As the light fell away she found herself staring into the face of a young woman who could only be described as a daughter of

No Bars and a Dead Battery

Frank Gilmore.

Neither woman moved. Erin couldn't help but remember a scene from I Love Lucy where Lucy convinced Harpo Marx that he was looking not at her but at a mirror. If Erin raised her right arm would the woman at the door raise her left? The daughters studied one another, neither speaking. They might have been twins with the exception of their noses. That was definitely Frank's nose mounted on her sister's face. Her *sister*—her *whole* sister, not just a fraction of one and before Erin could think, she found herself crying and hugging her and dragging her into the living room where they began to bond. As the streetlights blinked on, Erin was describing her childhood with Frank. When the pizza was delivered, Erica was talking about their grandparents. The last shots of tequila were downed while discussing their dad's condition. And by the time the streetlights fizzled the next morning they had finished planning their road trip to Colorado. Later, after Erica had gone to her hotel, Erin tried to catch an hour's sleep before work. Her brain was swirling like a Bollywood musical though and closing her eyes made it all the more vibrant and distracting. She had a sister! But more than that, she had a friend, an ally, a kidney donor (or recipient if it came down to it.) At least she hoped. For twenty-six years they had been apart and now Erin wished they could forego sleep for the next twenty-six in order to make up for the stolen time.

Two mornings later, the sisters drove east out of Phoenix. An hour into the trip the sun swelled like a blister on the horizon before bursting into piercing shafts of light. Erica drove slowly and blindly as the orb fought its way into the sky. Neither woman spoke. By the time the trip was done each would have said plenty.

Erin was still trying to sort information into piles. A lifetime of lies left her in constant doubt even when the words weren't coming from Frank Gilmore. Apparently her sister was rich. Or rather her sister's grandparents, were rich. Erin wasn't sure yet if that meant she was rich too but she had spoken by phone with her new family, Gram and Grand, and she had an idea that maybe her financial future was looking up. Maybe. She wouldn't let herself believe that yet. But Erica had paid to spring the silver frame from the pawn shop and she was paying for this trip so technically her financial future had already gotten a boost. Erin squinted at the road and tried to imagine how Frank was going to react. He would cry for sure. That was his new thing. When he saw Erica and realized she was his daughter, another bird of a feather, he was going to leak tears like a rusty sieve. She hoped the shock didn't kill him. If he had a damn phone at the trailer he would have had some advance warning. Nurse Janet's phone was rolling straight to voice mail and they would be driving down the rutted road to his place at least a day ahead of the mailman carrying their letter. So Frank was in for the surprise of his life, what was left of it anyway. And what was Erica going to think of their dad? This was the only Frank she was ever going to know and even though he was still a liar, he would have little time to prove it. Erica's knowledge of their father would be as false as Frank's pile of bullshit. His legacy with her would be untarnished like the silver frame. It would be truth-filled because Frank simply would not have the time that was required for the patina of doubt and deceit to spread and this just did not seem fair.

Erin glanced at her sister who was sitting up tall in the driver's seat where the visor might do some good. Over the past couple of days, she'd tried to explain their dad to Erica. But how could you explain the chaos of a hurricane? Unless you had actually seen one you couldn't imagine it to be much worse than a big wind. Frank was definitely worse than a big wind. *It's just that I want you to understand how he is.* This was the third time Erin had said this since they planned the trip. *Maybe he can't help it but he's hyperbolic at best. And I'm being charitable.* Erica fessed to not even knowing what that word meant, *hyperbolic*, and furthermore, she was tired of hearing it and couldn't Erin just leave it alone and let her experience

No Bars and a Dead Battery

Frank without all of the preconceived bullshit? The words sat full and heavy between them, demanding legroom and arm space like a portly stranger on an overbooked flight. Without the preconceived bullshit? You couldn't have Frank Gilmore without preconceived bullshit. The two were Siamese twins. Erin struggled to keep her mouth shut. Anything she said at that moment was not going to be helpful. They drove in silence until the sun had finally risen above the angle of interrogation before she spoke again.

You see, the thing of it is Erica...he lies. And then she described to her sister just how those lies looked. They were often disguised, camouflaged like poison ivy creeping thru an ornamental hedge. And it wasn't until later, once the noxious itch of it began to spread along your skin that you could go back and pick it out from among the greenery. *I was nine the first time he didn't come home all night or the next day or the next night. He said he'd be late and I believed him. I waited up as long as I could. I suppose you could defend him because technically he was telling the truth. He was late.* Very late. Forty-eight hours late. Erica kept on driving and did not speak or even glance at her sister. The silence was thick and angry. It permeated the cabin of the vehicle and Erin's tension expanded with every whiff that she inhaled. Her dad had never been one for silence. The waters around him were always crowded with talk and the flotsam of his lies. She had grown comfortable navigating in and around deceit but on Frank's rare, reticent moments she was without compass or rudder. She interpreted her sister's silence as accusatory disbelief. Erin continued, barely suppressing her rage. *And as far as preconceived bullshit goes? You don't know what you're talking about. But you're gonna find out. You're about to step in a big ol' pile of it and you won't even realize until it's too late and by then you'll have stepped in another pile and another. I'm just trying to help you, so you won't be too disappointed or hurt.* And because she had become very adept at spotting bullshit thru the years, Erin knew immediately that what she'd just said was untrue. The truth was that she wanted Frank to tell his biggest whopper ever. She wanted him to spin his windmills into a high-rise luxury condo complete with a doorman and a penthouse. And she wanted Erica to be all set to move in, boxes packed, key in hand, turning the lock and throwing open the door only to step across the threshold and plunge thirty stories down through thin and unsubstantiated air. Without the shared experience of their father's deceit, Erin didn't believe the sisters could ever truly bond.

The silent miles slowly bled out behind them. Erin thought of apologizing but she wasn't sorry and that would just throw more bullshit on the pile. Finally Erica spoke. *We're getting low on gas.* Thirty minutes later they pulled up to the pumps in Gallup, New Mexico. Erin offered to pay but didn't protest much when Erica refused. *You can get me a coffee though. Black,* which Erin gladly did. It wasn't until she was walking back to the car that she saw it. That morning, when they left Phoenix, it had been too dark to tell much about the vehicle. She could make out a light colored, large sedan and she hadn't given it another thought. Now she stared in disbelief at the hood ornament, the red and gold crowned crest of arms. Cadillac. Everyone knew that emblem, even a poor kid who had grown up in old and over-worked Buicks. She laughed and Erica frowned. *What's so funny?* Erin didn't know where to begin nor did she have the energy or the inclination to try. *This is a really nice car. My dad, our dad, is gonna love it.* Once they were back on the freeway, Erica began to talk and it was Erin's turn to stay quiet. The Cadillac is what started that conversation. Erica hated the car.

Who would keep a car like that around for that many years? It was a shrine just like her bedroom. Grand and Gram had bought the Eldorado brand new for Amy's graduation in '89. Their daughter used it to drive around La Jolla that summer but when she decided to escape Stepford, as Erica liked to think of it, she had abandoned the vehicle on her parent's driveway. They had kept the Caddy in their garage, driving it once a week to keep the battery charged, to keep it in tip-top condition for when Amy came to her senses and returned home. And she had returned home, sort of, six months pregnant and with Scott Stephens circling like a shark. After Amy died, the Erinssons became Erica's legal guardians and Scott's circles grew slower and wider. The last time she saw the man that she thought was her father was when she was twelve. *I always thought they had chased him off and I hated them for doing it and him for letting them. Now I wonder if he knew he wasn't my dad.* But it turned out that chasing Scott Stephens away wasn't going to be the worst thing they ever did. Her grandparents hadn't been the same since Amy died. Their friends had told Erica this more than once. *I don't know what they were like before but I can tell you how they are now. They're creepy, Erin. They want me to be her. They're disappointed I don't look like her.* They had presented Erica with the car on her sixteenth birthday—a big, boxy nearly two decades old Cadillac that no sixteen year old, southern California girl would ever want. *And the bedroom. You should see the bedroom!* When she was too big for her crib, they had moved her into her mother's old room which looked the same as it had the day Amy died. As Erica grew older she had insisted that the posters come down— U2 and The Cure were not her favorites—but she had been ineffective in getting them to allow much more than that to change. And though they weren't mean people, they never abused her, they were incredibly strict. They were not going to make the same mistakes with Erica that they had with Amy. They were not going to raise another wild child. *I didn't go on my first date until my senior year of high school and only then because they chaperoned. I got in to UCLA but it was too far away. They didn't want me living in a dorm so I went to San Diego instead.* Erin thought of her dilapidated Dodge and her two year degree from the Community College of Southern Nevada and she struggled to feel sympathy for her sister. Erica continued, seemingly unaware. *You were lucky, Erin. I mean I get that it was rough but at least you knew your dad and at least you got to have a life, your own life. I grew up in a bubble. I got shoved in the middle of someone elses half-lived life. It was like the only way I could get* out was to never make any of the mistakes our mother made and how could I even know what those were? I didn't know how to act on my own, like literally what to say or even how to sit or when to laugh or cry. I would always look to Grand and Gram to make sure I wasn't screwing up. I could see it on their faces when I was. They might as well have had a remote control pointed at me 'cuz I'd just look over at them and depending on what I saw, I'd make an adjustment until I got it right. I still don't know how to be me or who that even is. I'm still driving this goddamned car for Christ sakes!

Erin pushed a button and slightly reclined the soft leather seat. Then she adjusted the vent that was pouring icy, filtered air into the cabin of the vehicle. She stared out the window and began to consider her sister's life up to that point. Poor little rich girl? Maybe. She felt a morsel of sympathy for her younger sister. Growing up, the only thing that kept Erin from doing exactly what she wanted to do was money. It wasn't lack of imagination and it certainly wasn't a controlling father. By the time she hit high school, she knew the city bus routes by heart and she went everywhere. She haunted the libraries, taking advantage of free films and lectures. If there was live music or a poetry slam at a campus coffee shop, Erin was there nursing an iced tea until closing time. By the time she turned fifteen she was even reading her own angsty prose at open mikes about town. What if she had been stuck at home, looking to Frank for approval before she made a move? Well that idea was laughable, unfathomable really because Frank would have first had to have been home and second, had to have given a shit. So it came down to two crappy choices—an apathetic, pathological liar of a father or an over-protective pair of grandparents living out a twisted Tennessee Williams tale. Despite the doubt that was Erin's constant companion in adolescence and the debt which dogged her as an adult, she knew that she would not have traded her past for her sister's.

And just like that, she found herself hoping that Frank *would* be honest in his final days. The more she imagined growing up with the Erinssons the more sorry she was for Erica. Her sister deserved something real, a

No Bars and a Dead Battery

parent who would accept her as she was, regardless of the words she used or the way she sat or how she laughed and cried. And Frank could do that. He wasn't a critical man. If anything he was the opposite, too full of compliments. It wasn't just that *chuck steak* and *wonder bread* and *Buicks* were the best. Everything about *Erin* had been the best. *You're the prettiest girl in your class, honey* or *you're the smartest girl in the whole damn school.* The quickest, the sharpest, the funniest, the strongest…It didn't matter. Her father's compliments went beyond the way a normal parent bolsters their child. They were ridiculously effusive and overreaching so as to have been rendered meaningless, worse than meaningless really. The younger Erin had reasoned that since Frank lied the compliments were lies too and she would reinterpret them. *You're the smartest* must mean *you're the dumbest.* When Erin's boyfriend broke up with her the night before prom, the last thing she wanted to hear from her dad was how pretty she was. But Erica could never possibly know all this. Despite Erin's attempts to warn her sister, she knew the message hadn't been received. Unless you had lived thru Hurricane Frank for many seasons you couldn't begin to prepare for the torrent of lies. She was sure that Frank would be blessedly complimentary and accepting of her younger sister and Erin didn't care if it was real or not. She'd be happy to toss it all onto the *who the fuck knows* pile as long as Erica was buying it.

July days work overtime in central Colorado. It was after seven in the evening when they turned west off the freeway toward Frank's trailer. They had over an hour to go with the sun in their eyes. The drive had been easy once they'd got past their difficulties of the morning. The sisters had come to some sort of understanding or at least Erin had. For the first time in her life she didn't feel sorry for herself when she thought of her childhood. Perspective can be funny like that. Images distort or even disappear when the funhouse mirrors of memory merge with another person's sad reality. Where Frank had once been a grotesque buffoon she now saw a harmless, silly dork. She was looking forward to sharing him with her sister, warts and all. And she was especially looking forward to Frank's reaction when they drove up in the Cadillac. Erica hadn't let Erin pay for gas when they stopped in Pueblo but she had let her big sister drive. When they reached his place and the tires crunched and sprayed gravel on his steep driveway, she hoped he would come out and see her at the wheel. Frank Gilmore was about to meet a daughter he didn't know he had but Erin was pretty sure that the sight of the Caddy was what would impress him most.

In retrospect, she should have figured Frank wouldn't be home. He never was when she was a kid so why start now? But he'd left them a letter. *Dear Erin and Erica.* Well you had to hand it to him. He knew how to reel a reader in with a strong opening line. How in hell did he know they were coming and how did he know Erica's name? And there it was, right on schedule. That stupid feeling Erin always got around her father when his lies began to itch. Apparently he'd known about Erica since the early 2000's. *I actually did run into that SOB Scott Stephens but not recently. It was in Vegas a long time ago. He told me about her. Told me she had to be my kid, spitting image of me (poor thing.)* Erin glanced at her sister. She wasn't homely. She wore that Gilmore nose with class, like Barbara Streisand or a Caddy with an oversized hood ornament. *Erica was probably ten or eleven at the time. I wasn't sure what to do. I wanted to meet her and I wanted you girls to know each other. But I was also scared. What if they wanted her to come live with me? What did I know about raising kids, daughters? I* figured I was probably screwing Erin up real good. I didn't want to screw up another kid too. Erin blushed. She could feel Erica looking at her as she focused on the letter. *Also I was worried they'd want ten years of back child support. You know, that kind of stuff happens.* Good old Frank. He was spreading a lot of truth around. Erin wondered how he must have felt writing it. *In the end, I got ahold of the Erinssons. They didn't want anything to do with me which you can't really blame them. Anyway, they paid me to stay away just like they did Scott...* What the fuck! Payoffs? The sisters looked at each other, speechless and

No Bars and a Dead Battery

angry. Erica finally spoke for both of them. *How dare they?* Erin was seething. Her father, Scott, her grandparents, all playing deceitful games with other people's lives. It was a damn good thing that Frank hadn't unloaded this truth on her in person because she would have ripped his lying, conniving head off. *I wanted to say something all these years but I signed an agreement. They would have sued me. That doesn't matter now. I hope they do sue. I hope they spend thousands on fancy lawyers because the joke's on them. I'll be in the ground before they can even serve me papers.* Erin had started out the trip feeling jealous of her sister, jealous that she would have a true and honest relationship with their father where Erin hadn't. And that was what Erica *would* have because of this letter though it was nothing to be jealous over. Frank had finally told the truth and the irony was that without the lies it was a very incomplete picture of who he really was. *I was hoping I'd be able to hold out until you arrived. I knew you'd find her, Erin. I knew you'd be coming. But since you're reading this it means things got a little too rough for me to be up here on my own. I might go to a hospice or maybe to my sister's if she'll have me. Hell, maybe I'm already dead. Janet can probably tell you where I'm at if you even want to see me...* He had a sister? They had an aunt? Jesus Christ Frank, what else don't we know? Erin was a little afraid to really consider that question. *I want you both to know that I'm sorry. I really am. I should have got the two of you together long ago. I probably should have got the Erinssons to take you Erin. You would have had a better life. But I loved you and I didn't want you to leave. Besides you were half grown by then. I didn't even tell them about you. I guess that was selfish of me but there it is. I hope the two of you can forgive me.* And with that Frank signed off. *Love, Dad.*

Erin was driving too fast. Her sister sat in the passenger seat re-reading the letter and muttering under her breath before asking Erin to slow down. This was messed up. They didn't know where Frank was or if he was alive. She slowed the Eldorado to within ten miles of the speed limit and tried to figure out where they were rushing to. Somewhere with phone service and an internet connection would be a good start. Then she remembered the bills from the oncologist. Colorado Springs. They were going to find Frank that night if they had to call every hospice in the town. She heard her sister sniffle and looked over to see tears tracing her cheeks. *It'll be okay. We'll find him.* Erica nodded and gave a little smile. And they *would* find him, Erin was sure about that. They would call all the hospitals in town too. She'd do a search on Janet's phone number and also a search on Frank Gilmore. She'd never thought to look him up when she was doing the research on her mom. If Frank had a sister out there, Erin would locate her. Working for the paper didn't pay much but it had its perks and one was free access to the best people finding services on the internet. She focused on the road, speeding up a little, hoping her sister wouldn't notice. When she heard Erica's voice, she immediately slowed down. *I really want to meet him. I want this more than I've ever wanted anything and I'm afraid it's too late.* Erin sped up and really considered her sister's words. It might be too late. She knew this now though her dad hadn't seemed that bad when they'd said goodbye. That wasn't even three weeks ago. Erica was crying again and Erin would have stopped the car if she felt like they had a scant second to spare. Big sisters were supposed to take care of little sisters, even when they were well into their twenties. They were supposed to comfort and soothe the way a mother would or at least the way Erin imagined a mother would. *I really hate Gram and Grand right now. They had no right. If we're too late, if our dad is…I will never talk to them again. I will leave this fucking car on their driveway and take off without telling them where I'm going. That's what they deserve.* Erin considered how unlikely it was that she was driving a Cadillac in the middle of Colorado, wanting to see her father as desperately as her sister did. And unlike the first time she'd made this trip, she wasn't hoping for apologies or acknowledgment or reconciliation. She just wanted to hear him tell some lies. She wanted him to spin some tails for both of his daughters so that years from now, they could get together and say things like *remember when Dad said...* And though she didn't know them, Erin found herself hating their grandparents too. She tried to clear her mind and reached for the radio but stopped. Erica might be sleeping. She'd been quiet for a while but just then she spoke. *Look, fireworks.* She was pointing off to the right and Erin turned in time to see the flash. It was the third of July but people always started early. On the horizon they could see the lights of Colorado Springs and Erin drove a little faster.

The Marriot was nice and its internet was fast. It had taken her less than an hour to locate their Aunt Mary in Iowa City. And after the fear and then the annoyance at receiving a midnight call had passed, she had sounded as warm and wonderful as an Aunt Mary from Iowa possibly could. They were going to meet her the next day, actually that same day given that yesterday had crossed into tomorrow. But more important, they were going to see their dad. Iowa City was another eight hundred miles and though Erin wished they could just hop on a plane and be there by morning, she also relished the idea of the additional time in the car with her sister. Yesterday had been intense. Erin had never connected with anyone like she did with Erica. She had always been jealous at the relationships her friends had with their siblings. Some were estranged. Some were way too close in her opinion and some were just right. But they all had a shared history, a spider web of common memories with sticky strands that could never be brushed away. She and Erica were going to make those memories even if they got a late start. She closed her eyes and focused on sleep.

In the morning, both women were awakened by thunder. Normally Erin was thrilled when it rained. Phoenix could go months without a drop. Today she just wanted clear roads and clear skies so they could get to their dad as soon as possible. She glanced at the digital clock on the nightstand. Seven a.m. sharp. That seemed wrong but she didn't know why. She got out of bed and crossed to the window wearing nothing but a t-shirt and panties. A peek thru the curtains showed a bright sun lighting up the land, unhampered by any sign of a storm. No rain, no clouds. That could only mean no thunder. And then she remembered. *The parade! Shit! Shit! Shit!* She pulled on her pants, grabbed the car keys and ran out of the room, barefoot and braless. Erica was behind her calling out *what's the matter* as Erin hurriedly motioned her into the elevator. *The car. We have to move the car.* She watched as the realization drenched her sister's face. Last night when they'd checked in, the sleepy desk clerk had perked up when he was telling them about the Fourth of July festivities that began in the morning. First there was the firing of the cannon at Golden Hills Park and then the pancake breakfast which was capped off by the parade. *Now you don't want to be parked in our lot once they start setting up for the parade or you'll be stuck here for a bit.* Time was of the essence last night. They had needed to find Frank fast. They would move the car in the morning. Or better yet, they'd be on the road by the time the cannon was cheering them on. Maybe the alarm didn't go off or maybe they'd both slept thru it but now they were running thru the lobby of the Marriot as if S.W.A.T. was evacuating the building. They made it to the car and screamed out of the lot, dodging the orange vested volunteer right before he placed the sawhorse barricade across the driveway. Once on the street, they turned right, out of the parade route, parked and then scampered back to the hotel.

That was too close. Erin still couldn't figure out what happened. *Didn't we set an alarm?* Erica looked away and then in a small, scared voice confessed to possibly having turned it off. *It's just like sleepwalking. I can't help it.* Erin couldn't be mad at her. The poor kid was practically shaking with fear and it looked like she was going to cry again. *Hey, it's ok. I do that too. I got it from Frank so that means it's genetic.* Whoa! Where did that come from? Erin had lived her life being brutally honest, a little too brutal according to some former friends. And yet that lie had popped out like a hiccup. Maybe lying was genetic. She hoped not. And she didn't think it was but still there could be parts of her dad in her that she wouldn't be able to deny forever. Both women had grown up struggling with identity.

No Bars and a Dead Battery

Erica had tried to act like the mother she never knew while Erin had tried to act like anyone but the father she knew too well. They would get to know each other and maybe in the process they would get to know and nurture their own, deeply hidden psyches. They had the rest of the day to begin that process and the rest of their lives to complete it. Erin looked at her sister who looked so much like her and so much like their father. She couldn't wait to get a picture of the three of them together. Birds of a feather. She cringed at that a little, probably always would but still, that picture would be worthy of a second silver frame. What was it Frank had said about the crows? Something about them representing new beginnings or second chances. She had never fact checked it and wasn't planning on doing it now. Some things you just had to take on faith. She crossed the room and looked out the window. People were already gathering for the parade. Erin wondered out loud if they shouldn't all still be eating pancakes in the park but the sidewalk continued to fill. It took the sisters less than fifteen minutes to vacate the room and exit the building. This time, Erin remembered her phone charger.

They made their way through the crowd, and back to the El Dorado. And as they approached it, a crow flew directly over their heads and landed on the hood and then looked at them. They stood some distance away and watched the crow watching them. Another crow flew directly overhead and landed beside it. The first crow squawked and then both flew away. They watched the crows disappear, looked at each other, and then got in the El Dorado. Only one way to go this time, with five bars and full battery.

OPTIONS

Deborah Boller

No coverage, not even one bar, the battery was dead anyway. It was still daytime, but there was an overcast and the sky had a perfectly even dullness, so there was no way to tell what time of day it was, much less which direction was north or south or anything else for that matter. A two-lane blacktop road snaked up into the distance and disappeared into some trees, or a forest if you wanted to get technical about it. It also snaked down toward some lumpy hills and disappeared there as well. What sounded like a two-stroke chainsaw could be heard in the distance, but it was impossible to tell whether it was up in the forest or down in the lumpy hills. This had been happening more often lately. Two different ways to go, with a dead battery and no bars, and nobody left to blame.

Nobody but himself, anyway. Not that he wanted to be alone. He thought he could put up with anything Maggie dished out because of that and what they still had in bed every once in a while. But now he'd like to tell every youngster in the world that sex isn't everything and not because he was older. It just wasn't and especially when there's a kid involved. Those little guys have some kind of power. They throw up and everything comes to a standstill. Sure, he could have put up with playing second-fiddle to a baby, that's temporary after all and they're cute. But he gave up on the relationship because on top of Maggie treating him like shit, the baby wasn't even his.

Oh, Maggie was a good little actress, he'd give her that, and he wanted to believe her, wanted things to go back to how they were when he first

No Bars and a Dead Battery

met her. A year ago, she'd left him for almost six months, saying she needed to find herself, or something stupid like that. Then one day she was back, sitting at the kitchen table, like she was royalty, leafing through a magazine. Seeing her again was what he had been praying for but when it happened it wasn't like he imagined it would be, even though he went through the motions of being happy. But he had been alone for those months, just going to work and coming home, and he wanted his life back. He kept telling himself that the changes he saw in her—big breasts, no waist, crying over nothing—were all his imagination. But after a while it was pretty obvious that she had found herself all right and someone else too, no matter how much he lied to himself. And when she announced that she was having a baby, he acted pleased. But when she told him she wanted to get married, he acted like he didn't hear her. The reason for that was born five and a half months later—Lee Forester, Junior, eight pounds and two ounces. Premature, she said.

Telling Maggie he was unemployed was what finally set him on the road. She didn't care what his boss, that asshole Dennison, had said about him. A real man, accent on *real*, would have kept that job no matter what, because he had a wife and son to support. A *real* man wouldn't waste all morning looking in the want ads which are about as useful as a toilet in an outhouse, he'd go out and make some money. A *real* man would get that car fixed and throw in some new tires. And on and on. Besides being a great actress, Maggie could out-nag anybody. But he kept slogging and he tried to make it work, tried to ignore her, tried to ignore what his life had become. In the end, he stuffed some in a duffel bag, picked up his coat, and any cash he could find and left before dawn while the house was quiet and dark and just as lonely as when she was gone.

His first ride, an old farmer driving an even older pickup truck with a chicken roosting in the cab, picked him up fairly soon after he hit the highway. At first he was grateful for the company, but the guy never stopped talking. He told stories for too many miles that he probably made up as he drove about how big his house was and how young his wife was and how his other car was a new Cadillac. Lee finally escaped when the guy pulled over in front of a greasy spoon and said this place had pretty good chili but not as good as his wife made when she wasn't otherwise occupied, wink wink. Lee shook the man's hand and waved farewell.

He walked through town to a truck stop on the outskirts and waited around for a while and finally some young, fat, hairy guy got in a big rig that had naked girl mud flaps. Lee asked for a ride and the guy said that was no problem and for him to climb on up there and smiled. Big. He did a line of cocaine, just to keep himself awake he told Lee, and asked if he wanted some. Lee said he didn't and fell asleep as soon as they hit the highway. A few miles later he woke up to find his pants unzipped and the guy's right hand down them while he steered with his left hand, sweating like a pig. Lee punched him and the guy sat up straight and said to calm down, that it wasn't what he thought, and Lee asked him what was he doing then, looking for change? He said to pull over right here and took his duffel bag and got out. The trucker eased back onto the highway and stopped to yell out the window that hey, nobody rides for free, asshole.

Anyway, that's how he ended up on this two-lane road with the no options, except to turn left or right. He could smell rain far away and he felt a stab of nostalgia. For what, he didn't know. Nothing he remembered, that's for sure, and the loneliness of his life overwhelmed him. Did it really matter which road he took? Or anybody took? All roads seemed to lead to the in the same place anyway, as always. Well, no use feeling sorry for himself. That chainsaw sound meant there were people somewhere, but going toward the trees meant going uphill. He turned turned the other way, toward them.those lumpy, brown hills he could see far off in the distance.

The day was warmer than he thought and he hadn't eaten for hours. So it was no wonder that he saw the car before he heard it, coming right

No Bars and a Dead Battery

toward him, the driver hunched over the wheel, staring through the windshield at nothing. The last thing he thought as he sailed over the hood was that this was his punishment for walking out on Maggie and the baby. He landed in the ditch, his arm bent in a way he didn't know was skeletally possible. He lay there, moaning.

Up on the road the car had lurched to a stop and backed up and a woman peered down at him like he was a rodent. Then she cranked down the window and wanted to know if he was all right. He stared at her. Was he *all right?* He said that considering in the last twelve hours he had left his girlfriend and her kid that she said was his and gotten rides with a liar and then with a pervert, and now he was laying with a broken arm in a ditch after being hit by a car going two hundred miles an hour he was doing great. Oh, had he mentioned how he had been fired over a lie. She sighed and got out of the car and by the time she had climbed down into the ditch beside him, he was laughing hysterically about his shitty life and crying hysterically about his shitty life. She felt his arm and his shoulder, ignoring his laughter and his howls and his bad words, and slapping him on the head when he got in her way. Then she raised his arm and bent it behind him towards his other shoulder. He screamed like a banshee, but they heard a loud pop and the pain subsided. He would live.

She turned and was out of the ditch, half-way back to the car, when he called to her. She stood in the road, watching him haul himself out of the ditch until he stood at the top. She asked him how much he wanted to spit it out because she didn't have all day. He said he didn't want money, just a ride to the next town, and that she owed him that. She shot thought for a minute and then motioned for him to come on. She got in the car and stuck her head out the window and yelled at him to hurry up, that it was his arm that got dislocated, not his feet. Great. Another nagger. At least he'd be rid of this one soon.

He opened the door and eased himself onto the front seat. He saw a gym bag, full of something, in the back. She put it on the floor, gave him a dirty look and took off in a mass of flying gravel. Lee buckled himself in, preparing for a bumpy ride, and then looked at her: she was a big woman, not old, not young, not ugly, not pretty, but not the kind who would be doing two hundred miles an hour down the highway to get to the gym. She saw him looking at her when she checked the rearview and side mirrors for the fiftieth time and wanted to know what the fuck he was looking at. He stuck out his hand and said his name was Lee Forester and he appreciated the ride. She said to excuse her, Mr. Manners, but she was using both hands at the time or she would have slapped the shit out of him, and also, speaking of hands, he better keep his to himself.

Lee thought that would be no problem at all and wondered, not for the last time, if he had done the right thing by leaving. Better the devil you know and at least he had a home there, even if the last few years had been less than good. Plus, her boy needed a dad and he was there, feeding him and changing his diapers. If that wasn't love, what was? Who knows? He decided to call Maggie before he went any farther, and then remembered the charger was sitting on the kitchen table. He asked the woman if, by any chance, she had a charger that would fit his phone. She looked at him like he was crazy and said how about using a phone that's already fully-charged? Would that do? Besides, who was he going to call way out here, the president? She yanked open the glove compartment and dug around. He saw the gun, smelled the steel. He said that was okay, that there was no one to call anyway, and leaned his head back on the headrest and got as comfortable as he could. She wasn't going to talk him to death, obviously, and he was pretty sure he wasn't going to wake up to find *her* sticking her hand down his pants, although she might shoot him.

After a few miles, Lee woke up, startled out of a dream that she had run over something, something big enough to send the car spinning off the road, bucking into the air. He looked behind them. The road was flat and smooth and ahead of them it went on forever. But there was a

No Bars and a Dead Battery

thumping coming from somewhere in the car, methodical and regular. He hated to remind her that he was there, but he finally had to ask what that noise was and got no response. He said it could be dangerous, especially considering how fast she was going. Still no response. He said he should take a look because he could fix anything with an engine. She turned the radio on without looking at him, flipping the dial from one end to the other and finally leaving it blaring out static. He closed his eyes. She and her stupid car could blow up for all he cared, except that he would too and he wasn't, for some reason, feeling very suicidal.

She turned off the highway onto a dirt road, parked, and took the gun out of the glove compartment. She pointed it at him then, breathing like she'd just run a marathon, and said there was something she had to do and he had to help her or she'd kill him. Thinking that wasn't much of a choice and wondering how he was going to get out of this, he told her they could handle whatever it was without a gun. She motioned for him to get out of the car, took a deep breathand the gun, and went around to the trunk. He followed her, pretty sure something was coming that would make him change his mind about wanting a ride to the next town. She popped the trunk and he found himself staring at a man who took one look at them and tried to bite through the duct tape over his mouth. His hands and his feet were taped together behind him, and his head was bleeding from banging it against the inside of the trunk. He looked like a fat, furious worm, trapped there. She slammed the lid down, which resulted in another thump, and a muffled roar.

Lee leaned against the fender and took a few deep breaths and tried to speak but nothing would come out of his mouth except little puffs of air. She moved in front of him, pointing the gun at him, and said that now he could see why she didn't want to give him a ride and that it was nothing personal. He finally asked who that guy was and she asked if he wanted details or just wanted to know who he was he in general. He said in general would be fine. The man was her husband Bob and if Lee didn't help her kill him, she'd kill both guys and tell the cops Lee had killed Bob after he taped him up and stuffed him in the trunk, and then he'd held a gun to her head and raped her and kidnapped her. She was shaking.

Lee told her she obviously wasn't going to kill him or her husband or she would have done it by now. In fact, she wouldn't even have stopped the car after she hit him. She looked away and Lee asked her why she did it, was it another woman? She lowered the gun and shook her head and said that he had cleaned out the savings account. The other woman didn't matter. Lee said if it was just money, everything could be worked out. But they couldn't leave anybody in a trunk.

She said her husband's life was not worth saving, take it from her. Lee said that lots of lives weren't worth saving but if you started killing people it would never end and if one life didn't mean anything, no life would, including your own. He had seen it every time in combat. She sank to the ground and sat there, eyes closed, and began to cry. He sat down beside her and said how about if they untaped her husband's mouth, gave him a drink, and let him make one phone call. Not to a buddy but to someone like his mama, and then they'd leave.

She quit crying and was quiet and for a while there was no sound but that constant thumping. Then she pulled up her sleeves and held out her arms for him to see. Cigarette burns mostly. She said that they both used to drink but after a while he came up with this real fun game of wrestling and the winner got to put out cigarettes on the loser. She always lost. She quit drinking and took a self-defense class and that was the end of that.

Sweet Jesus. He hadn't even known this woman a day and already he was sick of the stupidity and brutality of her life. Worst of all, though he tried not to, he could see bits of his own life in hers, bits of himself in her. He wanted to be rid of both of them. Maybe go back to Maggie. Their relationship made more sense than this. Of course, that's probably what everybody thought about their crummy relationships. Anyway, he'd leave her, in the next town. But for now he racked his brain for

No Bars and a Dead Battery

something comforting to say, and finally said she must love Bob a lot to put up with that. She said that love was no excuse for cruelty and that she had no one to blame except herself for staying. Lee was quiet a moment and then he said the whole trunk thing was her call, that he'd do whatever she wanted.

She said she didn't know what she wanted and sat looking straight ahead, eyes like flint. A crow landed in front of them. He squawked and hopped back and forth until she smiled and Lee saw then that she was younger than he thought. And definitely not ugly. She just kept smiling at the crow and looking at it like she had never how their feathers glisten or how their eyes catch the light. The crow cocked its head and stared at them for a moment, until it heard another crow call far away and flew off, leaving behind only the grayness of the day. She said the bird reminded her of something she had read once, a poem, that everything is holy. She didn't remember who wrote it. It was something she had forgotten about until now.

She stood up and got her gym bag out of the car and tossed his duffel bag to him. She said that he sure didn't know her mother-in-law, tand Lee said he didn't want to know her mother-in-law, he just wanted her to come and get her boy, so they better get this thing over with. She popped the trunk, and Bob roared as much as you can with your mouth taped shut. Lee lifted him out, bloody head and wet pants and all, and set him on the ground. He worked on the tape and finally had to yank it off, taking a great chunk of beard with it. Bob screamed in pain, snarled at him, and then called the woman every name he knew, and some he had made up in his spare time in the trunk. He finished by yelling that she'd better run like hell when he was free because he was going to fry her up, he was going to barbecue- Lee slapped his hand over the man's mouth.

Then woman opened her gym bag and took out a phone and handed it to Lee. Lee told the red-faced, furious Bob that he would call Bob's mother and let him tell her he was okay and where he was. But Bob worked up all the saliva he could, which wasn't much, luckily, and spit it at Lee and said he wasn't okay and told him to go fuck himself with all that lily-white concern. Anyway, his mother knew where he was and she was probably on her way right now. The woman pointed the gun at him and said to use the fucking phone. He belly laughed then and said Lee was a pussy and she was a cunt and he was worried more about who'd win the Super Bowl than he was about getting shot. She clicked the gun.

Lee whispered that they weren't going to kill him, remember, and the woman said oh, yeah, she had forgotten and aimed the gun with both hands. He pulled her arms toward the ground just as she pulled the trigger. The bullet ricocheted off the hard dirt and went right through the gas tank of the car. A stroke of good luck since the bullet could have just as easily gone through one of them but also a stroke of bad luck because the car turned into a firebomb. They watched as flames engulfed it Then she picked up the gym bag and said have a nice life as she passed Bob. He called after her, saying he was sorry, that it was nothing personal, that he loved her but being in the trunk made him a little hysterical.

Lee hesitated, caught somewhere between his good intention not to kill anyone and his desire rid of them both and get the hell away from there. She told him to go ahead and help Bob if he wanted, that it had nothing to do with her. She said that life goes forward, not backward, and life without inflicting pain on yourself was her idea of moving forward. Even if Bob got loose and and killed her, one day of freedom was more than she had had with him. She walked toward the highway without looking back.

Lee dug a bottle of water out of his duffel bag. It was almost empty but he tried to pour what was left down Bob's throat. Bob sputtered, frantic, and begged him to please not leave him tied up and yes, he had a girlfriend but he loved his wife. A lot. He would never physically hurt her. Lee asked him about those cigarette burns and Bob said he didn't know anything about that. Honest. And would he please just cut the tape? Lee patted him on the shoulder and said that he'd be back with a car. He tried not to listen to the man's curses and cries and caught up with her. She didn't look at him or change her pace and said Bob would be okay, that he'd probably get to the next town before they did.

The grayness of the day had become night which gave them some protection from being seen and therefore from the revenge of Bob, if he should live through his captivity and who Lee felt would be exonerated by a jury if he did a drive-by shooting at them. But he sure had been an asshole of a husband, if she was telling the truth. Who knew what had happened? Who knew why people stayed together? Who knew why they left?

They trudged along for while, listening, getting off the road whenever they thought they heard a car and hiding behind scrub brush. But every time the sound turned out to be the wind or that the cars had turned off the road. Tired and hungry, they decided to stop and eat, although "eat" might be an exaggeration. They sat down against a spindly tree and she pulled some candy bars out of her gym bag. Lee hadn't eaten anything for almost twenty-four hours and those candy bars were like a high-fructose bomb. He wolfed them down and laid back to catch a few winks. In the dark, she started talking. Lee sighed. Now was not the time to get all chatty. Was it the trans-fat or what?

She said her name was Vivie and that she had cleaned out the bank account, not Bob. He was trying to get it back. She sat there in the dark with her head down and he asked her why she hadn't just taken out an account in her name. She said she couldn't because she had embezzled from a bank where she worked once and there were apparently no statutes of limitation on that one. They always found out and they always had an excuse not to hire her. She didn't blame them. She was young and stupid and Bob was convincing back then. So after she got out of prison she could only get low-paying jobs, caregiver, janitor, fast food, until that's the only kind she was qualified to get. But she put everything she could into that account.

Andthen he got his latest girlfriend pregnant. By this time, Vivie didn't care. Let him have another family, even move in with them. She'd babysit and have the whole bed to herself. But when she found out the first step in his new life would be a quickie-divorce from her and then putting his new wife's name on that bank account? No. That was a different thing altogether. Everything she had lived through came back to slap her in the face with shame and humiliation. She hadn't been a victim until he stole from her. Plus, she'd be handing out fast food until she was too arthritic to move.

Vivie stopped talking and sat staring at the mountains far away. Lee watched her and knew he had no right to judge. Jesus. The things every person lived with every day. He said nothing, didn't even think of any great advice, just listened to her. She talked some more and then lay down and put her head on his chest. He smoothed her hair until she fell asleep. He realized she wasn't big, she just wore clothes that were big. They lay there a while and he thought about the One Big Road. Would Maggie and her boy be wherever it lead, judging him, holding him accountable for leaving them in the lurch? Would Bob be there, with his bloody head and his dirty pants, still trying to kill Vivie? Or would they all be friends? Is that where Life led?

He was almost asleep when he heard the whine of an engine far off in the distance. Either a ride or another disappointment. Vivie shot her hand out over his mouth and listened. Then she jumped up, gathered their trash and stuck it in her gym bag. She said she knew that sound because the car was hers and if there was one thing she knew, it was engines. He grabbed his duffel bag and they held hands and ran to the biggest and lumpiest hill they saw. They lay side by side on their stomachs, listening, listening, listening to the whine become a roar.

The car screeched to a stop right where they had the little picnic. Had they left a wrapper? An imprint in the dirt? They heard the doors open

No Bars and a Dead Battery

and close. The sound was muffled and seemed to go back and forth. But they could hear a woman's voice and two men's. Vivie said that those voices belonged to Bob and his mother and his brother Jimbo who was as rotten as the rest of them. They listened, trying to make out what Bob and Mama and Jimbo were saying, and then they heard nothing, which worried them more than anything. After a long time of silence, Lee decided to climb up the hill and see if they were gone. Vivie tried to pull him back but Lee said he'd just have a look and let her know if the coast was clear. He climbed to the top and slowly raised his head and saw nothing but the emptiness of the desert. Then he started slowly down the other side to have a better look.

He turned to yell to Vivie that it was okay to come out, when he heard the click of a gun and he felt cold metal jabbing into his cheek. He jumped and Bob laughed and said he thought Lee was coming back with a car and that he had really looked forward to seeing him again and introducing him to the family. Four hundred pounds of stinky, sweaty flab stood behind Bob, grinning with no teeth. Lee guessed it was Jimbo. Some skinny woman that Lee figured was their mother stood by a bush, smoking two cigarettes at once. Bob looked like the normal one in the family, which wasn't saying much. He pushed the gun harder into Lee's face and wanted to know where Vivie was. Lee said how was he supposed to know, that she took the first ride that stopped and left him in the middle of nowhere. Bob said that sounded like that good-for-nothing-lying-whore Vivie all right and said she sure didn't seem worth dying for and that Lee wouldn't have to if he suddenly remembered where she was.

Lee said it wasn't about remembering, he just didn't know where she was. Besides, couldn't they just talk about this dying thing for a minute? After all he was the one that talked Vivie out of shooting Bob and leaving him in the trunk, and he was the one who gave Bob a drink of water. So, actually, he deserved a medal instead of being threatened with death.

Bob's mother put out one of her cigarettes and said to leave him be, that they were looking for Vivie and she would come home when she was readyto come home. And they needed to go because this night air was starting to make her sick. She coughed, loose and rattley.

Bob sighed and put his gun away and said maybe Lee was right and Mama was right and maybe Vivie would come back home like she always did, anyway he sure missed her. He sighed again and then put his arm around Lee's shoulders and asked if he wanted a ride to the next town. Lee said thanks but he'd kind of like to walk because he needed the exercise and besides, he really enjoyed the desert at night. Bob said he understood, he enjoyed it all the time, even at noon, but he was keeping these love handles. Hahaha. Then he asked if Lee would like to see the car. It was a classic. Lee couldn't see any way *not* to see the car and said real nonchalantly that yeah, he might as well since he was going that way anyway and wished he was sitting in the old man's truck, listening to his fish stories.

They walked toward a 1955 El Dorado. In perfect condition. Red. Beautiful. Jimbo said that it was Vivie's inheritance from her dad who was living in Mexico or Monaco or wherever he was from, which was probably where she was by now. They were sorry not to get to say goodbye to her but at least Lee could see the sights in style. Then he laughed like a hyena into the cold, dark night. His mother slapped him on the head, hard, and said he talked too much.

Bob put the hood up and asked if Lee remembered when engines were all V-8 and Lee said yeah, he did and bent over to look. Jimbo came up behind him and threw him on the ground and held him there while Bob covered Lee's mouth with duct tape and then wrapped it around his wrists and ankles. Their mother stood there, still smoking, and asked them what the hell good this was going to do since it that wasn't him they were looking for and they ought to get moving. Bob said yeah, maybe no good, but in the meantime Lee would find out what it felt like to be taped

No Bars and a Dead Battery

up like you were going to FedEx and then just left to rot like thrown-out garbage and that Mama should just mind her own business or she might get taped up herself. She threw down her cigarettes and got back in the car and slammed the door. Jimbo stood up and dragged Lee toward the car while Bob popped the trunk which was so huge it needed its own area code. He could hear Mama yelling that she was hungry and to hurry up goddammit.

Lee lay on his side in the dark after Bob slammed the trunk, trying to count backwards from a thousand and trying to remember to breathe real slow, when he felt someone tap him on the shoulder and whisper his name. Tears coursed down his cheeks and the crotch of his pants grew warm and soggy. If he ever got home, he would pay for Maggie to go on dates (well, he did that already, he just hadn't known) and pay for her boy to go to Princeton. The voice whispered his name again and he told himself okay now okay, they were all going to die someday anyway, even those jokers driving the car. The ghost, or whatever, pulled him on his back and stuck its face in his. Vivie. It was Vivie. He wanted to say thank you for being here, thank you for being alive, now get me out. He shook his hands and feet. She shook her head. She said she wanted him to calm down and breathe through his nose. He wanted to tell her that goddammit that was the only way he could breathe. She had a plan and she needed Lee to stay tied up for now and pushed him back over on his side. He felt her take his hand in the dark and he squeezed back as hard as he could, holding on for his life.

The car swerved and came to a stop suddenly and Lee heard Jimbo yelling to go on and Bob yelling back that he couldn't go on and just pull into the nearest town and open the trunk and haul out a guy who had duct tape all over him. That would be like taking him to the nearest police station. Jimbo should use his fucking, stupid brain, and not be thinking like his fucking, stupid father. Besides, Mama was hungry, so they just needed to hurry up and take care of business before all the restaurants in the whole world closed. Jimbo yelled that's why they needed to go on.

Lee felt Vivie pull her hand away. The trunk opened and the grinning, slick face of Bob and the angry, fat face of Jimbo and the pinched-up, disgusted face of Mama all peered in. Mama sniffed and said he must have wet his pants or something and walked away. Jimbo pulled him out and hauled him to the front of the car, by the headlights, and dropped him there. Bob said he would rather it was Vivie that found out he was nobody's boy to be traveling around taped up in a trunk but you had to make do with what you had. Besides, he'd make that point when she came home, like she always did, beat down and crying.

Lee got as ready as he could to die but there was really no way to get ready for that, so he just gritted his teeth and waited. He had always imagined his death would be a little more dignified than this or mean something to someone but instead here he was, surrounded by strangers who would just pull into the nearest burger joint after they put a bullet through his head. Then he heard a metallic click and waited for them to just do it and prayed that his death be quick and, he hoped, painless.

But that click belonged to Vivie, who stepped out of the shadows, pointing the gun at Bob and Jimbo. She said they better step away from Lee and kneel down or she'd blow them up and in fact she might just blow them up anyway, she hadn't decided. Bob laughed and said he knew she'd be back just as soon as it got dark and she got scared, poor baby. He walked toward her. She shot him in the leg and turned the gun back on Jimbo who hadn't moved, just stood there with eyes like full moons. Bob went down crying and calling for Mama. Vivie told Jimbo to tape Bob's hands and feet, which he did, against Bob's will. Then she told him to tape his own and hurry up. She moved in close while he grunted and sweated and taped his feet and then his hands, not tight but good enough for her to put the gun down and finish the job. He started crying and asked her not to tape his mouth please he'd do anything. She left his mouth untaped and dragged him by Bob and left them there crying in

No Bars and a Dead Battery

unison. Then she walked over to Lee.

It had been twenty-four hours of one bad thing after another, well, forty years and twenty-four hours if you counted his whole life, and he waited for the next bad thing to happen. But she said she was sorry and touched his face and said that this would be over in a second. She yanked the tape off his mouth. He was glad he didn't have a beard. She knelt and laid down the gun and untaped his hands. They were numb and he shook them while she untaped his feet and massaged his legs. Then she helped him stand and they turned toward the car. And came face-to-face with her mother-in-law, who was holding the gun Vivie had put down. She pointed it at them.

No one said anything unless you consider Bob and Jimbo still crying as saying anything. Then Mama asked Vivie if she hated them all so much to just up and take that money like that when they had given her a home, jailbird though she was. Vivie said no, that she didn't hate Mama and didn't even hate Jimbo, just Bob. Mama said she hated both of them sometimes, and at the same time even, and laughed alone. Then she said it was time to end this thing and that Vivie wasn't so easy to live with herself. And her boys weren't killers. End this thing? Lee was too tired to even fight an old woman. Especially one with a gun. She motioned to the car and said for them to get lost before they proved her wrong. They walked slowly to the car, trying not to run, trying not to throw red meat in front of Mama, when she called out for them to stop. They did, expecting bullets in their backs. Mama said she knew Vivie thought she had done a bad job of raising those boys but Vivie didn't know anything, not about the boys' lives or Mama's or about being a mother. No one said anything. After a few minutes, Mama said to just go on, just leave her here, just leave all three of them here, that she would take care of the boys just like she had always done. She started crying. When Lee and Vivie got to the next town, they felt like they could still hear her.

They pulled into the nearest restaurant. Lee figured they needed tacos, lots of them. He just wanted to stuff himself and make up for everything that had happened to him in the last twenty-four hours. Vivie ate a couple of tacos and then sat back and watched him. He was oblivious, eating, proof he was still alive. She thought if Mama herself and her boys had tapped him on the shoulder right then, he'd move over and tell them to sit down and eat up. She leaned forward and said she'd been thinking. This stopped him cold just as he was reaching for another taco. That could only mean trouble. He waited for the blast.

She said her father had moved back to Le Havre in France after her mother had died and she had married Bob even though her father begged her not to. She still had dual citizenship. She'd keep on putting money into a savings account, but she was thinking about buying a garage there with the money she'd get for selling this car in Miami. She hated to let the car go, she said, but she couldn't take it with her and she wanted to get as far away as she could from Bob and Jimbo and Mama. Le Havre was nice. And she missed her dad. Anyway, Lee could either just take a vacation for a couple of months or start a new life. Of course, if he stayed it would only be a marriage on paper, a formality, no ties, and she looked down. She said she couldn't think of any other way to make up for the mess of the last few hours and what did he think?

He just stared at her. She looked normal, but the older he got the harder that was to define. He said before he was shipped overseas, where he didn't exactly fit in with the locals, he hadn't even been out of the state, much less the country. Plus, he asked her if that wasn't a little risky to maybe marry somebody that she didn't even know? Also, he reminded her that he had asked her for a ride, that she didn't owe him anything. She looked up and said hah to all points, that she didn't care whether he was a world-renowned traveler and that nobody really knew anybody before they married them and also, regarding his last point, he shouldn't be so stupid. She started on another taco.

Lee just sat there, thinking. A vacation or a second chance. When had he had either? He said thank you, he'd think about it and they got up to leave. Just then an ambulance came roaring up, siren blaring, and stopped across the street in front of the run-down building that served as hospital, pharmacy, and grocery store. People streamed around the ambulance like a river, flowing from open-air restaurants and produce stalls and houses, excited to see what had happened to someone else so they could walk away, counting their blessings. Lee couldn't believe so many people lived in this tiny town.

They were swept by the crowd along to the ambulance. The drivers opened the doors and jumped into the human sea, fighting their way to the back to haul out the stretchers. First they brought out Bob, still and white, already dead from another gunshot wound. They were lifting Jimbo, who was heavy and bloody and on his way out, when another ambulance pulled up just as fast and screeched to a stop. The drivers jumped out yelling at the drivers of the first ambulance that driving around looking for customers who hadn't called you in the first place doesn't make you legal. The first drivers said these guys would have died if it weren't for them, and then noted that well, Bob did die, God rest his soul, and they all crossed themselves and then went back to yelling. Meanwhile, Mama, her face all red and wet and swollen, banged on the back window of the second ambulance, telling them to shut up and let her out and that they needed to get to the emergency room right now. Lee and Vivie turned around.

They made their way through the crowd, and back to the El Dorado. And as they approached it, a crow flew directly over their heads and landed on the hood and then looked at them. They stood some distance away and watched the crow watching them. Another crow flew directly overhead and landed beside it. The first crow squawked and then both flew away. They watched the crows disappear, looked at each other, and then got in the El Dorado. Only one way to go this time, with five bars and full battery.

RECALCULATING

Colin Brezicki

No coverage, not even one bar, the battery was dead anyway. It was still daytime, but there was an overcast and the sky had a perfect dullness, so there was no way to tell what time of day it was, much less which direction was north or south or anything else for that matter. A two-lane blacktop road snaked up into the distance and disappeared into some trees, or a forest if you wanted to get technical about it. It also snaked down toward some lumpy hills and disappeared there as well. What sounded like a two-stroke chainsaw could be heard in the distance, but it was impossible to tell whether it was up in the forest or down in the lumpy hills. This had been happening more often lately. Two different ways to go, with a dead battery and no bars, and nobody left to blame.

Nobody but you. So, snap out of it, pal. *You* are left to blame, the man who can't remember how he got here, or where he's heading to. *If you don't know where you're going, any road can take you there.* Who said that? The Queen of Hearts to Alice. You remember Alice, so that's something. Otherwise you're down a big old rabbit hole yourself and it's all your fault.

You never like to remember this part, but the doctors warned you it would happen unless you changed your ways. Eat properly, exercise and reduce your alcohol consumption, they told you. Now you call it your *stroke of luck* because it didn't kill you. But it left you with holes in your brain, gaps in your day and whole chunks gone from your life. Things you do, you forget like they never happened. Take right now—you drive all day and remember nothing. Your rear view's a blank—objects in the

No Bars and a Dead Battery

mirror nowhere to be seen.

Your odometer showed 256,704 miles when you left Great Falls. You wrote it down because you have to write everything down. Now it's showing 256,905, so 201 miles from Great Falls to wherever this is. You don't remember a mile of it. Not a town or a road sign of it. Is this even Montana anymore? The road you started on became a different road, the six-lane out of Great Falls a four-lane out of somewhere else then a two-lane and now a gravel stretch that's suddenly quit on you—like even the bulldozer gave up and went home.

Your GPS has no signal, not that you had a clue how to work it, and your phone's dead. Ashley gave you the phone so you were connected, and the GPS so you'd know where you were, but you're out of touch and lost anyway.

Ashley. Of course. You're driving to Billings because your daughter's in trouble. She left you a message to say she's finally pregnant and she's never been happier, but the voice said different. The voice told you she's afraid of Ryan.

You warned her before she married him that she was making a mistake. You could tell he was an abuser. Oh, he's done well for himself, but that doesn't amount to a hill of beans when a man has cold eyes. You could always read people and now you can read a voice when it's scared—you may have holes in your brain but you can hear fear in a phone message—so you're driving to Billings because Ashley's in trouble.

And so are you with the gauge on empty and this godforsaken place looking nowhere like Billings. You'll check out the chain saw first, so maybe someone can put you on the right road and tell you how far to the nearest gas station. Maybe they'll have a map. A proper map with Billings clearly marked, not a GPS that changes its mind every ten seconds so you want to reach into the glove compartment for your Ruger .38 Special and blow the freaking thing to bits.

You flip a coin. Heads for the lumpy hills, tails for the forest. Tails it is.

The noise gets louder as you get closer, so you lucked out. Now you wonder if it really is a two-stroke chain saw, or is someone flying a model airplane in the middle of nowhere, or maybe it's a hippopotamus with flatulence. But you won't find a hippo out here, or anyone flying a model airplane, so it must be a chain saw, and you wish you didn't think stupid all the time now.

You see a gap in the trees and a grassy driveway run up to an unfriendly looking house in a clearing. A '78 El Dorado's parked in front, a puke-colored two-door coupé, and there's a guy down the side of the house sawing up logs. He's wearing a red-checked shirt and matching cap with the ear flaps down, and you ask yourself who dresses like that anymore.

You get out of the car and wonder if you should take along your Ruger .38 Special because you wouldn't stand a chance against a chain saw if this guy wants trouble. But you leave it in the glove compartment because it's only directions you're after, which isn't much to ask, is it?

He looks up and kills the chain saw when he sees you coming. Right away he breaks into a stupid grin, which is a little weird because you're a stranger and for all he knows you could be planning malfeasance of some kind. Then something really weird happens. Out of nowhere, a couple of crows fly in and settle on his porch railing. He waves an arm to shoo the crows as he walks towards you. They look at him but stay put, so just like that he yanks the pull-cord on his chain saw and revs it at them. They fly off into the trees, and what was that all about, you think, especially how he whipped out his chain saw like he was Wyatt Earp or somebody.

He takes off his hat and wipes his forehead with his sleeve. Then he puts out his right hand, trying to act all friendly, but the chain saw's still sputtering in his left. One false move and he could slice your head clean off with a swing of his arm, so you grin back at him and shake his hand.

You ask him how to get to Billings from here, and where *is* here anyway. He kills the motor again and stares at you like you're from another planet. Then he takes off his dumb hat, scratches his head and points away off to his left. Billings is two hundred miles from here, he says, *here* being next door to a one-horse town called Twin Bridges. Where did you come from, he asks, and when you tell him Great Falls, he laughs—guffaws more like—then he asks how in hell you ended up at Twin Bridges when you were heading for Billings.

You tell him you must have taken a wrong turn sometime after you left Great Falls and he laughs again—harder this time—and says you *must have took* a wrong turn before you even left your driveway. He's on a roll now and says how you *must have took* highway 15 instead of 87 out of Great Falls, so you came southwest instead of going southeast and ended up at Twin Bridges which is as far away from Billings as you could get in one day. You probably set a record, he says. A record for what, you ask. For being clueless, he says. He's laughing even harder now, but his eyes are fixed on you, black eyes like a robin's, empty and cold. You know he'll start up that chain saw in a second if you don't laugh too, so you chuckle and nod at how stupid you are for spending the better part of a day driving in the wrong direction. You don't tell him you live in a senior's home, and not a house with a driveway, because he already has a low opinion of your intelligence. What you really want to do is stroll back to the car, take your .38 Special out of the glove compartment, stroll back and put all five bullets between his cold robin eyes.

He tells you that the black top road you saw from up the ridge is the 90 straight to Billings. Turn right when you get to the highway, he says, and just keep driving. He'd come with you as far as the blacktop to make sure you turn right and not left but he's got six cords of firewood to saw up for winter. He laughs harder than ever and you tell him it's okay, you'll manage on your own. He doubts that, he says, but what can you do. He had no call to add that last bit, you think. He'd already had his fun, and when he starts up his chain saw you turn around and stroll back to your car.

After you drive a couple of miles and come to the black top you remember to take a right. As you head towards Billings you think maybe it would have been simpler to look for his jerry can—he must have had a jerry can for his chain saw—and emptied it into your Taurus instead of taking the keys to his El Dorado because its gauge showed half a tank. But you didn't think ahead. Seems you can't think ahead any better than you can think back, and that's a whole new problem. Live in the moment, sure, but the moment's not a good place to live in if it's all you can manage. The moment can be kind of scary in fact. You try to remember what you did with the body and where you left the Taurus, but you can't focus with the ringing in your head. You pick up your .38 Special from the passenger seat—it's still warm and the five chambers are empty. You reach behind and shove it into your overnight bag.

He was right about the 90 taking you all the way to Billings because all of a sudden here you are. You don't even remember stopping for gas which you had to have done because the gauge is still showing half and the odometer indicates you've driven two hundred miles since you left the guy's yard. Maybe the gauge is stuck, so you had no idea how much gas was in the tank when you started, never mind how much you have now. Maybe you were lucky to get here at all, because you obviously didn't collide head-on into an eighteen-wheeler or drive off a cliff, things you could have done for all you'd be aware of at the time.

The 90 becomes Montana Drive as it heads into the city proper, and you see the sign for Pioneer Park—you remember Ashley's two-story faces the park. Five minutes later you turn down Virginia Lane and pull up at the curb by her house. You switch off, grab your overnight bag and get out of the car.

She's already at the door when you go up the path and she says the Lord's name out loud when you get near. You see that your shirt and pants are filthy and there's dried blood like rust on your sleeve and you remember now you dragged the body into the wood and covered it with a

No Bars and a Dead Battery

layer of leaves and dirt so the scavengers could still get at it. Now you look like you just crawled out of your own grave.

Ryan comes to the door and stands at her side. She takes his arm and holds onto him like she'd collapse if she let go. You wish she would let go—you'd hold her up. But her face tells you she's not letting go.

She asks what you're doing here, and look at the filthy mess you're in, and what's with the dinosaur you're driving, and why didn't you notify them you were coming. You tell her she sounded unhappy on the phone that one time, and she says what are you talking about. What else is she going to say with Ryan right there and her hanging onto him?

You tell her you borrowed the car from a friend because the Taurus is being fixed. You had a flat tire on the way here and got in a mess changing it yourself. You didn't phone ahead because you wanted to surprise her. But she looks more scared than surprised so you know you read her voice dead right on the phone. You ask if you can have a sandwich. It's getting dark and it's long past suppertime but you can't remember eating today.

She tells you to take a shower and change your clothes. Do you have a change of clothes in your bag, she asks, and you answer yes you do. She'll wash the ones you're wearing, she says, and you feel better now, because this sounds more like her. Ryan says he'll make you a ham sandwich, but you'd rather Ashley made it. He says he's perfectly able to make a sandwich, and you can see he's already getting testy, but you know he'll spit on the bread when you're not looking or use ham that's passed its sell -by date because he hates your guts and so no thanks, you don't want him to make your sandwich. Ashley says she'll make the sandwich if you go upstairs to shower and change your clothes.

Your room's all ready because she always has the guest room made up for anyone who comes on short notice, or even no notice at all like you. Ryan doesn't deserve her, but at least he won't try anything while you're here.

They're standing together behind the kitchen island when you come downstairs. She's made you a cheese sandwich, not ham, and that's weird, you think, as you sit down to eat it. You see the fear in her eyes and the cold in his, and so it's time to put it out there. You swallow a mouthful of sandwich and ask him why he abuses her. They go all stiff and grey for a moment like they've been injected with quickset.

She takes his arm again and glances up at him like she's afraid he'll hit her for snitching on him. Then she looks at you and says he's wonderful to her and what on earth are you talking about. She's in denial because that's where abused women go. They stand by their men like Loretta Lynn, or maybe it was Tammy Wynette.

You want to talk to her alone. She protests, but he tells her he's happy to go out for a while if she's comfortable with that. You ask him why wouldn't she be comfortable alone with her father, but he says it's time for Magoo's walk anyway. Magoo is their white Scottie that's blind in one eye and walks into the furniture a lot. Ryan grabs a leash and takes Magoo out the side door which he slams.

You tell her she should come back to Great Falls with you. She can bring Magoo because dogs are allowed in the residence. She looks at you and shakes her head. She's not sure she knows you any more she says, and you've upset her terribly by coming here with your accusations. She loves Ryan more than her life. Now she's pregnant with a daughter of her own that's due in seven months, all being well, so your coming here has set her right back. You see the tears in her eyes as she tells you he's the kindest most loving man she's ever known and she has no idea why you've *taken such a dislike to him*. This is part of her new way of speaking, all la-de-da, because she's been worked on by his family with their airs and graces.

You observe her while she speaks, but you don't see any bruises on her face or around her throat, or on her arms. This doesn't fool you. You know that emotional or psychological abuse is worse and can leave invisible bruises and scars that never go away. She's talking about you now, not Ryan, saying you need serious help because you're delusional and you've turned up in someone's ugly car looking like you've been dragged through a hedge backwards and why did you ever stop going to therapy. Ryan has put these ideas into her head.

Right on cue he comes in the door with Magoo, after a very short walk you think. He looks at Ashley and asks if everything's okay. She goes over to give him a hug, and stares at you to show that not only is everything okay but Ryan's one helluva guy and she wishes it was you who died in the car crash however long ago it was, and not her mother. Her face can be very expressive.

Now Ryan wants to talk to you alone, so she goes upstairs to get your dirty clothes for the wash. You left them on the floor and you hope she doesn't look in your overnight bag because you'd have to explain the Ruger. You're thinking about that when Ryan barks at you for not listening to him. Then he goes all soft-voiced and tells you it's not a good idea to upset Ashley, and were you aware how long it took them to conceive. You do remember vaguely because anything you remember is only vaguely, so you nod that yes, you were aware.

And now you're aware you've made a terrible mistake. You should never have come here, you're thinking, when Ashley appears carrying a laundry basket and says a police cruiser has just pulled into the driveway. The doorbell rings and you panic because there's only one reason why the police would come to the house of a pregnant woman and her loving husband who never broke the law and only do good things like adopt half -blind Scottie dogs, and that reason is you. Ryan stares at you like he knows it too. When he goes to answer the door it's Ashley's turn to look at you and not say anything.

Ryan comes back into the kitchen and says the police officer wants to talk to the owner of the El Dorado parked at the curb. You think you might make a dash out the back door, but you're too old to run through back yards and climb over fences anymore.

Then you think this can't have anything to do with the body in Twin Bridges because the guy lived on his own in the boonies, so no one could miss him already. You hoped by the time anyone missed him the scavengers would have found his body and devoured it. But you wish you could remember what you did with the Taurus when you took his El Dorado. You go to the door.

The officer's a woman so you relax a little. She smiles and says you have to move your car because tomorrow is the Thanksgiving Turkey Run, and the route is right along Virginia Lane. You didn't see any signs, you tell her, and you didn't even know it was Thanksgiving, but of course you'll act with full compliance.

Then she asks if you knew that the front headlight on the passenger side is smashed and you tell her you had no idea. Something must have happened on the way to Billings—you clipped a tree or another car maybe—but even if you knew it at the time you forgot. Now she asks to see your license and registration, which actually she's not allowed to do. You tell her she's out of her jurisdiction because you're inside the house and you haven't broken a law, only a headlight, which could have been a vandal. She looks at you, her eyes going cold suddenly, then she turns and heads down the steps. You watch the cruiser pull away knowing she's calling in the registration of a puke green El Dorado with a smashed headlight.

Ashley and Ryan have overheard everything, but before they can speak you hold out the keys to the car and ask her to move it into the driveway. If you even step into the car the cops will appear out of nowhere and demand to see your license and registration. She takes the keys like she was expecting this. Ryan goes with her so they can talk about you.

When they've moved the car into the driveway they come back in and she says they're leaving tomorrow after the Turkey Run's over. They're

No Bars and a Dead Battery

driving to Gillette to have Thanksgiving dinner with Ryan's parents, as was previously arranged. You aren't invited because you had a blowup with his family last year at Christmas. You'd been drinking and said things about Ryan you shouldn't have, so you and his family aren't on speaking terms. Anyway, you think you might have your own plans for Thanksgiving.

Ryan asks about the headlight and you tell them it was broken when you borrowed the car, but they don't look like they believe you. Ashley looks anxious and you know it's not about Ryan this time. She says they want an early night with their three-hour drive to Gillette tomorrow. You go to bed but can't sleep because you're the one who's anxious now, still having no idea what you did with the Taurus. The police will be back in the morning, so you have to dump the El Dorado altogether because they'll bring a warrant to see your documents. They might know everything by then, which would give them a real advantage because even if they knew only the half of it, that would still be more than you do.

Does Montana still have the death penalty, you ask yourself. That would be bad enough, but worse would be the shame and disgrace which Ashley doesn't deserve. You work out something like a plan in what's left of your head and then drift off.

In the morning, there's some commotion below your window. You look out and see a crowd lined up two and three deep waiting for the Turkey runners. By the time you shower and dress the runners have started coming through. Some wear turkey hats and others feathered tops. A woman is jogging in trainers painted to look like turkey feet. Most are running in outfits of orange and black because it's Thanksgiving, and after the run they'll go home to gobble down their turkey dinners and squabble with their families because everyone's had too much to drink. But right now everyone looks like they're having fun.

Your phone has recharged overnight, and all five bars are up again because you're in Billings not the boonies now. Not that there's anyone you want to call. You put the phone in your overnight bag along with the clean clothes Ashley has folded and laid on a chair inside the door. You've reloaded your Ruger .38 Special—five bars up there now as well.

The runners have thinned out by the time you head downstairs, and you see the tail-enders shuffling past the living room window. Spectators still line the street and cheer them on. When there are no more runners you ask Ryan if he would mind driving your El Dorado to a parking lot somewhere and leave it there with the keys. The police will be back with authorization and you don't have the right documents. He'll be happy to get rid of it, he says—he's obviously embarrassed having some redneck's rust bucket parked in his driveway—but he won't drive it anywhere with a headlight hanging off. He grabs a roll of duct tape and goes out to reattach the headlight.

While he's gone Ashley says they'll drive you to the bus station before they head off to Gillette because you can't stay in their house alone. She makes you promise to call your therapist when you get home. You watch Ryan back the El Dorado out of his driveway and park it at the curb. Someone in the crowd points at it and smiles.

He comes back into the house and tells Ashley she should come with him. He wants their car to stay in the driveway because there's strangers still milling about. They'll take a cab back, he says, but you know he doesn't want to leave her with you. You hear a police siren somewhere and you wish they'd hurry up. You give your daughter a hug and say goodbye. You hope she has a happy Thanksgiving. Ryan's already on the verandah.

She heads out the door and you go to the front window to watch. You want to remember this moment because it could be the last thing you *do* remember, depending on how things go from here. You want what happens now to be all that stays in your head. You open the window so you can hear everything too. The siren gets louder as you gaze at your daughter and impress the scene into your brain.

No Bars and a Dead Battery

You watch them walk down the path to the car, she clutching his arm, her head leaning towards his shoulder. Observe the details, you tell yourself. Her blonde hair wisping in the breeze. Her navy windbreaker and grey skirt. The brown leather shoes with toggles. What else do you see before they drive away? Take it all in so when you play it back this is what you'll remember.

They made their way through the crowd, and back to the El Dorado. And as they approached it, a crow flew directly over their heads and landed on the hood and then looked at them. They stood some distance away and watched the crow watching them. Another crow flew directly overhead and landed beside it. The first crow squawked and then both flew away. They watched the crows disappear, looked at each other and then got in the El Dorado. Only one way to go this time, with five bars and full battery.

GONE BUT NOT FORGOTTEN

Shannen Camp

No coverage, not even one bar. The battery was dead anyway. It was still daytime, but there was an overcast sky, which had a perfectly even dullness, so there was no way to tell what time of day it was, much less which direction was north or south or anything else for that matter. A two-lane blacktop road snaked up into the distance and disappeared into some trees, (or a forest if you wanted to get technical about it). It also snaked down toward some lumpy hills and disappeared there as well. What sounded like a two-stroke chainsaw could be heard in the distance, but it was impossible to tell whether it was up in the forest or down in the lumpy hills. This had been happening more often lately. Two different ways to go, with a dead battery and no bars, and nobody left to blame.

The two boys stepped out of the car, arguing about something. She couldn't quite hear them from her vantage point in the trees but that didn't stop her from watching. It was her favorite game: try to figure out the lives of those who had arrived.

From what she could gather, the boys were probably brothers. That would explain why they looked similar, and why a teenage boy would ever be caught dead chauffeuring a boy of about eight around. The older one looked down at his phone and frowned. It was the same frown she'd seen so many times before.

The fact that things always seemed to go generally the same way didn't discourage her from finding interest in those who happened across this long stretch of road. It always started with the car breaking down at the same spot. The driver would get out of the car, sometimes after blaming their other passengers for not filling up the tank, even though she knew they had. Then they'd look down at their phones and realize they had no bars. On top of that their battery would be low even though they'd swear they just charged the phone.

These boys were no different. Except for the fact that the younger boy didn't seem at all phased by this strange turn of events. Instead he immediately began walking away from the car, picking up a long stick in the process and brandishing it like a sword.

The girl in the woods tensed a bit as the young boy approached, but she didn't run away, just ducked down a bit lower in the bushes as he walked into the dense forest. He was humming a song and smiling widely, as if this sort of thing happened every day. His brother had started calling for him, more exasperated than worried. It seemed the young boy wandering off wasn't a rare occurrence.

The teenager looked down at his phone one more time with narrowed eyes, apparently cursing his bad luck. Giving an overly exaggerated eye roll for good measure, he pocketed the phone and did a little jog to catch up to his brother.

Following closely behind while still keeping enough distance to not be noticed, the girl listened to their conversation. It seemed to generally consist of the young boy asking a ridiculous and irrelevant question that had no connection to anything they had previously been talking about. Then the older boy would respond in a way you'd expect an exasperated older brother to. Often dismissing the younger one's questions. They went on like this in a cyclical manner for quite some time.

There wasn't anything particularly special or unique about the boys. Or at least, there wasn't anything unique about the teenager. The younger boy, though, was either incredibly optimistic and naive to the dangers of travelling through an unfamiliar forest, or he really was as fearless and unconcerned as he seemed to be.

The girl thought about travelling ahead of the boys to catch them off guard when they reached the old house, but something kept her in her place, sneaking slowly behind them as they walked. Maybe it was the young boy militantly walking with his stick that he had now transformed into a gun that was slung over his shoulder as he hummed his song. Or maybe it was the fact that their youth and innocence gave her pause.

All the others had been older. Harder. And usually much less innocent. They had always been the type who had gotten themselves into a bad situation through bad decisions. But she still wasn't sure how these two had ended up here. Maybe because of the bad decisions of others?

Considering these possibilities, the girl had gotten sloppy. She hadn't been paying enough attention to the boys and found herself passing them by through the trees. The younger boy stopped his teenage brother and whispered something in his ear, pointing to the place the girl had just been. She silently cursed herself for getting sloppy. Luckily, the teenager reacted how she'd expected him to. He shrugged off the excited interest of his brother and kept walking, checking his phone every now and then.

The girl breathed a sigh of relief. She hadn't been spotted. That meant she could get on with the proceedings, if she so chose. But something still held her back. The boys were nearly to the house now and a decision had to be made. She just wasn't sure why it had suddenly become such a difficult decision.

In the past, things had always played out in a fairly standard manner. People broke down on the road. They knew they could head toward the forest or the hills walking on the road, but instead, they always decided to walk away from their vehicle and the road and head into the trees.

The girl would watch them walk aimlessly around until they stumbled upon her old home. They would enter, ask if anyone was there, see the old rotary phone and try to get it to work. All the while, the girl would watch. She was usually in the woods alone and so having some company – even company that didn't know she was there – seemed nice from time to time. But she could only pretend for so long.

As soon as she felt herself fading, the desire to reclaim her place in this world would surface. It used to be something manageable. Something she could control that she'd compare to a particularly strong craving for chocolate. But over time, as she gave in to the "craving" it became stronger. To the point where the girl almost felt like it was in charge of her.

Once that temptation to stay in this world became too strong, she'd do what she always did. If they seemed like a nice enough person, she'd take what she needed without them ever knowing. She'd even do her best to only take what was absolutely necessary. Who would miss five years off the end of their lives?

The difficulty came when the person she was following let slip some undesirable detail about their life. Some shady past. Bad decisions. People they'd hurt. Five years for the girl didn't actually last her five years. And so to the kind people, she'd given up a part of her time in this world in order to spare them too much pain.

But when *these* types entered her forest, she didn't feel as bad for taking twenty years or more. Of course it probably wasn't necessary for her to include the theatrics of drifting through the walls in her full glory to scare the life out of them before she took what she needed.

In her full realization, she was a sight to behold. A thing of beauty that was every bit as terrifying as it was captivating. Her long silver hair, big doe eyes, petite stature, and full cheeks made her look sweet and harmless. It was when the dark circles under her eyes darkened even more, the veins under the skin of her face that went from being invisible to a ghostly dark blue, and the long mournful scream she released when she took the years she needed in order to stay in this world; those were the moments she could see why people had used words like wraith or ghost or banshee to describe the thing that lived in the woods.

But she was none of those things. She was surviving. And it wasn't her fault that she only had one way to do that. She could agree that it was her fault when she got a bit carried away with scaring the life out of someone who she deemed less-than-deserving of the years they'd been given.

And then there were these two boys. The younger one so full of optimism and faith in his older brother. And the older one, still trying to pretend he wasn't worried about the well-being of the both of them, all the while keeping a much closer eye on the brother he'd been so annoyed with only moments before.

It seemed that of the two of them, the younger was the brave one. The older was too jumpy. If he caught even a glimpse of her, she was sure he'd pass out. Then he wouldn't be of any use to anyone. Not to his brother, and certainly not to her.

She could feel the pang of her existence, reminding her that she needed to act. She could feel that pull towards the boys. The pull of survival. She'd done it a million times before. And it wasn't as if she was killing them right then and there. Instead she was just killing them in seventy years, when the time she took caught up with them. At least that was how she'd always justified it.

Watching the boys enter the old house and rummage through it, she felt another pang. But instead of survival, this one was of sadness. The young boy was still humming his song, smiling, and exploring the house as if it were a fun adventure and not a dangerous deathtrap. But the thing that actually got to her was the older boy.

The boy who had been so dismissive and annoyed before was looking at his brother with sadness in his eyes. Possibly realizing they were truly lost in a place that seemed hopeless. He was watching his brother explore and play when he knew he'd gotten them into this situation.

At that point, he was probably wondering why he'd chosen to go into the woods in the first place, rather than following the road to the nearest town. Of course, it wasn't his fault. He didn't have a choice in the matter. People were drawn to the woods. The girl had made sure of it. It was the only way for her to keep her life source coming. That and killing their cars and phones as they arrived.

The girl sighed, now torn as to what she should do. The older boy turned back to the broken rotary phone, fiddling helplessly with it even when he knew he couldn't fix it. But while his back was turned, the younger boy spotted her again. This time she hadn't been quick enough to move. She just sat there, peeking through the window.

The younger boy took a moment to register what he was seeing, but when realization dawned on him, he didn't scream or cry or gasp. He just let that same easy smile return to his face, lifted his hand, and waved at her. She put her finger to her lips, wordlessly telling him not to let his brother know she was there, though she still wasn't sure why.

Did she want to remain mostly anonymous so that she could take their years without them realizing it? Or did she do it because she knew deep down that she couldn't go through with it? Though if she didn't she was basically signing away her own life. Or what was left of her life she supposed. It wasn't as if she was really living anymore anyway.

The girl lifted her pointer finger and beckoned for the young boy to join her outside. He looked over his shoulder at his older brother, admiration obvious in his eyes, before he left the abandoned house to join her in the dark woods.

She didn't think she'd be able to resist the years the young boy had attached to him if she got too close. He was still so young. He had so many years to give. And the temptation to just scrape a few off the end of his life was too tempting. So instead she drifted ahead of him, close enough to be seen but far enough to discourage any conversation or contact.

The girl hadn't ever let anyone leave without first taking what was owed her, and now that she was seeing the result of this in full force, she, herself, was quite frightened. Around her in the forest, she could see the silvery wisp-like forms of those whose years she had taken. Standing silently in the woods, watching as she led the young boy back to the car, his brother finally chasing after him.

The young boy must have seen the entities as well, because his already large eyes got wider and more curious. He reached his hand out towards one of the forms but he quickly pulled it away as if the vapor had shocked him. He sucked on his sore finger and kept walking, still staring at the forms but knowing better than to try to touch them anymore.

The teenager called out for his brother, the concern obvious in his voice, but the girl kept her pace steady. She needed to lead them away before her need to survive overcame her. She didn't want to harm these boys. Even the annoying teenager had grown on her in a short amount of time. He had to be about the same age that she was when she'd become... whatever she'd become. This connection endeared the teenager to her.

The older brother called out once more and his sibling answered, though he continued to follow the girl through the woods. The silvery shadows of her victims still watched them. They were tall and pale and sometimes didn't even seem solid, but the thing that made her uneasy were the black gaping holes where their eyes should have been.

Perhaps taking years from them had a more dire effect than she'd realized. And as this thought crossed her mind, her still-unresolved question answered itself. She couldn't take these boys. She couldn't take their years. She wasn't even sure how they'd gotten here in the first place. The only people ever drawn to her road were lost souls. Whether they were lost because of their own wrongdoings or because of their internal anguish. But these boys were too young for any of that.

She had been doing this for... some time. Though she suddenly couldn't remember exactly how long it had been. Or how long she'd been this way. In fact, she couldn't remember what she'd been before this had happened to her, and her lack of recollection scared her more than the silvery ghosts who watched her with judgment in their black eyeless

No Bars and a Dead Battery

sockets.

The older brother had finally caught up to them, but when he saw the girl in front of them, he just stared silently. He kept pace with his sibling, but didn't seem to know what to say about the girl who was leading them back to their car. He'd glanced at the forms of her victims around them once or twice, but his main focus seemed to be her, which she thought was odd given the fact that the entities surrounding them were far more terrifying than she was.

The younger boy tugged on the jacket of his brother, getting his attention as the girl continued to try to ignore them as she led the way. She could hear the younger one whisper though it took her a moment to figure out what he had said. He seemed to think the girl looked like someone he knew. But not just anyone. His sister. Their sister.

The older boy looked back up at the girl in front of them once more, furrowed his brow, and looked back down at his brother. He seemed to agree, however reluctantly. All the while, the girl tried to ignore their words and remind herself that they were just strangers who meant nothing to her. She had one purpose in life and she was now ignoring that purpose in favor of getting these boys back home safely. Her logic had clearly gone out the window.

One word, whispered between the brothers, caught her attention, no matter how much she had been trying to ignore it. *Twin.* The younger boy mentioned a twin. A twin sister to the older boy. One who had been lost only a year before on this very road.

The girl shook her silvery hair, trying to convince herself that this was a coincidence. After all, she'd been doing this for ages. For as long as she could remember. The sheer number of her victims standing in the woods surrounding them and near the open road where the car stood were a testament to just how long she'd been like this.

But the more she tried to think about it, the more she realized that not only could she not remember anything before her time stealing the lives from other people, but she also didn't seem to have many memories at all. The time she'd spent in the woods could only be traced back about a year. Had her eternity really been so short?

All at once, her reality seemed to be crumbling around her. How could she not realize what had happened to her? Had she been cursed to stay here since the day she had died? And why did her brothers come to the very spot where they had lost her? It seemed like the memory would have kept them away for the rest of their lives.

The older brother quickened his pace to approach the girl, but she tried to ignore him, now unsure of everything she'd thought she knew. But as he spoke to her, telling her that they'd finally found her, she couldn't help but stop, right at the tree line, only feet from the vehicle she'd intentionally stranded on the road so that she could take life from these boys. Her brothers.

She looked at the car, which was now working once more. She looked over at her two brothers who watched her intently. She ignored the crowded bodies of her victims, which had gathered around the car in a wordless send-off. And then she remembered everything all at once.

It wasn't just her who had died in the car accident. Her brothers had died with her. They'd been separated as soon as they'd crossed over, and she'd been spending her time trying to come back to the side of the living by stealing years from others. All the while, her brothers had been on her side of things the entire time, just looking for their lost sister to bring them back home with her.

She wasn't sure how cell phones and cars fit into the afterlife. She wasn't sure of much anymore. But she did know that her brothers had found her, and they were going to be together now. She would be with them, wherever they were going next. And they seemed to understand that just as well as her, as they smiled at one another.

They made their way through the crowd, and back to the El Dorado. And as they approached it, a crow flew directly over their heads and

No Bars and a Dead Battery

landed on the hood and then looked at them. They stood some distance away and watched the crow watching them. Another crow flew directly overhead and landed beside it. The first crow squawked and then both flew away. They watched the crows disappear, looked at each other, and then got in the El Dorado. Only one way to go this time, with five bars and full battery.

1014'S NAME WOULD BE LOLA

Shelby Carleton

No coverage, not even one bar, the battery was dead anyway. It was still daytime, but there was an overcast and the sky had a perfectly even dullness, so there was no way to tell what time of day it was, much less which direction was north or south or anything else for that matter. A two- lane blacktop road snaked up into the distance and disappeared into some trees, or a forest if you wanted to get technical about it. It also snaked down toward some lumpy hills and disappeared there as well. What sounded like a two-stroke chainsaw could be heard in the distance, but it was impossible to tell whether it was up in the forest or down in the lumpy hills. This had been happening more often lately. Two different ways to go, with a dead battery and no bars, and nobody left to blame.

And yet, *this is all your fault* would have probably been the first words out of Paul's mouth, had he not been stunned at the abrupt death of the radio not halfway through what he believed to be a David Bowie power ballad. He'd been so ready to hit the high note, his throat was still tight as he sat there in silence, mouth agape, neck veins blue and bulging. Instead, as he finally collected himself, he swore at the dead battery of the El Dorado pulled so suddenly to a halt, and then blamefully looked at the sex robot beside him.

1014, the sex robot, asked Paul if he would like to know the latitude and longitude of their coordinates. He nodded. She told him she couldn't compute with no bars. She *could* have bars if she wanted to; it was only a matter of switching on her database signal. But it was often so much

No Bars and a Dead Battery

easier to say she didn't to keep Paul from requesting a new power ballad, or searching for the fifty best inspirational quotes of all time and having her read them back to him. Paul could be quite thick at times and not in any of the good places.

1014 rested her silicone hand on her silicone chin, staring into the void of scattered foliage and tiny hills surrounding the road they'd broken down on. A crow was sitting alone on top of a billboard advertising trailer hitches in offensive red lettering. It squawked once, and flew away.

Paul leaned against the steering wheel, and gently began to bang his head against it. 1014 counted to a total of twenty three seconds before he gave up on the banging (not an unusual trait for Paul) and cracked a beer and took a swig.

It had been Paul's mid-life crisis for the past year. He'd been on a banger of gambling, smoking, drinking, parties, expensive cars, and exactly one sex robot. The catalyst was the death of his wife, Lisa. She was all he could talk about. Lisa loved David Bowie. Lisa wore red dresses. Lisa wore blue dresses. Lisa loved movies. *The Notebook* was Lisa's favorite movie. Lisa used to twist the ends of straw wrappers and blow into the open end, spearing Paul in the heart like an arrow of love. All Paul could talk about was Lisa.

1014, purchased by Paul six months after Lisa's passing, was a robot manufactured for sex. She was a vessel for Paul to vent to, and occasionally fuck if he got horny after relaying the story of his wedding night, or anytime they passed a McDonald's because he and Lisa had done it there in the bathroom once. 1014 didn't mind so much, firstly because sex was her job and she liked doing her job, and secondly, because Paul wasn't a bad guy. He was just sad.

1014 often wondered about Lisa, and what she'd been like in the flesh. Completely and utterly lovely was the impression she got from Paul but no one is perfect. At least, that was what all the magazines said. The ones about people and stuff, that cost $4.99 and had smiling women on the covers flashing headlines about weight loss, home decor, and seven easy ways to treat anxiety and depression because *no one is perfect not even this model with B cup tits and teeth as white as her bleached asshole.* 1014 didn't know what those things were.

As robots go, she was pretty standard with her own thoughts and maybe even an idea or two but never any *feelings.* After being with Paul for a while, the feeling of *sad* did not seem pleasant. But then again, *horny* sounded like the best thing ever provided there's a friend nearby. So who was to say, really? The system was give and take. But even with that sadness, 1014 still wanted to feel. Something. Anything.

Sometimes, 1014 supposed that *wanting* itself was a kind of feeling, so she was practically halfway there already. Maybe, with a few more screenings of *The Notebook,* she'd work herself up to a real and true *aww* of emotion rather than faking one the way she faked her orgasms— because once again, she couldn't feel—while Paul burst into tears beside her the same way he did after sex.

Paul pocketed the car keys, and told 1014 he was sorry for being upset with her. It wasn't her fault the battery had died. Of course, it was her fault they didn't have bars but she wasn't about to share that information with him. Paul hadn't brought a map, so the way to Richard Green's cabin was uncertain at best. As 1014 understood it, Richard was a lumberjack, and a friend of Paul's from college getting married for the second time.

Richard's bachelor party was the third stop on Paul's Mid-Life Crisis road trip. After the party, they would be off to Vegas. Paul grumbled about the chainsaw noise, wishing it would sound again so he could at least pick a direction to start walking in. Chainsaws were the theme of the party, as noted by the invitation sealed in an envelope doused in gasoline, that, once revealed, displayed a chainsaw covered in glittering letters that read *On my way to the old ball and chain- saw. Help me go out with a bang!* The envelope was filled with flour, for some reason, and 1014 had figured it was meant to look like cocaine because Richard *used to be into that shit*, to quote Paul's explanation.

1014 had looked it up online, and found that lumberjacks hardly ever used chainsaws anymore, instead preferring the efficiency offered by the *feller buncher*, a motorized vehicle that could cut and strip trees in seconds. Upon asking Paul about the strange tool of choice, he told her Richard was all about taking matters into his own hands, and liked to be as close to the action as possible.

That was just how much he loved his job.

And then, like a jump scare during an otherwise silent scene halfway through the latest B-list horror flick, a chainsaw went off. Paul nearly smiled in relief and pointed to the forest, pinpointing the direction of the sound. 1014 and Paul got out of the El Dorado, leaving it on the side of the road. Judging by the recurring whir of what seemed to be multiple chainsaws, they weren't far from the bachelor party. Richard would probably be able to give them a jump when they were ready to leave. Hell, maybe even a new battery which he tended to keep on hand due to his habit of forever leaving the headlights of his truck on.

It was hot outside. The summer had been a dry one, with little rain but lots of sun. 1014 handed Paul his ball cap to protect his slowly balding scalp. You can never be too careful, especially in the middle of nowhere. 1014 inspected her arms. Like her legs, they were clear, showing off the silver wires and soft blue glow emanating from beneath the silicone skin. Her face, neck, chest, and buttock were tinted to be more skin-like in shade.

As it turns out, skin was sexy and silicone was not; as the research showed, nothing turned people off more than glowing plastic nipples. 1014 had very nice nipples. Very realistic looking. In fact, they were so nice that she was sporting a sheer white dress to display them to the world at Paul's request. Lisa usually hid her body due to her embarrassment of her low hanging breasts and stretch marks, but Paul had always tried to instill confidence in her. She could wear whatever she wanted and be just as beautiful and the rest of the world would have to deal with it. Of course, Lisa never got a chance to show off her body to the world because she died. But maybe she would have with some more time. There was really no way to know.

Paul and 1014 reached the place where the road turned to gravel and the trees got thick, creating a canopy of cool shade overhead. Tiny yellow circles danced down the path where the light broke through the leaves. A small clearing appeared on the left, revealing a bench and a rotting well. It looked like it may have been a romantic spot long ago where lovers could leave notes for each other under the cover of the forest or some shit like that. Now it just looked old and unused.

As Paul and 1014 continued to walk, thankfully, the whir of the chainsaws continued to get louder. Being thankful for chainsaws was not the thought 1014 had been expecting that day. But being thankful was a feeling, and 1014 would take what she could get. Being thankful for chainsaws was the best!

A conglomeration of black, red, and white trucks was gathered at the end of the gravel road. Voices and laughter carried through the trees. A house came into view, just behind the trucks. It looked like the house you'd expect to find in the middle of a forest in the middle of nowhere. Good craftsmanship, but as brown and boring as dirt, with a shitty satellite dish angled straight up to the heavens hanging precariously off the side of the chimney. A couple of crows were hanging out in the surrounding trees. 1014 could hear them squawking.

A man 1014 could only assume to be Richard began waving wildly, whatever was in his red plastic cup spilling over her flailing hands and down his arms. Richard yelled that Paul was late, but that they'd been waiting for him, the lucky bastard. Paul explained the car battery had died a little ways down the road, and as expected, Richard immediately sent one of his buddies, Tom, to retrieve a brand new one from his garage and

No Bars and a Dead Battery

hook it up for him. Tom saluted and sped off to complete the task.

A group of about ten other men appeared from behind the house and shook Paul's hand. They all took a good look at 1014, who stood a little behind Paul so as not to be distracting. Her amazing nipples were still visible though, so she ended up being pretty distracting anyway. One guy brought Paul into a hug and his eyes met 1014. He asked Paul, quietly, how he'd been holding up without Lisa, and then quite seriously asked if it was too soon for Paul to have acquired himself a sex robot. Paul looked at the man, full of gratitude for his concern, and was probably about to thank him or tell him about how he'd been doing, when Richard cut him off.

Richard loudly asked what the hell they were talking about, and if he had heard the other man, Bob, correctly in his asking if it was too soon for a *sex bot*. A sex bot! Paul was no pussy, that much was for sure. Richard assured everyone he got a sex bot not even a month after his first wife left him and hadn't regretted it since. Some other men raised their glasses to their own sex bots, or their girlfriends (none of which were at the bachelor party).

Bob patted Paul on the back and told him if he ever needed to talk, he'd be around. Paul laughed, half-heartedly, and told him it wouldn't be necessary but that it was *good to have a bro*. Richard winked at Paul, then poured him a drink, and handed him a chainsaw. They'd be cutting down trees with chainsaws, obviously, to commemorate Richard's last days as a free man (1014 failed to understand the symbolism if there was any). Paul told 1014 she was free to wait outside or in the house until he got back, it was entirely up to her.

The men waited around for a few more minutes until Tom returned a hero having successfully replaced the El Dorado's battery. They clapped him on the back, and then 1014 watched the men disappear further into the forest with chainsaws over their shoulders, and drinks in their hands. She wondered if Paul would choose a similar activity for a bachelor party, like Scrabble perhaps, because it was something he was good at and he liked showing off.

1014 sat on the front porch steps. She was facing the forest where the men had gone and the driveway full of trucks, five of which had the exact same pair of iron bull testicles hanging from the back hitch. One of them had a girl seated on the hood, quite inconspicuously.

1014 wouldn't have noticed her if the girl hadn't lifted her head. She looked about fifteen with stringy blonde hair and rainbow socks pulled up past her knees and a cigarette between her lips. The chainsaws revved in the distance. The girl looked 1014 up and down and told her she could see her tits like she wasn't stating the obvious.

Her name was Elizabeth, a reluctant daughter to Richard Green. She'd been trying to give a shit about his upcoming nuptials for the past three months, but he didn't seem to care all that much so she decided she wouldn't either. Elizabeth looked like she could use some cheering up, so 1014 told her a little bit about herself and Paul, and how she had sex with him, and how he missed Lisa. Elizabeth said the whole thing sounded like what she called a band-aid solution, but 1014 didn't know what that was.

Elizabeth took a drag of the cigarette and puffed out the smoke in saggy rings. A couple of crows had landed on the hood of another truck and were watching her. Elizabeth muttered something about how sad the fucking things looked, all droopy with ruffled feathers. She figured they were a sign of the apocalypse, and then leaned back on the hood of the truck, staring up to the canopy of trees.

1014 encouraged her to continue her thoughts. Elizabeth was way ahead of her. She was just content to have someone to talk to. She told the robot about the crows and how they'd been hanging around the house with nowhere else to go. She figured they knew the apocalypse was on the rise because Elizabeth had recently figured out how to masturbate, and she liked it so much she'd done it multiple times since.

Now it was the second coming of Christ or some shit like that. Fire was going to start raining from the sky soon, Elizabeth was certain of it. 1014 reminded her that she had sex with people all the time and it wasn't a big deal, the same way that masturbating wasn't a big deal. But Elizabeth wasn't having any of it.

1014 suggested she tell her dad about it, but Elizabeth shrugged her off. She told 1014 her dad was the type to not even realize women could masturbate in the first place. He'd ask her how it worked, and she'd try and explain the concept of the clitoris. He'd fail to understand and Elizabeth would abandon the cause. 1014 said Paul was very good when it came to knowing female anatomy, but Elizabeth didn't feel like talking to Paul. 1014 tried asking about Elizabeth's soon-to-be step mom, but she was gone on business trips most of the time so Elizabeth didn't know her very well and felt like she wouldn't really get a chance to.

Elizabeth's sister was the only other person she could think of to talk to, but she was far away like the intelligent woman their father never understood. 1014 wondered why Elizabeth continued to touch herself if she thought it would bring down the apocalypse, and Elizabeth told her if by doing it the first time she was already getting fucked she may as well enjoy herself. It grew quiet outside the house; the sound of the chainsaws had died down rather suddenly. Maybe the party had gotten tired, or bored. Then, in the quiet, 1014 asked if Elizabeth missed her mom.

Elizabeth looked up at her quite suddenly, eyebrows drawn together, her eyes crinkling at the edges. Her lips parted as if she was about to say something, or let out some sort of long suppressed noise, but instead she jerked her head down and crushed the cigarette under her boot on the hood of the truck. Then she told 1014 she missed her mom *all the fucking time*. All the fucking time.

The worst part was she didn't even want to miss her. It sucked so much, waking up some days and wanting to see her so badly but knowing she couldn't, that she'd puke in the bathroom from the anxiety and that would feel okay because it meant she wasn't thinking about how sad she was. Elizabeth hadn't been that sad in a couple of months though, there hadn't been any puking in the bathroom. But then 1014 had to go and bring it up and now Elizabeth felt like she was a zombie all over again.

Elizabeth wiped under her eyes to make she hadn't fully pussed out and cried any actual tears, then told 1014 she didn't look very empathetic. She was just sort of standing there looking like, well, a robot. But 1014 couldn't feel, and Elizabeth thought she was pretty lucky in that regard.

There was a crackle in the distance, and a shout and a cheer. 1014 looked up through the canopy of trees. A cloud was billowing across the sky in thick black plumes. All at once the smell of smoke hit her like a wave, washing over her circuitry and the glowing blue core wedged deep inside her chest.

Elizabeth stood up on the hood of the truck, and the nearby crows took off, squawking all the while. They were followed by what looked like hundreds more all flying for their lives to escape the glow of orange in the distance. Elizabeth swore and jumped off the truck. From the sounds of the cheering, the bachelor party had started themselves a fire, leaving Elizabeth and 1014 to burn in it.

1014 was adamant they get to safety, and took Elizabeth's hand in hers. They could both see the flames now, striking forward at an alarming rate. Their senses were overwhelmed with the stench of smoke and the feel of heat creeping closer, and closer, like an oven pre-heating to bake your grandma's favorite turkey that you know, deep down, will be too dry while your mother-in-law argues with your second cousin twice removed about the state of the nation and the right to free speech. Doesn't matter anymore. Your grandma's dead.

As they ran down the shitty gravel road, 1014 was looking for Paul. If the bachelor party had any sense they'd be close to the road, trying to move themselves away from the flames and exit the area. Elizabeth called out for her dad a few times, scanning the tree line as desperately as 1014.

Elizabeth muttered something about masturbating and the apocalypse,

No Bars and a Dead Battery

and then she spotted Richard. With music blaring out of multiple cellphones, the party was in the small clearing with the bench and the rotting well. Drinks in hand, they were laughing and wielding chainsaws and at least two of them had barbecue lighters and one had ripped his shirt and stuffed it into the top of an empty beer bottle to make a Molotov cocktail. Clearly, he wasn't sure how a Molotov cocktail worked. Paul was nowhere to be seen.

Elizabeth cried out for her dad, but he couldn't hear her over the chaos of the partying and the flames. Ash was raining down. Elizabeth let go of 1014's hand, and ran toward the clearing. A piece of ash caught her sleeve and immediately caught flame, startling Elizabeth so bad she fell to the ground and frantically patted at her arm and dragged it against the ground, but the flames were already wrapped around her elbow. She screamed for her dad, long and hard. She looked at him through the clearing, her arm on fire, as he waved around a lighter and howled at the trees.

A frantic crow flew across the path, it's wings on fire and its feathers raining down like molten raindrops. 1014 wrapped her own hands around Elizabeth's arm and told her to count to three. She counted. The fire was out, leaving 1014's hands warped from the heat. Some of the silicone had melted away, revealing the metal joints beneath. 1014 told Elizabeth they had to keep going, and they both stood up and continued to run. Elizabeth didn't look back. 1014 was still searching for Paul.

1014 and Elizabeth reached the end of the gravel road but didn't stop until they were nearly to the El Dorado, far from the forest and the flames, but still close enough that the smoke was unbearable. Sirens sounded in the distance from behind the lumpy hills, and a string of firetrucks appeared, lights flashing, and exceeding the speed limit. They pulled past Elizabeth and 1014, prepared to fight the beast that lay before them.

Thankfully, 1014 watched Paul burst forth from a cluster of trees. He was stained with ash and dirt and looked a little on the singed side but he was alive and that was something to be okay with. He ran for 1014 and doubled over, panting, when he reached her. 1014 told him how glad she was to see him and patted him on the back with her wrist where the silicone hadn't melted.

Paul said he phoned the nearest fire department the moment it started. He'd run back from the bachelor party to the house to use the landline, but 1014 and Elizabeth had already fled. He kept saying how sorry he was, over and over again. He should have kept things under control, he should have said something sooner about playing with the lighters, he should have done everything differently. But he didn't. And now here they were, with a raging fire and a lot of dead crows.

Some of the firefighters had located the rest of the party and were escorting them to safety. They also looked like shit. That one idiot was still carrying his stupid fucking empty beer bottle with the shirt stuffed inside.

Paul looked at 1014, and handed her the car keys. He told her to take the car and go wherever she wanted. Finish their road trip, or not, it was up to her. A couple police cars rolled up to the scene. Paul told her that he needed to stay behind. He needed to tell the authorities why half the forest had been obliterated, and take responsibility for his part in it.

Then Paul told 1014 he didn't want to see her ever again, but hoped she wouldn't take that the wrong way. She'd been a good friend to him, and Lisa would have liked her. That was for sure. He hugged 1014 goodbye, waved to Elizabeth, and headed toward the police cars, his arms in the air to wave them down.

A crowd was starting to gather, with the firetrucks, the police cars, and the few tourists on the road stopping to take photos, the once seemingly empty space was starting to feel claustrophobic.

1014 held the keys up to Elizabeth and asked her where her sister lived. Elizabeth smiled, and then she started to cry. And she hugged 1014

No Bars and a Dead Battery

and 1014 hugged her back, and maybe it was a circuit overheating but 1014 swore she felt a flutter deep within her chest. She asked Elizabeth if she liked music and switched on her database signal. Elizabeth told her she fucking loved it.

They made their way through the crowd, and back to the El Dorado. And as they approached it, a crow flew directly over their heads and landed on the hood and then looked at them. They stood some distance away and watched the crow watching them. Another crow flew directly overhead and landed beside it. The first crow squawked and then both flew away. They watched the crows disappear, looked at each other, and then got in the El Dorado. Only one way to go this time, with five bars and full battery.

SCHRÖDINGER'S PEOPLE

Savannah Cordova

No coverage, not even one bar, the battery was dead anyway. It was still daytime, but there was an overcast and the sky had a perfectly even dullness, so there was no way to tell what time of day it was, much less which direction was north or south or anything else for that matter. A two-lane blacktop road snaked up into the distance and disappeared into some trees, or a forest if you wanted to get technical about it. It also snaked down toward some lumpy hills and disappeared there as well. What sounded like a two-stroke chainsaw could be heard in the distance, but it was impossible to tell whether it was up in the forest or down in the lumpy hills. This had been happening more often lately. Two different ways to go, with a dead battery and no bars, and nobody left to blame.

They were coming. My voice was tense, my breath lost to the oppressive Midwestern air, as I informed Janie. She whispered back that yes, she knew. It barely carried over the ubiquitous, roaring sound of the saw, even as she leaned in and repeated herself, her lips grazing the shell of my ear.

I wrapped my left arm around her shoulders while jamming my right thumb into the home button of our phone. Felt the screen's glass practically buckle under its pressure, biting into the skin around my cuticle. I still somehow believed I could sacrifice pain for sanctuary. An erroneous, masochistic notion, but a brutally persistent one, especially now.

Janie murmured something against me. I couldn't make it out, yet I

No Bars and a Dead Battery

knew what she was saying: it wasn't going to work, the phone was dead. Her mouth formed my name: Maxine. I glanced at her reflection in the smudged obsidian—her expression no longer conveyed mere loss of hope, but heartbreaking lifelessness. Janie was resigned to the fate prophesied by our technology. I was resolved that I would use the last of my strength to keep her from it.

I dropped the phone to the dusty blacktop and crushed it beneath my heel, using my nails to scrape my hair back and secure it with a rubber band. Then I grasped Janie's hand and pulled her into the towering corn stalks on one side of the road, enveloping us in darkness as sudden and all-consuming as that which we feared the most.

♦

I met Janie in the back row of a compulsory writing composition class, both of us hiding beneath overlong bangs and false demureness. At first we only spoke under the ruse of swapping pieces; hers were much more eloquent than mine, and it's a testament to the intensity of my crush that I was willing to subject myself to such embarrassment just to talk to her.

My general approach, however, was one of caution. I sat next to Janie for months before I ever looked at her directly, choosing instead to glance fleetingly at her running shoes, her tawny legs, her chipped and chewed-off nail polish. I did this because I worried that her exhilarating gaze would strike lightning into my heart and I would be gone completely. Of course, I was eventually proven right.

She was still dating her high school boyfriend when we met. His eyes, she later told me, were just a little less green than mine. His name, incredibly, was Maxwell. She mentioned this casually three weeks into our relationship. Apparently she couldn't resist a good-looking Max. *As long as she never meets any more of us,* I thought at that moment, and I passed it off as a joke while her laugh sounded out like a songbird's. This was how

I told her I loved her for the first time. The four hundred and seventy-fifth time, I asked her to marry me. Her breath caught and she pulled out a ring; I'd bested her by a matter of hours. We were married in a courthouse a month later, surrounded by cheering friends and reluctant relatives.

My parents protested that we were too young. Her parents were in denial from the beginning, and that denial hardly wavered as we packed up our coastal, collegiate selves and crammed them into a newly refurbished two-bedroom in Omaha. We were twenty-three, Janie had taken a job at Berkshire Hathaway, and I had an undergraduate degree in animal science, which I promptly put to (reasonably) good use as an assistant aviary trainer at the Omaha zoo. This was another decision that bemused and distressed my parents, who'd hoped I would attend veterinary school near their hometown. But I enjoyed my unexpected new line of work, deriving great personal satisfaction from taking in wild, often wounded animals, nursing them with bottles and bandages, earning their trust. Most of the time it didn't take long; I could get a new bird to warm to me in just a few minutes, whereas my coworkers took hours or sometimes days. All the other trainers, even the aviary director, said I had a gift.

Janie would tease me when I'd arrive home with tales of wheezing owls and broken-winged macaws. She called me the second coming of Florence Nightingale, relishing in the perfection of the pun. I laughed with her; it was funny, and I was happy. Truthfully, even if I were forced to become a clerk or a waitress or a beggar, I would have followed Janie anywhere. As the case was, she led me to the middle of nowhere instead.

Only now did I realize the extent to which she had saved me—and not in the romantic, hyperbolic way that certain intolerable acquaintances ooze about their significant others. Moving to the Midwest with Janie had quite literally prolonged my life. Everyone on the coasts had been gone for months.

No Bars and a Dead Battery

Of course, everyone in Omaha was long gone now too. But we'd had a more advanced warning than other cities (I recalled the headlines flashing across CNN, notifying us who was on lockdown, in exactly the order you'd expect: New York, Los Angeles, Washington D.C.) and I attributed our survival to a combination of this auspicious timing and Janie's remarkable wilderness skills, acquired during her tenure as a teenage camp counselor. For all I'd learned about animals in captivity from work, I was woefully ignorant as to how humans might thrive outside their natural habitat. But Janie knew how to cover our tracks and smells, how to scavenge and keep warm without a fire. She knew where to obtain a miniature water treatment device, and she knew to do so before hardware stores and big-box stores and even online retailers sold out of them completely.

Even as we fled under threat of death, I was fascinated and impressed by the range of Janie's long- dormant knowledge, none of which she'd ever shared with me before. People say fortune favors the bold; I say the quietly prepared.

The one thing we were missing was a car. We'd always relied on public transport in Omaha, and by the time we realized we had to leave, we couldn't risk the excursion to purchase one. Our friends, everyone we trusted was traveling through back alleys and down dirt roads, trying to make it to the country, off the grid. Janie justified that a car would draw attention to us anyway, and so we set out on foot. All that was what had led us to corn stalks. All that, of course, being the culmination of the monsters themselves.

♦

The first few were manufactured in Ohio, in a small, rural town called Grinton. A particularly bitter slice of irony, courtesy of early news stories that showed clips from the local station: interviews with the earnest, unshaven factory fillers who were thrilled simply to be receiving minimum wage. The company, Imitantur, had promised to inject economic and scientific growth into the decades-stagnant town, and its residents had brightly, blindly accepted that promise like a list of unread terms and conditions.

The Imi, as the product was called, was invented by a Hollywood audio technician named Evan Spencer who'd graduated summa cum laude from MIT. Its intended purpose was to reduce the clunkiness of cinematic sound mixing, the inorganic nature of inserting sound effects into scenes where microphones couldn't pick them up, due to frequency issues or contextual inconvenience. The Imi would listen at the source and flawlessly mimic the scene's stipulated sounds directly into the mic, without any human intervention other than the initial programmed directive—a "mechanical mockingbird," as Spencer marketed it. (Oh, how I despised the comparison to my innocent avian companions.)

The Imi could and would imitate any sound, from something as benign as a child's laugh to as malevolent as a dying scream. And without even a thought as to the consequences, Spencer and the Imitantur team had engineered the Imi's most recent software patch (the *final update*, as it was chillingly referred to on the news) such that it would automatically gather all available auditory data, from the most authentic reference points possible. And if it wasn't available, the Imi would devise the circumstances necessary to produce it.

This nightmarish scenario alone might have hurt many people; it would have been tragic, but we would have recovered. The catalyst for the apocalypse was twofold. Firstly, that the Imis were mass- manufactured, with hard drives that were essentially limitless, such that they would be able to hold thousands and thousands of audio files without malfunctioning. And secondly, that all Imis were learning AIs from the outset, and that most Imis were being test-run on the sets of horror movies, in which sound mixing can often be so problematic. They

No Bars and a Dead Battery

learned to record sounds of torture, and to use these sounds in combination with true physical peril, in order to gain the cries of their victims.

The chainsaw impression was a standard technique to provoke sounds of stress and anguish from those nearby—an important component of the Imi's repertoire, as well as an effective means of locating their prey. When they had you within a twenty-foot radius, they'd blast sonic energy at you, your eardrums would bleed and burst, embolisms would form in your lungs, and you'd die of either respiratory or cardiac distress, desperately pleading for your life at the mercy of a machine.

A machine that had no idea it was killing you, that indeed had honed itself for this exact purpose, for it knew no other way. And when it was done with you, it would move swiftly on to its next victim, eager to accumulate more. Because, like fingerprints, the sound of each individual death is singular, unique.

◆

Janie and I emerged from the high-mounted crops roughly a mile from where we'd entered, tumbling out onto the dirt. The chainsaw sound still reverberated in the distance, but judging by its faintness—it no longer roared, but hissed—we'd bought ourselves a few minutes to regroup.

I unclasped the straps of my backpack and sighed in relief; I'd chosen wisely, though of course it had been pure luck. We'd sprinted downhill, and we were much closer to the hills now than to the trees, which meant that the Imis likely lurked in the forest above us. Though at this point Janie and I were seasoned surveilers, we still hadn't found a foolproof method to determine precisely where they were at a given time. Among the Imi's arsenal of ringmaster-like skills was a knack for ventriloquy, and if there was one within even half a mile, it could cast out a sound such that it was impossible to try and pinpoint its direction. In a way this was even more disconcerting than if they were absolutely silent as they approached. You had no way of knowing whether you had a chance at escaping until you'd already done it. (Janie sardonically referred to us as Schrödinger's people.) It was a troubling but undeniable fact that most of the decisions that had brought us to this point were the result of random chance. There was far too much that we couldn't know about the Imis without getting into closer proximity—and that was out of the question.

Janie was hunched over next to me, trying in vain to steady her breathing. I was familiar enough with both her and this situation to know that she wouldn't truly be able to breathe until we'd stopped in a safe place for the night, and that could take hours. Nevertheless I watched her, placing my hand at the crest of her shoulders, above her pack. Hoping that my touch would be enough to calm her, if only for a moment. A crow cawed just above us, reminding me of our former lives, and the tenuous threads that still connected us to it.

We had been trying to get in touch with another couple we knew from Omaha, Justin and Alec. They and their daughter Liza had left the city hours before we did, in a 1972 El Dorado that somehow managed to move and sound like brand new, though its mileage had to be in the hundred thousands. Ol' Reliable, Alec had called it, stroking its hood with deep-seated affection. Justin had called it Ol' Piece of Shit (or Junk if seven-year-old Liza was in the vicinity). But it really was a hardy vehicle for its age, not least because Justin, despite his claims to the contrary, had taken a great deal of care and effort to restore it. Indeed, the El Dorado had become a succinct microcosm of their relationship; no matter how Justin, naturally on the insecure side, tried to devalue himself and his work, Alec could be counted on to support him.

They were not only some of the handiest, but also the kindest people we knew, and I had worried for them and their sweet, intuitive daughter ever since they'd disappeared from their willow-flanked house on King Street. The last we'd heard they were heading northeast toward

No Bars and a Dead Battery

Minneapolis, where there was supposedly an underground shelter, impenetrable to the Imis thanks to a layer of titanium embedded in the earth. Of course, our knowledge of this place was limited to rumors swapped on the trails, fleeting whispers and vague texts from acquaintances with conflicting information; Minneapolis might in fact be St. Paul or Bloomington or even Ann Arbor, the sub-earthen headquarters might actually be a barricaded tower, or perhaps a houseboat in the middle of Lake Superior.

At this point it hardly mattered what was the truth, seeing as most of our contacts had stopped responding and our signal had been shot for days. Then there was the final nail in the coffin—the siphoned battery and my foot compressing the glass, rendering our phone well and truly useless. I'd actually wanted to destroy it ever since we'd lost signal; one of the many things that remained unknowable about the Imis was whether they were able to use technology to track us. The attacks we knew about seemed unrelated to virtual footprints so far, but then again, nothing about the Imis had proven predictable.

I'd only held onto our phone for this long out of desperation, waiting to hear from Justin and Alec through agonizing days of silence. They and the long-suffering El Dorado were the last concrete plan we had for getting past state lines. We'd traveled about a hundred miles hanging off of a dilapidated freight train, and a few dozen on foot, but every day we grew weaker, wearier, more vulnerable to an ambush.

◆

Janie was speaking to me now, asking me what we'd do next. These were the roles we had delineated for ourselves over the past weeks. I was the planner, the big-picture person; Janie took stock of our surroundings and advised me when I hesitated, based on the pattern of the clouds, the erosion of our path. Strangely, it was the reverse of our former dynamic, before the world had gone to hell. Janie had always called the shots and I'd followed in her wake—it was why I'd come to Omaha in the first place. But in the present state of emergency, it felt natural for me to be at the forefront of our mission. I was more mathematically, geographically minded, while Janie's attention to detail made her the perfect second in command.

I surveyed the brittle yellow-brown field that stretched before us. It was late fall in the Midwest, and while back in Omaha this meant luscious ripe scents and golden-leaved streets, the country was much bleaker for all its deciduous losses. Late fall also meant that temperatures were dropping, and Janie and I had dutifully stockpiled instant-break heat packs for when the weather grew more dire. These occupied the outer pockets of our backpacks, which also contained thoughtful proportions of lightweight reflective blankets, jackets of the same material, water bottles and purifier, Swiss army knives, medical supplies, trail mix, oatmeal packets, and protein bars. Janie had recently joked that if the Imis didn't get us, scurvy would.

It was getting to the point where I worried how much we were carrying, whether it was a worthy risk to slow ourselves down with the baggage. We'd already dispensed with a few unnecessary items we'd been carrying, mostly those of sentimental value like picture frames and old articles of clothing—all that endured from this category was our twin wedding rings. But we'd had several razor-close calls with the Imis in the last week alone, and I felt we had to shed more. What was the use of survival supplies if they no longer helped us survive?

Our plan had depended entirely on Justin and Alec, and as I attempted to rub the insidious Midwestern dust from my eyes, I watched the last remnants of it sputter and die. We were cut off from all potential contacts, and we had no means of transportation. The Imis were an omnipotent force gaining on us every minute, every second, and soon we would be coerced once more into playing their treacherous game. I was exhausted, deflated, undone. I knew Janie had begun to feel this way days ago, but she had held fast to my resilience, persisting for my benefit—the same way I'd hung onto our phone, our last pathetic hope. Now I'd let go, and we were both in free fall.

I looked at her, my brilliant, beautiful, bedraggled wife. Directly into her eyes, the way I'd been afraid to when we were still strangers. I had come to know her face so well, its gentle heart shape, its freckles, its frowns. I often experienced Janie as an extension of myself, the way you do when you love someone so deeply, for so long. Yet Janie still had the capacity to surprise me. She no longer wore the same expression of resignation and defeat, as I expected she would; instead she looked incredibly calm, almost dreamy. Her breathing had slowed, and she straightened herself, looking taller and more invigorated than she had in weeks.

She met my eyes with conviction and smiled. She started to speak, and once again I knew what she would say before she said it: that it was okay, that she loved me, that she had accepted what would come and she was no longer frightened. I pulled her toward me and began to cry. Our final role reversal, back to our roots—me as the lost, uncertain soul, Janie as my anchor.

Her body relaxed into mine, as it had so many countless times. Her breath glanced off the nape of my neck and tickled me slightly. I felt rather than saw her inhales and exhales, and I assumed she had closed her eyes. Until her soft, regular breathing suddenly sharpened into a gasp, and she half gestured, half forcibly turned me so I could see what she had seen just over my shoulder. So I could verify that it was, somehow, Justin and Alec's daughter Liza racing across that plaintive field toward us, gesticulating wildly with a glinting phone in her hand.

◆

As Liza drew closer, it became clear that the phone wasn't actually a phone, but some other small metallic device. She held fast to it even as she barrelled into my legs, her breathing loud and raspy post- marathon. Out of protective instinct and old habit, even though she was really too lanky for it these days, I scooped her up and held her against my chest. I was shocked by how light she was; she'd always been a thin child, but now she felt as delicate as a bird.

Janie pulled all of us in for a quick, reassuring hug, then broke away to look into Liza's face. She was still breathing hard, but she managed to choke out the essentials: her dads were close by, safe in the refuge of the El Dorado. One of them was hurt—it was impossible to ascertain which one, she spoke in such a rush—the result of twisting an ankle while trying to set up camp. This meant they hadn't been able to search for us on foot, but they'd been circling the area for hours, knowing we were nearby; apparently one of my last texts had miraculously gone through. They had a fully charged phone and a full tank of gas, and this, which they'd sent Liza to deliver. She handed Janie the phone-like appliance.

Liza explained that her dad (this time I knew it to be Justin, ever the engineer) had fashioned it out of parts from a disposable camera and pieces of wire ribbon. I inspected it as Janie held it up; it did remind me of a camera, or perhaps a tape recorder, with the external plastic shell stripped away. It looked dangerous to touch, like even a fingertip against the wire could send a deadly volt of electricity through your body. But Liza was telling us now, it posed no harm to humans. It was a sort of electromagnetic generator, and it could be used to incapacitate the Imis, if only we could get close enough to dispatch it.

This particular dilemma had been the undoing of the government as they'd tried to take action against the Imis. They'd been built like cockroaches, small and indestructible, such that even firepower had no effect. After realizing they couldn't blow them up or crush them through traditional military methods, the task force that had been assigned to the

No Bars and a Dead Battery

Imis began recruiting engineers to build disarming robots. In theory, these would be able to trek through the battlefields to manually reprogram the Imis without the necessity of human proximity. In practice, the Imis, these learning metallic monsters, realized quickly that the reprogramming bots were their enemies. Even without their sonic advantages, the Imis outnumbered the bots so enormously that they were easily able to destroy them when they came into contact. That didn't mean the emergency task force had stopped working, but I think by now even they realized their own fallibility.

So the challenge of demolishing, or at the very least decommissioning, the Imis was not only tactical, but practical. Even if Justin had managed to invent something that could be used effectively on them, there was still the critical matter of proximity. That old real estate mantra: location, location, location.

As Liza described it, the generator had to be within about fifty feet of them to work. Once activated, it would emit a series of electromagnetic pulses that would first mute, then hopefully disable the Imis completely. Its potency lay in the fact that its attack was not physical—like them, it relied on energy to trigger internal combustion. It would also be more wide-reaching if operating from above, which Liza suggested we try from the top of a tree. But even as she said this, she looked around and her voice

faltered; there weren't any trees for miles, they were in the opposite direction of where we'd been heading, and we were sure to run headfirst into a horde of Imis if we tried to go back. The chainsaw sound had been steadily increasing in volume ever since we'd stopped, and I estimated them to be about three-quarters of a mile from us now. Soon the sound would pervade every inch of air around us, and we would have no way of knowing from which direction they'd emerge.

Liza had grown quiet at last, and heavy in my arms. I set her down and she collapsed onto my bulky pack. I figured she was finished speaking, had delivered all the information she could. But then she looked up and said, like an afterthought, that if we could just figure out how to get the device near the Imis, our path would be clear to take the road across state lines, to safety. But not to Minneapolis, as I'd expected her to say; to Des Moines, in Iowa. Which was over a hundred miles closer than Minneapolis.

I looked at Janie. Her expression had morphed once again; her eyes now shimmered with hope. Getting to Des Moines was much more of a possibility than getting to Minneapolis, especially if we were traveling with Justin, Alec, and Liza. And if we were able to combat the Imis, we could turn that possibility into a guarantee. This idea fueled me, as did the *deus us machina* that Liza had brought. Here was my power to save Janie.

We had just one problem left to solve: the location issue. The approaching Imis must have just crossed the half-mile radius marker, because the two-stroke chainsaw sound was once again everywhere. They would be upon us in minutes, and I could see only one way to stop them. I knew what I needed to do, yet I felt remarkably composed, clearheaded. This was what was meant to happen, my ultimate sacrifice for her ultimate sanctuary; I had been right about that after all. I gently but firmly took the generator from Janie, ready to wade into battle. But before I could take a step, a crow landed right at my feet and cocked his small dark head at me.

I had thought I'd only been waiting for the god of the machine, but here was the god of nature beckoning toward me, offering up an unforeseen solution. As swiftly as I dared, I knelt down to meet the bird's eye line. I could feel both Janie and Liza watching me curiously. I cooed, cawed, and coaxed the bird with a couple of almonds I had in my pocket. After what seemed like an anxious eternity, I reached out for him, and he hopped aboard my arm.

Now came the tricky part. I ripped the rubber band from my hair and twisted it around the generator, such that the switch would remain

No Bars and a Dead Battery

flipped even if I let go. It began to make a noise that reminded me of a spinning roulette wheel, a constant click-click-click-clicking. This startled the crow, but he did not move from my arm. Holding my breath, I nudged him ever so slightly, prompting him to raise one of his legs. I quickly slipped the makeshift strap onto him, securing it tightly—our final, crucial stroke of luck was that the generator was light, and this was a particularly robust crow. With a nuzzle under his chin, I grabbed hold of his plump feathered body, took a running start, and launched him into the air. Our lives hung in the continuity of his trajectory. I knew our chances were slim.

Less than five minutes later, we caught sight of them. Rolling over the crest of the nearest hill, a crowd of at least fifty in a monochromatic metal wave. We'd had no idea where they would come from, but this was no longer because their warning sound was omnipresent; it was because they were absolutely silent as they approached. Convenient, too, because their noiselessness allowed us to perfectly register the sound of a long, blaring honk—still the sweetest sound I've ever heard in my life—coming from the horn of a gloriously restored 1972 El Dorado.

◆

So our story went. So it was told, first by us, urgently, vitally, to the rest of the world, via satellite from the shelter when we finally reached it. Then years later, to Liza's children, to impress upon them just how lucky they were simply to exist, much less to exist in times of peace. And finally, decades after that, by our biographers, and by the professors who used us in their science classes, their history classes, even their English classes—drawing parallels between Spencer and Icarus, between myself and Odysseus, with my Trojan crow and Janie as my faithful Penelope. So it was told; so it was written; so the textbooks read, immortalizing us as mythic heroes:

They made their way through the crowd, and back to the El Dorado. And as they approached it, a crow flew directly over their heads and landed on the hood and then looked at them. They stood some distance away and watched the crow watching them. Another crow flew directly overhead and landed beside it. The first crow squawked and then both flew away. They watched the crows disappear, looked at each other, and then got in the El Dorado. Only one way to go this time, with five bars and full battery.

PINE OVER DIRT

Helen Montague Foster

No coverage, not even one bar, the battery was dead anyway. It was still daytime, but there was an overcast and the sky had a perfectly even dullness, so there was no way to tell what time of day it was, much less which direction was north or south or anything else for that matter. A two-lane blacktop road snaked up into the distance and disappeared into some trees, or a forest if you wanted to get technical about it. It also snaked down toward some lumpy hills and disappeared there as well. What sounded like a two-stroke chainsaw could be heard in the distance, but it was impossible to tell whether it was up in the forest or down in the lumpy hills. This had been happening more often lately. Two different ways to go, with a dead battery and no bars, and nobody left to blame.

She'd known the county couldn't afford to pay a deputy a decent wage. Why expect more for an acting sheriff? They hadn't maintained their vintage squad car or supplied satellite radios. She glanced through her rearview mirror at the boy, anguish radiating from his handsome, almost angelic face, skin so pale his cheeks pinked when she'd touched his shoulder to guide him into the back seat. She'd worked as a dispatcher before the sheriff went out on sick leave and hired her as deputy. She wasn't bad at finding her way around but with no GPS, no map, and barely three months in the county, she'd have to draw on her army training. All she had to do was deliver the kid to the hospital. He'd sat still in the back seat while she checked out the engine, hadn't complained about the required cuffs.

He concentrated on holding it all in, looking away from the fire in his head, but when the car stopped, he got the idea she would unlock the cuffs, make him run, and hunt him down. The deputy, who looked like the Black Panther's movie girlfriend, muttered about the battery, but why would a car battery die in the middle of nowhere with the engine running? The engine in the El Dorado had chugged and sputtered along until they drifted onto the shoulder. He'd believed since sunrise that this would be the day of his death. If his stepmother hadn't taken the guns, it would be over, but she'd found the post on his laptop and called the county Crisis line. Night after night, they chose him for school shooter. His assignment. How they got into his head he didn't know, but he had to stop it. Do it, do it, and we'll leave you alone, they droned. He thought he'd escaped, but their mind-drills were sawing in the distance. Deliverance, do it, do it. They'd passed a store called the Do It Center.

She'd never driven this part of the county, but she'd heard the reports. Domestic assault. An old couple killed in the spring. Hunter shot by unknown assailant. Meth lab in the hills. Occasional escapees from the hospital. Not the best place to take off walking while black or while cop. And she couldn't leave her captive. But she didn't see any alternative. They would have to keep by the state road, and the boy would have to cooperate. He was fifteen, dangerous to self and others, but that face wasn't the face of a callous killer. He looked lonely and scared. Father killed drunk driving. She tried her phone again. No luck. No service. Her text to the secretary at headquarters undelivered. The sheriff had been dead two weeks. When she glanced at the mirror again, the boy's baby blues spotted her and looked away. When she asked if he was up for walking, he picked up his legs, clanking the chains.

If she hadn't clipped the chain on his wrist restraints to the child seat link, he could've brained her when she unlocked the leg irons, but he felt her breathing, smelled sweetness on her hair, which was a cap of black wool, with a few white threads. Soon she would order him to run, so she

No Bars and a Dead Battery

could hunt him down. What would he do? If someone asked him which role he'd choose hunter or hunted, he would choose neither, but that wasn't how the games were set up. No one ever gave him a choice. Every once in a while, the game masters revved their control beams. He could tell she heard it too, buzzing like saws. She made him promise not to run, but he wasn't going to fall into that trap. Tell him don't run and he does and she shoots. Payback for slavery.

She unlocked the leg irons, then the handcuffs. Vintage everything. Like being in the eighties. The boy avoided looking at her directly but his expression was so sad it made her heart ache. Reminded her of the terrified three-year-old she carried to the ambulance after he stepped on a landmine. Unless she'd spaced out, they hadn't passed any gas stations for at least thirty miles, so no use turning back. Better to head uphill into the forest. The sky stayed gray, but the air clung like warm soup. By the time they'd walked a few miles, both she and the boy were sweating. He didn't talk, so she didn't either. When they reached the woods, shadows crossed the road, and it smelled like pine. She was surprised not to see power lines. Would a psych hospital function off the grid? Buried power lines didn't seem likely.

The first turn off was a dirt road with a no trespassing sign and no buildings visible from the road. No rural mailbox either. Dumb trap by the game masters. The deputy wasn't that dumb, and he wasn't either. Run down there, and she'd taser, let him run, shoot to wound. Keep the game going as long as she could. The second turnoff went the other way and was so lame even she shook her head. All you could see was a falling down sign, Pine Lodge. No mailbox. No powerline poles. No visible satellite dishes. Pass.

The name was the same as the hospital, Pine Lodge, but if this was a back entrance, where was the front entrance? The boy hadn't spoken since his promise not to run, but his face showed everything, eyes on her, eyebrows making a question. When she aimed her jaw at the road to

143

mean let's get going, fear flashed in his eyes as if she'd told him to run ahead. If he was a brother, that would mean he expected her to shoot him for Jim Crow sport, but his ancestors must've been from Sweden or Holland. Skin pale. Hair dark blond. Let's stay together she said.

When they'd covered another three miles, tree-scalloped sky dimmed to a darker gray, the effect reminding her of a PTSD dream. Afghanistan canyon emerging in Hotlanta. An Army shrink once told her the dreams were nature's way to keep sharp but one way to stay sharp was to know when to refuse an assignment. She didn't have to keep the acting sheriff job, but this was no PTSD dream. The next turnoff was pine needles over dirt and gravel with a well maintained rural mailbox painted blue. Let's walk in side-by-side, she told him, and his face agreed, though he didn't speak aloud.

In the visible world, you would walk up the road and discover an ordinary place. He would be taken to a mental hospital where some counselor type would badger him to reveal the secrets of the controllers, which in the visible world were not real, yet controlled everything. He would take medicine which would sever the wormhole to the controllers. He would be sent back to the agony of daily life and live on through the drudge of day after day after day among the visible who cared about grades, dates, sports, and whether they got a buck the first day of hunting season. As the deputy ordered, he walked beside her. The canopy of greenery made it cooler. He listened for water and heard woodpeckers, songbirds, and the rustling of leaves. They startled a spotted fawn out of a patch of ferns. It leapt up and ran in fear downhill off the dirt road. Its spots lined up in rows that seemed almost fake. The road turned a corner, and he thought he saw a building through the woods, but then he didn't, and then he did: A modern log cabin of treated timbers, stone chimney, cedar porch with a rope hammock and two rockers. A satellite dish on the roof. Together, she said, meaning for them to mount the steps side-by-side to the porch.

No Bars and a Dead Battery

She called out, anyone home, before she knocked. She could have said, Police, or Sheriff's Office, but better not to spook whoever owned the cabin. It was well-maintained, expensive looking, so she didn't expect a pointed firearm, but better to be prepared. She listened and knocked again. Anyone home? Finally, she heard movement inside, then a high-pitched quaver asking who was there. The door opened a crack, then all the way, revealing a woman under five-feet with a square head and unreadable frozen-faced expression. She said something in Spanish a rush of words including *quien* and *por que* but also *ayudame por favor* which she recognized as help me, please.

He didn't speak Spanish but the deputy seemed to know what the woman was saying. Maybe come in. They followed her through a neat living room with a swastika rug in front of a stone fireplace into a bedroom where a pale old man with no eyebrows or eyelashes lay in a large cedar-post bed. At first it seemed the old man was dead, but then he blew a wheezy breath and turned his head to them. The only light was from the window. The Hispanic woman spoke to the man in the bed, her voice filled with questions but her face like a wood carving. The old man glanced past the deputy and stared so intensely he could have been a controller. The face like a death mask of something so familiar he felt as if he were dreaming.

The old man completely ignored her and asked the boy in American English why they were there. The boy looked at her for guidance, his face mixed question and fear, so she stepped up and answered in her generic Army brat accent that she was the acting Sheriff, their car had broken down, and they had been unable to phone for help. The boy stood silent beside her, but the man addressed him. Are you Eric? The boy nodded. Come over here, the man said, I heard you were being admitted. What happened, the boy whispered.

It didn't seem possible that the man in the bed was his old psychiatrist, whom he remembered with thick brown hair, a beard, and bushy eyebrows that went up when he was surprised. A month after he'd told Dr. Ward about the controllers, his stepmother informed him he couldn't go anymore. The practice was closed. He'd refused to speak to the new counselor who reminded him of a kindergarten teacher.

She explained her mission (deliver Eric to the hospital) and their circumstances (broken down car.) At the least, they needed a jumpstart or the use of a working phone. The old man explained that he knew the boy, had been his doctor but closed the practice before chemotherapy. He'd maintained his association with Pine Lodge Hospital, supervising nurse practitioners and consulting with a wilderness program nearby. Unfortunately, his phone had not worked for twenty-four hours. The home health nurse had not arrived to administer his chemotherapy dose, and the electricity was off. He spoke in Spanish to the short woman, whom he called Flora, and she brought chairs, which she placed close to the bed.

The bald face seemed different, too craggy, but the eyes beamed the connection he remembered. The old lady brought the deputy and him glasses of water. He gulped his. How far is the hospital, the deputy asked. Not far as the crow flies, his doctor answered. About ten miles by road. Can you call the hospital, the deputy wanted to know. I told you the phone's down, Dr. Ward said. Eric, I want to talk with you. We don't have much time.

She needed to use the bathroom. Will you stay here with him, she asked the boy, and he nodded. *Necesito saber si el trata de salir,* she said to the old woman, *pero...* She pointed to the bathroom. She thought of leaving the door ajar, but the woman seemed to understand her high school Spanish. She wanted to know if the boy got up. *Digame si el chico va a salir.* Through the closed door she heard only the murmur of hushed voices.

Did the shooting idea come back, the sick man asked him. Yes. The controllers keep putting it there. How do they do that? He explained as

No Bars and a Dead Battery

best he could that the orders came masked as other sounds. I think they are ideas, the sick man said, not orders. Only you can turn ideas into orders. Do you understand, Eric? You did right by telling your stepmother. I didn't tell, he said, I wrote it down and she read it. Maybe you wanted her to find it. Maybe, he answered.

She promised to send help after they reached they hospital, and, in return, Dr. Ward said he would call headquarters for her if his phone began working while he was still alert. Either way, Flora would call her cousin, who worked on cars. Flora fed them peanut butter sandwiches and gave her water bottles in a bag that she hitched to her belt. Dr. Ward wrote out admission orders for the boy, lab tests, and two drugs she'd never heard of. What's H&P, she asked. History and Physical. She buttoned the page of orders in her shirt pocket.

If the path was easy enough for Dr. Ward to walk it sick, surely they could hike fast enough to make it to the hospital before dark. He and the deputy were both strong. They couldn't walk side by side on the shortcut path, but Dr. Ward promised the deputy would not shoot him. He felt her presence on the skin of his back. He'd never thought of the running or the shooting as ideas. They were bam, bam, bam nightmares. The feeling of the woods had changed since they arrived. The trees had dimmed into shadows and the scent deepened. Smells like wet fur and bark tried to warn him about something. A large bird swooped almost silently over them. They started out on a steep downhill grade broken by roots and embedded stones. Halfway down to a small stream, the path was obstructed by a fallen branch. When he kicked it aside, a shadow scurried out from under.

The boy jumped back, her pistol out by reflex. She crouched, assessing the shadows. Nothing she could see. Maybe it had been a mistake having him walk point, but the path was supposed to lead straight to the hospital grounds. She'd thought the biggest risk would be some minor injury but realized a shooting would be the biggest risk. Him shooting her or her shooting him. She secured her gun in its holster. Chipmunk or something, he said and kept walking. There was still enough light to see the path, but shadows swallowed big patches. They approached a slender sluice of reflections running beside a fallen tree with a root disc still packed with fresh earth. A spring? The boy worked his way around and downhill beside the trunk to a several-yard-wide stream, and he, then she, stepped stone to stone across it. Not quite what Dr. Ward described. The tree must've fallen across the path.

He looked back at the deputy to see which way she thought he should go. Several mud slides rose from the stream where the path should have been on the near side of the hip-height barrier of fallen tree trunk. It was getting darker. The needles and broadleaves overhead seemed shades of gray and black rather than green. The controllers were quiet, which meant he could listen for enemies, but they might bark orders at any time. Lately they spoke in his father's voice. Don't you know your dick from a hole in the ground? When I speak you do what I say, got that? A mosquito whined around his ear. He smacked blindly, and it stopped.

She followed the boy up the bank, choosing her steps carefully so as not to slip. They didn't need stealth; her quiet was reflex and preference. Maybe better to be loud and warn away any bears. When they crested the hill, she asked him which of the three paths looked most traveled. In the dark, all three were broader than deer paths. She understood there were black bears in the area, coyotes, no wolves, and several disputed reports of catamounts. She agreed that the middle path seemed correct, but after they walked a short while they had to duck to avoid overhanging vines. Twice the boy untangled thorns from his shirt sleeve.

Only you can turn ideas into orders, he thought. What did that mean? Dr. Ward used to encourage him to resist the voices. Maybe that was what he meant. If you didn't think you had to follow orders, they wouldn't be real orders, like when his father told him to tell his stepmother that he'd stopped drinking. But that was the order he should

No Bars and a Dead Battery

have obeyed, so Dr. Ward was wrong.

Another tree blocked the path, this time impenetrable as if someone had laid a huge, untethered, fresh Christmas tree on its side. The boy backed up. She switched on her light. She told him which way to go, but the light made the shadows move and left afterimages. She couldn't tell what was deer path and what was real path. Maybe they'd gone the wrong way at the stream, but an officer shouldn't express doubts out loud. Besides, they were approaching a clearing, and she saw a distant light blink. She stepped backwards and saw it again. Moved ahead and it was gone.

Something far away yipped, and he stopped to listen. You could hear yips and yelps overlapping with howls as off-key as a dog singing with a piano. The deputy laughed behind him. He thought she must be laughing at him for stopping. It made him want to turn around and ask if she thought he was a coward. If not for his stepmother, he could have carried out his plan, armed his locker the night before with his father's pistol and rifle. He would be predator, then prey, but if the controllers didn't make him, why do it?

Unless the clearing ahead was part of the hospital grounds or wilderness program, they were lost. Were you laughing at me? the boy asked her. No, she said, she was laughing at the coyote chorus. She was sure she could lead them back to the cabin, but they'd better check out the clearing first.

A lightning bug rose over the path ahead of him and blinked off. Pretty soon the deputy would accuse him of leading her the wrong way. Or maybe she was prey too, and that's why the controllers chose a black deputy. It was better not to be the only prey. Good to have someone else to get lost with. He kept walking until he ploughed into a hedge of briars at the edge of a clearing. Thorns like eagle talons snagged his clothes, but he maneuvered through into a field of high grass that looked down on lumpy hills. The sky glowed way in the distance beyond the hills.

There was no sign of a hospital, just an overgrown meadow rolling in hills into a deep valley. The only light was sky glow through cloud cover and here and there lightning bugs. She let him pee into woods with his back to her. They drank from the water bottles. He drained his, and she saved half of hers. The sandwiches had taken the edge off, but she was hungry, tired, and thirsty. He yawned. It's late, she said. Let's stop here until sunrise. You can sleep. She didn't trust herself to stay awake. She would need to cuff him again but would play it by ear to avoid spooking him.

He touched a blackberry to his mouth. It was too dark to see the colors, but the ripe ones almost tumbled off their stems and smelled sweet. He pictured bears sniffing the wind, but they were probably sleeping. She shone her flashlight on the bushes while they picked enough fruit to fill her hat. Neither one of them ate until her hat was full and they were sitting on the ground. Then they took turns scooping out handfuls. She told him she would keep watch, but she had to cuff him. Not if you don't want to, he said, licking his hands. Not that simple she said back. She asked if many of those mosquitoes got him, and he asked her if she ever shot anybody.

She told him she didn't like thinking about it, but yes. She didn't confide her dream of finding herself in Atlanta, taking a sniper position, and suddenly not knowing who or why she was going to shoot. She didn't say she took the dispatcher job to see if she could teach herself to disengage. He told her she better put the cuffs on him, because sometimes he took the wrong orders. It was the same for her, but she wasn't ready to tell him.

She expected to catnap after he was asleep but jerked awake to sky dazzling with stars, the air cool and dry. A mosquito whined by one ear. The moon had risen, and the boy was standing. She'd looped his handcuff chains with his belt to a sapling, but he'd removed the belt and was free though still cuffed. She'd known he could escape but he'd kept

No Bars and a Dead Battery

his promise to stay with her. Move away from the berries, he whispered. Something rustled nearby. She called out, asking who was there. Not a catamount that was certain. Someone searching for them? Somebody from the wilderness camp working on survival skills? She smelled rank fur.

The bear snorted and shambled closer trailed by two cubs. He offered his wrists to the deputy, and she unlocked the cuffs, both she and he walking backwards at the same time. The bear snorted again and rose to its full height. Your hat, he whispered. That was what made the deputy smell like berries.

She tossed her cap onto the ground. It was her deputy hat, but after the sheriff died, the secretary transferred the gold sheriff wings from his cap to hers. The bear stepped toward them, cubs now out of sight, as the boy and she backed up. Shooting would just anger it, but her pistol was back in her hand. They kept backing up, hoping to find their way past the berries and disappear into the woods. The boy walked sideways looking from her to the bear. The border of meadow and woods was scalloped with the hilly terrain, so their view was blocked by trees. The bear moved uphill in their direction, watching. Over there, the boy said.

She kept her pistol trained on the bear. If she shot it in the eye, it might charge. If it charged without provocation, she would use lethal force, and the cubs might not survive. The boy tapped her shoulder and pointed to the silhouette of trees bordering the field. He was uphill from her. She sidestepped to his position, craned her neck, and saw what looked like a wide path into the forest. A few more yards, and, if the mother bear didn't follow, they would be out of her sight.

He and the deputy weren't prey for the bear, just threat. He led her to the path, really a one lane dirt road into the woods. She aimed her light, then swiped her phone to switch it off. Saving the battery, she said. Let's get going. She didn't need to say that. He wasn't afraid.

The moon was up, or maybe it was nearing sunrise. They followed the road, he in one wheel track, she keeping pace in the other. She heard a song bird far off and when she looked that way, glimpsed the face and neck of a turkey nested beside the road. It crashed upward battering foliage, but her pulse stayed rock steady. Turkey, the boy told her.

He and she jumped when her phone rang, breaking the spell of the forest. The deputy answered in a quiet voice, cupped her hand and mouthed the word headquarters to him. She listened, phone against her ear, and explained their situation, car broken down on the highway, him and her walking down a dirt road in the woods, his doctor expecting a chemotherapy treatment. When the call was over, she told him there had been a cyber-attack. A crow cawed, giving a spooky feeling to what she was saying. The FBI had sent a warning to reboot the router, but it was too late. The power grid had been down for the entire county. Power to the north was still off.

She didn't tell the boy his mental warrant had timed out. If she got him to the hospital, she could call for another. A crow cawed. Several more flapped overhead. The boy told her the crows were chasing an owl, but she didn't see it. He wanted to know if the nurses were on their way to help Dr. Ward. The deputy said she didn't know, so he asked her if they could go see. She said they should keep walking and see where the road went. You could hear mourning doves in the distance. He used to think they were called morning doves, because they called after sunrise. He asked her if she ever saw somebody die, and she answered that she had.

She asked him straight out if he'd been planning to shoot his classmates. By this time sun was up, and the canopy overhead was green. The road headed downhill and then veered sharply around a large boulder. That was the plan, he said, but it wasn't my plan. Whose plan then, she asked him, and he said he didn't really know who was in charge. He didn't care about shooting deer, though his father wanted him to.

She asked him what happened to his father. Nobody but Dr. Ward had asked that before. His stepmother didn't let him show the note to the police. She said the insurance company would take the money back if they knew his father crashed his car on purpose. He asked the deputy if she knew why the crows chased the owl. She asked him back if he thought owls ate crow eggs or baby crows. He didn't know. What if crows ate owl eggs or baby owls? He'd heard that sometimes crows warned other animals when predators came around. Then the crows came in close and stole food. He used to warn his stepmother when his father was drunk, and she took him with her to get away. His father hated his old boss.

When they turned another corner, you could see that the road opened onto another road. It was as if they were walking through a green tunnel. When they came to the end, the broken-down Pine Lodge sign they'd seen on the way lay tilted against a thicket of greenbriar. Less than a mile more on the paved road and they would be at the psychiatrist's house. She wondered what she should do about the mental warrant. The boy didn't seem dangerous to her, but she'd seen enough people lose it unexpectedly to know she shouldn't just go by what she felt at the moment. She asked him if he was suicidal.

He wasn't feeling suicidal right then, so he could have said no, but instead he told her that his father had been suicidal, but he'd really wanted to take care of his family which he couldn't do, because he got drunk at work and lost his job. She asked more questions, and he realized she thought he'd meant other kids were in charge of the plan to shoot.

You could see lights through the window of the cedar cabin. She rapped hard on the door, and Flora came right away and led them into the living room. *Esperame*, she told them. Wait. The rug in front of the stone fireplace must've been made by Native Americans. The design in the center looked like a modified swastika. The boy, Eric, saw her looking at it and blushed. He volunteered that he was not a Nazi, and neither was Dr. Ward. *Regalo de su esposa*, Flora said. The controllers aren't living people, Eric told her.

All that time, he'd been afraid that Dr. Ward had died and that somehow it was his fault. If you give into the controllers and hate people, maybe that made you into a predator even if all you were doing was trying to protect somebody. The son of his father's boss went to his school, but crows shouldn't eat the eggs of baby owls.

Flora took her into the bedroom alone. The chemotherapy nurse had not arrived, and the doctor was sleeping peacefully. When she touched the back of his hand, he opened his eyes and widened his dry lips in a fleeting smile. She asked if she should call the magistrate to renew Eric's green warrant. Dr. Ward whispered that the staff and campers from the wilderness program had been searching for Eric and for her. Some of the parents and the staff at the hospital had taken their family members home. There was no longer a bed available for Eric.

The Spanish speaking lady led him into the bedroom, and the deputy left them alone. I never told my father I loved him, Eric said. Someone had put Dr. Baker's eyes in the skeleton on the bed, eyes so alive that no words were needed for them to hold him. He said it out loud anyway. Dr. Baker once told him that saying you loved someone was not really harder than planning a shooting. This time Eric told him about the mother bear, and Dr. Baker said even bears weren't always prey or predator. But Eric didn't need anybody to tell him that.

Flora's cousin had reached the sheriff car. His phone was working now, the repairs on the El Dorado almost done. She and Eric headed out to the road, where they were joined by ghosts, some from the Middle East, some from the county where the boy had grown up. With each step, she felt more gathering, the girl with no legs, her fellow soldiers, the boy's drunken father, the friend who ate herself to death, the dead mothers, Eric's and hers. She didn't see them but felt their presence, none of them prey or predators, just people once intensely alive and now thronging the woods as owls, bears, vines, and more kinds of life than she knew the names for. She glanced at Eric, his face so determined and

No Bars and a Dead Battery

sincere, and let him walk point through the ghosts.

They made their way through the crowd, and back to the El Dorado. And as they approached it, a crow flew directly over their heads and landed on the hood and then looked at them. They stood some distance away and watched the crow watching them. Another crow flew directly overhead and landed beside it. The first crow squawked and then both flew away. They watched the crows disappear, looked at each other, and then got in the El Dorado. Only one way to go this time, with five bars and full battery.

JUST ASK NICELY

Peter Gikandi

No coverage, not even one bar, the battery was dead anyway. It was still daytime, but there was an overcast and the sky had a perfectly even dullness, so there was no way to tell what time of day it was, much less which direction was north or south or anything else for that matter. A two-lane blacktop road snaked up into the distance and disappeared into some trees, or a forest if you wanted to get technical about it. It also snaked down toward some lumpy hills and disappeared there as well. What sounded like a two-stroke chainsaw could be heard in the distance, but it was impossible to tell whether it was up in the forest or down in the lumpy hills. This had been happening more often lately. Two different ways to go, with a dead battery and no bars, and nobody left to blame.

Father and son sat by the road with enough dirt on them to say they'd done a fair bit of writhing first. A bit of grass popped up here and there, a helpful note that they weren't entirely alone or hopeless. Where grass grew and where it was green, water was around, a least a little of it, and water wasn't that poor a judge of character. It was the first thing any creature of any sensibility searched for when things looked tits up-ish. You could lure a monkey in the Namib with it, and with it you could tell if a planet was once friendly, and this was exactly the point, right now. Planets.

The last time this happened -- and he was quite tired of this, make no mistake -- they'd dropped Jeb off quite far from home. That was 1973 and Jeb could only hope at this point that it was all behind them. Not the event, but the year, because the second time it had happened, they'd dropped him off before they'd picked him up. The traumatic event was yet to come, yet he had already lived it. He'd become a little bolder the third and fourth time, and when he'd realized that this would be a thing, he'd spoken to them (with great difficulty) for the first time and asked two things.

First, if they were going to keep invading the planet and picking on him, if they could do it in chronological order, because this was how his and other people's minds worked, that would be helpful. While on the subject of the human brain, he had also asked them, if it was not so much trouble, to kindly give him some sort of *debriefing* to wash down the experiences, to explain them and tell him he'd be fine.

Closure, that sort of thing. They hadn't been painful but, again, his human brain -- and not the Pratt and Whitney of brains, mind you, maybe a Phillips -- his brain took these things he had seen back to bed with him. He couldn't sleep for months and his wife hated him for it as he always woke her up and tried to take her knickers off. She prefered to be prepared and braced for it, not surprised. Understood, and imagine Jeb's problems.

Secondly, he had asked for some company, so that at least someone else would believe him. So here they were now. Jeb and his teenage son Jake shaking like a noodle. Jeb asked him to breath and told him that everything would be alright, once they figured out where they were and where, in relation to that, the old El Dorado and their house were, in that order. And which day it was. Hopefully the same day they had left or near enough that they could square it with Jake's mom easily enough. Moms were tough with disappearances.

Jeb lifted Jake to his feet, dusted him off and made him look into his eyes. As far as his medical expertise went, his son's eyes looked about the right shape and colour, and weren't taking to the sun too kindly. That was fine then. He assured his son they would be alright, again, and asked him to put himself together and keep an eye out for rattlers. The last thing they needed now was a rattlesnake bite. Jeb and Jake went on rattlesnake roundups often, because there was good money in it and because young Jake's eyes could spot a rattler in a rope factory. Jeb was almost 70, and he wasn't taking anyone in when he said he'd seen a rattler, much less a flying saucer.

Which is why Jeb believed the boy when he said he could see an elevator, about 400 yards out from where they stood. They had their backs to the road looking out at the dark spot, what smart people might call perpendicular to the road. Seeing as they couldn't find their car, they walked out to what Jeb thought was a fuzzy tree stump, and what Jake said was an elevator.

It was an elevator, because tree stumps didn't open when you pressed the button. Inside, velvet covered the walls, warped and scratched all around the bottom two feet or so. Dust coated the brass railings and the floor. There were small footprints in the dust and hairs stuck to the walls, brown and grey and black and white. Some sort of small animal had been here. Dead ahead at about navel height was a small button with a green arrow clearly pointing up, with a plaque above it labeled Debriefing.

They pressed it. Well, Jeb pressed it. The doors hissed shut, which is when they realized the wind had been quite a howl. Its absence was almost louder, and when Jeb scratched himself behind his neck he almost jumped at the sound. The elevator dropped alarmingly about a half foot then squealed its way down, like an old train wailing through the turns out of a hill station.

Jake clutched his father's arm below the shoulder just then. He pointed to the plaque above the button. His father had to lean a little closer to read it. He really shouldn't have been driving the El Dorado at all, at his age, but it was his car and that was that. The plaque had somehow changed to say something else. Three words. *Just Ask Nicely*.

Just was the troubling part. The other two words were self explanatory, together and also in solitude. *Just* could mean a lot of things. When put before an action like *ask,* it could mean the request is trivial, that whatever you might need isn't at all out of reach. It's like saying *simply ask.* On the other hand, it could mean that you're only *permitted* to ask, that persuading, begging, cajoling, or forcing are strictly off limits. Like a genie might say to a mortal, to just ask for three things. There can never be any way around that.

Just, in that case, is a like a very large bouncer with a finger on your shoulder, a show of frightening and non negotiable power where the gentleness in itself is the threat. Now this was the more unsettling thought in Jeb's mind, as the elevator sunk ever deeper, that something very powerful was trying to hide its power plainly enough that he knew it was trying, and that it knew that he knew.

He found himself worrying about what it meant, and the elevator took its time. He supposed it could go either way, except for one thing. If the statement meant to *simply ask*, then it didn't really need the word *nicely*. The connotation in *just ask* set a polite nonchalance on the whole thing. Why would you add the word *nicely* unless… Jeb thought of the very large bouncer asking someone *nicely* to leave the bar. Someone was expecting trouble. Shit. There were no other buttons, and that moment, the doors opened and the elevator stopped, in that order.

They crept into a small carpeted room with more velvet on the walls, scratched as well, with a small coffee table in the center and two toddlers chairs on either end of it. A small writing pad and a feather pen in an inkwell sat on the table. On the far end of it a bookshelf pushed itself against the wall, with brochures and flyers propped up on it. The brochures showcased everything from the new hoover to exciting destinations the Trident now flew to, while the flyers invited concerned citizens to this or that march, most about the war in the rice paddies in the far east.

Someone who had never seen the inside of a room had tried their darndest to approximate one, likely out of a glancing description of it. This was Jeb's impression anyway, not least because a pocket watch hung from a hook in the far wall where a clock might have been. But also because next to it was a message in gold set in a plaque on the wall, like the one in the elevator, only a good deal wider. *We really are trying our very best.*

There was also the odd choice of a cat tower, the sort of thing city slickers bought their house cat. On its top rung sat just such a house cat, a large Burmese, coincidentally or otherwise the breed of cat which best effected condescension. It was Jake who spotted the cat and also the single antenna coming out of the rather Jewish *kippah* on the cat's head. A red light pulsed at its end in time with another red light on a grey panel in the upper corner or the ceiling.

Jeb was just then startled by the sound of wood sliding against wood. The plaque had changed. It now invited them to sit and write down their questions on the writing pad provided. They could jot whatever it was that they desired, debriefing or painkillers or otherwise. The plaque shifted again. It said that Nicely could read quite well and respond via the plaque, and he had even helped them with the room's content; they just hadn't figured out how to make him talk, or he didn't want to.

Father and son both looked at the cat and it looked back at them with naked contempt. The plaque shifted once again, and with a clear departure from the conciliatory tone it then told them in no uncertain terms and from the first person voice that Nicely didn't have all damned day.

Jeb went first, dipping the pen in ink because at least he more than young Jake knew how that bit worked. He scratched out a question on the writing pad and showed it to Nicely. The cat's eyes flicked to the paper and back at Jeb, who was just then at one height with its head. The plaque shifted.

Jeb clicked his tongue. Not because the answer was deliberately scant,

No Bars and a Dead Battery

saying simply that aliens were behind all this, but because of what Nicely had called him at the end of the sentence. Jeb didn't hate cats. He didn't love them much either, but they were, in their own way, like troubled orphans, understandable. It wasn't their fault they could be such cads. In the spirit of being in this together, he pushed the slight aside and put feather pen to paper with question after question.

He learned among other things that it was about a month after they had been taken, but that they had been returned to within two hours of the abduction. The plaque hastily added that it meant two hours after, not before. Great. They wouldn't miss dinner. Jeb was about to hand the pad to Jake when a thought struck him and made him snatch it back. He wanted to know if they had eaten while they were away, and what it was they had eaten and how often.

It was a sensible question and quite telling. It would reveal such things as how time had passed on board the craft, and whether the beings had a Noah-type scheme going, with beef and poultry and what not, all harvested to keep the subjects alive.

This was one of a few questions that seemed to bother Nicely. It took Jeb and Jake a while to guess at why that was, and when they did they were more than slightly offended. Nicely, an ordinary house cat, was a conduit for the interaction between two intergalactic civilizations, both much broader and more nuanced than the cat himself. The poor thing was clearly making a sandwich of it and not without cause. Whatever was coming out of the other end, it couldn't have had any similarity to the Latin and Germanic structures in English. It was probably closer to the sound of a dot matrix printer, an ink smear, or the crashing of waves. Both Jake and Jeb thought, in that condescension that humanity offers all other species, that they might have done better, given the same training and the same blinking *kippah*. At the same time, at least for Jeb, he was happy not to try.

Yes. Synthetics. Once. That was the answer to the food question. Ok, so it wasn't a Noah-type scheme. Again Jeb snatched the pad from his son as another question struck him, a sort of follow up. Jake at that point sat in one of the tiny chairs. It was equal parts resignation and the opportunity to think.

Jake was a large teenager. As a toddler he had had the kind of neck that could only grow a large torso and limbs as time went by. If his father hadn't been in the room just now, with the tiny chairs, the small table and the pocket watch, and with Nicely glowering up in the corner, this whole thing might have done well in Wonderland after the magic cookie.

Nicely glanced at the paper and then at Jeb. As the cat stared down the old man, the plaque shifted. It informed them that yes, there had always been something synthetic inside them, something which allowed readings to be collected from them, and that it wasn't up their anal cavity. At least, the plaque would add about a second after, not that *these* aliens knew about.

When asked to clarify, the plaque said that various civilizations conducted their handling according to various standards, with varying efficacies and varying subject-oriented care. When asked to add yet a little more clarity to the matter, however, the plaque didn't change.

Not immediately. The words *story of my life* made their appearance after a few moments. Jeb turned to see Nicely licking himself under his left thigh. At that time, Jake asked his father if he could now ask a question. His father apologized for hogging the moment and sat. Then he stood up again. It wasn't a moment for sitting, not for Jeb. It was moment for pacing, which he did a little.

The boy took a while to gather his thoughts, and then he seemed to write for a great deal longer, scratching out a few things, rewriting them and then in the end tearing out the paper and writing the whole thing out again, neater and more concisely this time. Jake was an untidy lad and a bit distracted. His writing suffered for it and sometimes he mixed up his words and letters. The school had given him agency for this trait by giving it a label, ADHD and dyslexia. Jeb thought it was more about giving a damn. Get your spellings better and listen to what you write as you write it, and clean your room. When Jake had finished, it was the second much neater paper that he showed Nicely.

Nicely looked at it and did his bit to act bored, but even Jeb, who was no vocal fan of cats and whose eyes were no gauge of subtle behaviours, even Jeb could see that the cat was impressed. This, finally, was something that even that wretched creature could stand knowing.

Is the earth ... You see, Jeb raised Jake christian, and wanted to name him Paul, actually, after the persecutor turned apostle, and in some ways the founder of the christian church. But his wife Gwen had been somewhat a rocker, a little wiccan perhaps in her earlier days. They'd agreed, when they knew she had a child in her, to raise it well but none too partisan.

Marrying was what people did, so they did, and doing it at the local church was fine for appearances. But Jake was to be raised morally, not religiously. That was the agreement. And it held, somewhat and pretty much mostly all the way except that Jeb took any chance to tell Jake everything he knew about the good book and about all the ways God and angels were looking out for them and how everyone was going to be hanging about Iran or Israel for the final battle between good and evil, that sort of thing. Jake was as close a name as Jeb could get to Jacob, the man who wrestled with an angel at the base of a ladder that went up into the sky. A fool, but one of Jeb's heroes and a staple of the Judaic corner of the scriptures.

Which is why Jeb was just then gaping at Jake as Nicely took his time to relay the question 'upstairs,' and why even Nicely himself turned to the plaque. Is the earth, Jake wanted to know, some sort of computational device, an organic machine, like an Atari, but a lot larger?

The question went on to ask if every creature was a sort of node in this calculation, each viable unit of flora and fauna a specific permutation of the same question designed to crunch through numbers towards an answer, and to arrive at that answer some time at a future which neither of them would be there to witness. Because, as the scribble ran on, the question would need to run through more variables, ifs, exceptions and consequences, and allow itself the timespace to arrive at such a complexity that would barely start probing at the original question (which had been asked when things were much simpler) and thus only then provide an answer.

There was more at the back of the page, which summarized the thing in a sort of shrug, asking whether they were all part of a large data simulation and whether Nicely, for example, was just an algorithm as well, bones, meat, fur, attitude and all. Nicely, it should be said at that point, was twitching his tail.

They waited a while, all three of them. After Jeb had satisfied himself that this was, indeed, his secular son Jake and not some creature from the spacecraft wearing him as a suit, he too turned to the plaque. All three waited then, the young man, the old, and the cat which had sat up for the first time since they had entered the room. This was going to be epic.

Nothing happened. They were clearly not going to get this answer. Jake had either broken the agreement or the cat's brain or the Jewish *kippah* or any combination of the above. This was where in some movies men in suits came in and took people away, and in others a laser incinerated the contents of the scene. And in yet others the wifi bars dropped from five to one and the stream halted, which reminded Jeb... They needed a good charge and some reception, somehow, if they weren't all about to be thrown into a human sized paper shredder.

The plaque shifted, but it got stuck. Revolving on its longer axis, the words were cut off at the lower third by the recess in the wall. It jittered back and forth, as if something were trying to force it out. In replicating a 'character' room the beings had certainly nailed the imperfections. With a

No Bars and a Dead Battery

shattering *clack* the thing slid down into place. *That's what we're trying to figure out too.*

There followed, then, a pointed lack of interest in whatever else might come from this conversation, such as it was. Jake slumped into his little chair, Jeb walked to one of the walls and gently placed his head onto the velvet. Nicely had a smaller range of theater to work with, and with a default which was already near to the expression he wished to convey, he could do little more than sit and stare at the small space between his two front paws, and wonder if even that little thing was part of some other being's calculation. He never sat any other way. Was that his choice?

If the earth was some complex abacus built to help another civilization answer its own niggling questions, well what did anything matter? Jeb took his head off the wall and wrote that it would be nice if they could get on their way now, if the alien beings didn't mind. They responded that that would be alright. They then apologized if this was not the answer everyone had been hoping for, to which Jeb responded with the truth, that they had only entered that elevator with the goal of getting home safely, for which they would need their electronics charged, a little help with directions, and their car.

The last thing took a bit of struggle, mostly on Nicely's part as he knew bloody well what a car was but translating that particular vehicle into the structure of the beings' language was for some reason quite a challenge. The beings, finally clear as to what it was, then admitted that they had tried speaking to the car as well and that the probe didn't fit in the usual way it fit humans. They quickly redacted that last bit and said the El Dorado would be waiting for them outside.

Jake wished to remember this while Jeb found no need to, but they both agreed that some sort of recognition of the ordeal by a third (human) party would be necessary, so that they might have someone to talk to without being labeled as crazy. That was almost worse than the experience itself, the stigma of bearing it alone and the ridicule offered by those closest to you. It was while they were pondering this that Jeb wondered out loud if the cat cared about any of all this, and what it might do now that it had this new insight, if some sort of revelation might have formed in its head. He had barely shut his mouth when the plaque shifted. *Different assholes, same question.* Well, that answered that.

Regarding their phones, the plaque explained that they'd been charged up already and the obfuscation removed, wirelessly. They would have bars again topside. Jake couldn't help but wonder what all that was doing to their brains, this whole wireless charging thing. Surely whatever charged a piece of lithium did something undesirable to a piece of meat. Would they rejoin the masses as one, brainless, slightly fried goo of human life? And then he realized that that was just what they needed. A mass of people. Only the most crisp of assholes (like the military) denied a mass of people its truth, whatever it was they said they saw. And even then, you had company.

Dyslexic Jake wrote a single word down to this effect and showed it to his father, who squinted at the word and then borrowed the pen to scratch out part of it and rewrite it. The problem was the D at the end. It had looked like an S, and this flighty lot might give them something else entirely. Jake then showed it to Nicely. The plaque soon informed them that they could have that too.

Jeb and Jake then stroked Nicely behind his head. They were awkward about it at first, not just because this was goodbye, but the creature had interpreted an alien language and presented it to them on a piece of wood in the wall. That sort of thing was difficult to patronise, but patronise was what you did with cats. Jeb asked Nicely if he might like to come with them, and the plaque asked them to piss off already. It almost immediately shifted again. The cat would come with them, on second thoughts, if they'd help it out of the *kippah*.

Now this is what happened. Jeb took the *kippah* off, which involved a little more work than he'd bargained as he had never considered there might be a clip hidden underneath the thing. The cat then hopped onto the floor and stretched out. As it stepped into the elevator and Jeb followed, something hit the floor behind them loudly enough that it might have cracked. It was Jake. He had donned the *kippah* and wasn't looking better for it. He had a lather around his mouth and his arms, hands, shins and feet were all doing whatever it was that they wanted and all at the same time without consulting each other about it. Here was Jacob wrestling with angels unseen. Jeb was ready to launch himself at his boy and wrench the bloody thing off his son's head, but Nicely stopped Jeb with a paw on his ankle. The look on the cat's face was calm. It said to wait, and do you know, Jeb waited.

The shaking stopped eventually and Jake, quite alright it seemed, propped himself up on his elbows and realized he must look a simpleton with all the bubbles crowding up at the corners of his lips and a dribble down his collar. He wiped that off unaware of the string of blood coming out of his nose, and then the plaque shifted. *Calibrated.* He then spoke directly to his father and said that he would be staying. This would raise an alarming number of objections in the old man's mind, but authority won over. So Jeb told the beings that no matter how many years they might keep his son, at the end of it he expected Jake at the dinner table that night or he would know the reason why. The plaque shifted to show a thumbs up.

Jake and Nicely arrived at the top and the doors opened. Jake's final request had worked. A crowd. They stood around the elevator taking pictures and gaping at the strangeness of it all, at however it was they got here and at here itself. Behind them parked in the dirt was a hop-on hop-off tour bus, large, clean, pink and odd for where it was. And behind that sat the El Dorado. Jebediah and Nicely stepped out of the elevator and the cameras clicked. Jeb couldn't look at it the same way, this crowd. He thought of cattle in a field eating. Pictures and cud weren't all that different now. He couldn't believe he'd never seen it before. He was thankful for one kind of math, the GPS, which now worked.

They made their way through the crowd, and back to the El Dorado. And as they approached it, a crow flew directly over their heads and landed on the hood and then looked at them. They stood some distance away and watched the crow watching them. Another crow flew directly overhead and landed beside it. The first crow squawked and then both flew away. They watched the crows disappear, looked at each other, and then got in the El Dorado. Only one way to go this time, with five bars and full battery.

THE MISFITS OF SUMO WRESTLING

Dianne Gorveatt

No coverage, not even one bar, the battery was dead anyway. It was still daytime, but there was an overcast and the sky had a perfectly even dullness, so there was no way to tell what time of day it was, much less which direction was north or south or anything else for that matter. A two-lane blacktop road snaked up into the distance and disappeared into some trees, or a forest if you wanted to get technical about it. It also snaked down toward some lumpy hills and disappeared there as well. What sounded like a two- stroke chainsaw could be heard in the distance, but it was impossible to tell whether it was up in the forest or down in the lumpy hills. This had been happening more often lately. Two different ways to go, with a dead battery and no bars, and nobody left to blame.

They had decided early on never to blame each other for anything; it was one of their two vital rules. The other was to never agree on anything; they would only make a move to do something when given no choice. Before making these rules, they had decided to travel together and had both agreed that this was probably a huge mistake. An additional rule—although realistically more of a guideline than a rule—they decided on a strict this-bunk-is-mine-and-that-is yours policy. No touchy-feely.

They met at sunset standing in the parking lot of a truck stop where they had stopped on their separate ways to the Grand Canyon. Although neither knew exactly how to get to the Grand Canyon, or even for sure, which state it was in, they both had the same goal in mind: There was a UFO festival that weekend at the Canyon; they wanted to attend. They had both made the decision on short notice and were not completely prepared. Their shared agenda didn't come up immediately in conversation, since, due to a regional power outage, they couldn't buy snacks or gas at the truck stop; these immediate concerns dominated their introductory chatter.

Steve, who had lost his nose when a spider crawled into it on a camping trip and injected flesh-dissolving venom into the cartilage, had plenty of gas, but he was hungry. Xery, who weighed close to 200 pounds had leftovers from lunch as well as a backpack stuffed with snacks, but was out of gas. Xery drove a battered up sardine can on wheels. It was so efficient that she just assumed it would never run out of gas; she didn't even own a gas can. Steve drove an ocean going vessel, it would seem, from the size of it, and was accustomed to having low mileage; his trunk was stuffed with red, plastic gas cans; three more were strapped to the roof rack. All were full. A merger seemed inevitable, and soon it was.

So many vehicles had pulled off the highway due to the power outage to get services and then stayed, the drivers not knowing what to do next, that Steve had pulled into one of the bays in the coin-operated *Pay-n-Spray* car wash. Xery, who pulled in shortly after he did, followed his example and was in the next bay. When the station manager noticed this, she ran out to shoo them away, shoo being perhaps too soft a word. The coin-op was a good money maker; as soon as the electricity came back, she wanted it ready to spray and *pay*.

Although neither Steve nor Xery had discerned anything especially menacing about the station manager upon meeting *her*, if that was the appropriate pronoun, perhaps given to excess or driven to it by the incessant questions about the power outage, she was running toward them brandishing an aluminum baseball bat. That alone may not have been a subject of concern, but the bat had been repaired more than once with jagged layers of high- tack, foil tape, and she knew how to shake that thing.

No Bars and a Dead Battery

Later, neither could remember the exact action that resulted in Xery grabbing her backpack and cellphone and casting her fate with Steve by jumping into the cavernous front seat, or more accurately, wheelhouse, of Steve's Eldorado. Steve thought it must have been his well-practiced 'come hither' eyebrow gesture. Xery, a *virtual* vegan—but, nevertheless, an avid consumer of snacks—the ingredients lists of which were epically long and impossible to verify—kept her from being a pure vegan—rather thought it was the lure of perverse decadence; the seats were *leather*. She had never once knowingly sat or trod upon leather. The reasons didn't matter so much when, once Steve stepped on the gas and accelerated, Xery turned to look back at what was happening in the coin-op. The station manager had been joined by a mob of men, presumably truckers or their zombie cousins, clad in colorful, pajama-like pants with stretchy waistbands, all wielding baseball bats.

Xery felt surprisingly little emotion watching her tiny car being bashed into a crumpled, red wad. She attributed her detachment to the fact that she had been driving it all through her undergraduate and graduate years—this road trip was part of research for her Phd dissertation—and had spent so much time in the repair shop with it that she was considering having her mail forwarded there. If she jammed too hard on the brakes, she could hear a strident tintinnabulation as loose parts fell off and hit the pavement. It was time to let it go, but, as a soon-to-be anthropologist, she was confused by the station manager's motives in attacking it and said so to Steve. He quietly explained that the station lost money on chump change customers like her; if she made a trip to the ladies' room, their overhead and expenses would cost more than they would earn from her at the pump. Steve had worked at a gas station during high school.

She was looking forward to possibly finding out more about a man who might have the means to cruise around rural America in a pristine, vintage gas hog while also having insights into the workings of life among earthlings.

For his part, Steve had already decided that he also would like to find out more about Xery. He found her attractive. This wasn't all that difficult as Steve had spent hundreds, if not thousands, of hours analyzing what he liked or disliked about women and discovered that only two or three features would result in his finding a woman to be unappealing: routine lack of attention to personal hygiene, cruelty to animals, and having ever initiated a chain letter. The first two were flexible—hygiene might be lax during a natural disaster, and people disagree on how to define 'cruelty' when it comes to animals—some think keeping pets is cruel—but the chain letter thing was not negotiable.

Yes, Xery was big; but as a body aesthetic, bigness served to exaggerate her exquisite feminine shape, not obscure it, as did her choice of stretchy clothing. Steve was, however, wondering how she would react once she knew the story behind the misshapen remains of his nose. Some women were reflexively attracted to the pathos of the story; those especially phobic about spiders often turned and ran, literally. He hadn't just been bitten by the arachnid, he had been partially *consumed*; to the hobby shaman, that made him part spider. He resolved, after his first experience with such a reaction, to never again reveal the unsavory denouement to the incident and how he knew for certain that it had been a spider. It's not like people could ignore the remodel; at more than six-feet tall, he towered over most people. When they looked up at his face, they immediately noticed his nose; he couldn't hide it by shyly ducking under the brim of a hat. Perhaps due to the dim light and the somewhat life-or-death circumstances, she hadn't mentioned it, yet.

The *hey-you* of their mutual interest created a cocoon of benevolence especially in the interior of the vehicle when contrasted to the scene of mayhem fast retreating behind them, and silence, at least during the liftoff. Eldo, as Steve called his vehicle, although not a rum runner, had about a Mach 7 acceleration when the gas pedal was leveraged skillfully;

No Bars and a Dead Battery

Steve was skillful. The highway morphed into a black hole and plummeting into it, Steve remembered a phrase from his maudlin, nihilist, high school creative writing: *the black back of death rises.*

Perhaps as a result of his disaster recovery training during his corporate years, once they slowed to cruising speed, Steve began to take inventory: one female of unknown origin, one day pack bulging with fat-salt-sugar food, 18 gallons of high-octane fuel, one mylar emergency blanket. Something was missing, but what? They had not a drop to drink. He pointed this out when Xery offered him a strip of soy jerky laden with sea salt; they agreed to stop and buy fluids as soon as possible. Due to the widespread power outage, that 'soon' didn't come until dawn when they crossed the state line and into an unaffected power grid. They stopped at the first truck stop spotlighted in the bluish blaze wrought by hyper-excited mercury vapor molecules. While Steve topped off the tank, apologizing for only buying 15 gallons, and answered questions about his classic wheels, Xery bought water and juice boxes. Xery noticed that Steve tipped the attendant.

Of course, every solution contains within it the germ of a new problem. Prudent hydration practices soon led to a need for a pit stop; as this was their first intimate act as road buddies; it was awkward. The two-lane highway stretched for miles in either direction through farmland as bland and featureless as any airport carpet without a shrub to pee behind, they had no choice but to pull off at the next exit. Once off the highway, the change from highway monotony to hills was so abrupt as to make them wonder if they were dreaming. They took turns relieving themselves behind a not-quite-abandoned vehicle; chittering bats were using it as a day roost. When they turned to get back on the highway, they discovered that the entrance ramp was closed, not just closed, but inaccessible. Ordinarily a trivial problem such as a road closure would not concern Steve, accustomed as he was to flouting rules as well as signs and wonders, but a sinkhole had devoured the road; workmen told them to follow the detour signs to the next entrance.

The detour devoured them. They followed the signs; the signs were bright and conspicuous; they were in many languages; they seemed to follow a logical sequence, and yet Steve and Xery found themselves coming literally to the end of the road. The pavement ended, and beyond it was hardscrabble land, a great spot to serve as a set for a stoic pioneer movie, but not likely to be a short cut to the Grand Canyon. The sun was setting on their first day and they had to make a decision. Steve's body made it for them; as soon as they stopped, he fell asleep, mouth open, head cocked back, hands still on the wheel. He hadn't slept for days.

With great difficulty, Xery shook him semi-awake and got him out of the car and into the back seat. Before he slumped into an awkward fetal position on the back seat and back to sleep, he pointed; there, under the front seat, Xery found an emergency kit with a few supplies—bandaids, aspirins, a pair of tick tweezers, thankfully, no condoms—it did contain one emergency mylar space blanket. Steve's body, all more than six feet of it, looked impossibly uncomfortable, so, after unfolding the tiny rectangle of flimsy mylar into a bed-sized, crinkly, microscopically thin, gold sheet, she spread it over him instead of using it herself. Xery's own body was soon faced with the prospect of trying to sleep upright in a bucket seat, a new experience for her. From that night on, her definition of a *luxury car* would only include one which would allow one to recline fully if forced to sleep in it. This *luxury* vehicle failed miserably; she experienced a night of countable and uncountable discomforts. It's amazing how cold the temperate zone can get even in the spring once the sun goes down.

When Steve woke as stiff as an old, cold garden hose, pried himself out of the backseat and staggered a decent distance from the car to relieve himself, he suddenly remembered the difference between a habit and an addiction. You might forget something if it's a habit, but you can't stop thinking about something when it's an addiction. He suddenly couldn't

No Bars and a Dead Battery

stop thinking about coffee; it had easily been decades since he had faced a morning without the magic elixir; the shock of this prospect was deadening. He was standing and staring like a kid who had just seen his new puppy carried off by a hawk when he felt a touch on his elbow. He turned, and Xery handed him a bottle of water with the cap already removed. Then a miracle happened; she reached under the flap of her black shoulder bag, like those used by bicycle couriers, and extracted a tube the size and color of a cigarillo; it was instant coffee. She tore open the tube, poured the precious grains into the bottle, and screwed the cap back on as he held it. He shook the bottle, opened it, and took a sip. It was surprisingly good. This good woman just might become misses, or more appropriately miss #3; Steve had been married twice; he automatically assumed a catastrophic end to any relationship.

Since there was no place to sit outside the car, other than on the ground, and said ground was strewn with generational layers of broken beer bottles, and, without needing to be told, Xery didn't want to eat inside a leather lined vehicle, they both sat silently on the edge of the seats with the doors open—she in the front, he in the back—leaning out to munch breakfast bars and jerky. When they were done, they both got up, and, like an Olympic, synchronized road-trip team, stepped away from the car, brushed crumbs from their clothing, then turned to face each other. The first rays of the morning sun travelled their millions of miles seemingly with but one purpose: to illuminate Steve's face, highlighting its extensive wrinkles and cracks.

The mirror of horror created by the expression on Xery's face made Steve wince; he then witnessed the most extensive and impassioned rant of his life, but when it was over, he could only laugh with relief. She wasn't repulsed by his *nose*, an uncle of hers had the same thing happen; she hated Steve because he was *old*—a boomer. Ever since the publication of that surprise bestseller *The Psychotrophic-opiodized New Age— A Social Necropsy of the Narcissistic, Entitle-Demented Generation* Steve had been meeting more young people who were repulsed not by his nose, but by his *age*. For him this was a great relief, but it bothered many of his contemporaries. The scathing book turned out to be a prank written using a prose generator fed with phrases from a Chinese-English dictionary, but the last sentence—and this *was* written by the author—stuck. It said: *Everything that's wrong with our world can be laid at the feet of the post-War generation; it's OK to hate them.*

Steve offered to drive Xery home, but she declined and explained that she really did want to get to the UFO festival as she was doing research for her dissertation. After declining, Xery pushed her lips into a tight, annular ring expressing social stricture and revealing a previously unnoticed collection of lip fangs. Steve made a mental note of the fact that Xery was likely to be over 30; and reminded himself of the fact that she, as a woman feeling the mortality of her youth, was likely to be more judgmental than the mean of him as a modern, aging hominid. Steve turned Eldo back onto the two-lane and they drove silently for the next hour.

Eventually they both realized that they still didn't know where they were. Xery snaked an arm under the flap of her courier-sized shoulder bag and extracted a cellphone; she explained that she was on a pay-as-you-go plan and that Internet access turned her phone into a highly efficient money-extraction-device but offered to do Google maps since they were passing a large lake. A snow- covered mountain peak punctuated the horizon. Scraggly, beaver- chew trees, looking like worn-out brooms with handles stuck in the ground, lined the shores; bank fishermen lurked beneath them. Using this geographic reference, they should be able to figure out where they were. Steve feared that they were on their way to Seattle; for most of his life, whenever Steve was lost, it eventually turned out that he was on his way to Seattle. They waited as the phone danced through its wake-up routine, Xery kept it *off* most of the time to preserve the battery, but when the wakeup was done, no bars.

No Bars and a Dead Battery

Since all American public school students receive exhaustive training in cartography, celestial navigation, and geography as well as philosophy to encourage independent problem solving, and world history to cultivate social empathy . . . *not*, they had no choice but to flip a coin. Many flips later found them on an east-bound highway headed to the Grand Canyon; they had found and begun to follow billboards advertising *Olympus*. That was the name of a recently opened casino that had been built under the suspension bridge now crossing the Canyon. The casino, built in the shape of a UFO, was suspended beneath the bridge, apparently by using cloaking cables that were virtually invisible; the effect had set off a wave of UFO reports and interest in otherworldly visitors. The interest resulted in the UFO festival being organized. Without revealing his own motives, Steve asked Xery why she thought people went to such events. This question was a magic key. Xery seemed to completely forget that Steve was a degraded member of the enfeebled effete and instantly started bubbling about UFOs. She told him the working title of her dissertation: *Sacred Stranger as Magic Mirror and Consummate Catalyst for Initiating the Inception of World Selfhood and Its Marketing Potential.* Xery loved alliteration.

Steve figured it would take them about three days to get to the Grand Canyon, assuming they were somewhere in Oregon and assuming that the Canyon was somewhere in Arizona. Neither was entirely sure of either, but Xery, thought the drive could be done in a day.

The scene that took place when Xery noticed that the Eldorado did not have a radio is too painful to describe. Steve once again offered to drive her back to her home, but she dialed it down and declined, citing the deadline on her dissertation. Once cooled, she plumbed the depths of her courier purse and extracted an ancient digital recorder as well as a digital camera to show Steve. He made note of the fact that she was at least five years recalcitrant in technology; for a thirty-something, that made her odd. To take her mind off media withdrawal, she asked Steve if she could interview him. Xery had her own style, instead of starting with the topic at hand, she invited people to tell their life story.

And so, Steve decides to jump right in and tell Xery that he is an alien-human hybrid, and that he has known this since wearing diapers and wriggling on his back in the crib trying to make sense of the whack-job kaleidoscope of sensory input assaulting his pre- verbal awareness. His multi-dimensioned alien side reacted so badly to the prison of a human body that he was assigned a special assistant from the Multiverse who appeared at his bedside from time to time. This being said his name was Harvey Gomantime; he wore a paper bag over his head so as not to frighten Steve. He explained, using remarkably good English, that there had been a molecular ambiguity leading to a singular phenomenological discontinuity; in the original instructions, the host humans were described as *big*. The technicians in charge of the implant, interpreted that to mean *tall*; they implanted an alien sequence compatible with *tall* parents, not parents genetically equipped to spawn a family of Sumo wrestlers, or more accurately, *Samoan* wrestlers; his parents met when his dad, air force mechanic, was stationed on Guam during WWII. Mom was Samoan. Xery interrupted to ask if both his parents were big like her, and he confirmed. He flipped down the sun visor to reveal a gallery of family photos. Big. The more his parents fed him, the taller and thinner Steve got, to their and his immense distress. He was as tall as a nine-year old by the time he was four.

Knowing from personal experience about the importance of clear instructions propelled Steve into becoming a top-notch, detail-oriented technical writer starting in aviation and then branching out into disaster recovery. Since retirement, he had been a UFO chaser. Although it slowed considerably, his body had never completely stopped growing; he was hoping to find an alien technician skilled enough to do a genetic retrofit. It wasn't acromegaly; his whole body kept growing proportionately.

No Bars and a Dead Battery

The first thing that comes to Xery's mind is the kid rhyme: They were passing out noses. I thought they said roses, And asked for a big red one. She does not recite this, but turns the recorder off and sits quietly listening to the reassuring, hypnotic hum of road noise, making note of the fact that a spaceship might just make the same kind of hum. A check with her inner bullshit detector convinced her that Steve was *not* making fun of her; he also did not read like a crazy person. This left two possibilities: that Steve had been exposed to a substantial deception carried out at an indelibly early age by his parents who were disappointed to have a lithe beanpole as a child but didn't want him to feel that it was in some way his fault and it was them who appeared by the side of his bed wearing paper bags over their heads or Steve actually was an alien-human hybrid. As an open-minded researcher, Xery did not completely discount the latter possibility.

When, after a long awkward silence, Steve added that he didn't usually tell people about the alien-hybrid thing, Xery was relieved; she couldn't help think this might be a social hinderance and had begun to feel sorry for him. She didn't want pity to dilute the raw hatred she was cultivating. When he further explained that the fact that she already hated him for being old made the alien-hybrid thing seem trivial by comparison and that's why he had told her up front; she felt slightly guilty, but not so much. She really did hold the Post War generation responsible for the impending end of life as we know it. How can you forgive that? They had to all be sociopaths.

Once again, Steve offered to drive her home. When she declined, he asked her to tell her story. Xery's story was more grounded. Her dad worked as a gas-company meter reader; her mom worked as an administrative assistant. Since Xery was first- generation college, her parents, extended family, and her church all agreed that she should go the distance and get her Phd. Xery felt beholden to them for the years of support; once a month, their church passed a graduation hat around for the collection and used half of it to buy US Savings Bonds; they were to help Xery pay off school loans. Because of her sense of obligation, she strategically included courses on business and marketing as electives. As an anthropologist, her plan was to study American *subcultures* and work as a marketing consultant. She would not eke out her career as a member of the genteel academic poor; she paid for her education and she planned to make it pay. Inspired by the substantive role that subcultures played in her extended family, Xery had begun at an early age to catalog subcultures and keep track of the likes and dislikes of each group, especially when it came to product preferences. So as not to jinx her business aspirations, she kept it a secret that she had already been making money as a consultant. For instance, she received a tidy sum when she was able to tell a beer company what brand Bowie hunters preferred to suck up after a boar kill. A marketing firm rewarded her for identifying a little-known but powerful market segment: perm culture. Most of her clandestinely powerful female relatives had never allowed themselves to be seen in public without a perm, regardless of prevailing style.

In Xery's family, there were Bigfoot hunters, rock hounds, ghost hunters, tole painters, generational flea market entrepreneurs, pinochle tournament champions, tent revivalists, bookies—it was limitless. The fact that these areas of American culture received so little academic attention, and when they did, were presented almost as pathologies, signaled a deep cultural bias, in her opinion. And yet, to get along in life, Xery had learned to be coy about revealing her social background. She looked forward to surprising her family by graduating with school loans fully paid and a book contract already in place, which it was. The working title was *Social Muzzle Firmly in Place: The Price of Admission.*

The more Steve learned about Xery, the more it depressed him to think that a little thing like a 30 or 40 year age difference would keep them apart. On the other hand, he had to admit that the fact that a merger was off the table added to the allure, that plus the fact that she

No Bars and a Dead Battery

was clearly 100% human; he had a secret aversion to anyone who might be a hybrid like him.

Xery took out her cellphone and tried it again; still no bars, but the battery was holding steady at 99. For the first time in years of living as an over-scheduled, plugged-in student and member of a huge, competitive family addicted to social media, nail salons, and drama, Xery felt boredom, mind-numbing, stultifying boredom. She didn't know what it was at first, and once she recognized it, she was surprised at how physical it was. The atmosphere was heavy and thick; when she moved her hand through the air, it felt like pudding. Her breathing slowed to the point that she thought she might pass out.

It was then that she noticed the mylar balloons in different shapes, mostly round or football shaped. Some were floating in the air and seemed to travel along beside them. Some were partially deflated and hopped along the ground. They were mostly silver, but the round balloons came in rainbow colors and moved about like butterflies. Some had writing on them: Congratulations, Welcome Home, Good Job, It's a Hybrid, and Happy Rebirthday. Although the appearance of the balloons was fascinating, she still felt numb. She tried to turn her head to see how Steve was doing, but she couldn't move.

Xery was the first to notice that it had been an incalculably long time since they had seen another vehicle along the road. As soon as she pointed that out, Steve realized that his butt was asleep and that he had to pee more than he ever thought possible. He abruptly pulled Eldo onto the shoulder and barely made it out of the car in time to open his fly and let loose with the most spectacular spew of yellow elixir that his hybrid hose had ever emitted. While he stood there in the middle of the blacktop so as not to splash the car, Xery squatted nearby and did the same into a drainage ditch. Steve realized this when he saw a vigorous rivulet of her urine trickle down the ditch. When she joined him, he was uncharacteristically unconcerned with the fact that he had not quite finished and *Good Buddy* was still out. For her part, Xery was uncharacteristically uninterested in the fact that, yes, indeed, all parts of Steve had continued to grow.

They were both ravenously hungry but didn't feel like being too far apart so they flattened out a cardboard box laying by the side of the road and sat huddled together on it as they munched their way through over half of their remaining food supply. From habit, Xery took out her cell phone; no bars, and this time, the battery was completely dead. She pointed this out to Steve and he started singing the first bars of a Bobby Bill country-pop classic; it goes like this:

> *I'm out here alone with my*
> *cellular phone. The battery's*
> *dead and I want to go home.*

If they had been allowed to remember their time aboard the space ship, this is what they would be reviewing: The *balloons* turned out to be alien space vessels and numerous small drones flying around at will; they were living machines. Instead of being utterly terrified, both voyagers felt joy, even bliss upon recognizing them for what they were. Had Steve and Xery been adepts, they would have realized that they had made a shift from the restricted dream of life on Earth and into their native multi-dimensional selves. They were neophytes in their understanding of the Multiverse, so they just felt happy, even happy together. They exchanged goofy smiles as the air filled with interlaced strains of cheerful 1960s songs; they bounced along with the music like Siamese bobble-head dolls.

They would also be remembering a warm reception given by beings in various colors, sizes, and degrees of luminosity displaying a spectrum of possible combinations of human and alien genetics. And they would remember the lusciously soft, sumptuously colored, truly one-size fits all robes, printed directly onto their bodies.

After greeting and robing, they had been ushered into a hall with

No Bars and a Dead Battery

sensitively done photo portraits of sperm and egg donors, surrogate mothers, hybrid children, alien foster parents, and special assistants such as Steve's Harvey Gomantime. They both spent a long time at the display for Steve's family; it contained photos of him at various stages of life. When Xery saw the poker- straight red hair he wore down to his shoulders in his college years when he was a full foot shorter, she shyly took his hand. This tender moment was interrupted when two technicians came toward them and explained that they had to be separated for a short time but that they would both go back to the same Earth dream soon. They were ushered into separate rooms.

Steve's technician, who was a taller and bean polier version of himself, was able to do a retrofit and stop his continuous growth. Unfortunately, age regressions—Steve was truly getting hooked on Xery—were limited to 20 years; both agreed that 20 years wouldn't make much of a difference to her. He really was that old.

Xery's technician looked like her perfect guy, and she had an instant crush on him until he told her that she had been selected to be a surrogate mother. She objected to this—meat sack, ain't going to happen—even when told that the child she would carry might be the one to save all life on earth from imminent demise, and that legally, they could draft her under the conditions of the Multiverse End-Times Protocol, and in addition seven billion of her Multiverse iterations had voted in favor of her serving in this way. The number of voters didn't matter since there were an infinite number of iterations; the only vote that mattered was Xery's, but the technician left that part out. They had a long argument too complicated to relate here, and Xery relented when he showed her video, dubbed with whale songs, of the potential future last man on earth—he looked surprisingly like Steve—he made a plaintive appeal and explained that the child would be a hybrid produced by mixing the best genes from multiple men; one of them would be Steve. Xery countered this with an offer to do some gene mixing the old-fashioned way with Steve, but only if it would save the planet and he were actually going to be the last man on earth. Suffice it to say that Xery went back to Earth dream carrying the makings of a hybrid child.

And they would have remembered the fabulous lunch after their separate sessions—flavors so fine as to produce bliss—washed down with copious amounts of space beer—the reason behind their desperate calls to nature once back in Earth dream. Instead, they remembered a frightening encounter with beings clad in what best might be called *hum-i-forms* to simulate bodies and wearing paper bags over their heads. They would never speak of this to each other or any other living being. Xery relented years later and told her dog. Since dogs actually understand almost everything we say—except for political newspeak—and only feign uncomprehending to facilitate noncompliance he immediately began to howl, bellow, and croon histrionically. As a rescue, the experience sounded all too familiar to him.

They were nearly out of food, but at the bottom of her bag, she found some tiny, mylar wrapped food bars with a hard-to-read brand name printed on them; they were clearly labeled VEGAN. She gave one to Steve; it would be days before they needed to eat again. The bars not only gave them an energy boost, but also exceptional mental clarity, and they appeared to contain psychotropic qualities. Steve looked both younger and shorter to Xery. When the molecular flood reached Steve's pre-frontal cortex, he realized that the traffic flow had resumed and that it was heavy. Most of the vehicles had some visual reference to space aliens and the UFO festival: flags with big-eyed faces on them, roof racks with models space craft strapped on, speakers blaring Strauss or the tone sequence from *Close Encounters*. Some vehicles were so packed with mylar balloons as to make it look as though no one were driving them.

Steve realized that they needed to get back on the road or they would never make it to the UFO festival. Steve no longer wanted to go, but Xery had to finish her dissertation and he set an inner resolve to get her

No Bars and a Dead Battery

there.

Having been brought up in Boston, Steve was a master in the art of traffic weaving. Only people who had never driven in Boston thought of Los Angeles as the spiritual hub for road warriors. Even high-plains rebels in tricked-out pickup trucks might learn a thing or two by watching him make his precision moves; his father used to brag of him saying that he could park a school bus in a bicycle rack. And yet, once he managed to nose Eldo into the flow, they barely made a mile an hour, even driving to the limit of his skill. Considering that the last billboard had given 38 miles as the distance remaining—Xery disagreed and thought it was *48*—the only way they were going to attend a UFO festival would be if everyone stuck in this epic traffic were to get out and stage one along the side of the two-lane highway.

It was then that Xery noticed an 'S' on the lever that controlled the semi-automatic transmission, and she asked about it. Steve had never noticed this mode, and in a trance-like state, he switched to it. Eldo began to emit a very pleasing electrical hum, the kind of sound power line transformers might make if musicians were assigned to tune them. Suddenly, where there had been no break in traffic, one appeared, and then another. The magical transmission setting when combined with Steve's road slithering allowed them to make better progress, but it was still apparent that it would be hours before they got to their destination. Steve was engrossed in driving, but Xery got tired of white-knuckling while trying to stay Zen with the potential for immanent death. So she asked Steve if he had anything to read.

When she got hold of the folder in the pocket behind the driver's seat and pulled it forward, she was surprised to see *Misfits of Sumo Wrestling* written on the tab. Steve explained that the folder contained a story treatment that he planned to send to a Hong Kong movie producer. He'd been working on it for years, and it was roughly autobiographical. When he graduated from high school, his parents, still hoping that he could be a

Sumo wrestler, had sent him to Japan where he met a blond, blue-eyed trans person from Santa Barbara who had the same aspirations. She@Sue had the right body type and had actually trained, but faced insurmountable esthetic barriers. One wrestling manager agreed to let them put on an exhibition fight as pre-match entertainment. They were met with tsunamis of laughter, but were paid enough to defray their travel costs. In the story treatment, the misfits went on to become wealthy comic actors in the Asian film industry. In real life, She@Sue came home and became a plus- size model, modeling fashions for both sexes. Steve became Steve. Xery read the story; pronounced it vapid and recommended that he submit it as soon as possible. It was sure to be a hit.

When they finally got to the UFO festival, neither of them wanted to stay. It seemed anti-climactic; they had already seen all the costumes and gear on the road. The attractions seemed ho- hum: T-shirt vendors, fake transporters, colorful mobiles with musical ascending orbs, refrigerated trucks carrying the cryogenically preserved remains of famous sci-fi actors, etc. The crowds were huge; it was impossible to get close to the Canyon or even see the UFO shaped casino that had inspired the festival. Xery hurried through her interviews while Steve stayed in the parking lot to clean and polish Eldo. As soon as Xery was done, they got ready to leave.

They congratulated themselves on leaving early and thought they had beaten the crowd as they got out of the parking lot and turned off the main road to a scenic route. Then they looked up and saw an enormous mylar balloon rising up from the distant wooded hills and headed toward them. It was in the shape of a silver disc, a space craft. Soon after noticing it, they could hear a distinct rumble; looking back, they realized that everyone at the festival had seen the craft as well. The rumble came from the thousands of feet pounding the ground as people ran toward them; the silver disc hovered directly over Eldo.

No Bars and a Dead Battery

What happened next was hard to sort out, but piecing it together later, this is what they arrived at: a man wearing either a camo suit or a cupid suit popped up from an underground hunting blind and shot the floating object with a crossbow. The balloon exploded into countless fragments; one landed squarely on their windshield. If Xery had not gotten out to get it, they might have made a getaway before the mob got to them. Instead, they were swarmed and, consumed by fear, they fled the Eldorado. Briefly, they both imagined an ignoble death, but touching the mylar fragments had an odd effect. Everyone who held a piece became instantly calm and centered; their faces expressing not bliss, but ease— paradoxically both focused and detached awareness, compassionate curiosity, kindness. When Xery looked at the fragment in her hand, she saw the image of a face with large, expressive eyes. She didn't want to ruin the memento, but nevertheless tore it half because she really wanted to share it with Steve. The image remained perfectly intact on both pieces. As they looked around them, the mob was no longer a mob, it was a gathering, a congregation, a flock—for the first time in her life—in both their lives—they felt at home, among their own kind. Xery found herself gazing fondly at Steve and thinking that she might like to stay in touch with him. If she ever did have children, he could be a grandfather figure. In an absentminded gesture, she laid a hand over the curve of her belly. Steve raised his eyebrows and offered to drive Xery home, and this time, she accepted.

They made their way through the crowd, and back to the Eldorado. And as they approached it, a crow flew directly over their heads and landed on the hood and then looked at them. They stood some distance away and watched the crow watching them. Another crow flew directly overhead and landed beside it. The first crow squawked and then both flew away. They watched the crows disappear, looked at each other, and then got in the Eldorado. Only one way to go this time, with five bars and full battery.

PUPPY FEET

Hannah Jackson

No coverage, not even one bar, the battery was dead anyway. It was still daytime, but there was an overcast and the sky had a perfectly even dullness, so there was no way to tell what time of day it was, much less which direction was north or south or anything else for that matter. A two-lane blacktop road snaked up into the distance and disappeared into some trees, or a forest if you wanted to get technical about it. It also snaked down toward some lumpy hills and disappeared there as well. What sounded like a two-stroke chainsaw could be heard in the distance, but it was impossible to tell whether it was up in the forest or down in the lumpy hills. This had been happening more often lately. Two different ways to go, with a dead battery and no bars, and nobody left to blame.

According to Aunt Baby, nobody was ever *right* to blame. She'd taught Ivy when Ivy was only a bud that she couldn't be pointing her finger all willy nilly like that. The fault of that one finger would just mean that three other finger faults were pointing right back at her. And young Ivy, she *felt* that. It made her anxious as she bathed in the kitchen sink, watching her mother bounce bills off her father's chest just before he'd bounce her head off the linoleum floor.

Over sitcom laugh tracks and repeat commercials of *Every kiss begins with Kay*, they would reconcile, her mother's legs across her father's lap as they whispered and they cooed. It all had to be somebody's fault, but they never blamed each other, and they never blamed Ivy. The trouble, according to them, was with Mama's stingy, selfish, greedy Aunt Baby.

No Bars and a Dead Battery

Panting, sweat beading at the edge of her cornrows, Ivy turned to check on her aunt. They had been walking for miles, and driving for more, but she was too afraid to stop now. The world around them now was as unfamiliar and wild as the one they had just escaped, and the distant but definite chuckle of that chainsaw could easily prove to be an even greater danger. Ivy turned around again and called down to her great aunt see if she wanted a break.

Baby was puffing along, just a little ways down the hill behind her. She wore a pink and yellow velour tracksuit that must have been all the rage in some prehistoric era, because that was the only logical explanation for Baby owning so many of them in such a wide array of colors. A small hand, colored and wrinkled like a crushed brown paper bag rose to wave off the girl's concern. By the time it dropped, Ivy was already behind her, arms wrapped around Baby's small body as Ivy took her aunt at the elbows and gently guided her off to the side of the blacktop road. There was a family of tree stumps that she could only guess were born of the chainsaw wielder, but she chased the thought from her mind.

Her main concern, as ever, was Baby's comfort. Watching the older woman wince as she lowered to the outer edge of the tree's rings sent Ivy's teeth sinking into her cheek. She checked the sky again, but there was no use. It hadn't grown any darker or lighter since they started their climb from the bottom of the hill. She was no closer to knowing which direction was which than she was to knowing which direction was right.

What Ivy did know was that she had driven herself and her aunt a hundred miles away from their home in Jersey City before her ancient station wagon exhaled to a shaky stop down at the bottom of the hill, empty of gas. She knew that everything up the road was an unknown, and that back down into the lumpy hills and past them into the horizon was home. Ivy had no clue whether it was safer to go forward, but she also knew it was too late for Aunt Baby to go back.

Everybody in a five block radius knew the story; an urban legend about as wide and as tall as a hidden safe with ninety thousand dollars tucked inside. This treasure was thought to be hidden somewhere in the bowels of Baby's house a few streets over from the Walkers. She was an epic hoarder and a complete shut-in; everybody in a five block radius knew that part, too. So, when the city finally condemned the property, leaving Baby with nowhere to go, everybody in a five block radius began to call, to check in and to come around, like vultures circling a dying thing.

Even at the age of seven, Ivy was fully aware of the fact that while the other kids had teachers, office workers, or firemen for parents, she was left with swindlers. The Walkers could talk themselves into houses, into fast money, into thinking they were in love. The other kids knew that all Ivy's parents did was take a vannage of the innocent. None of them knew what this meant, but they knew that it was bad, and that was the trouble.

After years of successful schemes, they were hard pressed to find anyone in a five block radius who still had a vannage for them to take. Fortunately for them, Ivy's mother was a distant cousin of Baby's as well as her next of kin. With their experience, it would be nothing to sweeten Baby's final days and reap the reward when she was reaped herself.

When Baby first moved in with Ivy's family, it was like a dream. Her father found a second job and came home every night after his shift. Her mother started doing nails at the salon downtown and served good, hot food out of the oven rather than out of soup cans. Next to best of all, the plumber was finally called for the upstairs bathroom, which meant no more baths in the kitchen sink for little Ivy Walker.

Best of all was Baby, because Ivy knew that her life was so much better thanks to her arrival. She didn't dare to trust a hope for change. At this young age, Ivy also knew that her parents were only preparing to take a vannage of Baby. It was to the Walkers' great surprise to learn that Baby left no advantage for them to take.

What the Walkers were expecting was a quiet, gentle and manageable old woman: a church mother type, of satin hats and pocket peppermints.

No Bars and a Dead Battery

Instead Baby was discovered, much to Ivy's delight, to be more of a gold-toothed gangster who loved to grow azaleas. An OG with the mouth a sailor and the wardrobe of a 90s rapper, Baby flung playing cards like darts, resting her pearl-handled pistol on the Spades tables as she collected books.

The Walkers had finally met their match, that much was clear. There was balance to their home; a hurricane to combat the volcano of their family life of running schemes. And little Ivy Walker, then, had no worries about her fearless Aunt Baby and her legendary fortune. She became enamored with her wildness and her wisdom.

At the annual campus cookout, it was Ivy who starred at the Spades table, making use of every trick she learned at her Aunt Baby's knee. She copied her attitude, her humor, and her old-school slang, right down to the way Baby called the clubs suit puppy feet. Under her guidance, Ivy learned how to drive, how to drink well, and how to study hard, and how to recognize true love so that once she escaped to school, her parents would never be able to lie her back.

Ivy pressed her finger to the home button on her phone and held it, to no avail. She leaned her head back against the nearest tree and shut her eyes tight as she mopped the sweat along her jaw with the back of her hand. This was not the turn of events she imagined when she set out to rescue her aunt two nights before. When she first received Baby's two-word distress call, Ivy was only aware of two things. One, that her parents still shamelessly and diabolically planned to inherit Baby's mythical fortune. Two, that they had decided to speed up the process by starving her.

Ivy knew their capability. She knew their track record. There was no other option for Ivy besides coming straight home and springing Aunt Baby in the half-dead station wagon. She carved her way across the state, driving until her tire rolled over the kiss of the curb outside the Walker house. Baby's huddled form sat squat on the front porch, her arms clamped around a black duffel bag, a long tan umbrella slipped between its handles, and something very unfamiliar nesting in her knowing brown eyes.

Ivy tapped her drained-dead phone against her thigh in the rhythm of a ballad she'd figured she'd long forgotten. None of Baby's usual steel and wit greeted her as she crept down the walk to the car, sat shotgun, and shut her eyes behind her tortoiseshell glasses. Baby said to drive. Ivy asked where? Baby said North. Ivy started the car.

That was three hundred and thirty miles ago. From there, Baby had continued to squint over a map of New York and direct Ivy from one roadway to another until the station wagon ran out of gas. Now that they were both tired enough, Ivy was ready. She waited until she had drummed up enough nerve to ask Baby the first question that sprung in her mind when Ivy had first pulled up to that curb.

Baby only blinked. She lifted her head and stared thoughtfully into the treetops, her fingers running over the grooves of her tree stump. When she finally opened her mouth, it wasn't to answer Ivy's question of where they were going; it was to tell Ivy that they should probably follow the hum of the chainsaw. That the tree stumps marked the start of a dirt driveway that had been conquered by young saplings, mossy rocks, and overgrown weeds. But, a driveway nonetheless. Ivy stood there stunned. Baby led the way.

The old path became clearer the further along that they walked. Baby kept mumbling to herself; something about being glad that the car had stopped when they were already so close. Ivy followed willingly but warily, clutching the tan umbrella in her left fist and the straps of the duffel bag over her right shoulder. There was no money in it, excepting what was on Baby's card inside Baby's wallet. Everything else was more velour suits, underclothes, toiletries, a pill organizer, pre-package insulin, a second pair of white sneakers and a pack of playing cards.

Of course when she'd first seen the bag settled on Baby's lap, she

No Bars and a Dead Battery

assumed that it was that legendary package of ninety thousand whole dollars. It didn't matter either way to Ivy. Baby's safety was the goal, and of course the money would be a viable tool to secure it. Still, the childish wonder of years ago in their five-block radius still found her. She often found herself sneaking glances at Baby, remembering how she and her friends would bike past the old woman's house and swap made-up mysteries.

Ivy broke from her trance to slap at her mahogany legs and then at her ears as swollen mosquitoes hissed into them greedily. When she looked up to complain to her aunt, there was a house ahead. Tucked into the heart of a small clearing was a little white cottage, clapboards stained yellow and gray from time and loneliness. A silver Jeep was parked in the grass in front of the house. Behind it was a small garage, before it a well, and beside it a fresh woodpile. Ivy's eyes immediately began to hunt for the chainsaw, and found it in the hands of a man, slim and hale, who came from around the back of the house.

Before she could scream, he started to. Having taken only a few courses of Spanish, Ivy could only make out a few words: *abuelita*, which meant grandmother; *lárguese*, which meant get the fuck out; *cuervo*, which meant crow. Ivy's mind went spinning, reeling as she tried to make sense of it all and find the words to respond at the same time. Her surprise was sealed as Aunt Baby called out to the man with the chainsaw, answering him in Spanish. Whatever she said, it made him lower the chainsaw. It also made another older woman appear on the front porch of the cabin. She called Baby Bernadine. Baby called her Carmen. Baby introduced Ivy. Carmen introduced Hernán.

After that, nobody said a word. Hernán stared at Carmen with the same searching look that Ivy applied to Baby, but neither of them responded. It was as if they had entered a world all their own, and the two visitors among them were nothing more than saplings, or mossy rocks, or swollen and hissing mosquitoes.

Ivy recognized the look in her great aunt's face. She had learned it from Baby after years of seeing it mimicked in her parents' mirrored faces. Ivy check Carmen's eyes. They were warm and clear and the color of tea, brimming with the same overwhelming love as Baby's. Ivy was finished. She had reached her last straw; the final nail in a velour-trimmed coffin. All her questions came spilling out as one: Babywhatthefuck.

Again, no answer came. Ivy had to forgive her aunt for that, because each time Baby opened her mouth to undam the truth, she trembled right down to her teeth, as if someone were physically holding her by the tongue. She tried again and again to speak, but nothing crossed her lips. They stood like statues, watching Baby try, until Carmen hastily invited them into the house for coffee, carting her oxygen tank behind her.

Inside was a two room set up, with a bedroom towards the back of the house. A sitting room couch and rocking chair shared the rest of the space with a cast iron woodburning stove, and a kitchen table with two carved chairs. There was a china cabinet, full of flatware and silverware, a white round-top Frigidaire, and a landline telephone.

What paused Ivy were the pictures. Along the wooden walls were framed photographs of the same three people, over and over again. She knew her great aunt immediately, reformed young and wildly gorgeous in black and white. Baby wore the same velour suits even then, with gold chains, huge hoop earrings, and crisp white sneakers. In most of the frames she was laughing the same squint-eyed, opened mouthed cackle, infectious even while frozen in time.

Subconsciously, Ivy had picked a favorite. Baby sat hanging out of the driver's window of a sleek Cadillac El Dorado that looked more animal than machine. Her long, curly afro was tied up in a bandana so that it curled down over her brow. Her left hand was raised in the air. Ivy would have figured she would form it into a fist, but all five fingers were wide open, free, swinging in the air.

She was always standing in the center of the three, a woman on one side and a man to her left. When she looked closer at these pictures, Ivy also came to recognize the woman as Carmen. There was the same beauty mark, in the same corner of her mouth. She also had the same hairstyle; cut close and smoothed so that it curled around her ears.

Without waiting for Ivy's attention, Carmen began to explain that this property was a private parcel they had purchased a lifetime ago, in case of emergencies. She explained that Hernán was her grandson. She explained that she, Baby, and the unnamed man were members of a California gang. *Lárguese. Abuelita. Los Cuervos.* Ivy could put it together.

Hernán apologized for scaring them, admitting he was scared. He told Baby and Ivy that he thought they were members of the Cuervos. He and his grandmother had been hiding out in the cabin for almost a week. When Baby and her niece arrived, Hernán had been chopping wood for the stove. He'd assumed that the crows had finally found him, leading him to grab the chainsaw he'd used to cut the trees down.

No matter how he turned his head, or the angle Ivy viewed him at, Hernán had an interesting face. She kept looking long after she realized she liked it. His hair was cut Caesar-style, and he wore a dark grey T-shirt with a T of sweat that formed in an even darker grey along his back. He dresses like a California boy, Ivy thought. Thick dark brows rested over deep-set eyes the same tea color as his abuelita's. When those eyes caught Ivy's watching them, they smiled without the help of his mouth.

Ivy immediately broke her stare and asked Aunt Baby if she knew Carmen would be at the cabin? Finally, Baby was able to answer, and told her that she didn't. She and Carmen hadn't seen or spoken to each other in over fifty year, and Baby hadn't been planning to start today. Every eye in the room fell on Carmen, who sat down in the rocking chair and laughed at Hernán. Shaking her head, she told Ivy that he looked nothing like his grandfather, the man in the photographs. Martín el Cuervo was much stockier, much hairier, much louder, much meaner. She told Ivy that she shouldn't be afraid of Hernán. Baby found her voice again, just long enough for her to mutter that Carmen shouldn't have been afraid of Martín either.

Carmen couldn't reply. Someone asked if Martín was the reason that Baby and Carmen had stopped loving each other? Only when every eye in the room was focused on her did Ivy realize she had spoken her thoughts out loud. After that, they turned to Baby. She was sitting on the edge of the couch, weathered oak-brown hands folded in her lap as if she were a first-time visitor.

She could have told them the story. She could have told them about the gambling shacks and the the violence and the promises made, both in California and in the cabin, too. She could have told them about Martín el Cuervo, and his complete control over both she and Carmen, and how Baby had begged Carmen to run away with her, where not even he would find them. She could have told them how she had waited fifty years in the same house, spending day and night indoors so that whenever the moment came, the one that would finally bring Carmen to her door, Baby wouldn't miss it. She could have told them that after the thirtieth year, she finally gave up and moved in with her half-smart niece and her husband, all because she felt ashamed every time she thought about Carmen finding her again: an old hoarding hermit, still clinging to yesterdays long past.

Instead, she told them that she had never stopped. The room went quiet with the weight of her words. A small sob, a brief, cracking cry broke the silence, and Carmen stood to her feet, snatched up her tank, and crossed the house to the bedroom, shutting the door behind her. Hernán sighed heavily and apologized again. He told Ivy and Baby, whose arms were now folded tight across her chest, that he and his abuela were on the run. He told them that she had tried for years to escape Martín and the gang they had built together, but she was either too loyal or too foolish. In the blink of an eye, the gang was a family; children and grandchildren, like him.

No Bars and a Dead Battery

He crossed to the kitchen table to retrieve a folder, thick with printed paper. The edges of the folder were creased and worn from being opened and shut and stained, but the contents had been carefully looked after. Inside was Aunt Baby's old address in Jersey City. She made the first trip many years before, but couldn't work up the nerve to knock on the door. A single pink azalea had been pressed between the folder's pages; a flower pinched from Baby's front yard.

The next time Carmen made the trip was many years later, when she finally managed to poison Martín. The house had already been bulldozed, and Carmen couldn't bring herself to search for a forwarding address out of fear that she would find an obituary instead. He told her that even now, with Carmen as a wanted woman, they would never be able to be together. Baby seemed to soften before Ivy's eyes. Without another word, she stood to her feet and walked softly into the bedroom, like Peter following across wild waters. Hernán cleared his throat and invited Ivy for a walk.

According to him, there was a town just on the other side of the forest; it was where he'd borrowed the chainsaw. There was a gas can in the garage they could use to fill up her car. Ivy was glad for that, because it also meant there was a chance for her to charge her phone and finally get something to eat. It wasn't long before they found the town, and after filling up the plastic red can, they found a small diner on the main street. As they waited for her food, Hernán loaned Ivy his portable charger, and when her phone turned on, she found herself at full bars. Her mood already much improved, Ivy's cheeseburger and fries arrived to send her through the roof. She squirted ketchup, mayonnaise and hot sauce on both before speeding through grace and tucking in immediately after. Hernán grinned for real then, not just with his eyes, and Ivy realized that he had dimples in cheeks, as deep as wells.

They talked about Spades. He kept a deck on his person at all times, and when he brought it out to start a game of Solitaire, Ivy pointed out that they had enough people to play a game at the cabin. Four players, in partnered pairs. She didn't look at him when she said it, though. Hernán warned her that he was competitive. Even though his grandmother *said* that he was nothing like Martín, he was quick to blame his partner if he lost a book.

No one is ever right to blame, Ivy told him, and realized just as quickly that he wouldn't understand the reference. That thought sobered her. Suddenly, Hernán started chuckling. He had finished part of the tableau already, making up the foundation for the clubs suit. At the moment, he told Ivy he was a real grandma's boy. Because of Carmen, he'd always thought it was good luck if he managed to finish puppy feet first in a game of Solitaire. Ivy could not even breathe.

Against her better judgment, she asked him how he thought this would all end? Hernán gave her a strange look. He shook his head and softly told her that it had barely even begun. The next moment saw a short but unmistakable fire engine race past the window, its siren blaring. Car after car came following behind it. It only took a look passed between them for Hernán and Ivy to toss bills onto the table and dash out of the diner and onto the street. Rising over the treetops, a plume of smoke billowed, as dark as night and growing thicker by the moment.

Hernán leapt in front of one of the passing cars and after a few moments of harried questions and answers, he and Ivy were invited for the ride up into the forest with the rest of the town. When they arrived at the family of tree stumps, there was more traffic built up on the old blacktop road than it was ever meant to carry.

When they reach the cabin itself, it was to a blaze of wild, licking flames. Ivy had never felt such a heat never without being able to understand it. She turned away, thinking of Baby, and of Carmen, too. She thought about the duffel of Baby's tracksuits, and how her insulin had to be refrigerated; how the heat would ruin it. Ivy thought about picture on the wall, the favorite she never knew she had. Staring at the

No Bars and a Dead Battery

ground behind them, Ivy found herself watching she and Hernán's shadows dance like demons, darker than she'd ever seen any shadow, ever. She turned back to the house, marching forward, full of the sudden and overwhelming need to put the fire out, immediately out.

Before she could, Hernán's hand reached out and snatched her elbow, drawing her back to him, hissing for her to wait. To look. The silver Jeep was gone. So was the wood from the pile. Ivy wet her lips, her heart pounding from fright, and she looked at him. Hernán was staring into the flaming cabin. His eyes bright and his mouth defiantly proud, he told Ivy that their ladies must have set it. Must have run.

Ivy realized suddenly that they were holding hands, tightly, and she wasn't sure who had reached first. When she looked back up at him, Hernán was staring right at her. He asked her if she'd ever heard tell of a hidden treasure; worth ninety thousand or more? Her stunned silence was answer enough. Hernán guided her around the house and the confusion of the townspeople. In the midst of all the commotion, he brought her to the garage. He flung open the door to reveal a dust cover, and the dust cover to reveal the Cadillac.

It was the same one from Baby's picture, just a sleek, just as beast, just as wild. Hernán explained that it was worth a fortune, if they wanted to sell it. Ivy was silent and watched him.

He was silent and watched her. As the fire roared, and the water hose from the firetruck bellowed right back, they pushed the car from its hiding place, following in the fresh tracks of the silver Jeep, which peeled out onto the road, turning left, back down into the hills. They went back to the yard for the gas can, and stared at the creaking, burning home for one minute more. Somehow, their hands had fastened to one another all over again, and Ivy knew this time that they had reached for each other.

They made their way through the crowd, and back to the El Dorado. And as they approached it, a crow flew directly over their heads and landed on the hood and then looked at them. They stood some distance away and watched the crow watching them. Another crow flew directly overhead and landed beside it. The first crow squawked and then both flew away. They watched the crows disappear, looked at each other, and then got in the Eldorado. Only one way to go this time, with five bars and full battery.

CROWDED

Luke Kingsbury

No coverage, not even one bar, the battery was dead anyway. It was still daytime, but there was an overcast and the sky had a perfectly even dullness, so there was no way to tell what time of day it was, much less which direction was north or south or anything else for that matter. A two-lane blacktop road snaked up into the distance and disappeared into some trees, or a forest if you wanted to get technical about it. It also snaked down toward some lumpy hills and disappeared there as well. What sounded like a two-stroke chainsaw could be heard in the distance, but it was impossible to tell whether it was up in the forest or down in the lumpy hills. This had been happening more often lately. Two different ways to go, with a dead battery and no bars, and nobody left to blame.

Bondo sat, frozen in the passenger seat of the El Dorado, watching as his husband— a word that had grown to become quite heavy— held the phone above his head, turning in slow circles while he smacked the side of it with his calloused palm. He could hear Tone cursing from inside the car, even over the roaring of a chainsaw that seemed to come from both everywhere and nowhere. It was louder than the caw of a crow that echoed so thunderously through the valley that it made the pine-tree fresheners on the mirror rattle. He shouldn't have answered the call. This had been happening more often lately, he thought, and The Blame Game was getting old.

Two years earlier, their son, Robert, disappeared during a stormy night. Someone— Tone blamed Bondo, while Bondo blamed Tone— had left his window open, screen and all, leaving no trace except for a single black feather on his pillow. But The Blame Game didn't start with the disappearance. There wasn't any concrete day they could pinpoint that the wedge had been planted. At some point, Bondo would wake up hoping that Tone wouldn't be there. At some point, Tone stopped sneaking behind and wrapping his arms around his husband's waist while he made dinner. At some point, Bondo started to hide in his classroom later and later. At some point, Tone started to drink. Regardless, they found themselves playing The Blame Game. It was always easy to blame Tone for everything, but this particular situation was all Bondo's fault.

A year after their son disappeared, they started to receive calls, all of them at three thirty-three in the morning, exactly one week apart. Every call was the same— static for a few seconds, followed by a small, quiet, prepubescent voice begging for help, and ending with the caw of a crow so loud it would kill the phone for hours. Before each call, Bondo's dreams were vivid. He could smell a strong odor of a wet, unwashed animal, and fresh rain, but it never rained in the places he'd seen— a BP gas station; a youth shelter; a dive bar called The Crow's Nest; a run-down Target. None of the places looked familiar, but signs could be seen and landmarks clear enough for him to put some sort of topography down. Bondo would beg Tone, a Pinkerton- turned-Private Eye, to go out and help him look. He had images, concrete images, with defining characteristics. Do your job, he'd yelled at him.

Tone pushed his reluctance to the side and followed the wild goose chase that seemed to send them to every corner of the country, but Tone had never heard any of the calls. He believed his husband at first, and wanted to believe him, but after each dead end, after each 'No, we've never seen him, sorry,' his patience wore thin. He knew when a case was hopeless, could see when the clues went cold and the suspects' silence was valid, but this was his son, his flesh and blood. He had his dark hair, his grey eyes, his beak of a nose that would eventually become just as, if

No Bars and a Dead Battery

not more, crooked. He wanted to believe, but dreams were not sufficient evidence, and everything pointed to one end.

Bondo knew his husband was at his wit's end, that he was ready to give up, which only upset him more. He'd been a wreck ever since, quitting his teaching job, leaving his forty-four fourth graders to the hands of some woman from Kansas. He'd let his blonde hair grow shaggy, let his facial hair curl. He'd lock himself in his room all day, staying awake all night, constantly checking the phone and reading every police report that could possibly be his son. Every single trip was like a scab being ripped open just as it was healing, making it bigger and deeper. There was a voice in him that told him, just before every trip, that it would be a bust.

But this trip was different. The call came in the afternoon that time, and Tone was the one who answered. Their son asked them both— by name— for help. The crow hadn't been heard. Bondo saw, in a vision of sorts: a spiral road; a red car in a ditch; a fork in the road; a thick wood with neon lights; an ashram; a chainsaw roaring in the background; a crowd of people; crows, by the hundreds. Bondo felt it in the bottom of his heart, knowing Tone had a hard time disproving it. But Bondo felt like he was to blame for getting them so lost, and for answering the call that would kill their only lifejacket in a sea of confusion. There was no seeable way to get back, he thought. They were lost, but they were not alone.

He rolled down the window to hear the rip of a chainsaw better, to try and figure out where it was coming from. Tone lowered the phone, joining in on the mystery. Bondo told him that it had to come from the woods— it looked similar to the one he'd seen in his dreams. But all woods looked alike, Tone said, not wanting to suspend his belief. He had always critical of elementary school teachers when he was working, because who had a better imagination— and a better bluff—than an educator?

But he was the one who drove them, the one who, against every bone

203

in his body, decided to pursue this madness. And, so far, everything his husband had seen was correct. Right off of the turn-off, the road curved down the side of the mountain like a water slide. Twenty miles down the road, a bottomed-out red Daewoo sat in the ditch, covered in vines and rust. Those things could have been coincidence, but... a fork in the road? A chainsaw tearing through a tree? A forest that, thanks to the dark sky, seemed to glow? Even Tone had to admit that, whatever was going on, it was true, and if that's true, then...

Bondo slid into the driver's seat with no trepidation, revved up the engine with no hesitation, and honked the horn with the most amount of agitation he could muster. The wielder of the chainsaw could only cut for so long, and, while the sky was as overcast as a sky could be, the little bit of light would be gone, covering the land in darkness so thick that the headlights of the El Dorado wouldn't even make a scratch. They couldn't afford to be lost— or more lost than they already were.

Tone slipped the phone into his back pocket and hesitantly got into the passenger side. He didn't like it when someone else drove his car— even if it was, technically, their car— but he could feel his husband's desperate energy, feel the fire that he hadn't seen for two long years. Bondo knew that their son was out there, somewhere in that glowing forest, and that belief fueled Tone, too. With another rip of the chainsaw, and another caw booming through the air, they followed the road upwards.

◆

The Lotus Eaters, Tone said after a long moment of silence. Bondo had asked him why this feeling he had was so familiar, this feeling of timelessness, like something he'd read in a book long ago. The thickness of the forest made it so no natural light came through. Their headlights gave out a while earlier, along with the clock in the car. The radio cut out

No Bars and a Dead Battery

during the opening of an old Dottie West song. *Would you hold it against me if I just see him one more time just so I can make certain I can leave him behind?*

Bondo felt like they'd been driving for hours; Tone felt like it had been days. One minute, it would be so hot and humid neither men could breathe, and their windows couldn't roll down fast enough, while the next minute the air would turn so crisp and cold they could see their breath turn into fog. Time was non-existent. In any normal situation, this would have been cause for panic. But nothing was normal, not anymore.

Guiding their way were two long strips of neon green lights, like some sort of creepy catwalk. The lights rose up and wrapped around the trunks of some trees, while other trees sparkled with neon pink through the leaves, flickering on and off like fireflies. The chainsaw had died some time ago. The only sounds that could be heard anymore through the rolled down windows were the hum of the engine and an even louder hum coming from the lights, as if they were breathing. Bondo tried to use the flashing as a sort of clock— one flash, one second— but they seemed to have no sense of rhythm. They couldn't have been driving that long— the gas tank was still at the half-way mark.

That's what Odysseus said, Tone was about to tell him, when the familiar caw of a crow crashed through the sky. It seemed to have come from everywhere, rising through the underbrush while echoing through the air. They could hear the heavy flap of wings and could smell the same wet and unwashed animal smell they'd smelled earlier. Bondo slowed the car down— but didn't stop— while they both looked, hoping to see something that could explain the noise. But the lights only illuminated so much, and their sense of direction so skewed that it was impossible to figure anything out. Tone thought it was coming from the left, while Bondo thought it was coming from the right. It had to be coming from above, they thought. If only there was enough light—

The high-beams suddenly started to flash at a dizzying speed, like strobe lights. They were able to make out little things with each flash— a squirrel the size of a dog darting across the road; the roots of the trees so long it could have been boa constrictors; stumps where once-giant trees had been cut to the very base. The flashing stopped as quickly as it started, causing another brief blackout, before the lights turned on again, only to illuminate a man, standing only meters from their car.

Tone shouted obscenities, while Bondo slammed on the breaks so hard everything in the car lurched forward, ricocheting off the windshield. The car stopped just inches from the man, who seemed completely unfazed. He was tall— impossibly tall— with a snow-white face and an oblong, bald head, almost like an egg. He wore a tight black suit, colorless from neck to toe, save for a white bow-tie, with harsh red lips, as if someone had painted them on. He looked both ancient and youthful all at once— as timeless as the world around him. In one hand, he held a bundle of cut logs, maybe a half-dozen or so. In the other, he held an old, rusted chainsaw.

The humming of the lights stopped, as did the engine. There was no chirping of birds, no rain dropping on the already wet plants, no breathing from the men. The radio turned back on, blasting Dottie through the car and out into the darkness. *Would it make any difference if I just called him once again? Now you know that I love you, but I have forgotten him.*

The man seemed as unfazed by the music as he was by his close brush with death. His eerily calm nature oozed into the car, permeating Tone and Bondo's thoughts. He ought to be trustworthy, Tone thought, or else he would have attacked by now. He must know where the ashram is, thought Bondo, knowing they were close. Where else would he have come from?

The man set the chainsaw carefully down on the ground— Bondo took it as a sign of surrender, perhaps— and motioned for the men to come towards him. They unbuckled their seatbelts slowly, at the same time, as if being controlled by the same puppeteer. In any other situation, Tone would have been beyond cautious. He would have had his right hand on the gun in his holster while running the other hand through his hair. But he'd forgotten his gun, and he'd lost his hair.

You boys must be lost, the man said, shifting the logs from one hand to the other with no effort. His voice was stiff, cold, with a fuzzy quality to it, like someone crying on a message left on an answering machine. It was comforting and unsettling, horrifying and haunting, wild, yet tame. It made Bondo think of his father, while Tone was reminded of his old partner, a man whose son also went missing, along with him a year later.

A little, Bondo said. Just a little. The man laughed, telling him that there was no such thing as a little lost. Being lost, he said, was like hunting. You either catch something or you don't. You either track the beast down, or you let him run back home, wherever home may be. Do you boys have a home?

Just as Tone was about to question the man— who was he? Where was his home? Wasn't he afraid that his tailored, expensive-looking suit would be ruined by the mud and sticks and animal fur?— Bondo spoke. We're looking for something.

You mean someone, the man corrected him. Or is it both? The man took a step forward and set the pile of logs onto the wet gravel. Tone noticed that his shoes— fine, black, patent-leather shoes that seemed to glimmer from the headlights— were spotless. So much for concern. The man pointed a hand, covered in a black leather glove, towards the pile of logs, seven or eight of them at most. Pick one, he said, his voice becoming more distorted, less like an answering machine and more like a HAM radio. But only one. I don't trust greedy people.

At first glance, they all looked the same—thick quarter-cut logs taken from the trunk of one of the many redwoods that surrounded them like a chokehold— but as Bondo looked closer, he noticed minor discrepancies. One of them had bark the color of rust, while another had a dark blue tint to it. One of them was covered in loose bits of wood, sure to give the one who picked it up a palm full of splinters, while another one was so smooth it looked like it had been polished.

Tone was about to question the man, the situation, the woods—everything— when his husband bent down and picked one up. The bark was as dark as the man's suit— either through moisture or natural shading, Tone wasn't sure— and the wood on the inside looked like it had been scratched up by something with three claws. Not like an animal had used it as a scratching post, but as if hundreds of birds had used this log to stand on after a long flight.

The man began to slowly nod, muttering something to himself while twiddling his thumbs. Bondo wondered if he had made the wrong choice, if he was able to drop that log and grab another, when the man interrupted his thoughts with a deep laugh. A someone, he said, but not just any someone. A child. He lifted a hand and pointed a gloved finger at Tone. Your child.

Bondo felt a shiver go through his spine at those words— your child— but he pushed past it. Have you seen him, he asked. He's six— dark brown hair, almost black, but brown in the right light— and he's only 3'3", but sometimes he likes to put his hair up into a mohawk so maybe 3'5", and he would be wearing bright red pajama pants with matching red rain boots with little ladybugs on them, and—

I haven't seen anyone, the man cut him off. I can't see anyone, he said, laughing again. I can't see anything. I have heard things, though. Scary things. I hear the Crow often. And I hear the lost ones, sometimes. I may have heard a boy, but it might not be yours. It could be anyone's. But I know who can help. The man picked up his chainsaw and pointed one end into the dark forest. My sisters, they live on the ashram. I'll tell them you're coming.

Tone didn't know what he meant. There was no ashram anywhere in sight. But Bondo knew—he'd seen it in his vision. The man pulled the starter cord with a force so strong the men thought he would pull it right out of the chainsaw. Holding it high above his head, with the guide bar facing to his left, he let it rip four times. Suddenly, not too far into the woods, a cluster of lights lit up. Through the lights, they could see the silhouette of a large, Hindu-style building sitting on top of a hill. A familiar strip of neon green lights flickered on, lining the road, which snaked its way up the hill towards the building.

Bondo turned to thank the man, but he, his chainsaw, and the pile of logs had all disappeared as quickly as they had shown up. Tone and Bondo looked at one another, and for the first time in a long time, their faces were not that of an unlucky, unhappy couple, but those of two men in love, filled with hope and a sense of adventure. They got back into the El Dorado, revved the engine, and took off. In the darkness, louder than Dottie, a crow cawed.

◆

The gates— tall, copper gates with intricate weavings of metal leaves and iron roses— were closed, but through them, the couple could see a crowd of people roaming around at a snail's pace, like some sort of abysmal merry-go-round. Tone couldn't tell if it was the harsh spotlights that circled the ashram like Grauman's Chinese Theater, or if it was the dark sense of foreboding that surrounded the place that caused the people to look morose and drab. Through the rolled-up windows, they could hear garbled chanting, a myriad of voices all talking over one another.

Do we knock, Tone asked from the driver's seat. He'd seen the way his husband was quivering the moment the strange white man left, saw the fear in his eyes, and knew that he would crash the car. He had no idea where their phone was— he didn't need another issue that would leave them stranded. Bondo said nothing, his attention focused solely on the building. It was exactly like he'd seen in his dream. He leaned across the divider and laid on the horn four times. Tone was about to chastise him, afraid that the crowd of people would hear this and swarm. But with a screech and a metallic moan, the gate opened outward, like French doors. Immediately, the crowd of people, all dressed in dirtied, sepia-toned clothes, turned to the car, slowly crowding around it.

Tone put the car in reverse, hoping to escape, but the engine started to stutter and kick back. No, he said, punching the steering wheel, no, no! His worst fears were coming true. The phone was still dead, and no one knew where they were. He didn't even know where he was. He went to lock the door, but Bondo had already opened the passenger side and was going into the crowd. He thought that these people would start to grab his husband and tear at his clothes, maybe even tear him apart, limb by limb, before passing his bits around for everyone to eat. But they seemed to completely ignore them both. The people all shuffled around, slowly calling out: Have you seen my daughter? Have you seen my son? I'm looking for my dog, have you seen her? Where's my mommy? Where's my sister? Hanging above them, free-floating in the sky, was a neon-green sign that simply said: "Welcome to the Land of the Lost".

Tone was reminded of a movie he'd seen once, in a time that felt so far away yet so recent. The Carnival of Souls. It was as if he'd found himself in that dilapidated dance hall, surrounded by colorless people with hollow cheeks and sunk-in eyes. It made his blood run cold, and, for the first time in years, he reached out for the hand of his husband to help him. Bondo wrapped the tips of his fingers around Tone's and pushed through the crowd, making their way towards the staircase that led up to the doors of the ashram.

The stairs seemed immense from the base— at least a hundred steps— but Bondo made the trek in what must have been record time. Robert was close. He could feel it in his joints like an arthritic feels an oncoming storm. His head hurt, and his chest felt like it was about to implode— all signs, he thought, good signs. At last, he stood at the doors— massive, marble, gold-plated doors as tall as a house— but something made him stop dead in his tracks. Something was in there, something that he didn't like. Tone reached around him and gave a tug on the gold handles. Surprisingly, the doors pulled open with ease.

Both of the men expected to find some sort of grand, gilded ballroom, with chandeliers and ancient, expensive furniture, but were surprised to find themselves in a room not even ten by ten feet. It was as plain as the lobby of a motel, with no artwork lining the walls, no plants in pots in the corners, no tables or chairs. In the windows that circled the room, crows sat, all pecking at little scraps of food. In the center of the room sat three women, all in black, all identical, each of them playing solo games of Cat's Cradle, in a semi-circle of chase lounges. And, perched behind them on a wooden stand, was a crow the size of a large truck.

No one seemed to have noticed the men enter until the door behind them slammed shut. All eyes darted towards them, including the crow, which let out a massive caw that almost knocked the men over. One woman— the one in the middle— turned around and shushed the beast, running a hand underneath its beak. It's okay, said the woman on the left.

Tone was about to interrogate these women, when, as if hearing his thoughts, the woman on the right cut him off. Who are you, she asked, dropping the strings that had looped around her fingers. The woman in the middle laughed. Miss Madness, she said, these are the guests we've been waiting for. Not possible, Miss Murder, the woman on the left said, we're looking for parents. Miss Murder clicked her tongue. Miss Mystery, these are the parents.

Tone felt as if his heart had dropped as low as his jaw. Madness? Murder? Mystery? He had no words for what was happening before his eyes. Bondo, on the other hand, had too many words. We are parents, Bondo said. We're looking for our son. He's six, with—

Dark brown hair, almost black, Miss Madness said with an air of annoyance, we know. Bondo's heart sped up. He knew it, knew that he wasn't crazy, knew that his son was here, somewhere in this land of chaos and confusion, the Land of the Lost. Tone's heart also sped up, but for all the wrong reasons. He knew his son was gone, lost somewhere in this carnival of souls, this Land of the Lost, unable to ever be saved.

Unfortunately, Miss Mystery said, you're both correct. He's here, but he isn't here. Not in the form you'd recognize him. He's still their son, sisters, Miss Murder said. Was their son, Miss Madness said. Oh, Miss Mystery said, sitting up in her chair, but what's the difference, sisters?

Tears began to well up in Bondo's eyes. What do you mean? Where is he? Miss Madness laughed. That is a question that has puzzled you two for a while. Miss Murder leaned over and gave her sister a slight pinch on the arm, causing her to cry out. We shan't tease them any longer, sisters. We've put them through enough. Look at them, she said, pointing towards Tone and Bondo's hands, which were intertwined, they've come far. This journey is not an easy one.

But this was a journey they put onto themselves, Miss Madness told her sisters, they are the cause! It wasn't a neglectful babysitter! It wasn't a door accidentally left unlocked! It wasn't a murder! Those people— she pointed a curled finger towards the courtyard of people— they don't know who to blame. They could blame the babysitter, they could blame the locks, they could blame the madman who killed, but their blame is fruitless. You two have no one to blame but yourselves.

Tone thought that these women must have taken their son. Miss Madness suddenly laughed, sitting upright in her chair. We didn't take your son! He came, willingly! He called out for help, and out little boy answered. He saw the way you two looked at each other, acted around each other. You— she pointed towards Bondo— he felt the bitterness you harbor towards your husband. Biology has nothing to do with being a parent. It's not his fault you and your son aren't flesh and blood. And you— she pointed at Tone— he saw the way you looked at him, saw the way you refused to touch him like he was no longer the man you fell in love with. Children pick up on things like that. Children, and crows.

No Bars and a Dead Battery

People change, boys, but vows don't. 'Til death do you part.

We don't usher death, Miss Mystery said, standing up and walking over to the large crow. We just welcome it. This was our son, she said, running a hand under his beak, once upon a time. But we, much like you, started to lose interest. We had other things on our minds, things we thought were more important. We fought. We bickered. We drifted, but it wasn't until he died that we realized everything was trivial. I swore up and down that I'd give anything to get him back. And get him back you did, said Miss Murder. But not as he was. You see, life is a circle. From life, comes death, and from death, comes life. No one understands death more than crows. They feast on death, follow death like a plague, bring death and take death at their whim. They collect death. They are death, but they are also us. Your son is like ours— a soul that you begged to come back, and come back he did.

Tone felt heavy, as if all of the blood in his body had curdled, weighing him down to the floor. He couldn't run, even if he wanted to. These women were right. Everything had been perfect before Robert, but he wasn't to blame. The man he loved had changed, grown angry and mean, and it killed him to admit that it was because Bondo's saw nothing of himself in the child. Bondo let his tears fall, looking over at his husband, the man he promised to love, in sickness and in health, for worse or for better. It was all his own fault. He wanted nothing more than to hug his husband and see their son, one more time.

Tone and Bondo looked around at the crows perched on the windows— hundreds of them, impossibly crowded together, all of them preening and pecking at one another. Anyone of them could be their boy. Then, looking at each other through tears, swallowing their grief and anger, they understood. They embraced, whispered their apologies and 'I love you's in each other's ears, and simply let go.

Miss Murder stood up and walked over to the men. She reached down into a pocket— Bondo wondered where in her cloak-like outfit she would have pockets— and pulled out the cell phone Tone had forgotten about. It was alive and glowing. She handed it over, wishing them each good luck. We wish you happiness, Miss Mystery said. Don't forget about him, said Miss Madness. Hand in hand, the men walked out and into the night where nothing but Dottie West could be heard.

They made their way through the crowd, and back to the El Dorado. And as they approached it, a crow flew directly over their heads and landed on the hood and then looked at them. They stood some distance away and watched the crow watching them. Another crow flew directly overhead and landed beside it. The first crow squawked and then both flew away. They watched the crows disappear, looked at each other, and then got in the El Dorado. Only one way to go this time, with five bars and full battery.

THE TORN CURTAIN

By Jon Krampner

No coverage, not even one bar, the battery was dead anyway. It was still daytime, but there was an overcast and the sky had a perfectly even dullness, so there was no way to tell what time of day it was, much less which direction was north or south or anything else for that matter. A two-lane blacktop road snaked up into the distance and disappeared into some trees, or a forest if you wanted to get technical about it. It also snaked down toward some lumpy hills and disappeared there as well. What sounded like a two-stroke chainsaw could be heard in the distance, but it was impossible to tell whether it was up in the forest or down in the lumpy hills. This had been happening more often lately. Two different ways to go, with a dead battery and no bars, and nobody left to blame.

Well, maybe there was someone to blame, at that. Crystal had told Bobby Joe to keep his flip phone charged, since they never knew when his lovingly restored candy-apple red '64 El Dorado would break down while they were tooling around the back roads of the Berkshires. But he hadn't. And as much as Crystal tried to practice the Christian charity she had learned in the one-room Mennonite schoolhouse in Pennsylvania Dutch country that was her true *alma mater*, she knew that Victor von Demme had landed them in this mess. And by failing to stop Bobby Joe from going to see von Demme, she bore some responsibility as well.

She and Bobby Joe had just finished their studies at the University of Western Massachusetts, in the town of Guthrie Junction in the Berkshires. Bobby Joe was everything she'd ever wanted in a boy —

handsome, resolute, of good character, and he liked Shaker furniture. Because he was good with computers, he'd be able to pay off his student loans before he was ready for Social Security. No such luck for Crystal, who had followed her heart and majored in French literature.

There was only one problem with Bobby: he had the worst case of athlete's foot she'd ever seen. There wasn't a dermatologist in the Berkshires who could successfully treat it. In desperation, one of them had recommended Victor von Demme.

Von Demme was an odd duck: a boy genius who had enrolled in MIT at 16, he had then gotten himself expelled for trying to use the university's atom-smasher to implode the universe. This had gotten him banned from the wine-and-cheese circuit of Cambridge parties, but such was his reputation for brilliance that people unable to find conventional solutions to their problems turned to him and the laboratory he operated in the back of a side-street record store (vinyl only) in downtown Cambridge.

One afternoon when a formless overcast much like today's overspread the Cambridge sky, rendering everything beneath it a formless, colorless, flavorless blah, she and Bobby Joe had knocked on the door of Von Demme Vinyl and gone in. Indulging in an occasional bout of sentimentality, von Demme was riffling through the Carpenters albums. He was dressed completely in black, like a punk rocker or a cat burglar, Crystal thought. His receding hair was closely cropped and his pallid skin suggested he didn't get out enough. Although his eyes were hooded, dark and harrowed, they also radiated a kindliness that put Bobby Joe and Crystal at their ease. That, she later reflected, was their mistake.

Looking up and seeing Bobby Joe and Crystal, he asked the musical question why do birds suddenly appear every time you are near, then asked a more pragmatic one, what he could do for them. Bobby, with the aw-shucks Southern country-boy manner that melted Crystal's heart like butter on a hot stovetop, awkwardly cleared his throat and explained the

No Bars and a Dead Battery

problem.

Von Demme examined Bobby's feet, doing his diplomatic best not to express the aversion he surely felt. After a few minutes, he got up and disappeared into his lab, concealed behind ochre curtains with a larger-than-life image of Jimi Hendrix sewn onto them by some flower child who had long since taken refuge in suburbia. The agile, lynx-like von Demme quickly returned with a thick, leather-bound volume with symbols on its spine neither Crystal nor Bobby Joe had ever seen.

He opened the book, recited some mumbo-jumbo, then closed it and told Bobby Joe and Crystal to go back to the Berkshires and everything would be fine in three days. They were incredulous, but von Demme had come highly recommended by Bobby's Joe's favorite dermatologist.

After three days, though, Bobby Joe's feet were no better. Something had changed in Guthrie Junction, though: there was a rash of chain-saw attacks. Slumber parties. Proms. Kids hanging out in haunted houses. The youth of their Berkshires town was being terrorized by slashers. And because the chainsaws were gasoline-powered, there was also more air pollution.

Bobby Joe and Crystal didn't make the connection until he called von Demme to ask why his feet were no better. Von Demme explained that, because he had been sleep-deprived, he had inadvertently cast the wrong spell, not one to ward off athlete's foot, but one that breached the fabric of the cosmos separating the Third Dimension from the Dimension of Slasher-Movie Villains. He offered Bobby Joe a redo as part of a two-for-one special promotion he was running, but Bobby Joe had had enough and graciously declined.

This was why it was so hard to determine if the two-stroke chainsaw was operating up in the trees (or forest, if you wanted to get technical about it) or down in the lumpy hills: there could be a psychopathic slasher operating in one place or the other, or in both. It was like an invasion of mayflies.

Crystal said maybe Bobby Joe shouldn't have gone to see that weirdo in Cambridge and he said he had just been trying to find a cure for the condition that grossed her out and she said yeah, some cure, and Bobby Joe said isn't it just like a Mennonite to say something like that and Crystal said at least she wasn't some idiot savant cracker genius from the hill country of South Carolina like Bobby Joe and he said maybe we should break up and she said yeah, maybe we should, but instead they climbed into the back seat of his El Dorado, threw the boxed six-volume set of Ove Knausgard's *My Struggle* he never seemed to get around to reading into the front seat and had sex in the back.

Bobby Joe said she sure had come a long way from Pennsylvania Dutch Country and she said he should be careful or she'd put a hex on him and he said let's never fight again and Crystal said that's just what she had been thinking while she was crying out oh God oh God oh my God and she was glad they weren't going to break up, but they still had to do something about the slashers.

Since Bobby Joe's flip phone was out of commission, they couldn't call the cinema studies library at the University of Western Massachusetts to see if it was open. The University of Western Massachusetts has a world-renowned cinema studies department, and Bobby Joe felt they might be able to find a solution to the slasher problem in their library. So they just drove down through the lumpy hills to the cinema library, hoping to find it open. Bobby Joe's penchant for vintage technology – flip phones, '60's-era Caddies – was one of the quirks that first endeared him to Crystal, but it irritated her when he forgot to charge the damn thing.

Crystal told him to make sure the windows were closed and the doors locked, what with all the slashers running around and sure enough, they saw one as they entered the lumpy hills, but the guy just waved his chainsaw at Bobby Joe in friendly greeting. Maybe they're not so bad after all, Bobby Joe said, but Crystal reminded him that they were now college graduates and slashers only went after high school and college students, hadn't he ever seen a slasher movie, and Bobby Joe said of course, what had he been thinking.

Lucky for them, the cinema studies library was open. Bobby Joe asked the reference librarian for the file of clippings on slasher movies. After they had pored over it for several hours, Crystal found an old article from *Cahiers du Cinema* that said that just as vampires are allergic to crucifixes and werewolves to silver bullets, slashers are allergic to high culture, indeed to any form of culture. But from a slasher point of view, high culture is the worst.

Bobby said that was weird because they were in the Berkshires and the Berkshires had lots of culture – they were always going to concerts at Tanglewood and had seen and listened to "Alice's Restaurant" more times than they could remember. How could anyone even hope to imply that the Berkshires weren't awash in culture?

But according to Crystal, the article said it had to be European culture. Hockey-masked slashers were a purely American phenomenon and required a European antidote. Bobby said of course they'd say that, it's *Cahiers du Cinema*, they're Europeans, and Crystal said they had all that American culture around them and the slashers were still running amok, so they might as well give the European longhairs a try. But how?

Bobby snapped his fingers and said a van Gogh exhibit had just opened at the UWM Art Museum: paintings on loan from the Louvre, they could soak up lots of European culture there. So they headed over to the museum. Both were magnetically drawn to the vibrant colors and emotional intensity of the tortured Dutchman, but the painting they kept gravitating back to was "Wheatfield with Crows."

The low, uncertain skies, roads leading nowhere, ambiguous, brooding mood with a hint of depression, even the crows flopping around, seemed just like Guthrie Junction. Crystal said maybe they should have a multi-media extravaganza, project an image of the Van Gogh painting onto the side of the County Courthouse, invite Don McLean to come sing "Starry,

Starry Night," that sort of thing.

Bobby Joe asked what kind of a Mennonite she was, trying to make things so complicated, the old way is the best way, that's what you guys always say, and she said that's the Amish, not the Mennonites, and if he still didn't know the difference between the two maybe she had no business climbing into the back of his '64 candy-apple red El Dorado with him and he said now wait a minute, honey, anyone could make that mistake and she said well I sure as hell wouldn't and he said since when do Mennonites swear like that and she said that slashers were running loose and all he could do was crack wise, he needed to get with the program.

Bobby Joe said the old way in this case would be to plaster posters of "Wheatfield with Crows" all over Guthrie Junction. They would create a force field that would drive out the slashers. It was a cheaper, lower-tech solution. They couldn't rent and set up the multi-media equipment they'd need on short notice or publicize it as an event and they didn't even know if Don McLean still did concert gigs, he must be older than God by now. They went to the copy shop, ran off thousands of copies of "Wheatfield with Crows" and headed for the town hall meeting that had been called that night to address the slasher question.

The meeting was chaotic, with badly frightened townspeople open to any solution that would rid them of the frightening invaders. Calls for torches and pitchforks were common, as were cries to blow 'em all away, whether it took Uzis, AR-15's, or military-surplus Sherman tanks. Someone said slashers were zombies and were already dead, so guns wouldn't help or even tanks, but someone else got up and said no they ain't zombies. Are too are not are too are not. The two men came to blows and had to be pulled off each other.

Crystal spoke up and told everyone about the *Cahiers* article and someone asked what *Cahiers* was and she said come on, this is the Berkshires. She said if they went out in the woods tonight with shotguns

No Bars and a Dead Battery

they'd just wind up blowing each other away and explained that the "Wheatfield With Crows" approach would be more organic and someone said let's do what the little lady says and she and Bobby Joe handed out posters to the townspeople, who fanned out across Guthrie Junction, brandishing them along with tape and staplers.

Bobby Joe and Crystal drove out along the road that runs through the woods above Gibson Creek just outside of town. They separated by a hundred yards and began working back towards each other, stapling the flyers to telephone poles.

Just after stapling her second poster, Crystal heard the sudden roar of a two-stroke chainsaw starting up behind her. Pivoting, the saw a burly guy in a red t-shirt and blue jeans wearing a white hockey mask with a maple leaf emblazoned on it.

She idly wondered if the maple leaf stood for the NHL team from Montreal or the one from Toronto, and weren't Canadians supposed to be reasonable people. Then she remembered: she had taken an incomplete in "George Sand and Her Circle," and could still be considered a college student. Just as she realized that, the slasher, who had started to stride grimly toward her, charged. Crystal screamed.

She started to run down the road toward Bobby Joe, but as she did, a drunk driver careened around the curve and headed toward her on the road's narrow shoulder. She leaped out of the car's path, tumbling down the hillside toward the creek. As she rolled down, she could hear the sound of a chainsaw following her.

Seconds later, Crystal found herself at the bottom of the hill in the shallow, murmuring waters of Gibson Creek, bleeding from a cut in her forehead. Although it was June, the water was cold. A few stars were visible through the canopy of trees and the nightly cricket sonata was in full swing until drowned out by the angrily ratcheting sound of Crystal's pursuer.

She raised herself up and started running through the creek in what she judged was Bobby Joe's direction. The slasher was getting closer and would soon catch up to her. Looking around, she saw a big maple tree on the creek bank and hid behind it.

But just as she did, a raccoon wandered out of the forest and sidled up to her, rubbing itself amiably against her. Crystal had always had this St. Francis of Assisi-like effect on animals. But this was the worst possible time.

The slasher reached the point in the creek where Crystal had jumped the bank, stopped and seemed to sniff the air. He even turned off his chainsaw, the better to commune with the creek-bed ecosystem. That's when he noticed the raccoon rubbing against Crystal's leg, fired up his chainsaw and charged her again.

Crystal only had time to grab a branch of the maple and haul herself up. The cut above her eye was starting to bleed more profusely. The slasher followed her up the tree. About 10 feet above the ground, he grabbed her ankle, but Crystal kicked him in the throat, just under his hockey mask, temporarily knocking him off balance, and kept going.

The tree was only twenty feet high, and when Crystal reached the point where the branches no longer supported her weight, she knew she had to jump. Having always been afraid of heights, Crystal steeled herself, told herself not to look down, and jumped.

Crystal's momentary relief at having escaped the clutches of the slasher turned to horror when she realized she had sprained her ankle on landing and couldn't go a step further. The slasher calmly and purposefully descended the tree and, as he walked toward her for what she assumed would be her last moment on earth, it seemed to Crystal he was whistling.

As the slasher stood above her, the rolling hills and wheat fields of her Pennsylvania Dutch Country girlhood – so much like those in Van Gogh's "Wheatfield With Crows," except they held fond memories for her whereas Van Gogh, let's face it, was a pretty depressed guy – flashed before her eyes.

No Bars and a Dead Battery

But at the instant when she expected to find herself on the business end of the slasher's chainsaw, she heard a loud "thwack!" and he unexpectedly keeled over. Behind him stood Bobby Joe, triumphally brandishing his boxed, six-volume set of Ove Knausgard's *My Struggle*, all 3600 pages of it. He had heard her scream, and had saved her.

The posters did the trick, and the plague of slashers was no longer upon Guthrie Junction. The rent in the cosmos was sealed up, and it was again safe for the town's youth to go to slumber parties and proms, and to spend graduation night in haunted houses.

A week later, the townspeople of Guthrie Junction held another meeting. Rather than being fear-addled and contentious, this one was festive and celebratory. Crystal and Bobby Joe were going to be honored as heroes, having saved the town from a fate worse than exploitation films. Crystal reminded Bobby Joe to charge his flip phone before they went.

One after one, on that bright Berkshires morning, the people of the town stood up to thank them. Perhaps the most heartfelt tribute, though, came from someone not even a resident of Guthrie Junction – Dr. Otto von Shtruppendorf, who was visiting from Wittenberg, Germany.

He was in the United States to spend a vacation with his daughter, an exchange student at the University of Western Massachusetts. She had had to lock herself in her dorm room one night to save herself from a slasher, and Professor Shtruppendorf was profoundly grateful. Since she insisted on going to college in the U.S., he realized she could still get blown away by a campus shooter, of course, but at least the slasher threat was behind her.

The best part, from Bobby Joe's point of view, was Doctor Shtruppendorf's medical specialty: he was the world's leading expert on athlete's foot. He had just invented a new cream that would control even Bobby Joe's athlete's foot and promised him a free lifetime supply.

In his remarks to the grateful townspeople, Bobby Joe admitted that it was his quest to find a cure for his athlete's foot that had triggered the crisis. But they seemed in a forgiving mood and didn't hold it against him.

Crystal said this episode had taught them humanity was not meant to tamper with the curtain separating the Third Dimension from the Dimension of Slasher-Movie Villains. That curtain had been torn with obvious consequences, but had again been rendered whole. It was just like the curtain between Victor von Demme's laboratory and vinyl record store, she thought: some things were better kept apart.

One of Crystal's professors said he'd be able to find an assistant professor position for her in the French Department at Boston College. Bobby Joe, with his degree in computer science, would have no trouble getting work at one of the high-tech companies along Route 128 circling Boston.

Just to be on the safe side, Bobby Joe told Crystal to finish her incomplete in "George Sand and Her Circle." She happily agreed and then, in front of everyone, Bobby Joe went down on one knee and asked Crystal to marry him. Crystal pretended to think about it, but after his decisive action along Gibson Creek, her answer was never really in doubt.

Back in Cambridge, Victor von Demme took delivery of a shipment of vintage Motown albums, wondered how the kid with the bad feet was making out, and started work on his next experiment, an effort to breed a genetically modified Kung Pao chicken.

As the meeting wound down, Crystal and Bobby Joe were presented with the key to Guthrie Junction by the mayor. Townspeople clustered around to thank them for their deliverance. But somewhere beyond the lumpy hills of Guthrie Junction lay their future, and it was time to go.

They made their way through the crowd, and back to the El Dorado. And as they approached it, a crow flew directly over their heads, and landed on the hood and then looked at them. They stood some distance away and watched the crow watching them. Another crow flew directly overhead and landed beside it. The first crow squawked and then both

No Bars and a Dead Battery

flew away. They watched the crows disappear, looked at each other, and then got in the El Dorado. Only one way to go this time, with five bars and full battery.

THE EASY THING

Juliana Lamy

No coverage, not even one bar, the battery's dead anyway. It's still daytime, but there's an overcast and the sky has a perfectly even dullness, so there's no way to tell what time of day it is, much less which direction is north or south or anything else for that matter. A two-lane blacktop road snakes up into the distance and disappears into some trees, or a forest if you want to get technical about it. It also snakes down toward some lumpy hills and disappears there as well. What sounds like a two-stroke chainsaw can be heard in the distance, but it's impossible to tell whether it's up in the forest or down in the lumpy hills. This has been happening more often lately—two different ways to go, with a dead battery and no bars, and nobody left to blame.

Zari always thought one thing really interesting—to blame somebody for something is to choose. To choose, for yourself, where that guilt should go, who should open up their chest and let it in. But for Zari, choice is a stranger. For as long as he can remember, there's always been something, *something* crowding Zari into this place of lonely inevitability, cold hands rough against his back and his neck when they force him to the only decisions he can ever really make, the ones that always wait for him heavy and patient at the fence of his confusion.

When his mom died, and then his dad followed her like he'd just been waiting for a damn signal, shutting the doors of himself, flipping that neon blue sign from *open* to *closed* seemed like the thing to do. No choosing. Foster care gave him deadbolts, made the house of him so secure back then that the folks at the Pentagon probably should have

No Bars and a Dead Battery

looked up one skinny, sulky black teenager for security pointers. No one could get to the middle of him, and so they just thought that there was nothing to get *to*. And he let them think that, because it was easier. No choosing.

So now, stuck in this car on the side of the empty road while it coughs and sputters like it has six months to live, asphalt black like the ocean when light can't go any further stretching for miles behind them and for a forever ahead of them, Zari's heart is trying to scale the walls of his throat. Smoke's coming out from the front hood of the car, and for a really weird moment, Zari kind of feels like the El Dorado is breathing out.

He has to choose—take Rem and keep going down the road towards those hills on foot, or walk back the way they came, hope that there's some gas station or rest stop that he'd missed when they'd been driving. The chainsaw, though it was holding tight to the background just a little while ago—noticeable but not that forceful—gets louder. Much louder. Zari wouldn't be surprised to turn around and see somebody revving up the thing in his backseat.

Zari looks over at Rem in the passenger's seat. Rem's brought his knees up his face, and Zari watches him wrap his arms around them. The kids staring out at the road in front of them, but Zari's wondering what Rem's actually seeing. He wonders how long Rem had been in that house by himself before he'd gotten there. He hadn't asked. He looks down at his phone, at the red *x* where the signal bars should be, and tries to remember what they'd driven past.

It comes to him how individual memories sometimes do for people, when they round that street corner in your head, come up the sidewalk towards you until you recognize in their face something familiar. Wait until you realize with a warm, steady pressure, like somebody grabbing onto your arm, that something *happened*, and what it left behind is inside you now, dangling from your rafters, waiting for you to help it down.

Zari recalls that they'd driven past what might have been a store. If Zari's right, it's a bit far back, but it's a sure thing—he knows that it's there, and he has a fair idea of how far away it the crescents you'd see if you dug your nails into the horizon's skin. It could be that she's at the end of this road, in Mayfair or Bailey or Attewood, maybe even Madison. Could be. Or maybe she moved. Zari doesn't know; he hasn't spoken to Auntie Ceto since he was like fifteen, hasn't seen her for even longer than that.

And sure, she could never really help him—she was always smiling way too much for him to trust her completely—but that didn't necessarily mean that she couldn't help Rem. Cynicism is loose ink for too many people, it stains and changes whatever it can reach, discolors whatever's closest.

If he'd ever said it to any of his foster parents they'd probably have had him sectioned, held for a psych eval, but Zari'd always thought himself a pen, negativity running dark and fluid inside his cartridge. You wouldn't ever really see it, unless you pressed too hard. So Zari knew that just because something had turned out real shitty for him, it didn't necessarily mean that the same situation was completely without hope for somebody else… for Rem. Maybe it was this weird, warped optimism that kept getting him jumped when he was younger, but he'd never really thought about it then.

He looks over at Rem again, sees him breathing hard, like there isn't enough air in the car. Zari knows a panic attack when he sees one, can almost feel his breathing falling off-kilter too, like he and Rem are sharing lungs. So he starts talking, knows they're the first words that have passed between them for three hours, the first ones since *where's your mom* and *she left* and *where are we going* and *Auntie Ceto's* and *who?* and *she's your mom's auntie, my kind-of-auntie.*

He starts talking, remembers that time a bunch of years ago when Chloe told him the only thing that could ever get two-year-old Rem to

No Bars and a Dead Battery

sleep was Prince's "Purple Rain" and takes a complete shot in the dark. He says to him, you know Prince changed his name one time? And after that he sees that Rem's still breathing pretty hard, so he keeps going, speaks in short, straight sentences to make sure he's making himself easy to follow—the last thing he wants to do is try to haul Rem into a protracted conversation. It could make things worse.

Zari says, he changed it to something people couldn't pronounce, and no one knew what to call him. And then he's silent, gives Rem some space, some quiet stillness to work against and hopes it helps. Rem's arms are still around his knees but his breathing's softening, and relief spins from the core of Zari's throat, calms his whole body.

Zari goes to roll down his window before he realizes that the engine would need to start for that. So he opens his door instead, tries to cut through the insularity of the closed car. When Zari used to have panic attacks, small spaces would always make him feel like the weak roof of his chest was about to come down, tear up his heart's floor. So he tries to make the El Dorado feel bigger than it actually is, tries to make it run seamless into the air and the quiet and the trees outside.

He still can't see Rem's face when Rem asks, voice just a little bit muted from the way his face is pushed up against his knees, so what did they call him? Zari replies, honestly? A lot of people just kept calling him Prince kind of just Road Ran right past the symbol.

Rem looks up then, and Zari wonders for a brief little moment whether he's dated himself—do kids still watch Looney Toons? But Rem doesn't seem to care about all of that, because he wants to know why people couldn't just learn to say Prince's new name? Call him by the right one? And Zari, with his memories snapping at the back of his neck, tugging on his sleeve, trying to get his attention, tells Rem that some people will always choose to do what's easiest.

But Rem is clever like Chloe, so he asks Zari why he didn't do the easy thing. And Zari acts like he's at a loss, acts like he has no idea what Rem's talking about. But Rem looks at him with eyes black like the darkness of a familiar room, makes Zari feel like he knows the truth and he's met the truth and now Rem and sincerity are on good terms.

Zari wants to tell him that he *is* doing the easy thing, he *is*—bringing Rem to some estranged, too-happy aunt, who Zari himself hasn't seen in years. Hell, he doesn't even know if Auntie Ceto and Chloe still speak to each other. Zari tells Rem that he does whatever's easiest for him too, and then he looks back to the outside of the car, at the smoke coming up from the hood a knowing haze.

He tells Rem that they're going to have to get out of the car and start walking, that he thinks he remembers some kind of store a ways back? Rem should want to know *how* far back, should look exhausted or annoyed, but he just looks kind of wary. Like he's waiting for Zari to leave him stranded here.

And Zari has absolutely no idea how long they're gonna have to walk to make it to this maybe-store. Just knows that he glimpsed something when they were coming down towards the hills, when Rem's three-hour-long silence made him think that the kid was catatonic, made panic wrap its arms around his waist and sit its chin on his shoulder. Made it stay.

The sky is still a steady gray, and Zari doesn't think he's ever prayed harder for anything than he does then for God to hold the rain. Rem keeps trailing behind him, and Zari is like eighty percent sure that he's doing it on purpose. So Zari slows down a little, gives Rem the chance to overtake him, walk ahead of him. But Rem doesn't fall for it, and when they're walking shoulder-to-shoulder Rem looks at him with suspicion, and Zari isn't really prepared for how much it hurts. It goes away pretty soon after, that cautiousness, but the look leaves Zari feeling raw, leaves him feeling like the sticks of his ribs are scratching at the walls of his chest. Zari doesn't know how long they've been walking when the chainsaw starts up again. Rem starts a little, and they stop.

And, okay, Zari can't really think of a horror movie set-up more

No Bars and a Dead Battery

perfect than this—two hapless kids stranded in the middle of the woods with a dead car battery and a phone that won't turn on. Some crows start circling overhead and all Zari can think is, great, the plot thickens. Here comes the choosing again. So now he's looking at Rem and the kid is trying to hide it, and he's doing a pretty good job of it, but he's scared. Zari knows scared. Plenty of people don't completely know what fear looks like. They'd know its face in daylight, but if the sun left, they wouldn't know it from their own. They might think its nose looks like something they've seen before, or its mouth, or its eyes.

But few people, Zari thinks, few, super unlucky people could ever bring all those pieces together, have them converge and settle into anything comprehensive. Zari's seen fear make people shake, like a bunch of years back when the kid in the house across from him had to sleep outside on the porch because his grandma thought he was trying to poison her. Zari's seen fear make people violent, like when his dad found his mom in their bedroom, still warm but quiet, and he broke a paramedic's nose when she couldn't be revived.

Rem is not moving. And a lot of people might say that this reaction is the most common when it comes to fear, especially if they've never really seen the other ones. But for as long as Zari's been around, for all the horrifying shit he's seen, and all the scary shit he's heard secondhand from other people, this reaction is the rarest, the last pick, the loneliest. When you're scared and you go as still as a summer street when it's raining, it's because everything else has left. The anger follows the desperation out the door, hostility climbs out the window and the sadness jumps out after it, feels the bottom of the pane bite into its hands as it flees the house of you. And what's left behind is this unassailable emptiness, this vacancy like a black hole, your very own singularity.

So Rem is still and quiet, and Zari's wondering why the hell the sound of the chainsaw isn't worrying him as much as he thinks it should. He's thinking that the chainsaw's too loud, too obvious to be dangerous (it's stupid to trust the killing thing to announce itself), so he decides to keep going. And he knows, with guilt pulling up an armchair to sit in the pit of his stomach, that Rem will follow him. Scared as he is, he'll follow him.

And he does. Zari has no idea how much longer they walk, but the sky never changes from that gray like craggy cliff rocks, so he assumes that it's still daytime. When they notice it, the huge cabin-style store coming up some fifty feet ahead of them, hazy but *there*, Zari is relieved that his suspicion has actually resolved into something concrete, something useful. It didn't always do that. Rem is still trying to fall in step behind Zari as they approach the store, and Zari does all he can to make sure that Rem stays shoulder-to-shoulder with him.

The building comes off every bit as rustic as Zari assumes its designers had intended—wooden logs the same deep, healthy brown as the dirt the place sits on, porch with its carefully hewn support beams whose sort of rugged beauty is almost enough to completely sell the whole authentically bucolic shtick. There's even a rocking chair on the porch, and the entire front of the store looks like a set piece that Quentin Tarantino would sell a kidney for with zeal.

But something splits that sweet little picture of rustic simplicity right down the middle. A huge, tricolored sign hangs from the store's awning, block letters cycling through a rotation of red and yellow and blue—*BIG BLOWOUT SALE!* The white, bubble letters of the store's name sit plain in comparison, just below the copycat birthday party banner. *AZ's Backwoods Equipment.*

The chainsaw is loudest here. Rem has gone still again, dark eyes big and unblinking, fists clenching and unclenching. And Zari is at a loss, has no damn clue what to do—he really doesn't want to leave the kid outside alone, even if it might be for just the few minutes that it should take to ask whoever's at the counter for a phone charger and the number for the nearest tow truck—when a man with deep dark skin and eyes like a warm

No Bars and a Dead Battery

weekend morning comes out onto the porch. Zari has the weirdest passing thought that this is what his grandpa might look like. Maybe what his dad could've looked like, decades down the road.

The man asks them if everything is all right and Zari tells him about everything that's happened, the car that won't start, the dead phone, how he and Rem walked back up here. The looks impressed at that last part, if not a little incredulous, but he doesn't ask them anything else about it, so Zari ignores the tiny, brief line of skepticism that ripples tremulous between his eyebrows. He introduces himself as Dave.

He remarks that Zari and Rem look tired, asks if their hungry, apologizes for the fact that all he has in his store is packaged beef stroganoff and dried noodles. From the corner of his eye, Zari sees Rem's eyes light up a little bit in interest. And he remembers that, like the idiot that he's proven himself to be, all he gave the kid to eat before the trip was a cheeseburger combo from the Five Guys two blocks away from Chloe's apartment complex. He'd found Rem alone in the apartment and he'd panicked, told the kid that Chloe's aunt would take him, that his mom could just pick him up from there. Rem hadn't said anything to that, just looked at him with a face that said *you're wrong* and came with him anyway.

Zari had, and has, no delusions about the situation then, when he'd gone to return a bracelet Chloe had left at his place on a stupid whim and found her son living alone, forcing rice to last much longer than Zari had ever really thought possible. The only reason Zari had been able to get into the apartment was that the door had been left unlocked. Chloe must've taken her key, and for some reason Rem had never gotten one.

So the kid had had to prop open the door with the edge of an old Casio calculator to make sure that he could come and go home unimpeded. Rem would've never opened the door for him, would've never opened the door for someone he couldn't fully recognize. Rem would've never trusted the distorted image a look through the peephole would've given him. That day, maybe the kid had forgotten to move the calculator after he'd gotten home, but Zari had found him on the sagging gray couch, asleep. Exhausted.

And when Rem had woken up, the wild, guarded look in his eyes told Zari, in no uncertain terms, that if the kid hadn't recognized him as somebody Chloe liked, somebody Chloe trusted, he would've taken his chances climbing out of that fifth floor apartment's window.

Rem is hungry, hungry enough to follow Dave, haltingly, with hesitation to spare, back into the store. They're walking towards the counter when Zari notices how Rem's attention shifts from one thing to another to another—from the tents to the sleeping bags to the hiking poles to the climbing ropes—and he realizes, with some warm, pleasant surprise, that this is the most energetic he's seen Rem be in the last few hours. So much like the toddler that Zari remembers.

There's a microwave on the checkout counter, right next to a mini-stand of beef jerky. Dave heats up the stroganoff and the noodles while Rem sifts through a shelf of climbing chalk. He's reading the back of each package with something two steps below awe sitting on his face. And Zari smiles.

Dave calls a tow-truck, and the driver agrees to swing by the store to grab Rem and Zari. The food's heating up and Zari's charging his phone with Dave's cord when the chainsaw starts up again. It's just one of those things, this chainsaw, one of those things you never really notice was gone until it comes back, full force. It's the loudest it's ever been. Zari watches Rem go straight and still again, watches the kid almost drop the hand-held fan he was looking at.

Zari turns to Dave and asks him about the chainsaw, finds that he almost has to shout over the noise. Dave is unphased, just stops the microwave and takes out the food. Tells Zari that it's his wife. His wife likes to build cabins. Zari turns to check up on Rem, finds that the kid looks only marginally comforted by the answer to this mystery.

No Bars and a Dead Battery

Zari repeats, cabins? And Dave nods, gives Rem a warm smile as he holds the bowl of noodles and beef out to him. Hunger wins again and Rem comes up to take it, face wary, movements stilted. When Rem takes the food, Dave comes from around the counter and walks towards the back of the store, signals for Rem and Zari to follow him. They do, and Zari feels some guilt coming up the hallways of his veins again as he watches Rem eat as quick as he can, like he doesn't trust the food to still be there if he pauses too long in between bites.

When they get outside Zari notices that the solid gray of the sky is breaking, snatches of orange couched in purple dribbling through the cracks above them. The sun's about to set. Zari doesn't expect the clearing that Dave leads them into. What he expects even less is the small collection of wooden cabins that they stop in front of. The chainsaw is all anyone can hear.

There are three small cabins, none of them large enough to be anything but single-room, and Dave gestures for them to follow him up to the one nearest the store's back patio. Dave knocks on its door, and Zari notes that Rem is the closest he's ever been; if the kid shifts, he'll bump right into Zari's arm. It makes Zari bizarrely happy.

Zari doesn't think that anyone would ever be able to hear anything over the sound of the chainsaw, much less Dave's casual knock. But the chainsaw stops, and the door opens. A tiny woman steps out, gray braids peeking out of her moth brown head wrap. She's a little shorter than Rem, would probably only come up to Zari's chest. But she's holding a two-stroke chainsaw, hands dwarfed by the thing, but calloused and sure all the same.

She smiles at them and Zari can almost feel his heart cracking inside his chest, softening and softening until only the tender can stay. She's beautiful. She's beautiful, and if Dave looks like what Rem's dad might've looked like if he'd lived longer, this woman, his wife, is who his mother would've been. He wants to cry, just barely manages not to.

She scolds Dave for only offering Zari and Rem the food in the store, and Dave's natural gentleness gives way to sheepishness. And Zari can feel Rem softening, softening, softening next to him, can feel the way this inscrutable calmness settles over Rem. When he looks over at the kid, Rem's looking up, towards the roof of the cabin, and his brows are furrowed. Zari looks too.

The cabin has no roof. When Zari meets the woman's eyes, she looks like she'd expected him to notice this sooner. But Rem is the one to ask, where's its roof? And the woman tells them that she's had enough with suffocation, that every house she's ever lived in has made her feel trapped. And Zari can hear a sound like Rem choking right next to him. When he turns to check up on the kid, he sees that Rem is crying.

Zari's not sure if he should touch him, doesn't want to make things worse. But this woman has no such compunctions and pulls Rem into her, hugs him, lets him cry into her shoulder. And Zari doesn't know what to do.

He doesn't, but when Rem looks up at him, eyes still wet, but *open* now, Zari's thinking that maybe he doesn't have to know yet. But what he does know, knows for a fact, is that he never wants to do the easy thing again. Which is just as well, because easy has never really been an option for him anyway.

After that, the woman gives them as much home-cooked food as she can find in the store (food that she and her husband had probably brought from home to eat here), and Zari unplugs his phone. When he looks out the store's front window, past the porch, the tow truck that Dave called is pulling up in front of the store. And a crowd's forming outside. Dave offhandedly remarks that people always wait until their last few business hours to show up.

Rem smiles, the first time Zari's ever seen him do it, and mutters *A through Z's Backwoods Equipment*, probably to himself. But the woman overhears him, turns to him with a smile on her face and says, A through

No Bars and a Dead Battery

Z? No, baby, *Az*. It's short for Azra, my name. And all Zari can think after that is just how much this woman's name, Azra, sounds like his own, Azaraiah. And after that, he's thinking about how Chloe had said to him, seven months into her pregnancy, Azaraiah… I want my kid's name to be creative like that… but I want it to mean something too… something big… And Zari, because he'd always found the notion of repair, the fixing of things, to be a comforting one, suggested Remedy. Rem.

They make their way through the crowd, and back to the El Dorado. And as they approach it, a crow flies directly over their heads and lands on the hood and then looks at them. They stand some distance away and watch the crow watching them. Another crow flies directly overhead and lands beside it. The first crow squawks and then both fly away. They watch the crows disappear, look at each other, and then get in the El Dorado, instead of the tow-truck. The driver seems okay with it. Only one way to go this time, with five bars and full battery.

FINDING DOLLY PARTON

Casey Lefante

No coverage, not even one bar, the battery was dead anyway. It was still daytime, but there was an overcast and the sky had a perfectly even dullness, so there was no way to tell what time of day it was, much less which direction was north or south or anything else for that matter. A two-lane blacktop road snaked up into the distance and disappeared into some trees, or a forest if you wanted to get technical about it. It also snaked down toward some lumpy hills and disappeared there as well. What sounded like a two-stroke chainsaw could be heard in the distance, but it was impossible to tell whether it was up in the forest or down in the lumpy hills. This had been happening more often lately. Two different ways to go, with a dead battery and no bars, and nobody left to blame.

Except for Dolly Parton. I totally blamed Dolly Parton, and you would too, honestly, if you were in my situation. I slumped against the side of the bus, my bangs sticking to my forehead. Everything about this moment felt very dramatic. If I'm being honest, I was already imagining how I would tell it to you. I wished I could think of a more dramatic way to describe the scenery—*lumpy* wasn't particularly dramatic, and all it made me think of was Mama's mashed potatoes—but the fact that I couldn't think clearly enough to be truly dramatic kind of increased the drama of the situation, a situation, in fact, that I wouldn't have even been in if it weren't for Dolly freaking Parton.

I knew, of course, that it wasn't really her fault—after all, what had Dolly ever really done to me?—but still, she was the easy scapegoat. If

No Bars and a Dead Battery

Dolly Parton had never existed, then she never would have created Dollywood, and then Mama would never have wanted to see Dollywood, and if Mama hadn't wanted that, then I wouldn't have been stuck standing against a tour bus on an empty road, sweat dripping down my neck. So much sweat. Honest to God, I could have filled a swimming pool with it.

In some ways, everything about that moment made sense. Everything about my grandmother ended with a breakdown. At first, it was her body; then, it was her mind; and then, at the most inopportune moment, it was this tour bus, which stranded me and about ten other tourists in the middle of Tennessee in a part of town that I was convinced I would die in because the only reason for a town like this to exist would be for me to die in it. If it was even a town. Maybe it was hell. Maybe we were all already dead.

Clearly, at this point, I was starting to panic. I plugged my phone into the portable charger I'd almost forgotten to pack, hoping to hear it buzz to life soon so I could scroll through my contacts and find someone, anyone, to come get me. A story wouldn't be a good story if I didn't live to tell it. The chainsaw sound rumbled in the distance, and I stuffed the phone, connected to its charger, back in my bag, next to the Pirouette cookie can lying across the bottom, on its side. I caught my breath, held it.

Despite my concern, no one else seemed to hear the chainsaw, or if they did, they weren't letting on that they did. One of the women, wearing a snug rhinestone denim jacket and a sparkly butterfly clip in her white cotton candy hair, suggested that if Dolly were here then she could lead all of us to the park herself. People laughed, and I didn't know why because it wasn't very funny. Then the woman's husband (who, I noticed, also wore head-to-toe denim) said that if Dolly were here then she'd protect us, or at least hold us close to her bosoms so we could feel some homespun comfort. He insisted, after his wife slapped him in the chest playfully, that it wasn't a sexual thing. I couldn't take this anymore. I had to get away from these people.

Everyone around me checked phones for service as they fanned themselves with gas station receipts, hats, Dollywood brochures. The bus driver, who had clearly given up on providing comfort, offered half-hearted reassurances as he ate pumpkin seeds out of a tiny plastic bag. I wished I'd brought a snack, but that's the trouble with losing your appetite for three months. You forget to make food a part of your life anymore.

I looked up to the dim sky and wondered what time it was and whether there were coyotes in Tennessee, and whether those coyotes' yells sounded like chainsaws, or maybe the coyotes knew how to work chainsaws. I didn't know what Tennessee coyotes were capable of, and I didn't feel like finding out. I grabbed the strap of my canvas bag, adjusted it on my shoulder. The cookie can inside felt like it was getting heavier by the minute, even though I knew that must be impossible. Right? Right. Totally impossible.

I slipped my hand into my bag absently, familiarly, the way a person might check her dead phone every two seconds just because she's used to doing it. My hand touched the cookie can, still cool despite the outside heat. I tapped it with my fingernails, the *clink clink clink* of it providing reassurance and memory.

More than anything else, I remember Mama's hands, the blue-veined maps of them. So different from my own smooth, incapable hands. I used to press against her cartography while sitting next to her in church, hot and sweating from no air conditioning, the backs of my legs sticking to the splintered pews. Those hands pressed coolness onto my forehead when I had a fever. Covered in flour, they pressed dough until it was unrecognizable, until, like magic, it became bread or cinnamon rolls. Those hands mixed paint into unrecognizable colors, pressed blocks of charcoal onto thick white

No Bars and a Dead Battery

paper, scratched lines that grew into feathers, beaks, little feet. My grandmother loved birds. Her sketches littered the desk where she also sat, hands shaking with arthritis, punching numbers into a calculator to budget money for textbooks, uniforms, field trips. She only ever framed one of her sketches: a small, barely-shaded image of two crows, one standing straight and tall, the other bent over as if searching for something. One crow, she used to say, meant death; two, however, meant good luck. I never understood the logic, and I never knew which was Mama and which was me, but I knew, without her ever saying it, who those crows were supposed to be.

Anyway, so the couple in denim stood in front of the group and announced, as self-appointed leaders of our motley crew, that the time had come to travel to Dollywood on foot. I thought they must be crazy, and I was sure everyone else must think so too, but no. In fact, one by one, people started agreeing that walking to Dollywood was the best plan of action. I considered them lemmings, every last one of them. Ludicrous lemmings. I could only imagine what Mama would think of them. I mean, I had a pretty good idea. I imagined she might say that the two of us were in our own, hellish version of *Cocoon*. Ironic, wasn't it, that I was in a situation that Mama would have hated because I was trying to take Mama to a place she'd desperately wanted to go. It seemed, in some way, that this was exactly how she wanted all of this to play out.

Before I go any further, you should know that the minute I was born, Mama became my entire world. A world when she wasn't my mother and father and grandmother and grandfather combined— well, that world, as far as I was concerned, never existed. When I was five, she used to sing "Jolene" in a soft yet strong voice, lulling me to sleep long before I knew what it meant for someone to take someone else's man. When I was ten, we watched *9 to 5* together. I remember pulling my knees close to my chest and tugging my t-shirt over them, then walking around the room with my knees, makeshift breasts, tucked under my chin. Mama told me she didn't like it, but she still laughed as I waddled across the tiny living room in an awkward squat, my butt grazing the floor every few steps.

It was like that for most of my childhood—the two of us, not against the world exactly, but clear allies in a world of people who mattered much less than the two of us mattered to each other. It wasn't until the last two years of high school that I started to venture out a little, make some new friends. Suddenly I wasn't as interested in Friday movie nights, breakfast in bed, long car rides listening to the *Rainbow* album. *Steel Magnolias* no longer made me cry, and I'd long outgrown my cowboy boots.

When I was seventeen, Mama asked where I wanted to go for my high school graduation trip. I knew she couldn't afford a trip, but I also knew she had one in mind. I knew she wanted to drive to Tennessee, wind our way around the Smoky Mountains and end up in Dollywood. It wasn't because she was trying to have a trip she wanted; she legitimately expected me to want this, too. And I should have wanted it. But what I wanted was to go to the beach with my new friends. I wanted to drink and lie on the sand and be with girls my own age, some of whom didn't even know who Dolly Parton was, let alone that she had a park.

So Mama used the money she'd saved for Tennessee and bought me a new swimsuit, some sunscreen, and a Visa gift card that I mostly used on booze. She told me to call her when I got there, and I did, but I didn't call her again until the day we left the condo, sunburned and drowsy and hungover. She never complained—she never even mentioned Dollywood again, not for years—but still, I know. I had kind of broken her heart.

So there we were, standing helplessly next to a useless tour bus, and the buzzing ripped through the landscape, this time louder. I looked around and saw no reactions from anyone else. I even asked the woman next to me if she'd heard anything. She was small, just barely taller than me. Out of all the people on this tour bus, she seemed the most normal. No rhinestones, no denim. Just a big straw hat and a kind of shapeless black dress, thin and linen. When I asked if she'd heard anything, she whispered that she thought she had, actually, but wasn't sure if it was real or in her head.

I didn't tell her that I'd had the same thought. I didn't tell her that this had been happening more and more often, and even when I wasn't out here, waiting for my imminent death. Sure, it was louder out here, but I had started hearing something like it even a few weeks ago, when I was holding Mama's hand, pressing the skin between her thumb and pointer finger to help her relieve a headache. We were watching *9 to 5*, and her head kept nodding forward, eyes closing and opening like a baby doll's with each movement. And even when she fell asleep, I didn't leave. I stayed and kept my hand on hers, and then I heard it. Quick and light but definitely there. A sound I wasn't able to immediately identify. It was just a whirring, spinning sound, distant but threatening, like something you'd hear coming from deep inside a woodshed, or from the back of a dark haunted house. I wish I could say it went away, but really the only change was in volume. Sometimes it was loud, sometimes it was soft, but it was always, always there, a persistent reminder, or maybe a warning, or, quite possibly, both.

It shouldn't have happened to someone like her. It was unfair, which I know is a super childish thing to say, but that's the truth of how I feel, and no one, not even you, could ever tell me otherwise. I searched endlessly for someone to blame—I still do. Isn't that the implication of saying that something's unfair? That there's a reason for the unfairness, something to blame for it? That someone took the fair option away from you, snatched it from your hands, denied you the truth you'd believed? I think so.

For three months, every day felt the same—gray, listless, nondescript. I started to wonder if it was really the world or me, like maybe the space between my cornea and my iris had grown a special film that made everything a milky gray. Or maybe the universe had just shifted in order to make me less interested in being part of it. I began to live only by technicality, a blinking, breathing robot suspended in animation.

So we walked, and when we reached the real fork in the road, the denim couple pointed towards the forest and said that was definitely the way to the park. As everyone followed—sheep, all of them—I made a quick decision and walked in the opposite direction, in the direction, I believed, of the sound. Constant or not, it definitely seemed louder when I looked towards the hills. I didn't need to follow those people. It's like I knew, even then, that this decision would make this a better story.

Not that that's the only reason I did what I did. I don't want you to think that. But, it's like, there are times when you're living your life and you just know, as you're doing something, that it's gonna be a good story. You know what I mean? And everyone loves a good story. Sometimes a good story is the only way we get through some things.

But like I said, that's not the only reason. I don't want to say the buzzing was calling me, but in a way, yeah, it was calling me. At least the sound meant someone might be nearby. And if no one was nearby, then I would know, definitively, that it really was all in my head. That it really was my fault that any of this was happening. At least the sound meant something might happen, something more than this stagnant limbo. I was tired of limbo. I was tired of nothing. I needed something.

Mama used to say that the two of us would be rich one day. She taught me to be independent, sure, but she still believed that if she found the right thing or person or people, then her life—and I guess my life, too—could be perfect. Sometimes it was a boyfriend, sometimes it was two weeks of the Atkins diet, and, most often, it was my happiness. As a kid, I didn't understand it. To me, our lives were perfect. To me, our lives were filled with options. To me, my life had no other option than to simply be what it was. Even when I grew apart from her, I still didn't want things to be any different. I loved her.

Maybe it's because I never felt like I didn't have a mother. By the age of thirteen, I'd figured out that Mama never knew hers. Not in a real way, anyway. There was one creased, gray photo on the wall, but other than that, Mama didn't talk about her much or tell me stories about her. As for my own mom, there were plenty of photos of her, young and beautiful, before, as Mama put it, her end allowed for my beginning. It was a pretty way of saying I'd killed my own mother. For me, my grandmother was everything. For her, I was one more person she could lose.

I never thought about it that way until one day when I was home from school, sick with a cold that stuffed my entire head with cotton balls, and the two of us watched Princess Diana's funeral. I lay with my head in Mama's lap as she stroked my hair. When William and Harry walked behind their mom's casket, she cried, silently, sniffing just enough for me to notice. She didn't want me to notice, but I noticed. I noticed and I even cried, too, just a little bit, because of course I did. It was sad. And it made me think, for the first time in a real, concrete way, what it would be like to lose someone—a daughter or a mom or an idol. Or the woman whose fingers moved, like magic, through my hair.

After leaving the group, I walked what I could assume to be about half a mile or a mile, up and down the winding hills. My thoughts alternated from curiosity to fear as I observed my surroundings. For one thing, I didn't hear any birds. Not one. No wind, either. Just that grinding sound that got louder, and louder, and louder. Even though I was used to it, it seemed more foreboding out here, more dangerous. Like a threat. I kept the bag close to my side as if something could come at any moment and snatch it away from me.

I became suddenly aware of a feeling like someone was behind me. I walked faster, keeping my back straight. I heard footsteps, light but definite, quickening behind me. I steeled myself, hand on my bag, ready to swing it if necessary. When I turned around, I saw the small woman from the tour bus, the one in the straw hat. She stopped, tilted her head to the sky, and for a moment her profile seemed familiar, the way her nose tilted in the exact same direction as her chin, like a sculptor got lazy. She told me not to be worried. She told me it could be a farmer constructing a fence. She told me that she'd heard about a man who owned a secret zoo somewhere near Pigeon Forge, a zoo with giraffes and zebras and pigmy goats. She told me he couldn't advertise because he'd get shut down and all the animals would be taken away from him, which really wasn't fair, was it, considering he loved these animals as if they were his own.

She told me all of this with a calm, clear voice, a voice that made it clear that she believed everything she was saying and that she knew she would make me believe it, too. And I did. I decided, right then and there, that she was absolutely correct about the source of the noise. A man with a secret zoo, building a fence to keep his animals safe. I thanked her, and that's when she looked at me, and the mold of her face struck me right in the gut. Mama.

She didn't like being alone. She never liked being alone. That's why I placed her in my bag before I left the bus an indefinite number of minutes ago, twisting the lid for good measure, just in case. I wasn't going to leave here there and risk losing her. I'd already lost her once. I didn't want the blame for this, too.

I wanted to tell the woman in black how familiar she looked to me. I wanted to tell her that except for the mole on her cheek and the fact that her eyes were more blue than green, she was the exact image of my grandmother, so much so that I lost my breath for a minute. I wanted to tell her, I so wanted to tell her, but I didn't, because that was the kind of thing that freaked a person out, and I needed her to stay with me. I didn't know why, but I did. So instead of saying something weird, I asked if she wanted to walk with me, and she nodded her head quietly before falling in step with my pace.

We walked in silence for a while with nothing but the crunch of dirt and leaves beneath our feet as a soundtrack for our journey. Can you call it a journey if you don't know your destination? I don't know. But we walked and it was never awkward. Just nice. Familiar. The overcast sky offered few shadows, but the trees kept the heat from becoming too unbearable. If I didn't know better, I'd think we were just two companions taking a walk.

The path wound, inclined, around a thick patch of trees. As we walked, I noticed we seemed to be approaching another highway. As we got closer, I noticed a bright yellow El Camino with the words *El Dorado* printed across the doors. It was beautiful and weird, like something out of a Tarantino movie. It stood, stark and bright against the otherwise dim landscape, its hood popped up. I asked the woman next to me if she thought we should check it out. She didn't really answer, just kind of looked at me, but I took that as a soft yes. We approached, and when we were a safe distance away, we stood by a tree and watched.

I could see someone standing under the hood and two other men standing next to the car. One, from that distance, looked a little like Santa Claus. The other, like he was going to a funeral. I wondered what time it was. Then I heard that chainsaw sound again and I froze, my eyes still on the car. It got louder and louder, but there was no way to see where it was coming from. I looked at the woman next to me, and she stood, hands over her ears, and her eyes looked pained. I wanted to hug her. Instead, I took her arm and pulled her with me behind a tree.

Santa Claus told the Funeral Man that they needed to just give this up and walk. He said that they needed to know when to hold 'em and when to fold 'em, and the time to fold 'em was now. Funeral Man told Santa Claus to stop being obnoxious and check to see how much money they had and whether they could afford to call a cab. Santa said that there would be time enough for counting when the dealing was done.

And I realized, watching this, that this wasn't a Santa Claus or a man going to a funeral at all. This was Kenny Rogers and Johnny Cash. Honest to God, I'm not shitting you, Kenny Rogers and Johnny Cash. I mean, they looked like them, anyway. If it wasn't Kenny and Johnny, then they were damn good lookalikes.

I know Johnny Cash is dead. You're not delivering new information or being helpful by pointing that out. So sure, probably a lookalike, but also, what if it wasn't? All I'm saying is that I saw Johnny Cash and Kenny Rogers next to a broken down car, and that's not all I saw.

The hood slammed shut and there, standing in a ruffled button-down, tight jeans, and cowboy boots, was Dolly Parton. I gasped. Actually gasped. She walked over to the men and grabbed their arms, looking first at Kenny then at Johnny. She told them, in no uncertain terms, that they needed to cut it out or else they would never get to the park in time for the show. She sounded so much like Dolly that I almost believed it was really her. Or I did believe it. I think it was her. Could it be really her? It was totally her. Then she looked in my direction, as if directly at me.

No Bars and a Dead Battery

The woman next to me grabbed my elbow, a gesture that normally might alarm me coming from a stranger, but I didn't flinch. I looked down at her hand and saw blue veins, stretching taut across her skin. My chest ached a little left of center, my breath caught in a net within me that I didn't know existed. I looked at Dolly, and I looked at my bag, and I looked at the woman next to me. And, god, she was beautiful.

Mama asked me three months ago, in the last truly lucid moment of her life. She reached her arm across the bed I'd rented from hospice, and she took my hand in hers, frail and weak. I traced a finger across her veins as she told me that she only wanted one thing, that she had one regret about her life. I knew, as she was saying this, that this was an important moment. This was a moment to remember.

I expected her, in such a moment, to say something about my mom, her daughter, or even her own mother. I expected something profound and important, something I could hold on to when the day finally came to say goodbye to her. I didn't think that would be the day. There was no way that would be the day. We still had time.

And what did she want? She wanted me to take her to Dollywood to meet Dolly Parton. And something happened to me in that moment, something not nice or gracious or any of the things I knew I was supposed to be in this moment. I was embarrassed by her request, and then I was embarrassed and angry that her request had embarrassed me, and I didn't know what to say.

I should have said yes. That's what I should have said. I should have said yes, and I should have promised her that dream. Instead, I became quiet and held her hand as she slipped out of clarity, letting her think I was considering it while quietly simmering with an irrational, misplaced anger. And I've never forgiven myself for that. For any of it. That's the honest truth.

So Dolly looked in our direction, and I had a little moment, but then my shoulder slumped, the bag slung across my chest suddenly heavier. I dropped it to the ground and lifted the pirouette cookie can out of it. I could swear something was moving around in there, which seemed just as impossible as it was likely. Nothing made sense anymore. The can seemed to be shifting even as I held it. And there was a banging coming from the inside. And a squawk. Was that a squawk? Oh my God, there was definitely something in there.

How an animal got inside a can of my grandmother's ashes was completely beyond me, but I knew I needed to get it out. The woman next to me stepped back, allowing me to squat on the dirt and pry open the can. Before I could even fully detach the lid, a mass of black feathers popped out, and the lid flung off. A giant, wide-winged crow flew straight out of the can and into the sky, and I could swear that it looked back at me as it ascended. I watched it until it was a black dot in the gray sky. When I looked back inside the can, I saw nothing. Not even a speck. Totally clean. I couldn't even begin to understand it.

I turned to my companion, but she was gone. All I saw were trees, and between the leaves and branches I saw the sky—was it brighter now?—and I couldn't hear the ripping sound anymore. It was gone, just gone, and if I didn't know better, I might have thought that I'd been transported to a different place. I might have believed this, really believed it, if the group of tourists didn't come walking through a patch of trees and, upon seeing the car and its owners, stopped in their tracks and gaped. The woman with the cotton candy clutched her chest with one hand and her sparkly barrette with the other, and, honest to God, I thought she might be having a heart attack. For a moment, all of us just stood, suspended in time, staring at these three people who couldn't possibly be the people we all, for our own reasons, wanted them to be.

No Bars and a Dead Battery

Standing in the dirt, an empty can at my feet, I watched as Dolly somehow, miraculously, got the car to start. One of the tourists clapped and yelled Dolly's name, which made her turn and smile and wave, the gracious country queen we'd all been waiting for, and if it wasn't really her then it really didn't matter. The three pseudo-celebrities waved and signed autographs, moving through the crowd and taking photos with their adoring fans. They were getting what they wanted, all of them, one way or another, and maybe that's what mattered.

I watched this, and I realized that it wouldn't have mattered which path I would have taken. Either way, I'd have ended up right here, with an empty cookie can and a broken heart and, for the first time in months, a quiet brain. I watched this, and I thought of all the things that had to happen in my life to make this particular moment happen. Maybe there aren't multiple answers or paths for this kind of thing. Maybe there isn't always more than one way to go. And maybe there's no one left to blame for anything. Not even Dolly Parton. Just me or fate or nothing. Nothing.

But you wanted a story, didn't you? And when you ask what happened next, when you beg for the resolution to this whole insane premise, what should I say? I've thought about this. I've thought about this a lot. And the truth is that people rarely really want the truth. They want a story, a good one that will explain the unexplainable. Like love, or loss, or the unbearable coexistence of both. You either want to know that these were really celebrities, or you want to know that everyone made it to Dollywood safely, or you want to know that my grief has changed form, has become something beautiful and symbolic and totally manageable. Even if none of this is true, it's nice to think it could be, isn't it?

And so here, if you want to know, is the honest-to-God, hand-on-a-Bible, swear-on-Mama's-grave truth: they moved through the crowd, took their photos and signed their autographs. Eventually, Dolly gestured towards the car, the engine quietly running, and told them they had to get going. As they did this, I felt a buzzing in my bag. I peeked inside and saw my phone, plugged into its charger and coming to life, full coverage and full battery and full bars. And I knew, then, what I had to do, where I had to go. I had to come back here. I had to come home, return to what I'd run away from, face what I didn't want to face—an existence without her.

They made their way through the crowd, and back to the El Dorado. And as they approached it, a crow flew directly over their heads and landed on the hood and looked at them. They stood some distance away and watched the crow watching them. Another crow flew directly overhead and landed beside it. The first crow squawked and then both flew away. They watched the crows disappear, looked at each other, and then got in the El Dorado. Only one way to go this time, with five bars and full battery.

TEAM 158

Tucker Lieberman

No coverage, not even one bar, the battery was dead anyway. It was still daytime, but there was an overcast and the sky had a perfectly even dullness, so there was no way to tell what time of day it was, much less which direction was north or south or anything else for that matter. A two-lane blacktop road snaked up into the distance and disappeared into some trees, or a forest if you wanted to get technical about it. It also snaked down toward some lumpy hills and disappeared there as well. What sounded like a two-stroke chainsaw could be heard in the distance, but it was impossible to tell whether it was up in the forest or down in the lumpy hills. This had been happening more often lately. Two different ways to go, with a dead battery and no bars, and nobody left to blame.

It was approximately noon. You hoped it was not later than that. You'd been searching for Team 158 since early morning. If you didn't find them soon, your number might be up, too. Eight o'clock tonight was your own appointment with Santa. The stress probably contributed to your inability to read the angle of daylight. If you thought about the lapsing hours, you might start to feel ill.

There was no real reason for you even to have checked the phone. Phones had never worked on this island since your arrival. There should have been reception here – there was an abandoned tower on the mountain – but it seemed the signal was deliberately jammed. A map would have helped you feel more secure in your journey but probably wouldn't have given you the answer. You turned the phone off again.

You'd been banished to this island with everyone else in your city, thousands of you. The rulers called it "quarantine" but, since very few of you were actually sick, that seemed like an excuse. It was becoming clearer that they were never coming back for you. And they had stopped airdropping food weeks ago. The food was nearly gone. The trees in the high forests bore nothing but pinecones. They were going to let all of you die here.

There seemed to be no way out, and then Santa had started to come. Although you had never been one to pray, others prayed, and Santa came. Santa gave, and continued to give, a brief, complicated hope. A boat would have been better. Santa was not a boat. You still needed a boat.

Santa was an unidentified flying object, a Drone that looked like a cooked black octopus settled into the shape of a dinner plate. It was about a hundred meters wide. It descended every night at eight o'clock over a barren field. What dropped from each of its eight arms was, remarkably, a PIN pad. Three empty digits and ten numerals to select with rounded buttons. No one knew the code nor what would happen if someone guessed it.

Because eight PIN pads were served simultaneously at the end of Santa's eight arms each night, eight teams could have a go simultaneously. The Drone got its name because it managed to visit these multiple households at the same time.

There was nothing to lose by trying, and, by that, what is meant is that you were all going to die anyway. Yesterday's pairs had checked out the usual way. It was Day 20 of the experiment, and they had been Teams 152 through 159, each comprised of one female, one male, perhaps due to a Noah's Ark complex on the island that you'd never heard explicitly verbalized. Most team members, when they

No Bars and a Dead Battery

went to meet Santa, chose to wear what little extra clothing belonged to them, although this had proven over and over to be a useless ritual. Probably what was needed was cryogenic suits, and not a single one existed on the island.

When Santa had come and lowered its eight arms, the teams entered their respectively assigned PINs. 152. 153. 154. 155. 156. 157. 158. 159. There would have been no reason to enter lower numbers because those had already been tried and had failed.

Because the eight-armed Drone dropped eight PIN pads at a time and because there were only one thousand possible combinations, your group had realized it could systematize its guesses. Teams of two began with 000 and counted up. What would happen when you hit the right one? No one knew. That's why pairs were sent; the person who punched the winning combination might need a buddy or a witness. So far, it was a costly strategy that only doubled the casualties.

What would you have done in, say, Team 153's place, if your number had been up last night? You would have entered the PIN assigned to you, of course. It was the right thing to do and the only honorable choice. It was the best chance of systematically solving the Santa puzzle and the only plan to get off the island. Running away to starve in the woods would not have helped.

Unluckily, just like all the other teams before them, all the teams on Day 20 perished. The screens had gone dark and human-sized pods on Santa's arms had opened, sucked in the pairs with a large vacuum, and closed the pod doors behind them, and, several minutes later, the pod doors had opened again and dropped their bodies. They were cold, hard, dead, apparently having been sprayed with something like liquid nitrogen, their sweaters having done them no good.

Except for Team 158, that is. Santa spit out all the other bodies except for theirs. Then Santa flew away. Morning came and their bodies hadn't yet been found. That made a big difference to everyone's outlook. Did that mean they had guessed the PIN correctly? Were they still alive? Were they still inside Santa? Everyone was searching for them. Until this mystery was solved, there was no reason for the next teams to continue guessing PINs 160 and higher. No one even knew if Santa would come back tonight.

You suddenly remembered a creation myth: *She and he were born with ten fingers, ten toes. Being good, to her and him, meant dying so that others would not have to suffer. They were good. They reclined and sucked a stream of light from each other's fingers. There were ten distinct and wholesome forms. They did not know the difference between life and death.*

Your number was 162. It was going to be your turn tonight. You and a female to whom you hadn't been introduced yet. You didn't want to meet her. If indeed the two of you were going to punch in that number at all, it's better if you don't think beforehand about what needed to be done.

It might not need to be done. Team 158 might have already solved the puzzle. You needed to find out what happened to those people. You and everyone else who had pulled low numbers in the draft and who hadn't died yet were highly motivated to find them alive.

You had been feeling a little more disoriented each day, stuck on an island where there was no meaningful difference between north and south, east and west. If any direction mattered, it was up: the Drone in the sky, a killer but perhaps also a rescuer. Your fate had been all but sealed, and now there was a ray of hope. You had to unlock "Rescue" in your video game.

Where to go? You were on your own, combing the field for signs of Team 158. Here you had come upon a two-lane blacktop road. In

No Bars and a Dead Battery

one direction, it headed up into the mountainous pines and, in another direction, it headed down through lower hills.

You looked up to the pines. Moving up would be to know the past and its origins: to see the conformities you were leaving behind, to admit you were motivated by your pain, to stop replicating ingredients so the story wouldn't repeat.

And you were ready to begin again: to pay attention, to take on challenges that fit what you could do today, to enjoy the work, to breathe and let the unconscious have its say, to be humble, to be noble, to comfort others through who you would become.

You looked down to the hills. Moving down would be to go forward your way: to avoid distractions that snatch your energy, to glide over the groundwater of worry, to choose the work of increasing skill with a vision of the home you wanted to see again.

And you were ready to pursue your uncertainty: a day when the sun would meet the earth with gentle flame and flower, where you were no longer broken, where you would hold and be held. It wouldn't be a return to the past. It would be new. A world made stronger because of its scars.

You fell to your knees and went nowhere whatsoever for a moment. To do this well, you suddenly felt, would be to transcend yourself, a pained being learning to sing out its fear and its last bit of joy, desiring that those you care about would survive or that something new, soft, resilient would be born.

You hadn't seen a bird in ages. Sometimes you thought you saw footprints in the dirt: three toes forward, one toe backward. Passerines, like crows, perhaps. But why would they be here, unless they were waiting to eat the dead?

It is nearly time, you'd been saying since arriving on this island for months that seemed like years, *but it's really time now.* You wanted to tell them: *What you used to be is irrelevant. Your credentials are meaningless here. All those who stood before Santa did so alone. It is time for everyone to own their joy and sorrow. Revaluate your naughty and nice deeds as you understand them. Live this last day. Figure out: What do you eat when there is no food? What do you burn when there is no fuel? Let Santa open you, right now, this day. Speak honestly. Die, and in your dying, live. Set yourself free and you will fly. You are the only one who can save yourself.* You wanted to fire off that text message but you didn't have the magic runes needed to hold a complex message and fit it in the box.

It's a Molly Bloom message. *Yes I said yes except that other time I said no. Desire is the tension between opposites except when it is the affinity of sameness. It's my efforts to "capture moments" without having the ability to photograph them. My actual self and my counterfactual self. To feel that I am not responsible for my naughty and my nice and to own it anyway. To intuit that other people are responsible for their actions and to stop blaming them anyway. The same meal tastes different when I am hungry and when I am full.*

Live or die? Was your fate open or shut? Does wanting an outcome change what is going to happen? *To want the tide to go in and to want it to go out. To want to go to the beach precisely because there is a tide that goes in and out. To want a boat that will take me off the island. To be self-protective and endlessly giving. To be honest and kind. To win and to have integrity. To be unique and march a united front. To want to live and to be willing to die. To know the difference between offensive and defensive actions. To feel deeply and remain calm.*

If you were to be honest with yourself about the full range of your possibilities, there was another reason you might not have to enter your PIN tonight. They saw you as male, but the more complete fact was that once you were female and that you now presented as male, so, depending on how seriously they took their Noah's Ark complex, this finding might disqualify you in their eyes from self-sacrifice in either the female or male role. Such an argument could have been made. But what would that have gotten

No Bars and a Dead Battery

you? Santa freezes you. The island starves you. You were not desperate enough to get out of your team assignment when the other option was a passive death.

You could still hear words of rejection, those voices you've internalized, criticizing you for having wanted to change your body from female to male. You could still almost see their eyes boring into you. Shame is the desire to hide. This feeling, still, even though everyone on the island now believed you to be male.

Those voices were always present: your ancient critics, telling you not to change your body, to stay as you are, and also to be who they think you were meant to be, a recipe they think amounts to being true to yourself. You know that being true to yourself and being true to their conception of you are two different things. They act as if this is a threat. They say they believe that the person you believe yourself to be somehow hurts them. That does not make sense to you. It is a form of crazy-making.

Be yourself, but don't act selfishly, those voices said. *Do not conform to systems that hurt me. Do not revolt against systems I'm using. You need some system. Use your own. I'll tell you what it is. It's the nail in your forehead. You didn't know it was there? I see it. Let me hang my laundry on it. There, it organizes my world. Don't you dare pull it. You are your body. I said don't change it because that's my nail. All right, you insist on acting like a no-nail, so, go on, pull it, quick. Here is a rope. Loop one end on your nail and the other on the doorknob. Slam the door. It won't be enough, I'm warning you. You can get rid of your nail but you can't change the fact that you were born with a nail. No? You won't pull it? Then act like you have a nail because I still see it. Why can't you just be yourself? What a privilege it is to have that nail in your forehead. Everyone wants to use it. I keep moving your goalposts but don't worry because they are always in my comfort zone. My God made you to be yourself. Here is a rope. Jump.*

This is the monologue you heard before the scheduled hour of your death. But you hadn't hanged yourself yet. You never had, and now you had other things to do. Whether anyone was female, male, or something else seemed mostly irrelevant these days, and you couldn't blame yourself or anyone else for arguments you conducted in your imagination. You had to find Team 158 and prove that they were still alive, or else you would likely go to your death sooner rather than later, testing PIN 162, which may not have needed to be tested, and hundreds more people were likely to die similarly.

Only the righteous man can repent and only the sinner needs to. This is what we have become and what we have always been. Will you be recycled in the sea? With paper or glass? Have you learned to say no and why would you want to say yes?

Given the uncertainties of the day, it was good that no one had working phones. What would they text each other? Questions like: *What was history?* What, indeed, was history, you wondered. What on earth was that question? *What was history?* is a broad question no one can answer in a tiny text message unless they have installed a keyboard with magic runes, runes that were originally inscribed in the crumbling cornice of the meetinghouse of a genocided tribe that no longer has a known name but from which they are genetically descended or spiritually adopted, and unless they climb into an ice pit grave of their elder warrior and find the translation tablet with a pronunciation code, and unless they drink absinthe and are visited by an angel who understands their new way of conversing and luminously nods.

Questions like *what were laws long ago?* or *how do ethics work?* were never appropriate conversations for text message. There was no magic rune keyboard to be installed, no one could read runes anyway, the phone battery would die if you turned it on again, and all of the survivors on this island, you noted, were still earning their merit badges from the ice pit angels. Searching, waiting, for Team

No Bars and a Dead Battery

158.

You had not yet risen from your knees when you saw it return in the sky. In came Santa, a prophetic sight, terrible and hopeful at the same time. Santa was flying toward the island for the first time in full sunlight. It was towing another vehicle through the open water. This one looked more promising. The other vehicle was not a Drone. It was seaworthy. If it could be used, it was exactly what was needed.

There was that sound again. That was it. What you had heard high in the pine mountain, the faint sound of a chainsaw, was the sound of the boat making its way to you. You did not know that liberation had a sound. You did not know that motors made music.

What Santa was pulling on a leash was an Ark big enough for the thousands of survivors. On its side was painted the name El Dorado. The deck was covered with a red awning, a kind of hood, and the sun gleamed through it. The water spread behind it in a large wake.

The wake does not touch the boat, you reflected. *It never does. The boat touches the water and sprays a story about the past. We see where we used to be, in a convoluted way, the white frills rising. We see everyone we pushed away, their faces in our memory. They cannot touch us anymore. They are paint on the canvas. They can smile or grimace at us.*

The boat touches the water and makes a wake. If people are dead, they are not awake. If we are awake, we are present to where we are now. Right now we are moving. We are trailing a wake behind us without touching it. The position we are in is the present. It does not have the past in it. A different force moves us into the future. We should know what it is. We should be in touch with it. We are looking back at the wake.

You were never one to pray, but you felt that you left the light on for Team 158, for the people who had not come home. You left a light burning fiercely for soldiers coming home from the war. You fixed a light so stubbornly for the people who were too stupid to come out of the rain. You poked holes in the lantern cover in crow shapes so people coming home would see illuminated spirits. You carried a torch for someone you remembered.

And now the people came home. Team 158 was alive, the female and the male. They stood on the deck of the El Dorado and waved. The other survivors on the island saw them now, too, and roared their approval. It was a homecoming and an outgoing simultaneously. You raced down the side of the mountain to join the crowd.

The first woman and man mistook breath for soul, water for unconscious. Now, tethered to wind and wave, was an Ark tied to a Drone. The Ark was called El Dorado and the Drone was called Santa. Below the ragged mountain line knuckled in prayer on the sky it hung. Every thread of soul was traced, remembered. They mistook the soul for simple wind, the labyrinth of the mind for shoreline, as if the knots could save them, could truly tie them down and lift them up.

They had ten fingers, and this had no meaning. They lit candles, tentative. The wax and flame shouted as it deformed. Now they thought they knew what meaning was. They were alive. They had once believed they could die in place of others, had once made sense of that.

The female and male disembarked and climbed ashore. The crowd touched their faces and wept from excitement but did not want to waste time. They were skeptical of Santa's intentions. They did not want the boat to leave again without them. *Go back,* everyone told Team 158. *Let us on board with you.*

And there was another shout of joy: Someone had turned on a phone, and it worked. The signal had been freed. Santa's eight black metal arms waved in benign gestures above them. There were going to be bars and battery again.

No Bars and a Dead Battery

You wondered: Why would Santa have let so many people die arbitrarily in cold and lonely deaths—Teams 000 through 157, a female and male on each team—only to then bring a boat to save everyone on the island? Why did Teams 158 through 999 get to live? Why had some people not drawn a number at all? And who was behind Santa?

The female and male counterparts of Team 158 assured everyone that they would explain everything in due time. Some of the crowd was already rushing ahead on the ramp. They grabbed bunches of grapes from baskets on board. The red hood shielded them from the bright sun.

They made their way through the crowd, and back to the El Dorado. And as they approached it, a crow flew directly over their heads and landed on the hood and then looked at them. They stood some distance away and watched the crow watching them. Another crow flew directly overhead and landed beside it. The first crow squawked and then both flew away. They watched the crows disappear, looked at each other, and then got in the El Dorado. Only one way to go this time, with five bars and full battery.

A MILLION DOLLARS

Amr Mekki

No coverage, not even one bar, the battery was dead anyway. It was still daytime, but there was an overcast and the sky had a perfectly even dullness, so there was no way to tell what time of day it was, much less which direction was north or south or anything else for that matter. A two-lane blacktop road snaked up into the distance and disappeared into some trees, or a forest if you wanted to get technical about it. It also snaked down toward some bumpy hills and disappeared there as well. What sounded like a two-stroke chainsaw could be heard in the distance, but it was impossible to tell whether it was up in the forest or down in the lumpy hills. This had been happening more often lately. Two different ways to go, with a dead battery and no bars, and nobody left to blame.

They had both seen enough horror movies to know not to split up, but they also knew that they were running out of time. Without a phone to show them the time, they had to rely on their mutual anxiety for a timer. Soon enough it would be dark, and there would be no escape. Jonathan was the first to say what was on both their minds. It felt as though they had just decided to stick together to the end, no matter what. But neither of them expected the road to break into two separate paths. They knew there was only supposed to be one winner, one survivor. One direction would lead to fortune, and the other to death.

Chelsea agreed that it would be better for one of them to live than for both of them to die. Someone had to tell people about this;

No Bars and a Dead Battery

warn them so it would never happen again. No one mentioned the money. It was easier to justify leaving the other to be killed that way. If it were brought up they would have to say that it would be wrong to take it after all that had happened. But it wasn't brought up because it was too much money for morality to get involved. After all, they could give half of it to a charity in order to atone for taking it out of so many lifeless hands.

Despite their agreement, Jonathan felt uneasy. Chelsea was younger than him and much smaller. Whatever was wielding the chainsaw would be a powerful force to reckon with. They had seen too much to doubt that it was only there to murder them. If it awaited down in the hills, a confrontation would be unavoidable. At least in the forest there were trees to hide behind. The thought of leaving Chelsea exposed to the killer was too much for Jonathan. Everything else was only tolerable because it wasn't his fault. Letting her go down the road leading to the hills would be as good as collaborating with the hidden murderer.

He could not tell her any of this. Even though he had only known her for a few hours, she reminded him so much of his younger sister that he knew exactly how she would respond to him wanting to protect her. As if to prove something, she would throw herself at the greater danger. Knowing this, and equipped by experience to avoid it, he asked her which road she wanted. Just as he expected, she told him to choose, and he obliged her, feigning indifference. They hugged, wished each other good luck, and took to their respective paths. Jonathan stopped and watched her until she entered the mouth of the forest. She did not turn around—just as he expected—and he wondered if tears were streaming down her cheeks, like they would down his sister's.

There was nothing along his undulating road except painful memories, and even more painful regret. Why did he respond to that advertisement? From the first time he read it, he knew it was too good to be true. *Do you want a million dollars?* Who doesn't want a hundred dollars, let alone a million? *All you have to do is survive.* How could anyone have thought to take it literally? Things like this only happened in movies, and yet here he was, seeing all that blood along the hills, and hearing all those screams in the stifling air. He shook his head and red became green again. The roar of the chainsaw returned. It seemed louder than before. Jonathan was eager to meet the person who would try to kill him. Then he would get the answers he wanted and the revenge he craved; and if he didn't, at least it would finally be over.

Each step he took away from everything that had happened brought his mind closer to it. *The contest is only open to the first three-hundred entrants.* When he submitted his application, he scoffed, ashamed of himself for entertaining something so ridiculous. It seemed like a careless submission of personal information to complete strangers. But he did it anyway because he had nothing to lose, and there was always the chance that it could be true. Receiving a congratulatory response a few weeks later was not enough to satisfy his doubts. He sent his confirmation and continued living as before, not daring to hope even in the last hours of night, when it is most tempting to compensate for disappointment with fantasy. His incredulity was even undaunted by the strict instructions he received soon after that.

In exactly two days from then, he would have to drive to a specific location and arrive no later than six in the morning. He was to come alone, dressed only in white—shoes, socks, dress pants and shirt, all white. To arrive a minute late or to wear anything else would mean immediate disqualification. Once there, he would park his car at the designated lot and be greeted by a masked man. After being searched and blindfolded, the man would guide him to a bus that would take the participants to the grounds of the contest. None of this seemed suspicious to him. The odd rules were explained by the eccentricity he attributed to the sort of person who would give away a million dollars. Besides, they were allowed to keep their phones. If something went wrong, anyone could just call the police. How was he supposed to know that by the time they arrived, his phone, along with everyone else's, would be dead?

He was led out of the bus and into a building crammed full of the people he was to compete against. No one said anything. They all felt the heat of each other's breaths as they waited in tense anticipation of further instructions. Until then he still suspected no malice. It was probably going to be a series of challenges like he had seen on television. As soon as he could see again, he would look around to size up his competition. That's all they were to him, competition, there for the same reason as him: a harmless contest for money that everyone wanted, but no one really needed. The thought that it was not necessity that had brought him there, but greed, stung him the most now. No amount of money would erase the smell of burning human flesh from his memory.

The stench, the shrieks, and the panic in the confined space overwhelmed him. He was caught in the mayhem of hysteria and could not even lift his arms to remove the blindfold. When he realized what was happening, instinct and adrenaline took over to protect him from being burned alive. There were no people in his way, just obstacles. With more strength than he could voluntarily summon, Jonathan charged through the stampede. They were not fellow beings he trampled, but obstructions, grasping and screaming like the doomed wights of perdition, trapped in fire and brimstone. There is no sympathy in survival.

Deafening blasts and blinding lights congratulated him for escaping the inferno. He was still gasping for air when someone overtook him with such violence that he stumbled and fell. The rushing survivors forced him to crawl forward, while the constant explosions maintained his disorientation. Before he could stand, a panicked sprinter tripped over him and tumbled. Jonathan barely caught of the glimpse of the figure: it recovered in an instant, resumed its flight, and vanished in a thunderous flash. Terror came with understanding. He had gone out of the frying pan, and into a minefield.

Despair numbed him to the pain of being run over. Why didn't he try to stop them? So many lives could have been saved if he had just warned them. Was the money worth so many deaths? He shook his head at the crucifying thought. There was nothing he could have done, not in that state of total fear. When he saw a dark path in the consuming lights, all he could think about was himself. Besides, who would have stopped to listen to him; who would have been able to hear him? Regardless of how loud he yelled and warned, his voice would have failed against the creaking, burning building as it echoed the groans of those who were stuck inside.

The severed limbs and disintegrated bodies he saw and felt as he crawled for his life did not start haunting him until now, when he was alone. Now, he could see them better than when they were scattered around him; he could feel them better than when they were cushions beneath his hands and knees. It didn't matter how often he shook his head, there would be no escape. He wondered how long it would be before he began envying the people who never even had the chance to remove their blindfolds.

No, he could not think like that. Life was too precious to envy the dead. The thought of his sister eased his heart. He had to not only live, but want to live. To burden with grief her whose very existence relieved and comforted him would be an inexcusable cruelty. For her sake, he would live in spite of the horrors of the

No Bars and a Dead Battery

interminable day.

The thought of his sister brought Chelsea to mind. When he first saw her, he couldn't believe his eyes. After being surrounded by so much agony and chaos; after narrowly emerging from the firestorm only to find such a vivid reminder of the last person he expected to see, the person he wanted to see most, he could not help but wonder if he had died along with everyone else. Hardly any white was still visible on her clothes. For a moment it looked as though the angel that was supposed to take him away had fallen, incurring upon itself all the filth of the world, and not knowing what to do, was now sitting, looking just as helpless and pitiful as him.

Her eyes assured him that he was still alive, and that none of it was a dream. There was too much fear and suffering inside them to belong anywhere but in reality. The relief that brightened her expression at seeing that she was not alone gave him new life. She pointed to the note pinned on the post, unable to say or do anything else. *There can only be one winner. You have until dusk to reach the end of the road.* That was it, the full extent of their instructions, explanations, and conciliations. The first sentence was more dreadful than the second. It lingered on their minds despite their attempts to forget it and everything else in conversation. They even made their pact to stay together in defiance of it. How could they have expected the split in the road? It felt like so much time had passed since then. The grating of the chainsaw was getting louder, making him relieved and hopeful for Chelsea. He wondered how she was doing.

The air beneath the trees was hot and thick. Each step she took felt heavier than the last. When she agreed to take the forest path, she had no idea it would be so dark. The resounding cawing of crows made her forget all about the chainsaw. Black plumes covered the ominous path, deteriorating her confidence the further ahead she went. The weight of countless little eyes fell on her from the sable canopy. She hated birds. How did it come to this?

Her father had told her not to go. If only he had not said that, she would be at home now. Home. It never felt so far away, so precious. She wanted to apologize to him for not listening, for leaving without saying goodbye. The last thing she said to him was that he didn't know anything. She said it with an enormity of contempt that pained her to think about now—so much so that she could think of nothing else. The crows chanted a chastisement that she would have given a year of her life just to leave behind. Disregarding the oppressive atmosphere and her shortened breath, she began to run in search of an exit.

The appeal of the money, and the independence it represented, perished in her remorse. Why did she want to leave her father's house anyway? There she had an endless supply of everything that anyone could want: food, comfort, love. Moreover she had time to read and write; to pursue her dreams and ideals with the support of those who cared about her most. How did a few arguments cause her to forget that her life was perfect; how were they enough to make her want to leave? As soon as she realized the danger she was in, all her loathing, anger, and frustration subsided. She dropped the pride that would not let her ask her father for help as she sprinted, spurred by guilt and fear. The atrocities she had seen did not disturb her more than the thought of never going back home. Death did not scare her—she did not even know what it was—but she would live to protect her father from grief. This was the least she could do. To seal her repentance, she would give him every cent of the million dollars. Escaping with her life, and a newfound appreciation for it, was reward enough for her.

Sprinting was easier than convincing herself that she was not lost. There was no end to the darkness. All around was the same grim black that offered no chance for relief. Her only solace came from

No Bars and a Dead Battery

an occasional beam of light that would burst through the living cloud to show that her steps were leaving faint prints on the otherwise concealed ground. Using these markers, she could always go back. But she did not take the thought further, lest she face the fact that there was nothing to go back to except a darkness worse than what was slowly digesting her in the belly of the forest.

Once her stamina began to fail, she kept herself going with the certainty that sooner or later there would be something, anything. But what if there wasn't? What if the other path was the right one, and here was only a gradual, painful death? Starvation and thirst elongated and worsened by artificial hope. Wouldn't it be better to give up now? All it would take was for her to climb a tree and then jump. If she were to be buried in the disdain of crows, would it not be better for her to make at least one final choice? The idea appealed as an irresistible last resort. She would take a feather and carve into her skin an apology to her father, and an assurance that none of it was his fault. Panic was delayed by these thoughts, which gave her at least some sense of control over the situation.

When she could no longer sprint, she ran; and when she could no longer run, she walked. The dimming of her solace reminded her of the futility of looking up for comfort. Night would soon consume even this simple reminder; soon the darkness would become absolute, and there would be no difference between going forward and going back. The forest itself confirmed the threat of the note: she had until dusk to escape. A feeling she could neither validate nor reject suggested that there was someone, or something else nearby. At first she attributed it to the prying presence overhead, but her unease grew worse the deeper she went. Birds had never made her feel so sick. Dread was dismissed as a result of paranoia, and caution was completely forgotten when she saw a faint glow in the distance.

Chelsea expected the light at the end of the tunnel to be white, but she was in no position to discriminate. Seeing that it was orange did not deter her from rushing towards it as though towards salvation. It grew bigger and bigger, yet remained just as faint, until she reached the log cabin from which it emanated. Candles stood on the sills of two square windows, as if to invite the weary traveler. There was no path, nothing to indicate its being there besides the flickering candlelight. Its exterior was made up of the same wood that her eyes had long adjusted to. She did not dare believe that her silent prayer had been answered—it was too good to be true. But at peering through the window and detecting a hunched figure, she felt the immense burdens of anxiety and dread melt away from her hitherto congealed heart. She breathed, even smiled, and knocked. The door creaked and cracked open.

A black blacker than that blackest of days peered through the opening, and through Chelsea. It stunned her soul as the moist miasma did her body. The shudder that ran up and down her entire being begged her to run, but she was tired of running. If the round and shriveled woman were any younger or taller, the danger Chelsea felt might have convinced her to immediately flee. But the old occupant of the cabin, in her thick cloak of feathers which concealed everything except her pointed, ashen face, seemed incapable of sudden movements, let alone threatening ones. Her crooked posture suggested a feebleness that belittled the terrifying effect of her penetrating eyes. The longer she looked down at the woman who winced and squinted as if pained by the effort it took to keep her head tilted back, the less afraid and more sorry she felt.

A few minutes or hours in the forest were enough to cripple her with dread and agitation, and yet here was a person somehow living in the nightmare. Sorrow became pity and instead of asking for help as she had intended, Chelsea stuttered and asked her if she needed it. The geriatric answered with a hideous grin beneath her pimpled beak, as discomfiting as the unyielding stench was nauseating. One resilient tooth persevered on her barren, blackened gums. But it was too late to turn back: before she knew it, pity had become guilt and her conscience was trapped. To leave someone so weak and defenseless in a place like that would be despicable. An inescapable sense of duty made her ignore the woman's devious cackle, and accept her drawled invitation to enter the cabin.

A sharp turn was all that was left between Jonathan and the roaring chainsaw. The rock he had picked up was the only weapon in his possession. With the element of surprise on his side, the rock was as good as a mace. From where he stood the deadly threat's exact position was indeterminable, but Jonathan was beyond discouragement. All his guilt and anger had been projected onto the unknown menace during his hike to reach it. His imagination had already supplied him with a vivid, indubitable picture of his victory, the questions he would ask, and the torture he would inflict. For the first time in his life, he would kill—immense suffering and implacable rage dampened the implication of this by numbing him to it. The rock dug into the skin of his clenched fist, but he felt no pain. It was do or die, there was no time for feeling. He jumped with his loaded arm cocked back, only for his feral cry to fade into a croak, as his fury did into bewilderment.

Instead of the murderous object of his expectation, there was a big, black box. In his excitement and confusion he thought that the adversary was inside it, waiting for him. He waited, listening to the raucous noise, ready to fight whatever emerged. Each passing moment chiseled away at the suffocating stillness. Eventually the lenses placed in front of his eyes by the survival instinct slipped off his sweaty head, and he noticed a cable running from the side to the back of the seemingly menacing enigma. Without relenting his vigilance, Jonathan slowly slid to see where it led. At perceiving a small generator, a bolt of realization struck the rock from his hand, and the agitation from his soul. The box was just a speaker.

Incredulity made him pace around in search of a decisive end to his unnerving confusion. Relief came when he saw a note taped to the back, and went once he read it. *The end is near.* What did it mean? He turned and followed the road as far as his eyes could go, but there was no end in sight. Maybe it was on the horizon, past his line of vision. Maybe he just needed to keep walking to reach the end; to reach the million dollars he had nearly died for. His proximity to victory disappointed him. The thought of it being that easy brought with it anxiety instead of alleviation. If he had really won, what had happened to Chelsea? The only reason he chose the road through the hills was because it seemed more dangerous. He could not help thinking that the absence of danger around him meant its presence wherever she was. No amount of money could convince him to forsake her.

Without remorse, apprehension, and rage slowing him down, Jonathan was able to retrace his steps with incredible swiftness. There was no fear for himself or desire for vengeance clouding his mind. Everything had been replaced by the urgent call of duty announced by conscience. It was easier for him to ignore fatigue and uncertainty when it was for the sake of someone else. Before he knew it, he was standing at the junction where they had split up. The forest path appeared darker than when he considered it safe. Somewhere inside, Chelsea was still walking; or she might have already reached the other side. He would not consider the alternative, nor rest until he found her.

Jonathan followed the faint footprints until the road turned into a black to which no eyes could adjust. Here he stopped and shouted her name, but could only hear the cawing of crows in response. Something about their blanketing insistence encouraged him not to lose hope. He looked up at the dying gray poking through the darkness, and saw the silhouette of a winged creature descend toward him. For the second time that day, he wondered if this was death. The seraphic apparition nearly struck him before it melded into the surrounding black. Jonathan was too enthralled to flinch. A proximal, piercing squawk blared with an urgency that only relented when he moved towards it. Even if this was death, following it seemed a better idea than standing still, alone, in the darkness.

The faint orange glow he saw at distance affected him like the comforting speck of a guiding star. He had already been in the dark for too long to think that the light might be a trap instead of a haven. Instinct possesses people and moths alike. When he reached the cabin, his excitement for seeing another person stripped him of all prudence. Without bothering to peer inside or suspect danger, he knocked, assuming that the resident would be eager to help after hearing about everything that had happened. All he needed were directions, or even a phone, and he would not feel so powerless. His desperation made it seem perfectly natural for someone to be living in that awful, never-ending shadow. His ebony guide perched on the door as it creaked open.

Jonathan's hopes drowned in the two fathomless black pools that stared up at him. The cadaverous face grimaced, shifting the deep wrinkles in which crumbled his expectation of help. As if regretting the reaction, the woman showed her gums and tooth in the closest thing to a smile that she could muster. His evident revulsion, as much a result of her as of the unavoidable fetor, called for a different approach. In a tone that creaked more than the door she only kept ajar, the woman conceded a single word, harder for Jonathan to hear than anything else she could have said. *Congratulations.* Ignoring or oblivious to his shuddering, she proceeded to tell him to turn around, take a right, go straight for a few minutes, keeping the light behind him, until he reached the end.

Every syllable she croaked worked in tandem with her expression and attitude to enrage him. She spoke as though he should be happy. His impulse to blame her and extract the joy of retribution he yearned for was checked by the aged woman's apparent frailty. A shove would send her tumbling, likely to her grave. She could barely stand; how could she be responsible for anything? It was impossible. But then, why would she congratulate him? He shook his head and told himself that she must be senile.

An expression of gratitude was nearly formed on his tongue when he thought to ask if she had seen anyone else. Her perfunctory, negative response left him wanting more. Not willing to give up so easily he said that he was looking for his friend, a young woman, and asked if she had come to the cabin. The answer was the same. Jonathan thanked her anyway and turned to leave when the perched crow that had not taken its inscrutable gaze from him descended with a vile cry. It tried to peck and scratch at the woman, who retaliated by swatting with a ghastly, varicose hand. She shouted and cursed as though the bird was no stranger to her. After inflicting as much damage as it could, the crow flew away, leading her in a chase that ended almost as soon as it started. This gave Jonathan enough time to peer into the exposed cabin and catch a glimpse of a familiar figure, barely illuminated by candlelight.

The woman slithered back to stop him from entering. Whatever she said was lost in the redoubled cawing above them. Jonathan shouted for her to move, but she refused to budge. His foot jammed the door, keeping it open as she pushed with her whole body to shut it. The contest came to an end with his patience. No longer constricted by scruple, he tackled the brittle barrier and heard a crash, then silence. He would not stop to think about what he had just done; he would not even look at it. Keeping his eyes and thoughts on the most reliable and effective of excuses, necessity, it was easier to see the life he was saving rather the one he had just destroyed.

Chelsea was sitting at a table with her back turned to the door. In the dimness of the enclosure and under the influence of adrenaline, he did not realize that she was tied to the chair, or that her mouth was taped shut. The frantic questions of whether she was hurt and whether she could stand were met with muffled attempts to speak that made him pay closer attention and detect the bindings. He freed her lips first, hoping to hear that he had not arrived too late. But as soon as she could talk, Chelsea exclaimed that the woman had a gun. Hearing the strength in her voice gave him the relief he had risked everything to find. The smile it inspired allayed her panic like no words could. It conveyed that there was nothing to worry about; that everything was going to be fine, and she believed it.

On their way out, Jonathan kept his head up to avoid the huddled mass of black on the floor. The sound of movement and clattering caught his attention. He turned and saw a cage on a counter, beside a steaming cauldron. Curiosity got the better of him. Inside the cage was a crow, its beak fastened with a rubber band. It threw itself against the wooden bars of its prison while staring at Jonathan, conveying a helplessness he could not resist. The closer he came to it, and to the nearby cauldron, the more he sick he felt. His nausea reached its zenith when he peeked at the bubbling concoction. Its greenish gray tint was almost as disgusting as its odious fumes. Pieces of swollen flesh surfaced and sank with herbs, feathers, and beaks. A human head appeared and disappeared in a convincing, accusatory instant that made him retch. It felt as though it was staring through him, crying. If he had been faster, he could have saved the poor victim from this fate, infinitely worse than mere death. The weight of guilt finally overwhelmed him, and he collapsed.

Chelsea had remained by the door, watching the fallen woman for any sign of life. At hearing Jonathan let out a sob she recognized all too well as the threnody for innocence, she ran to him. She did not need to look to where he was pointing to know what had done this to him: the woman had already uncovered every detail of her inhumane intention. For the rest of her life she would remember her fetid grin, and the way she licked her crusted lips as she described how the brain is most delicious when seasoned by its own hormones, secreted by prolonged fear and pain. But unlike Jonathan, she did not blame herself. She knew there was nothing that either of them could have done, and tried to convince him of this with soft words and an even softer embrace that, like a life ring, kept him from drowning in sorrow.

It took her a few minutes to get him back on his feet. Now that they had conquered both external and internal threats, it was time to leave. Another clatter alerted Jonathan of the life that still needed saving. He opened the crow's cage, removed the band around its beak, and set it free. They followed its hasty departure as far as the entrance, and then watched its evanescence into darkness. Jonathan hesitated to follow the directions given to him by the woman, but Chelsea assured him that it must have been true, if only because a lie might have given him reason to return. When asked why she did not make a sound to reveal herself; why she was willing to give up so easily, Chelsea dropped her gaze. Her brow furrowed and she muttered that the woman had promised to kill them both if she moved or made a sound. The silence effected by the grim revelation was broken by the cocking of a gun.

Fury flared in the two black pits that threatened to consume everything in the vicinity. Jonathan and Chelsea instinctively raised their hands in that universal gesture of placation. But the woman

No Bars and a Dead Battery

was beyond appeasement. Her intent scowl and the stillness with which she held the weapon guaranteed no mercy. She seethed a demand for Chelsea; Jonathan was given the choice to either leave or die. If it was not for the strain of discarding a corpse, she growled, he would already be dead. The gravity of her tone, mien, and bearing crushed any doubts of her veracity before they could emerge.

No sooner did the woman finish speaking than Chelsea told Jonathan to leave. He had not yet recovered from the shock of being held at gunpoint when this unexpected command stupefied him. Death appealed more than running away. A thousand gruesome deaths would not be worse than leaving her to the fiend—to the cauldron. Her readiness to sacrifice herself moved him to tears he tried to suppress, lest they be misattributed to fear. But there was no hiding anything from those severe eyes. The woman grinned at the cowardice she readily perceived and began to mock him, assuming his choice had already been made. She regarded him as a little boy, crying for a treat denied to him. Her scorn was palpable as she mentioned the money that was waiting just further ahead. All he had to do was turn around and walk, and his dream would come true. Every syllable she spat out fueled his rage until it grew into a conflagration, ready to engulf her even if it meant being incinerated himself. She would have time for one shot—the risk was worth the chance, however miniscule, of saving Chelsea. His dried lips parted for a final word or two to pass, but he was interrupted by a shrill squawk, followed by a scream.

Crow after crow darted at the shrieking woman. The gunshot was barely audible amid the cawing, unrelenting and tempestuous like the battle cry of a bloodthirsty army. They wanted to ask each other if they were hurt, but could not look away from the ruthless attack. One by one, countless ebony missiles struck their target. Their perfect coordination made retaliation impossible; their precision betokened festered hatred. At length, the shrieking waxed to an unspeakable pitch, and then there was only the squawking of birds.

When the assault was finally over, the victorious crows regrouped and rose to the sky as a caliginous cloud, taking the darkness with them. Jonathan and Chelsea received the leftover light of the setting sun that spilled over them as the radiance of an angel heralding deliverance. Bones and feathers were all that was left of the woman. The gun was buried somewhere in the abhorrent pile, but nothing could bring them to move any closer to it. In spite of everything, they both felt sorry for her. Neither of them spoke as they turned around and began to walk down the newly illuminated path to the end.

The silence went unbroken for the entire duration of their trek. There was so much to talk about, so much that had happened and so much more that could still happen—how could they begin to speak? They were alive, and that was all that mattered: nothing they could say would either add to or detract from this one simple yet most valuable truth so often taken for granted. The question of what the end even meant, if it was something to look forward to or dread, seemed irrelevant. Its inevitability reduced all preferences, expectations, and hopes to vanity. The only question worth considering was how that unknown but certain end would be faced. And with this question in mind they both quietly prepared themselves for anything. When they eventually came to a car in the middle of the road, an old El Dorado, they were too numb and tired to feel anything, let alone rejoice at finding the doors unlocked, the key in the ignition, and a note on the driver's seat.

You are the winner. Winner, not winners. One of them was supposed to be dead. They looked at each other, both inexpressibly grateful but unable to do more than blink and finish reading the

No Bars and a Dead Battery

note. A million dollars, the prize that was supposed to solve every problem, but which now meant nothing, was waiting in a locker. Attached to the note was a map and directions to a building in an unheard of town. Both of them loathed the idea of benefiting from the atrocity, but neither of them could deny that it was a lot of money. Splitting the burden of guilt would at least make it easier to carry for the rest of their lives. Somewhere along the barren road, they agreed that rejecting the million dollars would be a terrible offense to the memory of those who had died for it. But the heart is not so easily convinced as the mind, and they both hoped in vain that the other would recommend doing the difficult thing—the right thing.

It was well past night when they arrived in the small town, but there was nothing left to fear: they had already won. Fireworks and celebratory cheers welcomed them as soon as they reached the crowded streets. People were everywhere. The relief of being surrounded by so many witnesses, each one in possession of a phone that could be borrowed if needed, was distorted into disconcertment by the last line of the note. *We will be watching you.* They were not supposed to talk to anyone, or even look at them. Anxiety elongated the final minutes of the drive. What was everyone celebrating? Could it be that they knew about the contest? Was it possible for so many people to know and still cheer, as though it was the end of an innocuous soccer match? No. They preferred to believe—needed to believe—that it was all a coincidence. Neither of them could think of anything else as they parked the car and walked with their heads down into the specified, unmarked building.

No one was inside, but they could feel themselves being watched. There was no sound except for the pattering of their steps along the tiled floor. They dragged their feet to soften the maddening echo as they moved toward the end of the enclosure, expecting everything and nothing at once. The few steps separating them from the end were harder to take than all those that had led them there. Jonathan and Chelsea forgot to breathe once the locker was in sight. It was just like the noted stated despite their being together. Maybe whoever was watching had pitied them and decided to accept two winners. The time for conjectures had long passed—there was no point in finding excuses to hesitate. By the mere fact that they were there, the two were bound to complete the sale of their wailing consciences. They opened the locker.

Both their hands reached for the sealed envelope on which was written in golden ink, *Congratulations*. As if unable to do it without each other's help, they broke the seal together and took out the small piece of paper inside. *A Million Dollars*. There was no more than those three words, written in a cursive that seemed to laugh at every curve. They looked on the other side. *No one will believe you.* They looked in the locker again. A phone charger they had not noticed before begged them to challenge the audacious statement. They looked at each other, trying to figure out how to react.

The tense, silent stalemate was eventually broken by Chelsea. She chuckled, infecting Jonathan, who then invited her to guffaw with his own uncontrolled laugh. Relief, frustration, anger, gratitude, disbelief, terror, despair, and joy were all manifested in that laughter which neither of them could, nor wanted to stop. By the time they could speak again, both their phones were fully charged, and both their hearts were full of gladness to be alive. Everything else lost its significance in the light of that profound contentment.

They made their way through the crowd, and back to the El Dorado. And as they approached it, a crow flew directly over their heads and landed on the hood and then looked at them. They stood some distance away and watched the crow watching them. Another crow flew directly overhead and landed beside it. The first crow

No Bars and a Dead Battery

squawked and then both flew away. They watched the crows disappear, looked at each other, and then got in the El Dorado. Only one way to go this time, with five bars and full battery.

THEIR PLUMAGE STAINED WITH ASH

Jonathan Moyer

No coverage, not even one bar, the battery was dead anyway. It was still daytime, but there was an overcast and the sky had a perfectly even dullness, so there was no way to tell what time of day it was, much less which direction was north or south or anything else for that matter. A two-lane blacktop road snaked up into the distance and disappeared into some trees, or a forest if you wanted to get technical about it. It also snaked down toward some lumpy hills and disappeared there as well. What sounded like a two-stroke chainsaw could be heard in the distance, but it was impossible to tell whether it was up in the forest or down in the lumpy hills. This had been happening more often lately. Two different ways to go, with a dead battery and no bars, and nobody left to blame.

Ren sat back down in the car. The old El Dorado trapped the air inside like a greenhouse. It wrapped around her like a blanket, and her skin tingled as she began to sweat. The boxy car stank of two decades of dust collected in its upholstery, and the air conditioning was little more than a weak breath against the oppressive heat of July in the southern desert. The open door welcomed fresh air, but any cooling breeze must have missed the invitation. At least Ren had the shade the car offered. She turned the key in the ignition, her stomach turning over as she waited for the engine to do the same. To her relief, it sputtered to life. Her dad's college car was reliable, at least. She was trusting it to take her halfway across the country.

Ren had no idea where she was. She hadn't had a bar of reception

No Bars and a Dead Battery

since heading out of El Paso, and had yet to see a soul. It was time to take some chances. Ren urged the El Dorado in the direction of the forest and figured if there was going to be a chainsaw, it would be up there. She hoped there wasn't a clan of chainsaw murderers in these hills, but seeing as she had no way to find directions, she'd have to trust the chainsaw owners were of the non-murderous sort.

To call it a forest was generous— it was a stand of trees rising up out of the arid landscape. In fact, to call them trees was generous. They were ten, maybe twenty feet tall at best and no more than a few inches thick. The sparse growth made it easy to see the figures in among the trees, moving around with a couple of chainsaws between them. A pickup truck sat nearby, and two of the people loaded the trees into its bed. They all stopped and watched as her car rumbled up the path.

Ren stopped the El Dorado next to the truck and waved as she got out. Five people were working there, and for a moment, she wondered just what the fuck she had gotten herself into. Three were shirtless, one was wearing a white t-shirt and jeans, and one was wearing a vest with paint across his chest, arms, and face. It was what Ren imagined a person would wear to dress up as a Native American, if they had only ever had a Native American described to them by a person who had only seen pictures in history books. His eyes were painted with a black strip, and long lines went down his torso and arms. The three other shirtless men looked to this one as Ren walked closer. The only guy still wearing a shirt was staring straight at her. His face read a strange mixture of fear and relief, and Ren met his eyes briefly. She was more concerned about dealing with the Mad Max-looking guy first.

Fortunately for her, he spoke first and asked her what she was doing here. Ren waved her phone, explaining that it was almost dead and she needed directions to Tucson. She was driving to Los

285

Angeles, she said, and had gotten lost a little way back. Mad Max nodded and introduced himself as Jack Dawes. They had electricity and phone chargers back at Blackfeather, Jack said, and could send her on her way if she helped them with their festival.

Before Ren could agree, the guy in the t-shirt stepped forward and volunteered to ride back to Blackfeather with her. He was haggard. His t-shirt was transparent from sweat, and his face was sagging with fatigue. Despite this, he came to life to invite himself along in her car. As she looked at him, she saw the plea in his eyes. The guy needed help. She agreed.

Jack Dawes turned to the other three workers and ordered them back into the truck before climbing in himself. Three of them fit into the cabin, while one rode in back to keep the wood from falling out. Then they all pulled away, heading down towards the hills. White T-Shirt Guy came and leaned against the hood of her El Dorado, exhausted. He smiled weakly and asked her name— something she noticed Jack had never bothered to do. She told him it was Ren, and he shared that his was Andre. He put his chainsaw in the backseat of her car. It had no case and probably would get grease stains everywhere, but she reasoned that it wasn't the worst thing to have happened back there.

Before they got in the car, Ren pulled out a plastic water bottle and passed it to her new companion. It was half-full and hot, but he drained it in one long pull. The plastic collapsed and crinkled as he vacuumed air out alongside the water. Reaching into the trunk, she offered a pair of shorts as well. They were a bit small, being made for women, but he put them on anyway. With a cool breeze and a drink of water, Andre was already starting to look more alive. He sat down in the passenger seat with a deep sigh and told her he had been standing all day. Then he turned to her, fear in his eyes, and told her not to go to Blackfeather.

No Bars and a Dead Battery

Ren asked him what Blackfeather was, and he explained that this musician—he put emphasis on "musician", as if he didn't believe the claim—was holding a festival. The only problem, he explained, was that only a couple hundred people were attending and they were all batshit crazy. According to him, they believed the crows were nature spirits that could be appeased by a burnt offering. This would take the form of a giant pyramid built using all the wood they were collecting, which they would ignite tonight to complete the festival.

As for how Andre was out here, he was hitchhiking from El Paso to Los Angeles and was excited when he heard that she was going the same way. He begged her again to leave Blackfeather behind and carry on to Tucson. Ren hesitated. She looked at the anxious kid next to her and for a moment thought about going on, letting the strange guys from the woods have their little party without them. Andre did seem to have his head on his shoulders about all this. But her curiosity was piqued, and she couldn't help herself. Besides, she explained, she needed to recharge her phone if they were going to get to Tucson, and they had to return their chainsaw. Andre put his face in his hands, but acquiesced.

It wasn't too late to follow Jack's truck, and the breeze coming in the window as the car started rolling put her in a good mood. Ren began to talk about her trip coming out of West, Texas and her plans for Los Angeles. She was sick of the desert's heat and dryness, she said. She gestured out at the scrubland that spread in all directions. She was going to live by the ocean and swim every day.

That put Andre's spirits back up. He had been stuck in El Paso for all of his twenty years and, as he told her, was hitchhiking out to Los Angeles to be an actor. The last person to pick him up had been heading to Blackfeather and he figured that getting closer was better than staying still. Ren asked him if he had done a lot of acting up to now. He said he had never done a day in his life. She kept quiet. If she was moving out without a plan, then he could too, she reasoned to herself. Like he said, getting closer was better than staying still.

They drove down to a path where Jack had turned moments before. If Ren hadn't seen him go down it, she would have never noticed it at all. It wound into the hills to where she could see a stage in the distance. It looked so out of place, out in the desert like an ancient temple. The stage was elevated just a few feet off the ground, but was framed by metal scaffolding that held speakers up high. The struts glinted dimly in the sunlight. She took this time to look up and realize that, as the day went on, the cloud cover was burning off. It had to be early afternoon.

Jack's truck, the red paint now even more obscured by the dust, pulled around the side of the stage. Crowds of people sat in the hills. Those who came prepared sheltered under tents and umbrellas. Others had crawled under the stage for shade. From the lazy way they watched the El Dorado approach, Ren was reminded of the monitor lizards she had seen in nature documentaries. She hoped they didn't get hungry. Andre twisted to look at the hillside and muttered something about them being freaks.

He turned back in time to see the structure they were building. His jaw dropped. An enormous frame made of milled lumber rose twenty feet into the air. Ren realized she hadn't seen it before because its color matched that of the dusty ground beyond it. Around the base, Jack Dawes and his crew of marauders were lashing their gathered wood to the frame. Unlike the effigies she had seen at other festivals this one was simply a sort of pyramid. Actually, a lopsided dome was more accurate. Still, it was impressive how they had begun to put this together with what appeared to be minimal tools.

Jack flagged their car down. Ren parked behind him and stepped out of the car, wasting no time in asking for a charger. He waved his

No Bars and a Dead Battery

hand towards the pyramid as explanation. She would need to give him a couple hours of work, and a charged phone would be her pay. She was welcome, Jack added, to stay for the festival. Ren tried to gauge if he was hitting on her, and decided he was doing a bad job of it either way. Giving no answer, she took the hammer out of his hand and stepped towards the structure. Andre came up behind her and asked one more time that the two of them leave before the festival began. Ren shrugged at him. He was young, and hadn't had many chances to make crazy decisions. At worst, they'd wake up with bad hangovers and weird memories, she said. He didn't seem so sure.

Nevertheless, she and Andre got to work. It went slow with the sun beating down on them. Fresh-cut trees were not exactly the easiest building material to work with. They sprung back, rejected her attempts to nail or tie them down, and generally gave everyone a hard time. Andre and Ren worked together on the opposite side of the pyramid from Jack and his boys. From time to time, Ren would catch one of Jack's workers looking her way. They seemed to watch for too long, studying her as if she was a strange animal whose behaviors were unknown to them. Andre nudged her with an elbow. He said he noticed them looking too, but at him. Meanwhile, the lizards sat and watched, unmoving.

By the time the western sky had started to turn from blue to yellow, the builders had finished the pyramid. Ren sat atop a platform and watched the sky in the east start to darken. It was a veil being pulled back, exposing Earth to the deep void that surrounded it. This time always made her feel cold and distant. She never felt more alone than when the setting sun revealed the secret it was hiding. A voice floated up from below, which she recognized as belonging to Jack Dawes. He was mentioning someone, a guy who he said no one would miss. In her reverie, the thought passed through her mind like a distant cloud and left no trace.

A hand jolted her. Andre had climbed up to join her, and mentioned that she looked lost. Ren shook her head. Just daydreaming, she said. He smiled at her, and she smiled back. Having removed his soaked shirt and wearing only the pair of pink jogging shorts, he looked like he was just another partier here to have fun. Andre gestured to the ground, and they helped each other climb down.

On the stage behind them, a woman stepped up to the microphone. She called out to the crowd to gather. As they congregated before her, the woman introduced herself as Blackfeather. She certainly worked for the name. She was dressed in a massive Native American war bonnet, done entirely in black feathers. Other than a pair of tight, torn, black jeans it was her only clothing. The bonnet's two long strands draped over her pale shoulders and breasts, provided some semblance of modesty. Like Jack, she was also painted in long lines across her chest, face, and arms.

She welcomed everyone to her inaugural music festival, and promised it would be a desert romp that would never be forgotten. This festival, she announced, was a way to honor the spirits that once filled this land. These spirits now manifested as crows which would grace the festival if their sacrifice was deemed worthy. Blackfeather waved a hand at the pyramid behind her. The crowd stood without making a noise, and Ren felt tension building in the silence. With a sigh, she added that they would be serving dinner before the music started.

This earned the reaction Blackfeather was looking for. With a roar, the crowd erupted into cheers. Jack Dawes and his crew came out from either end to guide them towards the food. Long silver buffet trays sat on plastic tables—Ren thought of them as beer pong

No Bars and a Dead Battery

tables from college. From her vantage point close to the stage she could see piles of rice. They were mountains really, stretching off along the twenty feet or so of beer pong tables and stacked into buffet trays. Barely contained, the partiers were corralled into lines so the staffers could serve them reasonable portions.

Ren made her way into line between two slender people in fishnets and rainbow leotards. She pried a Dixie paper plate from the stack, snapping it apart from the one below it. She realized the whole setup, with the plastic tables and buffet utensils, reminded her of Sunday luncheons after church from when she was younger. When she turned to remark on this to Andre, he was gone.

A wave of panic washed over her, and her eyes darted across the crowds, looking for her new friend. Past the leotard-clad person behind her, she saw him. He was sandwiched between an anonymous person dressed like a disco ball (the outfit must have been sweltering) and a girl wearing a bikini and an enormous amount of glitter. His running shorts reflected the sunlight and glowed neon. To the apparent relief of the person behind her, she slid out of place and cut back in next to Andre. He smiled when he saw her. He was worried she had abandoned him.

Ren gave Andre a pat on the shoulder as they went down the line. She might be his only way out of here, but she was the only person who wanted to be here less than her. She wasn't going to give up a connection to sanity that easily. Andre visibly relaxed and laughed in agreement. The two went down the line, allowing the half-dressed staffers to pile their plates with rice. Ren realized it wasn't just rice, however. It was flecked with little pieces of what she realized were mushrooms. Most of them appeared to be button mushrooms, but others were wrinkly and had a golden-brown color.

She picked one out and nibbled it. It was slightly chewy, and had little flavor beyond the salt they had used to season the dish. Ren shrugged. She told Andre it wasn't bad, but she didn't care for mushrooms. He pinched one out of his dish and nibbled it, mentioning he had never seen one like it before. The two of them carried on through the line, which dispersed quickly once all the attendants had received their bland portions.

Ren and Andre sat on the hood of the El Dorado as the sky grew darker. Overhead the minute lights of stars began to blink to life. After a while of picking at her dinner Ren set the plate aside with most of the mushrooms picked out. She turned to Andre, gesturing mildly with her plastic fork, and remarked that she could only eat so much of the bland meal. He set his down in agreement, asking if she had anything else. Ren hopped off the car and opened the door to the backseat. She rummaged around in the back for a moment until she found what she was looking for, and stopped still for a moment. The orange overhead light made her feel a little safer. Incandescent lights always did on summer evenings like these, when it felt like nothing was holding you back from falling into the sky.

With the bag of beef jerky in hand, she returned to the hood of the car and passed it to her newest friend. The change of texture and flavor settled her stomach. Andre mentioned that he was glad she had it, and he felt much more satiated now. They continued to chew their jerky in silence as the dome of night slowly spun overhead. The Milky Way blossomed above them, a flowering branch among the darkness.

Suddenly Ren was filled with a sensation she had never known looking at the night sky. It was no longer an expanse, an abyss into which she could fall, but rich and deep like a dense forest. The universe teemed and glowed with possibility. Purples and oranges danced around the edges of the Milky Way and Ren was filled with the sense that everything was going to be all right. Her life in Los Angeles was going to work out but, if it didn't, she would find her

No Bars and a Dead Battery

way. She began to reach a hand out to the welcoming galaxy above her, feeling the cool night air between her fingers.

The lights of the stage snapped to life, casting a glare across the night sky and into Ren's eyes, temporarily blinding her. The crowd screamed in joy. She brought her hand back from where she reached out and shielded her eyes. At the same time, a harsh caw met her ears and a crow flew low over her head. It landed on the dirt in front of the El Dorado and looked at the two of them with an inquisitive, intelligent eye. Ren stared at it, and for a moment felt like the crow was about to speak to her.

With a booming voice that echoed across the desert, Blackfeather called out to the crowd. She welcomed them to the real party, and without any further interlude began to blast electronic dance music. The crowd began to scream with delight, and Ren watched as the lizards came to life. The whole crowd, small though it was, writhed in the laser lights coming off the stage. With their hands in the air, their bodies pulsed in time with the hypnotic music. Overhead, a few crows had ignored the noise and perched on the scaffolding. Ren turned to Andre to mention how unaffected the birds seemed, but he couldn't hear her. After a few tries, she took his arm. Sensation tingled down from her fingertips, a mix of friction and warmth that coursed straight into her body and sent a wave of pleasure into her core.

She looked at her arm confused, and Andre did the same, realizing they had both felt the sudden sensation. Ren dragged her fingertips across Andre's forearm. Once again, the feeling of skin on skin gave them both shivers. Andre started to reach out to her, and she felt a slight shake of anticipation.

A crow calling—two, actually—broke through the daze. The black birds were sitting in the headlights of the car watching them, and Ren could see dozens of the crows had come to roost on the

strange pyramid and the scaffolding on set. The crowd reached up
and cheered when they saw Blackfeather, who was dancing on stage,
pointing up towards the birds.

Head cleared, Ren gestured to the rave and suggested they join.
Andre seemed to see the stage for the first time, but his eyes flitted
back to Ren for just a moment before he agreed. The two of them
scooted off the hood of the El Dorado and made their way over to
the pounding, flashing festival. Before they did, Ren crossed to one
of the generators, where one of Jack's boys finally supplied her with
a phone charger. She left the phone slightly out of sight behind the
generator, then took Andre's hand and led him away. Approaching
from behind the stage, they easily slid into the front of the crowd as
Blackfeather played her set.

Up on stage, Blackfeather was gyrating and twisting to the
pulsating music. The tails of her headdress flailed wildly, exposing
her to the crowd, although no one seemed to mind. Ren fell into the
groove of the music, waving her hands in the air and relishing the
sensations all around her. The bodies pushing against her felt like
the embrace of friends, the cool desert night counteracted the heat
pressing around her, and the music in her ears began to take her far
away from the festival. She swayed to the music until time slipped
away from her, and the stars overhead rotated without her noticing.

An elbow in the back shuddered her. Ren turned to look. One of
Jack Dawes's shirtless workers was standing there. She watched as
he pushed his way towards the edge of the crowd. As Ren turned
back to the stage, the beat receded into nothing. A quiet fell over
the crowd as Blackfeather held her hands out, grinning. Sweat
coated her body, dripped down her arms and covered the stage
around her bare feet. Once more, she welcomed the crowd to the
first Blackfeather festival and raised her arms high. With a cheer
from the gathered crowd, she pointed to the crows perched high in

the scaffolding and introduced her guests of honor. Then, she stepped aside to offer the culmination of the night—the lighting of the pyramid.

To either side, Jack Dawes and his employees pulled aside the metal barricades and encouraged the crowd to surround the structure. Ren turned to Andre, only to realize he was no longer there. A shiver pulsed down her body, and she felt sick to her stomach. The music, the festival, and the crowd around her no longer felt so friendly. Her experience of love and acceptance bottomed out like she had a plug pulled in her belly. Ren started to crane her neck as she was pulled along by the tide of the crowd. The partygoers spread around the stage and the pyramid beyond, and Blackfeather began playing the music anew.

On this musical cue, there was a spark and an orange glow from the base of the pyramid. The crowd began to scream so loud as to drown out the music. Ren looked back at the stage, and noticed the crows were fewer. They now watched the growing bonfire, rather than the gathered crowd. The smell of smoke wafted over them. From where she stood, Ren could see small piles of scraps—branches from the woods, discarded paper plates—starting to catch and burn around the base of the rickety structure. As the embers became flames, Ren traced the smoke trails to the top of the pyramid, where she saw something had been lashed to the top. For a moment, she stared at it, lit only barely orange from below, and wondered what it could be. A spotlight from the stage flashed over the figure on top, and she saw a glimpse of a familiar neon pink. The pyramid was not the only burnt offering being made tonight.

At that moment, Blackfeather's modulated voice began to wail over the speakers, and the crowd began to pulse and sway, shifting Ren with it. She tried to focus on Andre atop the pyramid, but couldn't see him anymore. Without another thought she turned and fought her way through the rocking crowd. To Ren, it felt like she was moving through a dream. Her arms and legs didn't want to move like they should, and smoke was filling the air, obscuring her vision. Strange faces, lit by pulses of colorful lights, grinned out at her through the smoke and throbbed with the alien beat.

She was momentarily dazzled by one of the disco ball-headed dancers, when someone grabbed her. Ren jumped. It was one of the rainbow-dressed partiers from earlier. They asked if she was okay, and the two of them locked eyes. Ren took a deep breath and a swig from the offered bottle. The water refreshed her parched mouth and cleared her head. She smiled, and thanked them for their concern. A friendly face had shaken her out of her dreamy confusion, and the beat from Blackfeather's music now drove her onward.

Ren broke through the crowd, taking a quick gasp of clear air, and ran to the El Dorado. She stopped short when she saw the plates of unfinished food still on the hood. The unfamiliar mushrooms, which she had only eaten half of, made her remember the strange tingling she had felt when she touched Andre. Blackfeather's plan was suddenly clear. In the El Dorado, Andre's chainsaw rested on the backseat. She grabbed it and started to head back, but remembered she needed her phone if they were going to make a quick escape. The time told her she had been dancing for four hours—four hours which had felt like forty-five minutes. Ren pocketed her phone and sprinted back to the throng.

She stopped at the edge and tapped one partier on the shoulder. Gesturing with the chainsaw, she mentioned that she needed to get to the center. Whether or not he heard her, she was unsure, but he saw the chainsaw and stepped aside while grabbing another dancer and pulling them. The dancers began to part, eyes turned to Ren, as the light from stage began to strobe. In stop motion, the waves of people spread to let her through, and she ran down the parted path

No Bars and a Dead Battery

like a zoetrope's figure.

The pyramid rose up in front of her, ringed in orange flames. They had already started to lick up the outer frame, sending glowing spider webs up the scavenged wood. Andre was squirming at the top, although from a distance his movement could have been mistaken for a trick of the smoke and firelight. At the clearing surrounding the pyramid, Ren searched the crowd. Jack and his goons were at odd intervals around the edge, alternately watching the crowd to make sure no one got too close. She wouldn't be able to saw down the pyramid where they could see. Ren inched her way around to where one of the shirtless guys was watching Blackfeather's performance, entranced. In a moment, the smoke billowed towards him, blocking him from sight, and she took a deep breath to ready herself. Clutching the chainsaw tight, she ran and jumped over the fire, between the outer wooden beams of the pyramid and into its innards.

The fire was spreading into the center of the pyramid, filling the structure with smoke. Ren tried to breathe, but was choked and fell to her knees, coughing. Down there, at least, there was a little more room to breathe. Crouching and working quickly to escape burning alive, she set the chainsaw down and began to crank it. The first pull met no resistance, and neither did the second. Ren cursed, and used her whole body to pull the cord. A grumble from the chainsaw gave her the strength she needed, and two more pulls urged the motor to life.

In the flickering light of the space, it was nearly impossible to see. Wooden struts loomed out of the swirling smoke like a forest in fog. Ren wracked her brains to remember the layout of the structure she had helped build only hours before, but the cocktail of exhaustion, smoke, and mushrooms blocked it. She hefted the chainsaw and began to cut through the first post she saw. Flying sawdust did little to help her visibility, and when she cut through the pyramid seemed unfazed. They had built it sturdier than she thought.

With one hand to hold the chainsaw and one to pull her through the smoke, Ren made her way to the next post. She jerked her hand back when she grabbed it. It was burning hot. Though it hadn't caught fire yet, it could at any moment. Keeping her distance, she sawed through this one as well. Now the pyramid seemed to shift, just barely. Heartened by this slight progress, she pressed on. One by one, the beams fell to her chainsaw, and the pyramid began to rock as she removed its supports from underneath it. Finally, she made it to the first post again. The space where she had cut it was smoking and turning black. Even though she had cut all of the posts, the pyramid was still standing.

Frantically, Ren dug the chainsaw into the central column, made of five trees bound together to support the main structure. The chain had no more than bit into the first tree than the chainsaw sputtered and died. Out of gas. Ren tossed it aside and looked up. Flames had made their way up to the second tier and were starting to singe Andre's toes. With nothing left to do, she threw herself at the column. The whole pyramid rocked, sending up a cry from the crowd. She did it again, hearing the column groan. The whole weight of the structure was resting on it, and it rocked when she had hit it.

With one final push, Ren threw herself at the column. The entire pyramid's momentum strained against it, and the wood cracked under the stress. It could no longer hold up the weight alone, and toppled with a splintering crash to the ground. The crowd let out a gasp, then an ear-splitting cheer. Before the smoke could clear, Ren had grabbed Andre from the pile and hauled him to his feet. The whole festival had their eyes on them, and Ren stared back. From the corner of her eye, she saw Jack Dawes and his boys start moving

No Bars and a Dead Battery

towards them. Looking back at the waiting crowd, she lifted her arms in victory, and the partiers rushed in to celebrate. Ren held Andre tight against the surge, and began to push through. She'd had more than enough, and was sure Andre had too.

They made their way through the crowd, and back to the El Dorado. And as they approached it, a crow flew directly over their heads and landed on the hood and then looked at them. They stood some distance away and watched the crow watching them. Another crow flew directly overhead and landed beside it. The first crow squawked and then both flew away. They watched the crows disappear, looked at each other, and then got in the El Dorado. Only one way to go this time, with five bars and full battery.

IN THE SHOE TREE

Syche Phillips

No coverage, not even one bar, the battery was dead anyway. It was still daytime, but it was overcast and the sky had a perfectly even dullness, so there was no way to tell what time of day it was, much less which direction was north or south or anything else for that matter. A two-lane blacktop road snaked up into the distance and disappeared into some trees, or a forest if you wanted to get technical about it. It also snaked down toward some lumpy hills and disappeared there as well. What sounded like a two-stroke chainsaw could be heard in the distance, but it was impossible to tell whether it was up in the forest or down in the lumpy hills. This had been happening more often lately. Two different ways to go, with a dead battery and no bars, and nobody left to blame.

Marti didn't want to leave the El Dorado sitting out on the road, but she didn't know what else to do. Despite the clouds, the air was hot, and the humidity pressed down on her, full and heavy. She looked through the car, trying to decide what was worth carrying with her, and what she might find useful. She filled a tote bag with two half empty water bottles that had been rolling around in the backseat, a granola bar, a thin cardigan sweater, and a pen and crumpled paper.

If she was a kid, she would have done *eeny meany miny moe* to decide which direction she should set out. If she was a more competent adult, she would have been paying attention to the road and would have known more about the landscape she had just

No Bars and a Dead Battery

driven through—like whether there had been any sort of house or building or road leading off to a town. But—better admit it now, whether she liked it or not—she was still a little bit drunk, and she had been focusing on keeping the car between the lines, and hadn't been studying the countryside.

She looked up the road, and then down once more, and then picked down, because walking uphill was more than she could face. Her head was beginning to pound, and after a few steps she turned around and went back to the car, looking through the detritus in the center console one last time for a spare travel pack of aspirin. She found one, dry-swallowed the two pills inside, and walked away from the car.

As she walked, Marti realized that the road was misleading. It had looked like a half mile, maybe, to the hills she had seen. But as far as she walked, she didn't seem to be getting any closer to them. She didn't know if it the sprawling landscape was deceptive, or if she was drunker than she had originally thought.

By the time she got to the first slight incline, it was getting darker. The clouds still covered the sky, but the gray was deepening, and the heat was relaxing, slipping off her like a heavy satin shawl. A breeze picked up and her skin drank it in. She stopped and took a drink of water, painfully aware that she didn't have much between the two bottles.

She crested the first hill and looked back, but there was no way to pick out the car where she had left it. Not for the first time today, she thought about her choice back there—picking between the two different directions—and wondered if she'd chosen correctly. Then she turned and followed the road around a bend.

A large tree swelled up in front of her, dripping with moss and dead leaves. There were huge nests built up in the forks of branches, balls of sticks and debris. As she looked, she saw a large black wing extend out of one of the nests, and then fold itself back up. She moved closer to the tree, and saw in the fading daylight that some of the decorations on the tree weren't actually leaves at all, but shoes. Pairs of shoes tied together by the laces and flung into this tree, out in the middle of nowhere.

Now that she looked more closely, she could see tire tracks in the dirt here, as if someone (or many *someones*) had pulled over in the mud, gotten out, hurled their shoes up into the branches over and over until they found purchase, and then turned around and driven back the way they had come. That thought reassured her—there must be a town somewhere nearby.

She tugged experimentally at a shoe hanging on a low branch, and found that the laces were so tangled around the tree that it didn't move an inch. She stood below the branches and looked up, gazing at so many soles she couldn't begin to count them all.

A rustling, and then a flapping, came from one of the nests as a large black crow took off, out into the twilight, without sparing Marti a second glance. She watched it disappear into the gray sky, a black speck in nothingness.

For a second, Marti was overcome by a desire to take off her own shoes and hurl them into the tree. But she was wearing slip on boots with no laces, and there was no way they would stick in the branches. She shook her head to clear it—and reminded herself that she also needed her shoes. For walking. To find a safe place and someone who could help her.

But even as she was forming the thought that she needed to keep moving down the road—nightfall was approaching more rapidly now—she found herself picking her way closer to the tree trunk, stepping over tall humped roots. She ran her fingers over the tree's bark, thick and twisted, a layer of armor. She knew that others had felt the same way about the tree—wanting to triumph over it,

No Bars and a Dead Battery

exercise control, show their superior power as humans over nature—because there were decades of carvings etched into the trunk. She ran her fingers over the words and symbols, wondering what they all meant, who had needed to leave them here. One phrase stood out to her, whether because of its size or the depth the letters had been carved, or because it seemed newer than the others. *They're souls*, the graffiti said, and Marti thought, *The shoes?* She was wrong but how was she to know? The crows called to each other in the branches.

Marti shivered and pulled her sweater from her tote bag, sliding it up her bare, goose-bumped arms. The cotton was thin, but did make her feel warmer and a little safer, more secure. She was reaching back toward the tree trunk when she heard scratching through the tall grass behind her, and she whirled around.

A boy was making his way up the bank from the creek that ran behind the tree. He looked up and saw Marti, and looked alarmed, but just for a moment. Marti waved to him, smiling, looking as friendly as she could. She knew she would be better equipped to put the boy at ease if she was able to speak, but that was one trick she had never learned. She tried some sign language with the boy, who looked blankly at her. Marti assumed he didn't recognize what she was doing as communication. She went back to smiling, trying to put him at ease. She turned back to the tree.

Suddenly the boy was there at her side. He looked up at her, watching her run her fingers across the tree. He reached up and did the same, imitating her, looking at her for approval. His face and hands were dirty and grass-stained, and his feet were bare. *He must have walked here from somewhere nearby*, Marti thought, but she had no way of asking him where he lived or if he could help her. She pulled out the note she kept handy in her pocket, the one giving her name and saying she didn't speak, but the boy just glanced at it and then went back to picking at the bark.

He got a fingernail under one chunk of bark, and pulled. The piece came off in a long strip, longer than Marti would have expected. It popped off with a surprisingly satisfying crack. He studied the moss that grew on it, the back suddenly exposed to the light, and then tossed the entire thing out into the grass, over the bank. Marti heard it splat against water. She peered through the tall grass and saw the low glimmer of a slow creek. The crows cawed disapprovingly above them.

Marti realized that once the sky had darkened completely, it wouldn't be safe for her to be walking around out here, in the unfamiliar landscape. She could have slipped down the bank and fallen into the creek, which might be a foot deep, or ten feet. She could hit her head on a rock. She could twist her ankle. Without knowing where she was and without the ability to call out for help, she could die out here.

She faced the boy again, determined that he would help her. He must have a family out here; or, if somehow he was living on his own, he must have shelter. If she could only ask him to share it with her. She waved to him to get his attention, but he was staring past her now, back where the creek was.

She felt more than heard a noise from the creek bed, a shuddering intake of air, as if something very, very large was crouched down there, trying to breathe quietly. Something was listening back to her, waiting to see what she was going to do, if she was going to strike out on her own, away from the boy, become an easy target.

She couldn't bring herself to turn her head, afraid that she would see one great eye looking back at her over the edge of the ridge. Instead, she stared at the boy, who was slowly raising one hand, palm out, toward her. She heard a branch crack behind her and then

No Bars and a Dead Battery

a shifting, maybe in the dirt, maybe in the trees, maybe in the water itself.

In the shadows of the tree, Marti saw a light issue from the boy's raised palm, and push itself out, as if pressing out through a membrane. The light swept past her, enveloping her, and she felt both calmed and pleasantly tingly. The light pushed to the edge of the ridge, and she heard whatever was down there move away, quickly. She could look now: it was too dark to see anything, but she felt the air rush back in to the space that had been occupied by whatever was stalking her.

The boy beckoned to her and she moved closer to him, and he withdrew the light with her so that it tightened in around them. She realized then that the crows from the branches were swooping down, diving close to the light although not penetrating it. They seemed to be drawn to it even though they couldn't enter it.

The boy covered his eyes with his hand and gestured for her to do the same. She obeyed him, and she heard him take a deep breath, and then, even behind her covered eyes, there was a flash so blinding that she saw stars—and then they were back in darkness. When she opened her eyes, the ground was littered with dazed crows. Their wings twitched and their tarry eyes glinted at her as if this was her fault. In a moment, they began standing up and hopping away, looking back at her, as if they were shaking it off. Within a minute all the crows were tucked safely back in their nests, murmuring softly to each other, and the only movement left in the tree was the gentle swaying of the shoes on their laces.

Marti was grateful to him. She shook out her tote bag onto the ground, found the granola bar from her glove box, and unwrapped it. She held it out to him, and he broke off a piece and then pushed her hand back toward her. They sat on the ground and ate together, sharing the water from one of her bottles. Afterward, he scraped together a pile of leaves and pushed it toward her, then made one for himself. He laid his head down on the leaves, hands behind his head, looking up at her.

She couldn't see much, but she realized she could see him, because of a faint light that was constantly emanating from his skin. He was like a night light, keeping the crows and the scary things at bay. She smiled at him, and he smiled hesitantly back. It had never occurred to her to think about having her own kids, but she liked this one.

From habit, she pulled her phone from her pocket. She didn't remember that it had been dead until she hit the home button...and the screen lit up. She sat up in surprise. The battery icon said 34%, when she was positive that it had been completely dead when she left her car. Of course it had been. She'd watched the battery trickle away, counting down the last 5%, hoping against hope she would get to a town before it died. So how was it now charging itself?

The boy had propped himself up on one elbow and was looking at the phone curiously. She held it out to him, and he brought it close to his eyes. He didn't have any of the child's normal impulse to swipe or click, and Marti thought he must not have seen a phone like this before.

He handed it back to her, and she noticed the battery now read 36%. How was it charging itself? As she held it, it fell back down another percentage. She thought of something, something crazy, but why not, and she pressed it back into his hands, keeping the screen where she could see it. In a few minutes, the battery had climbed eight percent, and she realized it was the boy who was charging it.

That blast of light must have started it, she thought, and she looked back at the screen to see if she had any bars of service, but she must have been in a—*Don't think it, Marti,* she admonished herself—dead zone.

No Bars and a Dead Battery

Still, battery was something, and she felt much more positive about her chances of finding help tomorrow. She was almost cheerful enough to sleep, and she laid back on her leaf pillow once more. She was drifting off when she realized the boy was shaking her arm, and she sat up.

That feeling was back, the full feeling in the air, the sense that something was watching—no, stalking her. She couldn't tell this time the direction it was coming from. She looked at the boy for help, but he also looked confused and scared, like he knew something was wrong but didn't know how to handle it this time. She felt a sudden fierce need to protect him.

She realized then that the crows were completely silent. She looked up, and saw only the soles of a thousand old shoes, hanging from their final resting place. The laces whispered together as they swayed gently. The boy was looking up too, and she felt like he was pulsing the faint light that came from him, pushing it outward into the branches to try to see further.

Suddenly a crow dive-bombed them, swooping so close she actually gasped out loud. Its wings brushed her head and she felt one talon scrape across her shoulder. She rubbed the spot as if she could erase its touch. The boy ducked the crow with a fluid grace that surprised her.

Another crow, and another. They were after the boy, not after her, and she realized in a moment they were after the phone. Some of his power had been poured into the phone, and they wanted it. Once she realized what they were after, she felt their want, sensed them craving the phone and what it contained.

They were coming faster now, and she was getting pushed away from the boy. She felt sure that at any moment they were going to scoop him up and carry him away from her forever. She began to fight through the crows, feeling their talons scratch her arms and face, feeling their musty wings brush across her cheeks. She felt like she might be sick.

The same light that had protected her from the thing in the creek blazed outward from the center of the crows again, blinding her momentarily and pushing her back onto the ground. Her head pulsed, and she felt each beat of her heart rush the blood through her temples. When she was able to open her eyes again, the crows had retreated and the boy was huddled on the ground, his light again reduced to a dim glow.

She crawled to him and cradled him in her lap, feeling his hot skin begin to cool in the night air. The phone was clutched in his hand and the battery was now almost full. His eyes were half lidded, and his cheeks flushed, but he still shivered in her arms.

Marti didn't want to stay there any longer—didn't want to risk the crows or the thing in the creek (or were they one and the same?) coming back for them, especially when the boy was so weak. She stood, still holding him (he was so light), and then kicked their piles of leaves apart, as if to not leave any sign of their being there. Then she made her way carefully over the great roots of the shoe tree, back onto the blacktop road that wound through the hills. Even in his state, he cast enough light in front of her that she could follow the road, and in the east, an orange moon was rising over the hills.

As they got further from the tree, she felt her spirits lift. The boy seemed to breathe easier, relaxing some of the tension in his small body. At the same time, she felt like he was gaining weight, although she couldn't tell whether that was strength coming back into him or her arms just getting tired. After a few minutes, he opened his eyes and smiled at her, then turned and gazed at the moon, which had broken over the hills.

Marti also rose over the final hill, and stood on the open ground now. It would be an uphill climb to the car from here, but she did

No Bars and a Dead Battery

feel better being away from the shoe tree. The shoes had felt so whimsical when she first saw them, but she now felt a humming discomfort about them, an eerie sense they didn't belong there… and they didn't want to be there.

The boy struggled to be set down and she gladly put him on his feet. Together they began to walk up the long, slow slope to where she knew she'd left the El Dorado. It seemed like a lifetime ago. There was no reason to expect that the car would be miraculously fixed—but she also had an idea that, like he did with the phone, the boy might be able to help with the car.

And what happens after that? she thought. She was in no state to be taking in an orphan, even one as miraculous as the boy was. She didn't even have a home herself, much less anything to offer a child. But she had an idea that he would gladly accept her company even if that was the only thing she could give him.

They trudged up the hill together, not speaking. It had been years since Marti had felt the need to break a silence with someone, but this was different somehow. Even without speaking, she felt like they were communicating, sharing their thoughts and emotions in a kind of conversation.

A rush of wind passed overhead, and the boy flinched. Marti looked up and saw a crow, a big one, circling in the moonlight. It seemed to travel with them in lazy loops, tracking them up the hill. She didn't like the breeze that came from its ragged wings each time it swooped lower toward them. The boy pressed himself into her side and they both picked up their speed.

The crow uttered a low caw and Marti heard another one answer it, from behind them—but not too far back. She turned her head quickly and scanned the dark sky, picking out three—no, four— more shadows flying their way. The boy groped for her hand and she took it firmly, trying to reassure him as well as herself.

The car was in view now, still parked on the side of the road, and she could hardly believe that it had been just earlier that day that she'd left it there. It looked older than she remembered, dust-covered and sagging, and she thought of the thousands of miles she'd covered in the car. *Not much more to go now,* she thought to herself, *so please let it work.*

The boy seemed to know what she was asking, and he was ignoring the crows now, directing his attention toward the car. She could feel him pushing at it, feel a flow of something from him toward the car. She let go of his hand so he could concentrate. As she watched, the car seemed to sit up straighter, to shed some of its dirt, to look more real. They had almost reached it now, and she was ignoring the flock of crows circling them, hoping against hope that they would be able to reach the car and disappear.

The boy suddenly slumped where he stood, and she turned back to him. He looked at her and nodded, and she understood. He was going to get them out of there. She took her keys from her pocket and they were shiny, brighter than everything else around them. The boy looked triumphantly back at the birds, who were swooping ever closer. He glowed a little brighter for a moment and they hesitated in their flight, seemed to retreat. Marti realized the crows were surrounding them, on the ground, in the air, filling the night with the musty smell of dusty wings.

They made their way through the crowd, and back to the El Dorado. And as they approached it, a crow flew directly over their heads and landed on the hood and then looked at them. They stood some distance away and watched the crow watching them. Another crow flew directly overhead and landed beside it. The first crow squawked and then both flew away. They watched the crows disappear, looked at each other, and then got in the El Dorado. Only one way to go this time, with five bars and full battery.

CUB

Andrea Poniers

No coverage, not even one bar, the battery was dead anyway. It was still daytime, but there was an overcast and the sky had a perfectly even dullness, so there was no way to tell what time of day it was, much less which direction was north or south or anything else for that matter. A two-lane blacktop road snaked up into the distance and disappeared into some trees, or a forest if you wanted to get technical about it. It also snaked down toward some lumpy hills and disappeared there as well. What sounded like a two-stroke chainsaw could be heard in the distance, but it was impossible to tell whether it was up in the forest or down in the lumpy hills. This had been happening more often lately. Two different ways to go, with a dead battery and no bars, and nobody left to blame.

Catherine corrected herself: there is always someone to blame. She sat on her suitcase, watching her ankle swell by the minute. The drone of the chainsaw tapped into a memory that was lodged close to the surface, just past skin deep, where slivers find a resting place. The whirr and whine of tools in her father's workshop had been her lullabies, the rhythms of her childhood. Until they weren't. Yes, Catherine thought again; there's always someone to blame.

The young sheriff's deputy let her know that her car would be towed to a local repair shop later that day and reminded her to call her insurance company when she had cell coverage again. He figured the whole thing should be settled quickly since the other driver had been ticketed. When Catherine refused medical attention for the fifth time, he nodded and said he'd pick up a pair of crutches at Walmart before dropping her off in town. She breathed deeply as she got ready to stand on her tender ankle, pushing up against her suitcase and raising the handle for support. The shiny deputy reached for her backpack and shot her a look of what-the-hell? before hefting it to his shoulder. She shrugged an apology as she hobbled toward his SUV, knowing better than anyone the true weight of the past. Pausing before getting in the vehicle, she examined the road. Downhill looked so easy and inviting, but that had never been her fate and she didn't have any better feeling about the days ahead. It was uphill, toward Knollburg.

Catherine had never spent time in the upper Midwest but Knollburg fit her small-town stereotype. The downtown was four blocks square, surrounded by a lattice of modest residential streets, and a tangential highway for the indispensable big box stores and chain restaurants. The deputy stopped in front of a mom-and-pop motel called the Highwayman that anchored one end of the downtown main street and stayed with her until he heard her turn the lock on the door of her musty room.

Lowering herself to the stiff mattress, Catherine eased a pillow under her foot and quickly fell into a fitful sleep, startling every few minutes to the muscle memory of the car crash that was only hours behind her. She finally gave up on sleep and tugged at her suitcase, which the deputy had left on the other side of the bed. Pushing aside her few folded clothes, Catherine retrieved a worn manila envelope, pulled off the tape that was sealing it shut and held the envelope upside down, letting a half dozen or so printed pages glide to the quilted bedspread. She arranged these articles by date, the earliest ones being the briefest, as if the facts accumulated every day to add weight to the evidence against her father.

The first was a posting she had seen online about a dramatic

No Bars and a Dead Battery

rescue in a far-off state, the kind of feel-good story that ricochets around social media in a futile attempt to balance out its depressing bulk. Catherine would have been blind to the story if not for the photo of the rescuer that was posted right next to the photo of the rescued, a 13-year-old girl, pulled from a flaming car where her older brother had perished. The rescuer, who also perished, was the man who had been her father.

Catherine picked up that first online article and examined his face, as if she would find something new since the last time. Dust had settled on his hair and mustache over the years, but his reluctant smile was unchanged. Where had the photo come from? Who knew him now? A new family? Friends? She had followed the online stories from the local newspaper, which lasted less than a week, then faded. None of the articles told her anything about her father, as if he had no life, no history beyond this one heroic act. At least no history since he vanished from their family home without a word nearly twenty years ago.

Catherine's mother tested theories over the years, making up stories of what might have happened but never settling on any one of them, as if hope lay in keeping the options open. She died knowing nothing more than the day she raced through the house and yard screaming his name. Catherine wove a story of her own when she was a kid, sure her father had met an extraordinary death, maybe a drowning or an explosion, with no remains left to identify him. As a teenager, she branded him a worthless coward. By the time she read about the rescue, she had no opinion, having decided to delete this defining narrative of her life. The photo and newspaper articles rebooted the old anger. When her internet searches yielded nothing more, she rode her rage to Knollburg.

In the early afternoon, Catherine crutched her way down the main street to the local pharmacy, and then sank into the bench outside the shop, opening a bottle of water and downing a handful of anti-inflammatories. She turned to look in the window of the shop behind her with its grab-bag display of office supplies, sunscreen, reading glasses, drain cleaner, and hand-sized china figures of girls painted in outfits to match each month of the year. Automatically, she searched for November and turned back to the street.

The first thing she learned about Knollburg is that everyone says hello to strangers. On the downtown sidewalks, people entered the stores or offices in ones or twos and no one seemed to be in a hurry. Catherine wondered if her father had walked these streets, worked in one of these businesses. She watched a man talking on his phone outside of a florist shop. Was he a friend of her father? A business associate? Did her father have a lover, a bigamous wife? Could that redhead on the bicycle be his daughter? The thought that Catherine might have been replaced shut down the questions.

A bell tinkled over her shoulder and a shadow fell over her lap. She looked up at the man leaving the pharmacy, who asked if she needed help with anything, gesturing to the crutches. Catherine shook her head and he touched his index finger to the bill of his Minnesota Twins ball cap before walking on.

Watching him fade down the street, Catherine knew she should have talked with him, taking any chance to find connections to her father. She fell into a mental reading of the newspaper articles, scouring them again, making sure there was nothing she had missed. Her thinking was interrupted by a trio of crows resting on the roof of the building across the street. She nodded to them. You're right; no time to waste.

The office of the *Knollburg Herald* was two short and painful blocks from the pharmacy. Seeing Catherine struggle, a passerby rushed to open the heavy wooden door. The receptionist gestured toward a seat and perched next to her, ready to help. Catherine pulled out the clippings, surprised to see the paper shaking in her hands. The receptionist's eager expression faded. She so wished she could connect Catherine to the reporter but he had moved on to Billings right after the rescue, wasn't it a miracle? She wondered if the county death records might help? Or the funeral director? The girl's eyes shone with apology and hope, but Catherine doubted that information about her father's death could illuminate his life. She forced herself to stand on her crutches and moved on.

Catherine passed the county courthouse, which was now a museum, and hobbled another two blocks down a side street to track down the current county offices, a building that looked like conjoined railroad cars. The clerk in the Vital Records office had been in her job too long, skillfully deflecting Catherine's request for her father's death certificate, even after demanding a ream of completed forms and Catherine's own birth certificate as proof of ownership. Finally, shuffling into an office behind the counter, the clerk returned without another word and shoved a copy of the legal document across the counter. Catherine dropped to a metal bench in the hallway and began reading.

His name was full and formal and his birthdate was correct, in November, just a week after hers. Although the newspaper had reported he was declared dead at the scene, the place of death was listed as the county hospital. The cause of death was sanitized, with none of the drama reported in the newspaper. The informant was a sheriff's deputy, maybe the same one who had helped her today, whose name she couldn't remember. The typed words in the rest of the boxes were of no help. No address. No next of kin. But still, this statement of death proved that her father had lived after walking out of their home.

Catherine rose and made her way through the string of boxcars until she found the Registrar of Deeds. This clerk was as serious about his work as the other clerk was bored with hers. Flashing the official death certificate like a passport, Catherine explained that she had just learned about her father's death, that she was his only child (although she didn't know if this was still true) and that they hadn't been in contact for several years. She wondered if he had owned property in Knollburg.

The clerk leaned too close to assure her that property documents were public record and he would be happy to look up her father in the files. Catherine winced as he slid the unexpectedly precious death certificate from her fingers. After poking at a computer keyboard for a few minutes, he attached a yellow sticky note to the document and wrote out her father's name and an address. The clerk offered his condolences for her loss and returned the death certificate with the solemnity of an undertaker. The address flashed at her like a dare.

Catherine's ankle was throbbing and she hadn't eaten all day. Making her way back to the diner she had passed earlier on the main street, she wondered how a such a small town could have so many blocks between everywhere she needed to go. By the time she pushed through the restaurant door with her crutches, she was breathless and sweating. She backed into an empty booth close to the door, groaning as she raised her leg to the bench.

A mother-hen of a waitress clucked over Catherine's swollen ankle before taking her order and returning with a towel filled with ice and what seemed like an urn of iced tea. Catherine held the glass with two hands, resting it in her lap between sips and damning her father for every painful step she'd taken in this town. She mulled over the two pieces of information she had, unsure if they would amount to more than characters on paper and wondering if she really wanted them to.

No Bars and a Dead Battery

A voice came over her right shoulder, remarking that she had made some progress since this noon. Catherine turned to see the man from outside the pharmacy sitting in the next booth. He gestured toward her crutches, his eyes smiling between a surf of white hair and the grey stubble on his cheeks, like a morning mist. She knew she should reciprocate but instead she only stared ahead as a single mortifying tear fell from the eye he could see best from her angle in the booth. He reached a napkin out to her.

Catherine wasn't sure why she did it. She wasn't a person who confided in anyone, really, and the man hadn't asked a single question. Maybe it was seeing him across the back of the booth that seemed like a neighbor's fence in this friendly small town. But she heard herself telling him about her search, sparing him the backstory but starting with her shock at seeing her estranged father's face on Facebook and then reading the local newspaper articles.

The man in the booth said he knew about the rescue, but he'd never known the man involved and hadn't heard much talk about him after that. Catherine raised the death certificate with its flag of an address then pointed to her ankle, explaining she had crashed her car this morning and had no way to get around. He asked to see the paper, nodded that he was familiar with the road and offered to take her there, if that's what she wanted.

Catherine debated whether this was the stroke of luck she had been waiting for or a foolish risk, getting into a car with a strange man in a strange place when she couldn't even run. But it was all foolish, risky and foolish, just coming here had been a foolish idea to begin with so there was no sense in trying to distinguish the two. The man said his name was Stan, that she should take her time with her sandwich and he'd be waiting in the El Dorado parked out front, with plenty of room for crutches. She watched as he stood to pay his bill at the register.

Howell Road was outside the grid of the small town, not exactly rural but lacking curbs and lined with broad, mowed lawns where crops and livestock used to be. The houses were small and seemed untouched since they were built. On the asphalt ahead of the El Dorado, what looked to Catherine from a distance like a discarded black garbage bag broke into a scrum of crows picking over the corpse of a racoon. Stan braked the car as the sleek birds considered leaving the car's path.

Catherine voiced a memory then, a story her father read to her about an old Indian legend. Rainbow crow, the most colorful bird with the most melodious song, flew to the Creator and brought fire to the earth to melt the snow that was freezing the animals. The price it paid for this selfless act was losing its beauty and its voice to the heat of the fire. Stan nodded at the story as he moved the car forward again after the crows' exit. Catherine thought how she had always loved crows because of that, was grateful to them, until the day the stories stopped and she came to understand that the crow had saved a magical world and not her own.

Stan said he wished he had a dollar or even a dime for every time he had to learn that lesson again during his long and sorry life, every time he took something at face value and didn't take the time to look deeper, at what was underneath. Catherine turned her face to the window and started to call out addresses painted on mailboxes dotting the edge of the road.

They lost the late day sun as they drove through a wooded break between houses, with shallow standing water along the road. When they emerged back into the light, a red mailbox with her father's address stood out like a stop sign. Stan pulled the car to the side of the road, leaned forward to examine the house, then asked if he should turn off the engine. Catherine hadn't thought through what to say or do, so they sat in the humming car, the elongated hood

No Bars and a Dead Battery

shimmering in front of them for a few minutes before she grabbed her crutches.

Her father had been dead about a month, but the house looked like it still had life. A hanging basket with flowers in a spectrum of pink to purple hung from a pole in the front lawn. The paint on the stairs was worn in the center, but there wasn't so much as a leaf or a pebble on the porch, as if it had just been swept. Two rockers held blue corduroy cushions, comfortably dented. Catherine used the railing to hop up the steps and raised her hand in a first knock against the screen door. She had no idea who might answer or what she would say if someone did. She knocked a second time, her falling gut telling her that no one was in the house. She knocked a third time anyway, and heard the knob turning.

An older man stood on the other side of the screen, his expression cautious but not unfriendly. When Catherine didn't say anything, he frowned and asked what he could do for her. She decided to answer simply: she was looking to talk with someone about Tom Candell. The frown deepened and for a few moments the man stood still and silent. So Catherine explained she was Tom's daughter. She understood this was his house. She was just trying to…she didn't know how to finish the sentence. The man backed away, saying he had nothing to tell her, and closed the door.

Stan had been leaning against the El Dorado and held the door open as Catherine approached. She studied him, knowing he was older than her father but thinking this is what it might have felt like to know him, to have him waiting for her, in some magical world saved by a rainbow crow. She dropped into the passenger seat and Stan collected her crutches before gently closing the door to secure her inside.

Seeing Stan's questioning look, Catherine shook her head. Stan told her then that he didn't know the man at the door but he knew *of* him, that he owned a cabinet shop in town—kitchens, bathrooms and such. He figured some of these houses were rentals and if the man wasn't friendly, maybe he was worried that a new owner would put him out. This was a new thought for Catherine, that she might own that house, that her father might have had a will, and the will might mention a child. That the will could be proof that he had not forgotten her. Proof but not justification.

Lulled by the comfort inside the El Dorado as they drove back to town, Catherine began to think out loud. She was sure the man knew something, that he had been too quiet, not friendly like everybody else around here. She had two more leads to follow now: checking whether her father had a will and going to the cabinet shop to try again with the man from the house. Opening the car door for her at the Highwayman, Stan wrote his phone number on a receipt he pulled from his pocket and said to call him if she needed anything else. She nodded but turned up the walk before he could see how his kindness was crushing her, this simulated father who was giving her everything she wanted but had convinced herself she didn't need.

The next morning, still armed with her father's death certificate, Catherine faced yet another worker at the county offices. This one confirmed that her father did not have a will, at least not filed in this county, but he rambled on, proud to be in control of this information, reciting that any assets would go to Probate Court and the court would search for legal heirs. So if she would provide the county with her birth certificate, it's possible she would be deemed the legal heir of such assets, to be divided among any other legal heirs, of course. The clerk beamed as Catherine turned away, seething to know how completely her father had erased her, not only during his life but even now in death.

She fingered her phone, which was low on juice again. Catherine sensed that everything, even the little things, were slipping out of her grasp in this unreal place where it was all seeking and no finding. A text told her the car would be ready the next day. She headed back to the motel, plugged in her phone, and rested her foot, which was feeling good enough today to go without crutches. Her next stop would be the cabinet shop. It was beyond coincidence that the owner was living in her father's house, her father who had been an expert woodworker. Confronting the man again would be the end of her search, she decided. If her father had wanted to disappear, he did a damn good job. If he hadn't wanted *her*—then maybe it was better that way. If she came up empty again from the cabinetmaker, she would just quit, and ask Stan to let her know if he ever heard anything more. Or maybe not.

The cabinet shop was six blocks away. Catherine struggled under the weight of the backpack, wishing now she had brought her crutches, stopping to rest against a fence or building from time to time. The shop was one in a row of industrial businesses along the street and its exterior was as welcoming as the house had been, with light blue siding, flowers in a window box, and a sign written in charming Old English script. When her eyes adjusted to the fluorescent lights inside, she saw the balding head of the man from her father's house bowed over a drafting table in the back. He looked up as she limped forward but didn't stand. She shimmied out of her backpack and set it on the counter.

Catherine told the man, across the expanse of his shop, that all she wanted was information about her father. Unzipping the backpack, she presented his remains: a smoothing plane, a wooden mallet, and a set of chisels. She laid the tools side by side on the counter, as corroboration of his previous life. She told the man her father was a fine carpenter. She told him he could build anything. And in that moment Catherine was a little girl again, her anger and betrayal falling away and leaving in their place her desperate desire to be a daughter of a father. She asked the man if he knew her father. She wondered if he worked here.

The man came to standing as the tools appeared. He walked toward the counter, shaking his head and telling her again that he couldn't help her, continuing to shake his head as he stared at the display of tools. Then he walked back to his seat at the drafting table. After a pause, Catherine returned the tools to the backpack and slid it over her shoulders. When she glanced at the man before exiting the shop, he had yet to pick up his pencil.

Catherine was finished. Lying on her motel bed with her foot throbbing, she left a message with Stan, telling him that she had reached a dead end, asking if he would drive her to get her car the next day, and offering to pay him for his help. Setting down the phone, she set her jaw. She had lived without her father for nearly twenty years. She would go back to her life that didn't include him, discarding his heroics to the archive of short-lived social media stories and relegating the reality of a father to the stuff of childhood dreams, magical legends that inspire but leave a girl with nothing of substance to hold, to be held by. Wills, houses, inheritance— Catherine wanted none of it. She glanced at the backpack, allowing herself the option of leaving it all behind in this stifling motel room.

Although it was afternoon, Catherine slept well, waking only to the notice of a text. Stan gave her a time to meet him at the bench in front of the pharmacy the next morning. They would pick up her things from the motel on the way to the car repair shop. Not caring to unscramble the illogic of this request, she fell back asleep.

The man was perched on the edge of the bench, hands clasped between his knees, squinting through his metal-framed glasses at Catherine's approach. Oh no, she thought, glaring at the man; you had your chance. Her father had a lifetime of chances. It's over. She summoned her anger as a barricade against the door she had closed the night before. Done with it all, and enraged, Catherine started to turn back the way she had come.

Then he called her Cub, with a shaking voice that hovered between a question and a wish. She drew up at the sound of her childhood name, a name that would only be known to people who were now dead. He said the name once more, a statement this time. He said her father was a fine carpenter. He said he could build anything. He opened his mouth to speak again, stopped and leaned back against the bench, lifting his hands to his mouth to staunch any more words.

Breathing hard, Catherine came closer to the bench but stayed standing. The man lifted his eyes to her, tears gleaming brighter than his glasses. He moved his hands away from his mouth to say her father had always loved her, then replaced them over his lips like a lid on a jar.

Catherine told him she didn't believe him. She accused him of using her own words to try to steal the house. She called him a liar, all the while knowing that no one could have called her Cub except someone who had known her father intimately. She started to cry. The man moved his hands from his mouth, reached them toward her, then patted the seat next to him. She sat, defeated, her anger unable to keep her upright any longer.

There were more people on the sidewalk now, all going in the same direction. A group of preschoolers was passing, adults in front and back, with each child holding a loop on a rope, their happy shouts competing with the noisy crows that were again stationed on top of the building across the street. Catherine sunk deeper into her confusion at the sight of children, happy and protected.

She turned to the man, who was looking at her, his chest rising and falling with shallow breaths. In a whisper, he told her they had met at on a hunting trip, had a natural affinity over woodworking. The man stopped and worked his jaw before continuing, telling her that somehow it became more than that. He repeated the phrase—more than that—looking away then back again. He told Catherine her father couldn't stay with her and her mother and live a lie. But he didn't have the courage to tell them. Her father was ashamed. The man said that's how it was back then, people like us were ashamed, and until he saved that girl—and here his voice cracked and he was forced to stop—her father lived in shadows. He used her name Cub again and said her father loved her too much to burden her with this; right or wrong, he thought she was better off without him. The man paused before whispering that her father's very last act on this earth was to rush in and save a girl, a girl who might have been like her. The man told her he thinks about that every day, how the whole purpose of Tom's life came down to saving not just one, but two girls.

The man wasn't hiding his tears now. Catherine turned toward the people passing by without seeing them. She had expected narcissism. She had expected cruelty. Even a life of crime wasn't out of the question as she thought about her father's motives and state of mind. She had not expected shame. She rolled this around on her tongue, feeling its sharp edges, its bitter taste. This man would have her believe that love and hate were in a constant dance, like parts of an atom; that it was this polarity that allowed her father to maintain equilibrium. If Catherine were willing to accept his explanation, the love that brought her father here—the love of this man—had led to such self-hatred that he was compelled to reject the one he loved the most—her—just to be able to live with himself. Could a person be so consumed with shame that he felt others—a child!—were better off without him?

The anger began to rise again, but it was tinny now, as if bravado were creeping in where certainty had sustained her for so many years. Catherine thought how her father had always been other-worldly: first her god, then her demon, now a community's superhero. The man had offered her a way to understand him in the real world. But the thinking seemed too convoluted, implausible, even for the most flawed of mortals. To Catherine, it sounded too convenient; there is always someone to blame. She knew she couldn't navigate her way from anger and betrayal to pity or compassion using this man's reasoning—her father's reasoning, if it be true—at least not yet. If ever.

Catherine rose without saying another word. The man reached in his shirt pocket and held out a business card, printed in the same welcoming Old English script as the sign on his shop. His name was Roland. Her father had been in love with a man named Roland. It was a fact and one of the few she could hold in her hand right now.

Certain Stan would be waiting for her at the diner, Catherine turned up the street. She threaded through a crowd on her way, as big a crowd as can be assembled in a small town, children and adults spilling out of a park where a fair of some kind was in full swing, with a bouncy castle and colorful tents arranged in a large circle. Stan was sitting in a booth in the front of the diner, watching the fair-goers. He turned as she tapped on the window, raising his eyebrows. She nodded. He smiled and stood, grabbing his coffee cup from the table. In a few moments, he joined her on the sidewalk and pointed toward his car. She thought she might ask him to stop by the house on Howell Road on the way out of town, maybe leave the backpack with her father's tools. She would decide once they were on the road.

They made their way through the crowd, and back to the El Dorado. And as they approached it, a crow flew directly over their heads and landed on the hood and then looked at them. They stood some distance away and watched the crow watching them. Another crow flew directly overhead and landed beside it. The first crow squawked and then both flew away. They watched the crows disappear, looked at each other, and then got in the El Dorado. Only one way to go this time, with five bars and full battery.

AS THE CROWS FLY

Christopher Schiller

No coverage, not even one bar, the battery was dead anyway. It was still daytime, but there was an overcast and the sky had a perfectly even dullness, so there was no way to tell what time of day it was, much less which direction was north or south or anything else for that matter. A two-lane blacktop road snaked up into the distance and disappeared into some trees, or a forest if you wanted to get technical about it. It also snaked down toward some lumpy hills and disappeared there as well. What sounded like a two-stroke chainsaw could be heard in the distance, but it was impossible to tell whether it was up in the forest or down in the lumpy hills. This had been happening more often lately. Two different ways to go, with a dead battery and no bars, and nobody left to blame.

The two humans looked up above their heads to the power lines that stretched in both directions alongside the road. All they could see was the electricity running through those lines, at the end of which would be a way to plug in their one phone and get a recharge. What they didn't see were the two crows sitting on those lines, watching the men as they trekked off away from the forest. The crows looked at each other seeming to know what lie ahead of them in that direction. One crow shook its head. The other nodded and almost mournfully watched the men amble slowly down the hill.

Bob was the headstrong one of the pair. He'd wrestled in college, was pretty good too. But a shoulder injury cut short his career – whatever that would have been. Made him bitter just to think about it. Which was all the time. Now his shoulder ached when the weather was about to change, like today. He looked up at the overcast sky and cursed under his breath.

Jerry huffed a little trying to keep pace with Bob. Jerry was out of shape. Well, that's not really fair. He was in pretty good shape for a short, overweigh guy who didn't exercise. His job didn't demand any and he wasn't one to do more than was asked of him. So excursions like this weren't in his forte, usually. He padded along a step behind Bob's long strides and tried to keep up. He knew better than to make small talk, especially when Bob was in one of his moods. Like now.

The road bent and undulated under their feet as they walked in silence. That's not really true. Though they didn't speak, there was lots of noise if you listened. The wind through the trees in the distance behind them gave a rustling undertone as it faded into the background. Somewhere off to one side was an almost imperceptible bubbling of a brook, creek or stream heading merrily on its way down the hill. Overhead, if the men cared to listen, they'd hear the distinct flapping of bird wings from behind, above and then ahead of them. And then there was the chainsaw-like, coughing engine noise growing distinctly louder as they continued down the road. But they didn't even really hear the crunch of their shoes on the loose asphalt as they walked on. They were lost in thought, and somewhat lost in general as well.

The crows landed in a lone elm in a bend in the road, a good perch from which to watch the next events unfold. The men moved slow, but, then all humans did that. They'd likely be even slower if they realized what was ahead of them. The crows knew, but, didn't speak or understand human. So the crows kept it to themselves. And watched.

Jerry was the first to see it as they rounded the bend and a small

No Bars and a Dead Battery

hill but he didn't point it out to Bob. Eventually Bob looked up from watching his feet and saw it too. The Cadillac sat in the middle of the road. Just sat there. Not running, not moving, not anything. It was a 1972 Cadillac El Dorado in nearly mint condition, a rare thing to find just about anywhere, let alone in the middle of the road out in the middle of nowhere. Odd that.

At least Jerry and Bob could see why the El Dorado hadn't gone any further. The road was blocked and in a very odd way. Odd because it was blocked by a pile of freshly cut down pine trees laid across the road in the style of a beaver dam. Exactly in the style of a beaver dam, come to think of it. But we'll get to that. The dam was odd partly because there wasn't a pine tree grove or copse or whatever they call a collection of pine anywhere near this turn in the road, at least, not anymore. Severed tree trunks equal to the number of trees in the dam were strewn all around the little hillock and valley area.

Bob could see that the dam was freshly built, somewhat because the saw cuts to the trees were still oozing sap and somewhat because he could see the one cutting down the trees still at work. Explains the chainsaw sounds from earlier. But not with an explanation that made sense. Standing beside one of the few remaining pine trees with its back to the men was the obvious culprit, a regular sized adult beaver with a full-sized chain saw in its hands or claws or whatever beaver had. Bob wasn't at all versed in animal husbandry.

Jerry was about to make comment but Bob shushed him, silently. He pointed to the car and the two made their way beside it while the beaver continued to cut. The chainsaw was having trouble staying running so was taking all of its attention.

The two humans made it to the car. Bob looked in. The inside was as pristine as the outside was. Bob smiled. Not only were the keys inside, dangling from the ignition, but, in the cigarette lighter plug was the cord of a phone charger. Bob looked to Jerry who shrugged and tried opening the passenger side door. It wasn't locked. Bob opened the driver's side quietly and got in. Jerry plugged their phone in the charger cord and Jerry tried the ignition. The engine turned over and purred like a kitten. Correction. Purred like a very loud and out of place car sound that got the attention of the chain saw armed beaver.

The crows watched as the beaver turned from the tree it was cutting and stared wide eyed at the men in the car. Neither crow could remember if they'd ever heard a beaver scream before, but, they heard one this time. They didn't understand beaver speak either but it was clear as day that the beaver was not happy. The men must have understood at least that much because the car they were sitting in suddenly lurched backwards, screeching tires and making a racket of its own. Until it hit the bear behind it.

It didn't stop making noise then, but, it stopped moving backwards for sure. The bear held it in place. And it didn't look like it took much of an effort from the bear to do that. It was impressive to say the least. So impressive that the two humans fell out of the doors of the car and stared in disbelief back at the bear. One of the humans, the shorter pudgy one, did as the crows had suspected he would and started to run off. The other human surprised the crows by what he did. He surprised the beaver and bear as well. He stood his ground and yelled at the bear.

Jerry didn't look back to wonder at Bob yelling at the bear or see the reaction he was getting. He was too busy stopping in his own tracks as fast as he could so as not to run into the pack of wild, man-eating wolves growling and baring their teeth right in front of his getaway path. They were man eating for sure. Not only because that's what Jerry normally thought wolves would be, but, also because of the evidence they presented since one of the wolves in the back of the pack was still chewing on what looked very much like a human femur. Or, at least a leg bone of some sort. He never paid much attention in high school biology to be able to tell bone from bone. But it definitely looked like a human one from here. He decided getting a closer look wouldn't help determine it so he began to back up slowly. The wolves allowed this.

As the car stopped its screeching of tires and resisting in its paws, the bear let go of the bumper it had been holding and turned its full attention to the screaming man. This was an odd reaction, even for a human. The bear was puzzled and took a few strides toward the man to investigate. This caused the man to scream even louder at the bear. The bear looked around at its other animal companions to see if they were as perplexed by this development as it was. Yep, the beaver was as curious, even dropping the now out of gas chainsaw beside the half cut tree and moving in to get a closer look at this curious man-thing reaction. The wolves were keeping their man at bay but snuck looks and perked ears towards the other loud one, all but the wolf with the bone. That one kept chewing as its main occupation and only half-heartedly joined in with the others. The bear couldn't blame it, man meat did have a nice flavor, even the bones.

The crows thought this was getting interesting. It might even have a different outcome than before. They flew over to the half cut pine tree and perched on a good limb to get a better view of the goings on. None of the animals or humans noticed them there.

Bob kept screaming. He'd heard somewhere on some nature show that the way to survive an encounter with a bear was to be as big and as loud as possible. He guessed the theory was to make the bear decide that a large, loud meal was less appetizing. Jerry never truly believed the theory enough to try to put it into practice before, but, now that he found himself in a perfect test situation, he'd give it a good old college try.

It didn't matter what he yelled. He doubted whether the bear would understand a word of it, but watching enough professional wrestling in his youth he had a pretty good banter of smack talk that he could spew without having to think too much. So there was Bob dissing the wimpy weight training and lackadaisical wresting style of his bear opponent as well as his questionable lineage. His rapid delivery of zingers would have made any fight manager proud to have him on the bout card. It was so good that it nearly distracted Jerry from the immanent death that faced him. The wolves growled a reality check, though. Jerry moved around the car nearer to Bob who continued to scream insults.

Even the non-meat eating woodland creatures were attracted by the ruckus. The crows were the first to notice when the moles burrowed out of their holes to be able to listen better. And the family of chipmunks scurried past the crows on their way down the pine tree's trunk. They might have been using the opportunity to escape the imminent demise of their chosen tree house to go find another, but, when they got to the bottom they paused, enraptured by the aural ballet being performed. It was getting to be quite a crowd down there.

The beaver was perturbed. It was already miffed not being able to finish building the dam. Though to be honest, beavers never really feel finished building a dam. They tend to keep working on them, fixing things here, adding elements there, all the time. In a flowing river constantly trying to tear the work apart a constant builder's attitude is a good thing. A dam built on dry land across a road bed between two sides of surrounding hills didn't have those pressures knocking things askew.

What this one did have, though, was a pack of wolves climbing all over it, clawing it up as they shifted positions trying to find the best attack angles to get at the two humans if the opportunity arose. One even settled down in a natural divot among the trunks and branches ignoring everything else to concentrate on finishing up a good chew on its tasty bone. The beaver didn't like the wolves. It considered it did a lot more work than they did and deserved a bigger share of the collective spoils. The beaver determined that once it finished building the dam it would have to have a sorting out with the wolves and work out the hierarchy again.

The kid chipmunks couldn't help themselves. Being small they had trouble seeing the ruckus from the ground by the tree so before their parents could stop them they ran off up atop the dam as well and were quite pleased with the perspective they gained. Their parents followed and hovered near their children, wary of the fangs of the nearby wolves but also drawn to the spectacle as well.

The moles stayed where they were. Since they couldn't see worth a damn anyway, they didn't need line of sight. They could hear quite fine where they were. And there was lots to listen to, even if moles didn't understand human speak or bear speak either for that matter.

And the bear did speak just then. Or roared. It was loud. Louder than the human had been screaming. It shook the trees. And, to be honest, probably shook the human too since he seemed to stop in mid-sentence and the color left his cheeks. The crows noted that this was probably a flaw of general human anatomy. It's usually not a good thing in nature for there to be a telltale sign of how scared you were viewable to those rising up to challenge you. And they were right.

The bear noticed the fear signs and got emboldened. It stood up on its hind legs and towered over the humans below. The chubby man-thing dropped to his knees, then into a fetal position. The bear was pleased with this. But the once screaming man regained his color and screamed even louder than before. The entire gathering watched in awe. The bear was taken aback. No one had ever stood up to him when he both bellowed and stood up high. This man was either crazy or might have some hidden skills giving it confidence. The bear wanted to go with crazy, but, still, there might be a reason to pause here and rethink.

Jerry looked up from his balled up position at his friend with curiosity. Had Bob lost it? He knew that Bob was one to usually side with passion rather than rationality in most things, but this was a bear. This was a pack of wolves. This was not the time to channel an old rerun of Hulk Hogan in spandex. Their lives were on the line here. Jerry seriously worried about his friend almost to the point of forgetting to worry about himself. Almost.

Just like what had been happening pretty regularly lately, Bob's choices were reduced once again to two options. But this time both of them seemed to point to the same result, him getting eaten. He could cower and resign to it like Jerry seems to have done quite willingly. Or he could stand and make a valiant, yet likely futile attempt to fight for his life. It was almost cathartic when he realized that finally he couldn't seem to make the wrong choice from the two options available to him. For once, both choices were wrong. He wouldn't be blamed either way. He wouldn't regret whatever decision he made either. Mostly because he'd be dead, but, still. So that's why he decided to fight. And he'd make this the best wrestling match there ever was.

The crows were perplexed by what happened next. If they'd ever had the opportunity to watch a college wrestling match they'd recognize the moves the human was making. But to them it just looked like a series of squats, then a jump to one side or the other, then a squat, thump of the chest and more shouting. It was confusing the crows. At least one of them. The other seemed to be concentrating or coming up with something momentous to say about it all at the right time. The man's antics were confusing to the bear most of all.

The bear's mother often told it not to play with its food. Kill it, eat it and be done. The bear had thought her advice silly, but, never once had it considered that the food might deign to play with it instead. But here was the man-thing hooting and jumping, squatting and feigning attacks. It was a curiosity that made the bear hesitate.

Of course, the wolf pack leader was familiar with a good fight. It participated in quite a few of them. But what it was watching wasn't like any fight it'd ever seen. At first it didn't even look like any fight ever before.

The skinny man-thing lunged at the bear like an idiot. Without a pack that would be suicide for a wolf. But the human didn't seem to know this or care. This tactic, though, surprised the bear, who probably hadn't ever been lunged at in its entire adult life by anything other than another bear. It just stood its ground bewildered. The man-thing bounced back and yelled again. It made the wolf pack leader wonder if it understood man speak this would make a bit more sense. Probably not. This man creature was crazy.

The beaver was convinced of the lunacy of these men as well. Or, at least the fighting one. The other human was prudently making itself smaller and smaller, cringing into a ball. That's a good strategy in these situations. Inevitably, it won't save him, but, it won't make things worse. But the flailing man – the beaver couldn't bring itself to think of it as fighting – wasn't doing anything that would assure survival in a fight with a bear. Exactly the opposite.

The beaver was intrigued, though, in the actions of the flailing man. So much so that he perched himself on his own dam next to the youngest chipmunks to watch the outcome. And what happened next surprised the entire crowd, participants included.

Bob had of course never faced off with a bear. It's not something you train for in even the best college wrestling preparations. But he'd half-watched a few nature shows while doing other things and seemed to remember a few things about bears. He couldn't quite remember whether they were good things or bad things to do when encountering a bear, though. He really hadn't been paying close attention to the show. Still, he might as well try them out. It's not like he'll have time to re-watch the episode, or anything else, soon.

Jerry peaked up at his friend's antics from his cowered position through the gap of his arm covering most of his face. He'd known Bob in college and had even attended one of his wrestling matches before realizing how boring those things can be. What he was seeing was not boring this time. Just at this moment, the cell phone still charging in the car received an e-mail and announced it with the ceremonial loud ding. To Jerry it meant they surprisingly had cell coverage here. To Bob the bell started the match.

The crows had the best view. Even the crow trying to think of the perfect thing to say about this historic occasion was distracted by what they saw. The human crouched low and growled, yes, growled at the bear. The bear looked perplexed, cocked its head and just stood there. Then suddenly the man leaped from his crouch through the air right at the bear, reached up with one hand and slapped the bear's nose. The bear blinked, which was the only indication that the bear was touched at all. He otherwise didn't move. The man, on the other hand continued his flight up then crashed into the bear chest, bounced off and tumbled back. He ended up losing his balance and collapsed all the way to the ground ungraciously onto his butt. He bounced back up and into a crouch and yelled again. The bear blinked once more. The thoughtful crow got back to work, thinking.

The bear was furious and confused. Both emotions were battling for dominance. It's embarrassing to have your nose slapped in any

No Bars and a Dead Battery

situation. It's infuriating to be embarrassed by a clearly lesser opponent in a fight. But how it all happened was baffling. This puny man was clearly the lesser, one of the least worthy opponents he'd faced in recent memory. But, he'd gotten a good- ineffective, but, good- shot in first. That the bear could not abide. It's mom didn't want it to play with its food so the bear would oblige. This fight was now on. The bear rushed at the crouching man and roared a roar that showed that a shouting contest with a bear has a clear winner.

So far Bob was still alive, which was a surprise to most watching, but especially to Bob. He'd gotten in and slapped the nose of the bear. He'd done it. Soon after realizing that it was probably a documentary about what to do in a shark attack he'd watched, not a bear one. He realize this when the bear didn't swim away. He really should pay more attention to nature shows in the future. If he ever had one.

Still, he'd started a fight with a bear and hadn't been mauled to death before getting in a blow. Yes, his blow was trivial and wasn't even a legal wrestling move, but, he'd been first. That's something at least. But he wasn't dead yet. And he wasn't done yet.

The eating wolf stopped eating. This fight was getting good. All the wolves watched with keen interest. They were so interested in the fight that one of the wolves didn't even notice that the smallest chipmunk had crawled on top of its back to get a better view. The chipmunk mom noticed, scolded the child and dragged it down by the scruff of its neck, and then with her errant child still in her clutches, they both watched the fight with the rest of the crowd.

The beaver was familiar enough with the underdog mentality. After all, beavers are notoriously underappreciated for the amount of work and destruction they're capable of. Felling whole sections of forests and damming fast flowing, wide rivers are all in a day's work for these relatively tiny and sedate creatures. So the apparent imbalance between the fight opponents wasn't as straightforward to the beaver as it might seem to the others.

And the human proved a capable fighter. Or, at least a limber one compared to the bear. The bear lunged. The man evaded, barely, the charge and shifted its weight at just the right moment as the bear passed, catching the bear's foot just so. The bear actually stumbled, a bit. But then turned and growled. And the man wasn't there. At least it wasn't where the bear thought he'd be. The man had taken the bear's stumble to his advantage and actually climbed the bear's back as it regained balance. Once the bear realized the man wasn't on the ground anymore it surmised where he'd gone and began thrashing about. But the man grabbed hold and wouldn't let go. The beaver couldn't tell what the man was trying to do, but, it looked like it might be succeeding.

Jerry recognized what Bob was trying to do. He was crazy to try to do that to a bear, but, Jerry knew not to put anything out of the realm of possibility when Bob was riled. Jerry'd seen this maneuver at that same wresting match he gone to all those years ago. In that old match, Bob managed to get behind his bigger opponent and get him in what Jerry later learned was a sleeper hold. Bob rode the big man to the ground, into unconsciousness and the win. Jerry didn't think it would work this time, though.

First of all the bear was at least three times the size of Bob's previous opponent. Traditionally the sleeper hold, as it was explained to Jerry, is all about the arms wrapped around the neck of the opponent, restricting the breathing of the opponent until lack of oxygen makes them pass out. The bear's neck was so big Bob had to improvise and bring his legs, back and everything else into it to achieve a similar effect.

But then there were the other things that Bob hadn't had to deal with on the wrestling mat. Jerry was pretty sure that having razor

No Bars and a Dead Battery

sharp claws and fangs was frowned upon in college wrestling. The bear didn't mind breaking the rules. It scratched and bit at every bit of man flesh that came within range. Jerry wasn't sure that Bob would be able to stay attached to the bear long enough without blood loss taking its toll. But there were signs he just might.

The moles heard it first. How moles experience a fight is mostly by sounds, since the world is just one big blur to them. But their hearing is keen. They began to hear the bear's breathing slowing, rasping, getting more desperate. They could tell the end was nearing. Soon the bear would be heading towards the ground, hard. And, since they couldn't see where he'd land, they decided to play it safe and listen to the rest of the fight from deep enough underground not to get squished.

The wolves and chipmunks were more surprised when the bear's legs started to wobble. Surely the human didn't weigh that much that he was too much to carry. And there was no way they thought the man could be winning. He looked like a flea on the bears back. All the wolves started involuntarily scratching at that thought. Could the man actually win this?

The collapse of the bear to the ground was the loudest thud ever heard in this little valley. Louder than the beaver's felled trees, louder than any bear bellow. A giant oof sound escaped from the now unconscious bear as he lay on the ground in a cloud of dust. The man victor slowly extracted himself from his pretzel hold around the bear's neck. Blood oozing from several wounds on his arms and legs from the scratches and bites, but, surprisingly still alive. The other man-thing rose from his ball.

The contemplative crow looked smugly at its companion and sort of *hurumphed* in an I-told-you-so way. The other crow shrugged. They watched as the chubby, smaller human helped the victor human walk towards the car. The crows flew off the pine branch and followed the humans.

They made their way through the crowd, and back to the El Dorado. And as they approached it, a crow flew directly over their heads and landed on the hood and then looked at them. They stood some distance away and watched the crow watching them. Another crow flew directly overhead and landed beside it. The first crow squawked and then both flew away. They watched the crows disappear, looked at each other, and then got in the El Dorado. Only one way to go this time, with five bars and full battery.

SUPPLY AND DEMAND

Jeff Somers

No coverage, not even one bar, the battery was dead anyway. It was still daytime, but there was an overcast and the sky had a perfectly even dullness, so there was no way to tell what time of day it was, much less which direction was north or south or anything else for that matter. A two-lane blacktop road snaked up into the distance and disappeared into some trees, or a forest if you wanted to get technical about it. It also snaked down toward some lumpy hills and disappeared there as well. What sounded like a two-stroke chainsaw could be heard in the distance, but it was impossible to tell whether it was up in the forest or down in the lumpy hills. This had been happening more often lately. Two different ways to go, with a dead battery and no bars, and nobody left to blame.

Marks glanced at her and asked which way they were headed. She looked up and down the road and finally jerked her chin towards the tree line. He took one last look around; he had more questions—like how far they would be going—but experience had told him that his guide was a one-question-an-hour kind of woman. He just nodded and walked around to the back of the car while she pulled out her old-school cigarettes and put one between her chapped lips, scanning the horizon. He remembered her saying *no one is welcome there.*

The car clicked and radiated heat. Somewhere, someone was missing their El Dorado. There were a multitude of Virgin Marys on the dashboard, tiny statuettes glued to the top, magnetic images affixed everywhere, one solemn, sun-faded bust dangling from the rear-view mirror, all of them together a choir of immortality, promising there was more to come. Marks knew better than most the way mortality inspired devotion. People could go their whole lives not thinking much about it, then one day they had a cardiac event or a bad test result, a nasty fall, a senior moment and they started collecting icons. Or searching, putting out feelers that eventually led to someone like him.

He popped the trunk. The Client stared up at him with red-rimmed eyes and said something through the gag. He couldn't make out the words but it sounded like a bad job performance review, which was to be expected. The Client brandished his bound hands, thinking they were at the end of the line, thinking he'd be cut loose. Marks told him they were walking from here and dragged him out, rolling him onto the dusty blacktop.

Their guide watched wordlessly as Marks cut the zip ties around The Client's ankles. He set him upright and knelt down, still holding the utility knife in one hand. The Client was an old man, white-haired with an air of depleted strength. He still had big, calloused hands; he still had the wide-shouldered frame that was still imposing. But there was a hollowness to it, a fragility. Marks met The Client's gaze steadily and told him that if he ran, he'd get the exact opposite of what he'd contracted for. That sobered him. The Client studied him for a moment, his ancient face a map of lines and sagging, too-pink skin. An overfed face, jowly, imperious, a Roman Emperor writ small. Finally, he squinted and nodded, once. Marks sighed and twisted his head up to look at The Guide, told her to lead the way when she was ready, then stood and hauled The Client to his feet.

The Guide took one last drag on her cigarette and flicked it onto the pavement. Without a word she turned and started walking, sending a cloud of bluish smoke into the clear air. He gave The Client a gentle shove that sent him staggering forward. The old man twisted around to glare at him, but Marks just stared back. No one ever understood who they were hiring, he thought.

The Guide set a murderous pace. He marveled at the way someone who smoked liked a chimney and was shaped like a pear could *move* like that, so he asked her about it. She shrugged and didn't even break pace. Her people, she said, were born here, in the mountains, in the woods.

He nodded. He understood. He felt the same way about his own people, shadowy and unknown as they were. They'd been born in the alleys and sewers of the city, and that's where they always returned, that's where they always felt most at home. Out here, with the stiff, brittle trees closing in around them he was sweaty and irritable, eyes stinging and ankles aching. He didn't let any of it show, though. You couldn't tie a man up and stuff him in the trunk of a stolen car and then show any sort of weakness. It would be bad business.

When she steered them off the road and into the trees, he realized he'd worn the wrong shoes. So had The Client, whose progress slowed until Marks had to give him a few good shoves to keep The Guide in sight. This time the old man didn't even turn to glare at him, concentrating on breathing around the gag.

The Guide paused to let them catch up, then shook out another cigarette and offered one to Marks by holding the pack behind her as she walked. He plucked one wrinkled stick and caught the lighter she tossed over her shoulder as she asked him if this was what he did, kidnap old rich guys and march them into the hills.

He told her the truth: People hired him to do things. Sometimes that meant getting information no one else could get, proving the unprovable. Sometimes it meant attaining things for them, situations, objects, whatever. And the process of getting those things sometimes took both of them into unexpected places. And sometimes his clients didn't understand what they were getting until they got it—but he always delivered. You hired Philip K. Marks, you *paid* him, and he *always* delivered.

She grunted. He spent a few too many minutes trying to parse the sound, looking for inflections and subtleties. He came away with the impression that The Guide used that grunt as an all-purpose sound with many meanings, most of an interior nature.

He gave The Client another shove. This one had come to him, like all his wealthy clients did, thinking that he'd achieved something by tracking him down, securing an appointment. As if it wasn't his business to take meetings with rich assholes just like him. They all did the same things, men and women or otherwise, rich people who thought money was a signifier, that money meant they were super smart or super lucky or super something. They barreled into his office and acted like he already worked for them, sneered at any mention of money or terms, and then told him—in excruciatingly dull detail—what it was they were looking for. These people found anything they couldn't simply buy to be intolerable, and he'd built a good business offering to get whatever it was they lacked.

It took you into some strange scenarios, his work. What was truly remarkable to him was that it didn't take any special talent or skill. All it took was *work*. Effort. Sustained and exhausting. There was nothing that The Client couldn't have done for himself over the course of a few months—he simply didn't want to. Because the ultimate point, even when facing down your own mortality, was that the rich never did anything for themselves.

The Guide grunted again, and asked what The Client wanted, what Marks was getting for him. He lit his cigarette and pocketed the lighter, shoving it next to his useless phone. The cigarette smoke

No Bars and a Dead Battery

was harsh and bitter, and reminded him why he'd quit. *More life*, he told her.

She nodded; she knew where she was leading them. She asked him what he got out of it, and Marks told her the simple truth: Money. He got paid. She nodded again—a practical woman, wearing clothes that had been hand-sewn a few times, her hair cut painfully short and her hands grimy and calloused. A practical woman. She glanced at The Client, who was following their conversation carefully, his sharp, yellow eyes bouncing back and forth. Then she started laughing, shaking her head.

It was hard to believe there was a road behind them, any sort of civilization. It was just trees and moss and rocks and dirt, sinking sun and scumming clouds. There was no trail, no markers that Marks could see. And almost no sound—there were no birds chirping or insects buzzing. Just the crunch of their shoes, The Client's heavy breathing, the wind in the branches. Yet The Guide plunged on, leading them up a steady slope, choosing her steps without hesitation.

The Client was struggling. Forced to breathe through his nose, a thick line of snot was running down over the gag, and his gait had become rubber-legged, his trajectory kind of random as he pinged one way and then bounced off a tree or rock, staggering diagonally. If there were any apex predators nearby, Marks thought, their ears were filled with the sweet sound of a soft bit of prey warbling about. The Guide turned her head and glanced back at him, her face impassive. She pointed out that rich assholes had hearts made of paper and bones made of wax, and that if he died *en route* there would be no deal to make. And then she laughed, another bark, the sort of rough noise someone made when they'd never once in their lives considered whether their sense of humor was shared. Then she noted that he seemed upset.

The Client had stopped and turned to glare at Marks, nostrils flaring in damp outrage. Marks wanted to pull his phone out to check the time, then remembered it was dead. He asked The Guide, standing uphill from them in casual glory, if there'd be any way to charge his phone. He needed it to transfer the payment, anyway. She nodded and shrugged simultaneously, a tilting of the head that communicated immense disinterest. He studied The Client and decided he looked robust enough. With a shove he got them moving again.

Marks thought The Client had been awfully proud of himself when he'd found his office, just like all of them, the whole overfed lot. Money gave you the illusion of competence, of mastery. Because you could exchange numbers for just about anything, you felt like you controlled some portion of the world—but in reality you were just hiring people. People who hired plumbers weren't masters of their bathrooms, and The Client wasn't *his* master—something he might have started to figure out when Marks knocked him over the head and put him in the trunk of a stolen car. Although he hesitated to give any of the Ruling Class any points for cleverness. They were, by and large, an inbred and useless group.

The Guide said, we're here. Marks found himself looking at a rough wood cabin, small and weathered. The slanted roof was covered in solar panels, and an array of junk was spread around it like bizarre yard decoration—rusting wheel rims, ancient metal box springs, a collection of old satellite dishes arranged like flowers pointed at the sun. There was just one door, crooked and too-small, and now windows. A plume of white smoke leaked from a brick chimney.

He nodded, pulling a wad of currency from his pocket, currency that had until recently rode on the hip of The Client. He eyed it now, sullen, as he peeled off several bills and held them out to The

No Bars and a Dead Battery

Guide. Half now, he said, and half when you get us back to the car, and no offense. She took the money and sketched a sardonic salute. None taken, she said.

He gave The Client a shove. Go on, he said, she's waiting. Which wasn't strictly true; you didn't exactly make a reservation. But it *felt* true, which in these low times was something. And a man like The Client, Marks thought, expected to be expected, to be *anticipated*. With a baleful glance Marks hoped he enjoyed, The Client turned and headed for the tiny door, trying to straighten up and have a modicum of dignity despite the way his thin white hair stood up from his head. The Guide took a seat on a stump, pulling out her cigarettes. Marks followed The Client inside.

It was hot and dark, and smelled like wet cardboard. It was just one small room, a squat black oven in one corner blasting smoke and heat into the space, a small cot next to it, a huge television propped up against the wall, a card table and two folding chairs. The whole place gave the impression of a DIY fort built by a bunch of kids one boring summer afternoon, a DIY fort about to collapse in on itself, killing everyone inside.

The Client took three steps in and stopped, blinking around, blind. The Witch was sitting at the card table, a small spirit stove and a tiny metal cup in front of her. She was north of fifty but south of dead, a huge mass of gray hair spilling everywhere, her face deeply lined but from weather, from sun and wind, not from age— although she also looked like she hadn't seen the sun or felt the wind in decades. She looked like she was sealed to the chair by cobwebs, a strange mushroom in the shape of a wizened old woman. Her hair had been braided a long time ago and left that way,, a thick rug yellowing on the fringes.

She glanced at The Client, then at Marks, running her eyes over him and then again, up and down, up and down. She snorted and asked him what he'd brought her, then warned him if he said the old fart she'd make him regret it. He nodded and pulled out his phone and dropped it on the table. He told her the amount The Client had given him access to. All he needed was a charge and a routing number.

She stared at the phone for a moment, then looked up at him without lifting her head and asked him what The Client wanted in exchange. He told her the old man wanted to live forever, and was willing to pay exorbitant prices.

She laughed, throwing her head back, and The Client shot him one more really bitter glance and turned, shuffling awkwardly for the door, having decided—Marks assumed—that he'd been brought here to be murdered and turned into Soylent Green or sold into Rich People Slavery or something. He spun and hunched down to try and grab the door handle with his bound hands, but couldn't seem to get any purchase. The Witch appeared unconcerned, but Marks assumed she didn't have much of a refund policy. She gestured at a power strip that had been nailed to the wall near the door and asked Marks if The Client knew what was going to happen.

He shrugged, taking back his phone and pulling its cord from his pocket. He told her that The Client was going to get exactly what he'd hired him to find: More life. He'd shown up in Marks' office smelling of death, his own cells turned against him in irrevocable, irreversible revolt. He wasn't that old a man, he should, by rights, have decades left—*poor* people were going to live longer than him, was the unspoken but heavily implied subtext. People who had never created a job in their lives, people who couldn't be bothered to make a better lives for themselves. It seemed to him that someone, some vagrant, some piece of shit, had stolen his years from him. But it was okay, he would get them back, he would buy more, and Marks was going to broker the deal for him. And Marks had agreed. And he would stick to the letter of the deal.

The Witch began putting things into the spirit stove, pinches of things she pulled from the pockets and folds of her clothing. A too-orange flame sprang up, and the air got even thicker with the smell of something rotten and aggressively unpleasant. He asked her what form it would take. She shrugged. Whatever is nearby, she said.

He looked at The Client, still struggling mightily to open the door. Marks wasn't sure what he intended. Even if he could get away, even if the door would open for him, he had weeks, maybe less. Marks could imagine it, because he'd seen it, bearing witness. Blood in the sink in the morning, pain all the time, a low-grade feverish feeling of mild agony that had spread everywhere and ruined everything. Food tasted like sand, thirst never got quenched—but then, he probably thought that he could snap off a few million and start a foundation later this afternoon which would build him a cyborg body by tomorrow, and then fly a team of neurosurgeons in from Sweden to effect the brain transfer. Why not? Was he not the man who'd once turned a modest inheritance of a few million dollars into a vast fortune using only his old family contacts and some admittedly sweetheart interest rates?

Giving up on the door, The Client turned to look back at him with such a naked plea for mercy that Marks almost faltered. Why not let him die? He might be realizing how much better that option might be. A man like him was used to reading the tea leaves and making bets, but part of the job was to know when to pull those markers.

Then the air thickened, and she was telling Marks to step outside, telling him that to remain in the room with her would complicate things and she could not be held responsible. And he wondered what *that* meant, and imagined myself being crowded internally by another presence, another mind fighting for control. He approached the door, eyes watering and lungs burning from whatever she was burning. The Client tried to shout at him, eyes bulging, but Marks pushed him aside and tore the door open, slamming it behind him and leaning back against it, sucking in air.

He heard The Guide say, *told you no one was welcome here.* When he'd cleared his vision, He saw her perched on the stump where they'd left her, smoking. She chucked her chin upward and added that they were going to have some trouble.

At first he thought she meant the crows, big, ragged-looking one sitting on the rusting chassis of an ancient truck. He wondered how in the world anyone had gotten it up here—even when it had wheels and an axle it would have been nearly impossible—and then wondered if crows were dangerous. They looked malevolent enough, certainly, inky black, somehow irregular and asymmetrical, their tiny eyes steady and unmoved. But they weren't very large, and He couldn't imagine being torn apart by a pair of small birds.

Then He saw the people. A few dozen, men and women, all of them just standing there in the trees. They looked grubby, sweaty and grimy, their clothes old denim and torn T-shirts, ragged flannels and loose, stretched-out knit caps. Their hands were blackened with grease, their fingernails torn and bloody, their faces cracked and impassive. These were folks who lived out here, far away from his sewers and street corners. And they didn't look happy.

The Guide exhaled smoke and rubbed her cigarette out on the stump. She said the locals didn't like The Witch. He looked back at them and thought there was an implied violence in the crowd, a cumulative stance and posture that hinted that they might find it difficult to leave the general area. He'd seen mobs before. The transition from an orderly protest to bloodthirsty terror took a second, less.

No Bars and a Dead Battery

The Guide told him not to worry. They wouldn't come near the cabin. She said they all thought there was some kind of radiation or something that The Witch gave off, invisible and poisonous. Or that they all thought she'd turn them into something. He asked if she got a lot of visitors and The Guide shrugged. Couple a year, she said. Some she turned away. Some never came out of the cabin.

He looked at the place. It seemed to absorb more light than it should have, like someone had placed a filter between the structure and his eyes. There was a high-pitched, keening sound from within, muffled and cut-off suddenly. This was followed by a sound like wind in the tall grass as their audience all shifted their weight uneasily, breathing in sharply. He noticed the two crows were gone.

The Guide looked up and squinted at the darkening sky, pulling her pack of cigarettes from her shirt pocket and packing them against her palm. You can go back in now, she said, gesturing. It's done, and she'll be wanting a few words with you.

He rolled his shoulders and scanned the crowd again. They all stared as he approached the cabin door, and He wasn't going to give them the thrill of seeing him hesitate. He forced myself to walk right up to it, suddenly uncertain, with all these eyes on him, of how his legs worked, how gravity worked. Every step felt dubious and provisional, as if the mental image of him stumbling and falling onto his nose somehow made the reality of it inevitable. Then he was pulling the door open and stooping to reenter, breathing in something like burnt flesh and candle wax, his throat closing up.

The Client was slumped over in a corner, eyes open and glassy. He'd chewed through the gag, his lips bloody. His hands were clenched into fists. His trousers were stained. Marks stared at him until The Witch made a noise that was almost but not quite entirely unlike any noise a human being had ever made.

He turned. She was sitting right where he'd left her, smoking a clay pipe, exhaling clouds of dense white smoke. Your phone, she said. He blinked at her. He gestured at The Client and asked her what happened. She plucked the pipe from her mouth and pursed her lips, yellow eyes resting on him. You got him what he wanted, she said, shrugging. More life.

More life. Marks rolled the phrase around in his head. He counted the dollars he'd been paid. Considered what they represented. He did the math—his bills, his groceries, his rent. Six weeks, give or take, of existence, he decided. Twelve if he cut back on everything. Fifteen if he went on starvation rations, and who could tell the speed difference between starving to death and just the normal slide into death? More life. The Client had gotten more life with his money. He'd gotten more life by biting through a gag and shitting himself.

He picked up the phone; not only was it fully charged, it had five bars all of a sudden, placidly informing him of the time and weather. It too had more life. They were all, rich and poor, animate and inanimate, locked in a bloody struggle with entropy, and Marks was unsettled as to which side he represented in this puzzle. He thumbed it on, navigated the baking App, punched in the numbers as The Witch recited them, and deposited her fee. Then he shoved the phone into his pocket and left as quickly as he could, wondering if the smell would ever get out of his clothes.

Outside, he nodded at The Guide and told her they were done. She put the cigarette between her lips and stood up, saying that he should stay close. Marks looked around at the blank, sun-faded faces around them and told her that wouldn't be a problem.

Progress was slow. The crowd didn't give way, exactly; they bent, leaning this way and that to avoid direct contact, as if he'd been infected with something dark and viscous, something that clung to him. But they didn't shift their feet. The woods had become an obstacle course of human bodies. He stayed in The Guide's shadow and treated it like a minefield; when she twisted herself sideways to slip between two glowering people, He did the same, keeping his eyes down, pushing his feet into her prints.

They were all older, he realized. No one under fifty or sixty, although they were leathered and permatanned, dried out like smoked meat. The smell when they had to thread their way between them was overpowering, a mixture of sweat and feces and dried blood from skinned rabbits and squirrels, cleaned fish and plucked chickens. It all made him yearn for his sewers and his sidewalks. More of his own life.

The crowd started to move behind them, slowly falling in and trailing them until he felt like they were being pushed along by a wave of humanity. Like they were sealing off the mountain. The Guide looked at him sideways and asked if he did a lot of work like this, in this vein. He told her he did. A lot of people wanted more of things they didn't have any natural right to, and he had a knack for finding deep veins of it.

She nodded as the crowd formed up behind them, silent but drilled, in perfect sync. She took a drag on her cigarette and suggested he take this off the menu of services, because this way would be closed to him. He was known, now. He looked around at the blank, unfriendly faces and nodded back.

They made their way through the crowd, and back to the El Dorado. And as they approached it, a crow flew directly over their heads and landed on the hood and then looked at them. They stood some distance away and watched the crow watching them. Another crow flew directly overhead and landed beside it. The first crow squawked and then both flew away. They watched the crows disappear, looked at each other, and then got in the El Dorado. Only one way to go this time, with five bars and full battery.

THE POETRY IN LEAVING

Ansley Vreeland

No coverage, not even one bar, the battery was dead anyway. It was still daytime, but there was an overcast and the sky had a perfectly even dullness, so there was no way to tell what time of day it was, much less which direction was north or south or anything else for that matter. A two-lane blacktop road snaked up into the distance and disappeared into some trees, or a forest if you wanted to get technical about it. It also snaked down toward some lumpy hills and disappeared there as well. What sounded like a two-stroke chainsaw could be heard in the distance, but it was impossible to tell whether it was up in the forest or down in the lumpy hills. This had been happening more often lately. Two different ways to go, with a dead battery and no bars, and nobody left to blame.

The radio, which had been blasting '90s smash hits, began fading to static with a beat just perceptible enough for Charley to continue yelling the lyrics. Earlier, Ezra had tried switching the station but she'd given him a withering glare and turned it right back. The yelling was only partially invested in the song itself. It was also serving as a suitable vent for her frustration, mostly at the fact that they were lost deep within the hinterlands of Illinois, likely nowhere near Chicago.

As a result of the deafening static-singing combination, Ezra's other senses had become heightened. So he was the first to perceive a vague scent of tomatoes, disappearing just as quickly as it had arrived. Of course, this gave him a moment of pause. *What did they have with them?* A stack of cash. A pistol. A Yorkshire terrier, which

No Bars and a Dead Battery

was presumably still sitting in the backseat. No tomatoes. They'd overlooked packing any food in their panic. Ezra's panic, really— Charley had been eerily calm. The scent drifted into the front seat once more, sending a deluge of chills down Ezra's spine.

This could only mean one thing. Turning down the static one notch, in a urgent whisper, he suggested Charley pull over to the side of the road. She listened; this was the first time he'd spoken since they'd left. Once the Prius was safely parked, Ezra nodded in the direction of the backseat. They both swiveled around to take a closer look.

On the left side was the sleeping Yorkie—*Skippy*—according to the collar, a small ratty-looking dog with a pink bow tying back the fur in front of his eyes. In the middle rested Charley and Ezra's backpacks, which contained the aforementioned goods. However, the right side was hosting a large object of some kind covered by an Aztec-print blanket Ezra had only taken vague notice of earlier. Looking at it now, he somehow instantly *knew* what it was, though it seemed inconceivable. Charley, both less patient and less intuitive, whipped the blanket back like a hostess of a TV game show revealing the mystery prize behind a curtain. Except in this case, the prize wasn't a goat or a jet ski or even a worthless prank item, though it felt like a twisted version of the latter.

Under the blanket was Headmaster Salisbury, almost unrecognizable in a Hawaiian shirt and jeans, salt-and-pepper hair unkempt, gel-less, a half-eaten tomato sandwich dripping onto his lap. The heart-stopping silence was finally broken by Charley spitting a chain of expletives. *They were over.* Ezra's pulse had skyrocketed initially and was just beginning to drop when their former headmaster spoke. Maybe it was a delayed response to the shock or a side effect of not eating in a day or some unsavory combination of the two, but Ezra felt his consciousness slowly slip away from him, breath-by-breath, spiraling headfirst into oblivion.

Seconds? Minutes? Hours? later, he reopened his eyes to find Charley had navigated them back onto the highway and the radio was tuned to the local sports station. When Ezra inquired about the station, Charley told him it was Brad's hour to decide and when Ezra inquired about "Brad", Charley rolled her eyes and said that while he'd been unconscious, Headmaster Salisbury thanked them for what they'd done because he'd been looking to get away from Beaumont forever but never had a good excuse before. It was, like, a midlife crisis thing. He wanted them to call him Brad now, she added a minute later. Ezra glanced behind and smiled tightly at "Brad", who was spread across the entire backseat with Skippy perched at attention atop his lap.

It was the kind of smile, though, that vanished a millisecond after its appearance. The kind of smile that indicated a minor latent concern about being trapped in a stolen car with two people who seemed not quite sane, one of whom was driving. Ezra fiddled absently with the zipper on his jacket as he contemplated the scenario. *Where were they actually going?* He looked over at Charley with her hands squarely at 10 and 2, nine miles over the speed limit, ultra-concentrated on the road ahead. Earlier, when he'd asked, she'd simply said *Chicago* and evaded a further explanation. *But why wasn't Brad driving his own car? How could Brad be "good" with what had happened?* Ezra knew what a midlife crisis generally entailed: A new motorcycle. A sudden interest in collecting cheese labels or snorkeling. Maybe a spontaneous vacation to Aruba and perhaps, for the more adventurous, a secret paramour. But *none of the above* applied to what Charley had claimed Brad accepted as his midlife crisis. Not even close. In other words, Brad's mansion had been burglarized—his dog had been stolen, along with a thick roll of cash, a gun, and other various and sundry items. His mansion was

No Bars and a Dead Battery

later burned down, his Prius taken as the getaway vehicle while he had been conveniently hiding in the backseat, and it was all "good" with him? Not only this, but the burglars/arsonists were also two of his students, neither of which had a particular vendetta against him. *It's really not personal,* Charley had said while she'd soaked his antique Persian rugs in kerosene, *it's supposed to just be a statement against the system, you know?* "The system" presumably being Beaumont—their elite boarding school now hundreds of miles away in Rhode Island. Of course, it was a distant possibility that Brad hated the system just as much as his students, but *he* was the one who profited from it. Was it really that simple for him to just leave behind his entire life's earnings and start over, completely new, with no real plan as to where to go from here? Not that the "where" was even in his control. But what if Brad decided to have another "midlife crisis" and call the police on them? Ezra was seriously vexed, first, by how he'd even come to be entangled in this mess, but equally at the fact that Charley seemed totally fine with how much danger they were all in right now. The police would be looking for someone to frame for the incident. And when they inevitably found Brad to be missing, there were only two plausible conclusions: kidnapping or murder. They wouldn't even consider the possibility that the victim had fled willingly with the perpetrators, because that was something that literally *never happened.*

Now the radio had been switched off and Brad was musing about how, deep down, he'd never really felt like the type of person who would end up working for an institution. Trapped. He'd always been more "let life unfold organically". In college, he'd been a hippie and he found that kind of lifestyle to be more fulfilling. Perhaps that was why he never married or had children. Ezra had been paying attention at first but dropped out soon after Brad began a long explanation of some Sanskrit philosophy called *prajnaparadha—*

"crimes against inner wisdom"—which supposedly meant people should stop choosing things that don't bring them peace and balance, like staying in an unsatisfactory job. Ezra rolled up his jacket against the window as a makeshift pillow and watched the city rush by, wondering how Charley could tolerate another minute of Brad's spiritual enlightenment Ted Talk.

Charley Adler was by far and indisputably the most interesting member of the Beaumont Class of 2019. Her real name was Charlotte but no one ever called her that anymore. Though she was an only child, Charley had the personality and appearance of someone's kid sister. Freckles. A loud laugh and a permanent impish grin. A tendency to wear tie-dye on free dress days. She was unquestionably pretty but only beautiful to those who were in love with her, and most people who met her were, at some point or another. She always wore her wavy auburn hair down to her waist, a vivid contrast against the white sweater/green skirt uniform. In hushed discussions within the boys' common room, she'd been likened to some kind of mythical fairytale creature—maybe a forest nymph, a pixie, a wood sprite... There was some kind of intangible magic to her, perhaps in her dreamy gaze, her ever-parted lips or her waterfall-blue eyes that made her look as if she was raised on a steady diet of honey and dew. Charley was a flitting image of magazine cool—liked primarily for her prankster attitude, her spontaneity, and her unabashed willingness to wear her heart on her sleeve. She laughed as she talked and she talked a lot about how she hardly ever went to school. So really, it should have come as no surprise when she suddenly wanted to leave Beaumont last Friday, but there was still some unexpected element to it all. Mainly the fact that it was Ezra she wanted to leave with. Ezra was neither the boy she was in love with nor one of the friends in her *circle*, as she liked to say.

No Bars and a Dead Battery

The reason Ezra had agreed, unlike almost every other male in their class, wasn't a shot at the futile dream he'd win Charley's affections. It was because she wasn't like the rest and she was offering a perfect avenue out of school. Had pre-midlife-crisis-Brad— in all his tyrannical, glorious power from sentencing yet another first year to morning detention— asked Ezra to accompany him on a day's excursion to a headmaster convention, he wouldn't have objected either. The sheer drudgery of sitting in a classroom with 25 kids his age in various degrees of consciousness all copying down the same (mostly worthless) facts from the overhead projector—50 minutes a period, 8 periods a day, 5 days a week—had become so insurmountably dull that any second spent away from the place was a second of greater value.

Ezra had been silent the entire trip because he knew if he tried actually talking to Charley, she wouldn't like him anymore. Charley only liked him for the mystery. She'd said it, just like that: *you're a mystery, Ezra. Come with me?* Ezra had long accepted his status as local enigma. He was a quiet yet intelligent boy who had only a few close friends and often wrote poetry in public. Floppy hair. Soft smile. A tragic past that could practically be read in the archival depths of his warm green eyes. Being mysterious coupled with somewhat attractive is quite the paradox, as many people will want to know you and act as if they care about you, but really, it's just selfish curiosity and when the mystery is gone, so is the interest. Ezra knew he couldn't risk losing her interest, not when there was so much at stake and so little of it in his control.

A few hours later, Charley pulled into a murky plaza just outside Chicago city limits. Ezra picked his head up and surveyed the area. It wasn't particularly picturesque. There only seemed to be a drugstore, some kind of deli and a run-down vape shop in the immediate vicinity. Still, Charley instructed them to stay in the car while she headed into the drugstore. Ezra was beginning to feel uneasy about letting her go in alone, when she popped right back out, rolling her eyes and saying they didn't have anything. What she was looking for, she wouldn't tell.

They hit every drugstore on the outskirts of Chicago until Charley collected all her mystery items. A pair of scissors, a razor, cheap tortoiseshell reading glasses, black eyeliner, and *Tru-Hu* hair dye— two boxes in a metallic auburn that matched Charley's almost identically. With no regards to the "Men" sign, Charley ushered them both into a single-stall bathroom and began tearing open the boxes. Brad raised his eyebrows but knew better than to object. It's just easier this way, she explained impatiently. The idea was that strangers would think Charley and Ezra were siblings, Brad their father— a mere aesthetic nuance which would dredge up considerably less suspicion than two unrelated teenagers traveling with a random middle-aged man.

The process of bleaching and dying Ezra and Brad's hair took about an hour and stretched Charley's patience to a level it had never previously reached. This wasn't even the extent of their disguise. Brad was ordered to shave off his weak mustache and beard to look younger. Charley spent fifteen minutes bending over Ezra, applying the black eyeliner with a surgical precision to give him an "urban androgynous edge". He would have washed it off when she wasn't looking but he kind of liked it. Charley's disguise turned out to be just the reading glasses and a haircut of about one inch, though really, not even the glasses. When Charley first looked in the mirror, she swore they were already messing up her 20/20 vision. After dismantling the scissors into two separate blades, she punched out the prescription lenses and kept only the frames.

Charley's unpredictability made her almost predictable in a way. Ezra and Brad learned to expect exactly what they would think not

No Bars and a Dead Battery

to expect. So when Charley's next stop turned out to be the city Main Hospital, neither were necessarily *surprised*, though both were curious. Charley, in her typical unrelenting reticence, claimed she wanted to say goodbye to her mother (a surgeon?) before the next part of their trip, but she only wanted Ezra to come in with her. Brad, who had given up jealousy and cynicism as part of his new zen lifestyle, merely shrugged and headed for a nearby sandwich shop. *How exactly does a person become like Charley?* Ezra wondered as they hurried along the crowded pavement leading into the hospital. Really, he'd been wondering all along. He was looking forward to meeting her mother to see if she was part of the reason. Maybe, maybe not. Ezra knew things weren't ideal for the two of them (they were still, indeed, both fugitives and murder suspects), but in that moment, skipping over the sidewalk cracks with Charley, surrounded by strangers who seemed kind and pleasant for no reason in particular, he'd never felt more alive. Like everything was possible and there was more beauty in the world than he could ever notice. Serotonin overflow.

Of course, this feeling came to a crashing halt at the doorway. Charley suddenly took Ezra by the shoulders and steered him off to the side to let a couple wielding half a greenhouse of flowers pass through. She had to tell him something depressing but important, she said. Her mother wasn't part of the hospital staff, though she used to be a nurse at a different hospital. She'd actually been in a prolonged coma here for 8 years, ever since Charley was in Year 2. No one knew why. It was a medical anomaly, but she was still technically alive, though... unresponsive. Ezra could tell Charley was skirting around the word "vegetative", as she described her mother in about 30 other ways, none of which really made much sense. Anyway, Charley had made it a tradition to visit every year on her mother's birthday and she guessed this would be the last time it'd happen for a bit since next year, Charley would be living too far away. Where? She wouldn't say. This was part of "the grand plan" that would be revealed later. The point was, Ezra wasn't *family* so he couldn't go in and see Charley's mother himself. He'd have to wait outside, which Charley assured him wouldn't be for very long— usually her visits only lasted about 20 minutes. Charley knew which room was her mother's but she needed to find a doctor for permission to go in. So Ezra settled himself in a blue vinyl chair in the corner of the hallway and gazed out at the limelit night city looming behind the small circular window. There were no visible clocks near him, but he could tell when it had been longer than 20 minutes, perhaps twice as long. Luckily, a nurse happened to be passing by at the moment, who he flagged with a brisk wave.

No, he couldn't go in. No, she didn't know how much longer Charley would be. Wait. She checked a folder full of loose papers under her arm while Ezra waited patiently. Probably an hour, if she had to guess, giving him a quick smile that didn't reach her eyes.

The minute details of Ezra's ventures during this time aren't particularly interesting, but for the sake of clarity, he spent 13 minutes looking around the gift shop, 24 minutes talking to a friendly new grandmother who'd lost her glasses and needed him to escort her to her pregnant daughter's ward, 11 minutes searching for a vending machine before he realized there were, in fact, none, 7 minutes waiting in line for coffee at the cafe downstairs and an additional 5 minutes waiting for it to cool to a drinkable temperature back on Charley's mother's floor. It took him 30 seconds longer to realize something had gone seriously wrong.

Ezra could hear a sort of muted angry shouting—Charley's shouting—emanating from behind the closed door of her mother's room. Clearly, it wouldn't make sense for her to be shouting at her unresponsive mother, so Ezra set his coffee down in the windowsill and cautiously turned the doorknob of 4AE, which had been left unlocked. The scene at present was unsettling, to put it lightly. Charley's usual mischievous, jovial pixie face was flushed red and streaked with tears. She froze, mid-sentence when she saw Ezra had entered the room. To her right was the hospital bed where a woman who admittedly looked too much like a corpse to bear any relation to Charley was lying, eyes closed, hooked up to more tubes than he could count. In the far right corner was the doctor who'd likely been the subject of Charley's frustration. When *she* noticed Ezra standing by the door, her eyebrows shot up and she told him in a very calm voice that he'd better leave right now if he wasn't family. Suddenly seeming to remember their initial plan, Charley insisted he *was* family, tapping her hair as evidence. The doctor cast Ezra a skeptical glance but he quietly confirmed it was indeed true. He was her cousin, Jeffrey, from Pennsylvania. (Brother felt like too much of a stretch.) As it seemed a logical follow-up at the time, Ezra inquired as to what was going on. Of course, this was apparently the worst question he could have asked, because it inspired a second round of tears and yelling so angry it was still mostly incoherent. And entirely nonsensical. The first tear-warped phrase he could make out from the cacophony was *Ezra, she wants to kill my mother* and the second was *It's all about the money.* Ezra just looked at her worriedly. *What was she talking about and what did she expect he could do, anyway?* The doctor simply shook her head and ushered him out into the hallway, one arm around his shoulders. They took a seat in the two vacant blue chairs at the end of the corridor. This was a typical reaction, the doctor explained, to what was going on. It was natural and even expected.

Hands clasped tensely together, she elaborated on what that meant. As he knew, Charley's mother had been in a coma of unknown origin that had progressed into UWS (unresponsive wakefulness syndrome) for the past 8 years. Up until last week, she'd been "fine", obviously a quite relative "fine", but it meant there were still brain waves even without any response to external stimuli. Throughout her time at this hospital, they'd tried nearly every technique to treat the UWS in hope of a miracle cure. They'd tried surgery at first. Then physical therapy. Then deep brain stimulation. The most recent effort was a drug administered last year known as Zolpidem, a new breakthrough in medicine that'd allegedly caused a full recovery for a few patients in its trial run. But it did absolutely nothing for Charley's mother. If anything, it only worsened her condition. Last week, they'd taken some tests that measured the electrical activity in Charley's mother's brain and the results had come back from the lab a few hours ago. There was no sign of electrical activity this time, which meant she was legally brain-dead. In this case, the doctor continued (not making eye contact with Ezra anymore), the next move is to decide whether—or when—is the right time to disconnect the patient from the life support machines that aren't really doing anything. You're only allowed to "pull the plug", as the euphemism goes, when someone no longer has brain waves and any hope of a quality life. But you still have to contact a representative of the patient for their legal approval. The doctor cleared her throat before glancing up at Ezra: *Your uncle.* Ezra's first thought was *but I don't have an uncle?* before realizing she meant Charley's father and correcting his quizzical expression. I don't know how well you know him, the doctor proceeded, but he didn't seem particularly invested in the patient's life and he approved... the unplugging almost immediately and without question, which is... rare. Still, his permission proved unnecessary because one of the nurses found a copy of the patient's living will in which she'd indicated that in the unlikely chance of this situation ever occurring, she would prefer to be disconnected instantly. Living wills haven't

No Bars and a Dead Battery

really become a common practice yet, but Charley's mother, of a medical profession, sensibly happened to be one of the few who had prepared one. So... earlier, when the doctor had informed Charley of everything she'd just told Ezra, Charley became irrationally, understandably resentful and aggressive, claiming it was the hospital's fault for not caring about her mother's life because it was just costing them to keep her around so they killed her off to save money. While this wasn't true, they indeed *had tried everything*, and it was Charley's father who was paying the lofty medical bills with no complaints, Ezra could see how it made sense in her head. He couldn't imagine how awful she must be feeling right now. The doctor seemed to read his mind. She stood up, heading back for the room, and told Ezra gently that Charley would need a bit more time to say goodbye and she'd let him know when Charley was ready to leave, but in the meantime, he should just wait where he was and not try to come back because that would only make things harder for her.

As Ezra sat there alone in the hallway, staring at nothing and everything under the flickering city lights, he couldn't help thinking of a sort of cheesy quote that the Kindness Club had taped up in various places around his school: *Everyone you meet is fighting a battle you know nothing about. Be kind. Always.* Unfortunately, it felt like Ezra had been the only one to actually read it. He wondered if people would have treated Charley differently knowing her mother had been dying this whole time and her father didn't care. And he wondered if people would have treated *him* differently. Ezra's father, an Englishman, had died from a drug overdose before Ezra came along and his mother, of Estonian descent, remarried a born-and-bred New Yorker a few years later. His name was Marc and he was some kind of high-profile agent for a business firm that dealt with sourcing materials for luxury cars. It was the type of job that gave

Marc a gratifying sense of self-importance but also the same type of job that if aired as a TV show, would be cancelled immediately, as it would primarily involve endless meetings full of middle-aged white men who interrupted each other's every sentence and sipped thin glasses of water allegedly bottled somewhere tropical.

Anyway, Marc kept Ezra's mother shacked up in a $16-million dollar Manhattan penthouse, where she supposedly ran a middlingly -successful jewelry business, but really, she was a housewife who watched reality television more often than she dealt with jewelry and spent most of her time reclining on a white settee with a glass of overripe Cabernet, never once spilling a drop onto the pristine patent leather. Ezra had never actually visited this penthouse. All of the previous information had been gleaned exclusively through a tiresome series of phone calls, usually only once per year. Imagine not seeing your mother for a week and then catching up over coffee on the weekend—perhaps a two hour affair to patch up the minute holes punctured in your relationship. However, Ezra's mother preferred this to be a yearly occasion, but with the same comprehensive agenda. Therefore, the conversation would last typically from 7 to 10 hours, until Ezra's phone would overheat and turn itself off and he'd have to ask his roommate to borrow theirs so he could keep talking. The most recent time was the longest and most unsettling. His mother had called him in the late afternoon and continued talking throughout the entire evening, into the early hours of the next morning. Ezra knew well enough how to carry on a drawn-out, seemingly endless conversation while doing schoolwork, studying, eating dinner and going along with normal life, but it had never lasted this long before. He'd finished his schoolwork hours ago, studied for all his tests in the next week and now he just wanted to go to sleep. Through his blinds, the first gasp of daylight was creeping into the room.

No Bars and a Dead Battery

Mom, he interrupted, his voice husky from disuse, *Mom, I have to get up for school in two hours.* But she kept on talking right over him, perhaps oblivious, perhaps because she had to. Ezra tried to focus on something to stay awake— the phone's vague buzzing from being on for so long, the lightbulb in his desk lamp, the—it was useless. His eyes were the first to surrender and his mind soon followed. When Ezra woke up an hour later to his alarm clock, he picked up his phone (which had slipped beside the edge of his bed, to hear his mother's muffled voice still echoing through the receiver). She'd been talking for an entire hour without even pausing once to hear his response.

It was 6am and once again Ezra put the phone to his ear. Now she was talking about how she'd cut her wrist slicing some vegetables for dinner the other night and how it'd taken forever to stop bleeding. Nineteen stitches. Three doctors. *Maybe I shouldn't cook anymore*—her voice suddenly broke... and stopped altogether. On the other end, tears were silently gliding down Ezra's face because of what he'd heard, because of the raw despair of the entire situation. He hadn't cried in three years, even when he'd broken a rib. And here he was, listening to a story about a mishap chopping vegetables and he'd never felt more helpless. His mother didn't cook. She said this every time they talked. They *always* ordered Postmates—her and Marc. So what had happened wasn't a "kitchen accident". Evidently, she had been talking to her distant, quiet son on the phone for 11 hours straight because she had nobody else who would listen to her. Who cared to hear anything she had to say. Or how she was doing. Or if she lived or died. The kitchen story was, as Ezra realized in that moment, a thinly masked shout into the void. She'd tried to kill herself. Marc clearly hadn't picked up on it; would her son?

Now she was sobbing almost imperceptibly into the receiver,

probably thinking he'd fallen asleep hours ago. Her last hope—dashed by the sound of silence. Ezra took a deep breath, swiped his sleeve over his eyes and cleared his throat: *Hey, Mom, yeah, I'm still here. Are you... all right?*

After a few more hours (he'd skipped breakfast and assembly that morning) they said goodbye and vowed to talk before the next year. Later that day, Ezra found Marc's number on LinkedIn and rang him at work. He'd answered impatiently, saying he had to be at a very important meeting in 5 minutes, but once Ezra filled him in on who he was and why he was calling, Marc seemed to re-evaluate his priorities.

Never having a real father sucked for reasons that are presumable. But having Charley's father, a man who cared so little about his ex-wife, his child's mother, he signed off to her death without the slightest hint of regret... might even be worse. Ezra couldn't decide who it was sadder for, Charley or her mother. Running through his mind now was something half monologue and half a pleading invocation to a person he'd never met and wasn't sure he ever would. *Amor vincit omnia. (Love conquers all.) Or love is ~supposed~ to conquer all. Including tragedy. Including death and the fine print you didn't bother reading. I hope you stay, for always and after, and never because you felt you had to. Because you wanted to. And when a machine keeps me alive, I hope you have it in you to walk away.* Who would this person be? Ezra didn't know, but definitely not Charley. He knew he wasn't her type, despite how *mysterious* she found him, because a girl like Charley would only ever fall for a lacrosse player sort with insultingly long eyelashes, someone who'd give her his jerseys to wear to school and call her "my girl" in front of his friends. Also known as Asher Belaire. Everyone knew Charley was in love with Asher. Every student, every teacher, even Brad knew, because she'd announced it over the school's PA system the morning after

No Bars and a Dead Battery

Columbus Day. It wasn't uncommon for students to run the morning announcements, but Charley was never part of that crew. The girl who was supposed to do it had been absent (hungover) that morning, so Charley took matters into her own hands.

Good morning Marauders, this is Charley Adler reporting live from Studio A! I hope you all had a wonderful long weekend and you recover from your hangovers as quickly as possible. Especially you, Salisbury. The weather today is 59 degrees, sunny with a 30 percent chance of rain, so plan accordingly. The lunch today is leftover special, so make reservations for Pauly's early. (A popular nearby restaurant) There was a long pause, then a sigh. *Now I guess... I'm supposed to lead you into saying the pledge. Well. We're not doing that today. Yesterday, I'm sure you all know, we had the day off to celebrate an illustrious national icon known as Christopher Columbus, who, as legend goes, "discovered" America. Yep. We raised our red cups to a man who enslaved, mutilated, and destroyed an entire indigenous population and due to his white colonial male privilege, is still being honored as a hero today. Cheers.* Pause. *So I don't think most of us are feeling particularly patriotic. Anyway, now that we're not saying the pledge...umm, what else what else. Stop judging women based on how they dress. Love is love and love always wins. Health care should be a human right. The only minority destroying America is the rich. Immigrants aren't an issue in this country and if you really think so, come talk to me. Black lives matter and if you're one of those people who responds with "all lives matter", again, you better come see me. Climate change is real and we need to demand action now. The police are corrupt and school shootings are an epidemic and you can put a silencer on a gun but not on us. Last thing... everyone tell Quinlyn Young happy 16th if you see her today! Huge thank you to the storks for bringing this one to earth! Happy birthday, baby!! Umm. All rightttt, one more thing. Hey, Asher Belaire, I'm in love with you.*

To put it mildly, the school was shook. After that day, morning announcements were sent in the form of daily email blasts. Ezra wasn't exactly sure how things unfolded with Asher afterward but he knew the narrative everyone knew from a friend who'd heard it from a friend of a friend and likely at the base of the chain was a distorted but somewhat accurate version of the truth. During the long weekend, Charley had met Asher at some party and immediately fell in love with him. He was a fourth-year and she was a second, so their circles didn't really Venn much. At said party, they'd talked and agreed to go out at some point because Asher, like the rest of Beaumont, found her exceptionally adorable and interesting. But then the party ended early and they said goodbye and somehow forgot to exchange numbers. Later that night, though, a mutual friend of Charley and Asher informed Charley that Asher had a massive crush on her and wanted her to come to his lacrosse game the next day. Charley couldn't make it for some reason, but she didn't want Asher to think she wasn't interested... which led to the announcement. In the hallway afterward, she'd run into Asher, grinning shyly like her typical magical, radiant self, but he coldly pushed her aside this time, saying nothing more than a line everyone in the school knew had been quoted verbatim: *You were only ever a consideration.* In truth, this line hurt Charley more than she'd ever admit. If she'd been anyone else, she would have been bitterly offended and cried for 4 hours while watching an embarrassing rom -com and carving through an entire pint of Butter Pecan ice cream. Instead, she played it off as a joke—the biggest joke Beaumont had ever seen, a joke that became so hallowed, so revered, it would inevitably become a tale for future generations of Marauders to tell in hushed tones to one another, as if some mystic secret.

Asher was the first boy Charley had ever liked at Beaumont who didn't fall head over heels in return. After the announcement, dozens of other boys had approached Charley saying how brave she was and how they admired that quality in girls, which minorly revolted her. Their directness. Their lust. Correspondingly, this only

No Bars and a Dead Battery

intensified the degree to which she wanted *him*. So as for the joke, she decided to hold a party with the theme of her non-relationship. The day of the party was dubbed Charley-Asher Day and *everyone* was on board. Shirts had been sourced from an anonymous donor that simply read "Ashley" (their combined "couple" name) in a red font with hearts dotting the letters and everyone (minus Asher and Charley, of course) wore these over their uniforms on the day of. And the fact that the administration was totally clueless and bemused as to why the entire school was suddenly obsessed with a mystery girl named "Ashley" only intensified the scope of the joke. The concept had become so widely circulated that there were *30* pre-parties held before the actual party, which was at a warehouse off-campus. This party shattered school records as the event with the highest participation rate since 1909—higher than prom and homecoming combined. Even chronic introverts like Ezra knew this was a social event they didn't want to miss.

When Charley arrived, the crowd cheered, cued the DJ to start the music, and hoisted her up on their shoulders. But when Asher arrived, the crowd went *wild. Ballistic.* Many people had made bets as to whether he'd actually show or not and indeed, he showed, high-fiving all his lacrosse pals and blushing under his ridiculously long eyelashes Charley drove herself mad thinking about. The rest of the party was really just a standard Beaumont rave, ten times as loud. However, the very last song had been programmed to be slow—comically, the Twilight theme song: "A Thousand Years", and, as these things go in high school, the crowd began to chant "Ashley!" until Charley and Asher were located and shoved together into the center of the room and forced to dance, much to everyone's delight. *Look at this,* Charley thought while examining Asher's eyelashes up close, *look how much everyone loves me and us and this joke I created as a defense mechanism for the heartbreak you caused.* Everyone loves me, *Asher, so you're in the minority now.* While Charley enjoyed this moment immensely, she also knew there were many people who had bet on whether they would kiss or hook up, and she didn't really want her love life to become a source of her classmates' income. Luckily, Asher seemed to feel the same way. He leaned forward and whispered into her hair: *come to my game tomorrow, no announcements?* The next morning there were no announcements. But later, at Asher's game, there was no Charley—she'd left Beaumont hours ago with Ezra and Brad.

Charley!! Ezra leapt up and out of his seat, shaken abruptly from his thoughts. He'd just turned around to see her flying out of the room, heading in the opposite direction. So much for a warning. *Was she trying to avoid him?* Probably. *Should he bother going after her?* Like he'd ever stop bothering. Like that was something he *could* stop... Impossible, he thought, with a slight shake of his head. Impossible as catching up to Charley when she wanted to leave a place. He'd lost sight of her now but there was only one staircase and elevator at the end of the hallway, and in typical Charley Adler style, she'd slid down the 9 railings, thereby beating Ezra's time sprinting down the 120 steps by at least 30 seconds. From this gain, her lead had increased by so much he couldn't see her anymore, let alone know which direction she'd gone. Definitely outside. But from there, the possibilities were infinite. He tried putting himself in her mindset to see if that gave any better indication. Where would *he* go after seeing his mother die at the conclusion of 8 years of getting his hopes up she'd recover? Probably as far away as possible. The farther, the better. Best not to have any reminder of the unspeakable shock of that day and anything that played a part in it. The place. The people. Which included Ezra but he wouldn't let that happen. So the next step was how—how to get as far away as possible? Considering Charley had no money (Ezra'd pocketed the stack

No Bars and a Dead Battery

during their drugstore shopping), Brad's car was the only real escape. Hopefully Brad was somewhere nearby so they could grab him and leave immediately. Ezra then recalled with a note of frustration that Charley was the one with the keys, so there was a possibility she could just take off without either of them. Without money, though? Unlikely. But no, actually, no, none of the above. Once Ezra finally reached the sandwich shop lot where they'd parked hours ago, the most obvious ending to this terrible, endless day crossed his mind for the first time. They'd parked in the third row, four cars from the left curb. Ezra had a near photographic memory so this wasn't something he'd ever misremember. Now the shop was closed and there were no cars anywhere in the parking lot or along the adjoining streets. It was pretty self-explanatory. Brad must have had another set of his keys on him and he'd bolted when he saw the chance. In all likelihood, calling the police on Ezra and Charley like any sane person would. Of course. It was idiotic to have trusted him in the first place. Now both of them were completely screwed over. And Charley—*there she was*, or at least someone her size. Once Ezra's senses had adjusted to the dark, he could now perceive a vague outline of someone bent over on the curb facing away from him. As he drew closer, he *knew* it was her. Not wanting to frighten her even more, he called out her name from a few meters away. Charley jumped up instantly and swiveled around like he'd whispered it in her ear.

She was looking at him, but she wasn't looking *at* him. She was looking past him, at some scene from earlier, or at the hospital masked by the skyscrapers behind him, a mile or so from where they stood. It was the single-most hopeless expression Ezra had ever seen on a person. Eyes wide, lips slightly parted in a kind of disbelieving, stunned disappointment, like when, as a kid, you first find out that magic isn't real. Her arms hung limply at her sides, shoulders caved in, thin frame slanted forward as if she was one strong gust away from being carried off with the wind. Ezra wanted to hug her, to soothe her that it would all pass in time, but he couldn't find the words and he knew she wouldn't listen anyway. Sometimes all you can do is watch powerlessly as your entire world unravels in front of you. Ezra could see words forming on her lips, but she had to repeat them five times before they became audible: *can we get dinner?* This wasn't exactly what he'd been expecting, but nevertheless, he told her of course, where? She just pointed her shaky hand at a dimly lit Chinese chain across the street. Ezra knew that Charley was far from all right, but pretending she was would inevitably only make things worse. She wasn't even necessarily *pretending*, just refusing to talk about it and refusing to express any actual emotions. Silent as they crossed the street. Silent as they walked to the restaurant. When they got into the place, the man behind the counter asked her what she'd be ordering three times before Ezra realized she wasn't planning to answer—apologized and ordered her the same thing he was having. Apologizing for her felt wrong the second it'd come out of his mouth, but Charley didn't even look at him. *Should they eat inside?* She nodded. Luckily, there were only a few other customers so their food was ready almost instantaneously.

They brought the paper bag with their dinners to a two-seater near the front window. Neither of them reached in to take anything out. Charley seemed more absorbed in whatever was going on outside. Ezra felt like he'd been shoved into a movie as the lead role without being given the script. He had no idea what to say to her and all the cliché, greeting-card sympathies seemed stiff and unwanted. But what else could he say? Sorting through the greeting cards he'd just rejected, he settled on a quick, painless *I'm sorry*, which came out as a frustrated sigh. Charley looked over at him and

No Bars and a Dead Battery

shrugged.

Don't be. It wasn't his fault. Yes, but—She reached into the bag and took out one of the boxes of rice and a pair of chopsticks. She was a vegetarian, apparently. So much for ordering her his sesame chicken noodles. Ezra half expected her to start inhaling the rice as a presage she wasn't in the mood for conversation, but no, she was eating it extraordinarily slowly, almost one grain at a time. Which meant what, then? Apprehensively, Ezra began eating his own dinner and they continued in silence as people passed in and out of the restaurant—waves of laughter and cheerful banter. Every loud laugh, every overheard joke felt like a stab in the chest to Ezra, as if he was Charley's defender and so he should find some way to block out everyone else's happiness until she too could be happy. It was cruel, sadistic even, that all these strangers were flaunting it right in front of her face.

The silence was growing unbearable. Every violent tick of the clock felt like it was adding to an invisible cloud of tension hovering over the two of them, threatening to turn tempestuous at any moment. Impulsively, Ezra decided to say something without really thinking about what he was actually going to say, only that he should say *something*, and it was too late to backpedal—he'd gotten out one word, "so...", when Charley brought the chopsticks halfway up to her mouth and just stopped. Froze. A sharp breath escaped her like a gasp, which all at once turned into sobs, racking her body in the kind of uncontrollable misery he'd seen earlier, before she'd even been through the worst of it all. People could at least have the decency not to stare... Shaking his head, Ezra led Charley outside and away from the windows of all the restaurants and shops. He finally let go of her at a deserted street corner. In between her sobs, he tried to put together what Charley was saying. There was a lot and it was kind of a whirlwind of anger and frustration and disappointment. She'd already figured today was going to be the last time she'd see her mom, because of the moving thing, but it was different knowing her mom would have been alive even if unresponsive. It was hard to explain. Did he understand what she was saying? Kind of... Then just imagine having a dog all throughout your childhood that you can't bring to college with you and so you just leave him with your family. Except when you leave, you break off contact with your family permanently for whatever reason and a lot of years go by, like a decade, and you know that the dog can't possibly be alive anymore because they only live 12 to 15 years and he was old when you left, but you still always picture him alive anyway, barking whenever your father comes home, sleeping on his favorite blanket after dinner. Because that's the last version of him you knew and so that's how you preserved him in your memory.

And it's different when it's your mother but it's the same idea. Charley wanted to be able to preserve her mom forever as someone with a heartbeat, still existing somewhere, still able to listen even if she could never talk back. But now that was impossible because she knew it wasn't true. And now the last version she had was a mock up in a flowery hospital gown she would have hated if she could only see it, given to her by the people who killed her. And they'd probably charged her for it. *Charley...* Exactly. What was wrong with her? Why did he even follow her when she left the hospital? She was a horrible person and nobody actually knew that because they all thought she was the person they wanted her to be and so no one ever saw her as who she really was. And something was clearly wrong with her because she'd only ever liked one person in her life and it was mostly because he didn't like her back and when that changed, she immediately stopped liking him and ran away because she was sick of him and everyone else so how could she ever fall in love with anyone? She'd never be happy. And why didn't Ezra ever

No Bars and a Dead Battery

talk? Why couldn't he ever be the one to initiate anything? Didn't he have any opinions? She'd been waiting this whole time for him to disagree with her or say *something* just *once* but he never did and that made her sad for a reason she couldn't explain to him because he wouldn't get it. Or was that part of the *mystery*?— not talking ever. And now they were screwed over because the police would track them down and arrest them and so the dream would end before it even started. What was the dream, Ezra wanted to know. It *would* have been to move to this quiet town by the sea in California— M. — and live there as writers forever. And if they got bored they could bounce around the country and meet other writers. But that was never going to happen anymore and both of them would be miserable for life and in prison and would it *kill him* to say something for once??

After a 5.97 second pause, Ezra determined it wouldn't. And then he just wrapped her in his arms. They stood there for a while on the street corner, motionless, full of emotion. Ezra knew he was still very much treading a fragile line and needed to be ultra-careful with what he decided to say next, so as they walked to the nearest car rental place, he told her a funny story about when his roommate Chaz had been caught smuggling beer into the dorm. Somewhat surprisingly, but much to his relief, she laughed at all the good parts.

They reached the car rental shop within 12 minutes, luckily, because it was closing in only 3 more. For a moment, Ezra wondered if it'd be too suspicious that two kids were looking to rent a car a few minutes from midnight and were also paying in all cash. It wasn't, apparently. They were given a navy Cadillac El Dorado, a few maps Charley'd asked for, and told to have a good one and stay out of trouble. Ha. Charley hopped into the front seat and they sped off into the night together. She was back to her usual self, thankfully—a little quieter, a little more serious—but still a lot closer to the Charley of days past. The good thing was that now Ezra didn't have to worry about censoring himself in front of her. As if she would leave him now. As it turned out, she even seemed to enjoy the talking version over the silent, mysterious apparition.

At 2 a.m. they'd reached Iowa and stopped at a roadside diner to order decadent blueberry pancakes without a side of tension. After all, neither of them had really eaten dinner. Charley wanted to keep driving afterward but Ezra refused on the principle that no matter how much coffee she'd consumed, she would eventually fall asleep at the wheel and steer them both into a telephone pole and the police wouldn't exactly be on their side. An hour or so later, Ezra pulled over in a small, deserted break in the road near some kind of field. Charley wanted to get out and sleep under the stars but the sky had cracked open and it was now beginning to drizzle, so they settled for the front and backseat of the El Dorado instead. The next day felt like an everlasting blur of fields and cows and energy drinks and 90's pop charts. And the next night, once again, Charley begged to carry them through the final stretch, but Ezra wanted to play it safe. They'd get to M. in the morning. At least this time they could sleep outside. Charley unrolled a blanket that'd been in the trunk (along with a flashlight and first-aid kit) and smoothed it out flat on the sand of whatever desert was at the western edge of Nevada.

It was nice to be able to look up and see a clear sky full of constellations, rather than city smog. Was he sleeping? No. A long silence. What was he thinking about, then? Mm, nothing in particular. The next question was a total non sequitur, still, not much of a surprise from Charley. Was he gay? Ezra wasn't quite sure how to answer this. He'd never had a real relationship with anyone, apart from the time Zoë Forrester had declared him her valentine in Year 3 and proceeded to hold hands with him under

No Bars and a Dead Battery

their shared desk for the remainder of the day. Charley folded her arms around her knees and tipped them both backward onto the blanket. They just laid there for a while, memorizing the stars and soaking in the quiet desert night sounds. An orchestral symphony of crickets. Cicadas rattling distantly. The cool baritones of what sounded like owls hovering nearby in the darkness. Charley was the first to break the peace, with a pressing follow-up. Well, who did he find more attractive: her or Asher Belaire? There was a telling moment of hesitation. *You?* Charley just laughed.

Liar. They both laughed this time. Ezra suddenly felt like he was on the verge of tears, but out of relief, maybe. Was that even possible? He could see Charley looking at him askance and she reached over and tousled his hair. Then she hugged him, in the awkward but comforting way someone hugs someone else who's lying right beside them. Now that Charley felt it was acceptable, she proceeded to talk about Asher's eyelashes for the next 20 minutes and while Ezra considered them a worthwhile subject of fascination, he was too tired to stay awake any longer and drifted off a few minutes later.

The next morning, when they arrived at the off-the-grid seaside town M., things seemed fairly idyllic. The tepid air lifted their spirits with a cool, salty breeze, the sky a promising cerulean. No people anywhere nearby, as far as Ezra could tell. There were only a few houses in the area and Charley assured him they'd all been abandoned for multiple decades. Why? Nobody knew. (She'd read all this in some travel encyclopedia a few years back.) Therefore, without any qualms, she busted open the door of a small bungalow on the water and started sweeping dust out of the place. This was the perfect writers' retreat, Charley claimed, because real writers always seemed to complete their magnum opus in a place where there were zero distractions. Incidentally, all the best books were either written from a quiet seaside hideout or from prison. Ezra laughed. If they *hadn't* relocated to a quiet seaside hideout, it very much could be prison for them. So they were both destined to become great writers either way. The days lapsed blissfully in tandem with their prospective works: Ezra, a collection of poems about homesickness and Charley, a novella about a young girl in Lebanon. In the time they didn't spend writing, they hung out by the ocean, or went on morning runs or played cards. Once, a raft had drifted onto shore mostly intact, so on a whim, they spent the evening paddling a mile west and back as the sun sunk behind the waves, radiating hues of crimson and deep violet. And when the sun resurfaced in the morning, the enchanted cycle started over.

Did he want to go swimming this afternoon? No, not really. Well, let's do *something*. The initial thrill of sudden total independence had come and gone quicker than Ezra could ever have imagined. Privately, he'd always harbored the notion that he could get along perfectly fine without internet but now that he'd been thrust into this reality with no foreseeable escape route, it felt as if they'd almost teleported themselves back to the 1700s. (There was also no electricity.) Things were still going on *out there*, in the real world. Wars. Scandals. Fluctuations in the stock market. News for headlines. Maybe a nuclear war had just been triggered, and now, they'd be the last to know. It wasn't even the psychological change that bothered Ezra most. It was the dust. *Everywhere.* One of the clear and presumable side-effects of moving into an abandoned house is that everything is old, rotting and dusty. He'd been expecting it and it'd felt kind of Robinson Crusoe to him at first, but that was before he was practically inhaling dust wherever he went. Even his writing desk had a layer of cemented sand that he could never seem to shake out of his hair and clothes and papers. If this was the fabled "hero's errand", the "writer's burden"—sacrificing

No Bars and a Dead Battery

any sense of self to focus solely on your work—maybe he wasn't cut out to be a writer. He just couldn't get out of his head like that. As every hour ticked by, the ever-present dust, the oppressive sense of nonexistence bothered Ezra more and more, but there was no way he could let Charley know.

For a reason he couldn't fathom, she was *so genuinely happy* here. She hadn't stopped smiling since they'd arrived. And Ezra thought she'd be the first one to snap. Her usually immaculate copper locks had become somewhat tangled and dusty within 24 hours but no, this could be remedied. The next day, she simply clipped them off in the fractured rearview mirror of the El Dorado, scissoring a jagged line along her collarbone. It was really kind of a shocking alteration, but it framed her face well. Ezra thought about how girls always seemed to do that. Get a drastic haircut when they wanted to come across as changed on the inside, whether to themselves or everyone else, or both. Like when Camila Edmonds had been dumped by her boyfriend of 5 years; she'd chopped off her long golden curls and kept chopping until she had what was essentially a buzz-cut. The next day, she'd sat at a different lunch table and inexplicably began speaking with a slight British accent.

While Charley's haircut might have been more an offensive tactic against the invading dust, Ezra knew part of it was also an attempt at self-reinvention. Transmogrification. Logically. She was a girl who'd been endlessly mis-imagined, by him and by everyone else. Partially because of her appearance, but mostly because of her words and actions. Of course, this raises the question of whether a person can ever be *truly* seen as who they are, but regardless, since what'd felt like an eternity, Charley had been trapped, every day playing the role of a character that other people greatly enjoyed, but also a character that she herself couldn't root for, and now was the time for her to pick up the pen and use it to write her own story. No point in hiding anymore.

As it turned out, Charley indeed loved living as a writer in M. but she was intuitive enough to observe that Ezra had come to hate it. Later that day, as they raided their rations for dinner, they realized they had nothing left but one can of soup, a few assorted stale donut holes, and three bottles of Sprite. It was time to venture out, at least temporarily. Checking the maps, the nearest pinprick of civilization appeared to be a 7/11 about 10 miles east.

Once they arrived, Charley began sweeping the shelves clean of Twizzlers and ginger snaps, but something more important had caught Ezra's attention. Perched in the front corner of the store was a small TV reporting national daily news and at that very moment, the yellow ticker-tape headline had switched from some state test update to *Beaumont Headmaster Accidentally Burns Down Own Home. Whattt...* Ezra dragged Charley over to see what had happened. *Yes, folks, you heard that right,* the grinning reporter read somewhat unconvincingly from his teleprompter, *We are here with Bradford Salisbury, headmaster of the renowned preparatory boarding school Beaumont. On October 21st, Salisbury's $3-million-dollar Rhode Island mansion was reported by a neighbor to have seemingly gone up in flames. Salisbury was missing at the time, along with his car and dog, Skippy. A week later, he returned from what he called 'an unannounced sabbatical' visiting family in the Midwest to find a can of kerosene he'd left open in the garage prior to leaving had somehow tipped and caught fire, perhaps from a chemical reaction with another spilled fluid, which later spread to destroy the entire central and east wing of his home. A direct quote from Bradford here: Well, it's certainly a fine thing I have homeowners insurance, even better that I wasn't home at the time. And really, I couldn't be more grateful to return to my wonderful students and staff at Beaumont.*

Brad's midlife crisis was over—the end of an era. Which meant two things. Brad hadn't actually reported them to the police. He'd

No Bars and a Dead Battery

taken the blame, committed a crime against his inner wisdom. All so Charley and Ezra could be safe. Maybe they'd head back to Beaumont now that they were free to return to society. Charley agreed this was probably a better idea then roaming the country in a rental car with an ever-thinning stack of 20s, if they wanted to actually make a living someday. Yeah, they'd go back. But first, there was one place Charley wanted to take Ezra that she knew he'd love. She made him close his eyes for an hour (blindfolded for extra certainty) as she drove with the radio on full blast so he couldn't hear any atmospheric sounds that would give away their surroundings—city or country. Okay, Ezra could take off the blindfold now. He obliged and peered out the window to find himself looking at a place he'd never imagined he'd actually get to see in real life. It was a miracle and a half in itself that Charley even knew him well enough to know that. *City Lights Bookstore, San Francisco*—the birthplace of the Beatnik movement and the eternal commons of a million legendary authors and poets. But that wasn't even all, Charley hinted. There was an event scheduled for that night, a poetry reading by S.K. Linneman—an author Ezra revered. Whattttt. How could she possibly have known? Without the Internet...? Charley had never bothered to find a charger for her phone which had died the very first day. But oh, no, unbeknownst to Ezra, she'd been planning it all along. Ever since she'd noticed him reading a collection of Linneman poems back at Beaumont. Ezra glanced at her curiously. Yep. She'd always been able to tell that there was something intangibly different about him. That he was someone she would meet once and never be the same person afterward. Because some people are one-in-7-trillion in the way that they shake you out of your small, familiar bubble into an infinite universe you never knew existed, one you can never go back from once you arrive. And those kind of people, Charley finished grandly, deserve an adventure of a lifetime. So he'd better get out of the car soon or they'd miss it.

Inside, the bookstore was crammed wall-to-wall with a vivacious, eager audience. It was a world just like the one Ezra'd always envisioned. Everyone seemed vast and interesting for a reason he couldn't place. The air hung a bit stiffly around them and appeared hazy though no one was smoking. Perhaps it came from the tapering candles positioned haphazardly around the perimeter of the room. Soon, a thin glass of champagne and some kind of petits fours were thrust into his hands with a brisk *welcome!* before he could protest—cueing the return of Charley's coy smile. They seemed to be the only guests under 21; most were at least twice their age. This was no matter. A warm, smiling man in his late sixties wearing a thin scarf over a checkered dress shirt was suddenly shaking both of their hands at once, saying how *glad* he was that they could join him tonight, two young dreamers like themselves. What had brought them here? As one of the youngest, Ezra didn't want to be written off as a naïve dilettante. He began rambling about how he'd loved Linneman's prose in *Ellipses, The Art of Hopefulness* before Charley elbowed him sharply, smiling almost conspiratorially at their mysterious greeter, who then introduced himself... as Linneman. So much for the naïveté. Ezra blushed. It wasn't like the man had included a headshot in his book jackets. They were all laughing now. What had brought them here, Charley began to explain, was a combination of wanderlust and a false belief they were fugitives. This seemed to capture the poet's attention. An unplaceable glint came into his eye and he swiftly raised one arm in the air, snapping loudly.

The crowded room became soundless in an instant. *Tonight,* the poet started, *we are here together to listen to a live recitation of my latest piece 'Lover is a Question'. However, as I've made my way around the room, it's*

No Bars and a Dead Battery

become clear to me that most, if not all of you, already own a copy of 'Ellipses' and an therefore access the poem at any time you please. These days, poetry is a truly rare language to come across in spoken form, but even rarer is an epic story that has never been written down and never will be. Like I mentioned previously, I had the opportunity to meet many of you. I don't usually shake hands *with everyone in my audience but I did today because there was a second agenda besides learning 100 names I've already forgotten.* Laughter. *I was probing, respectfully, I hope, for a story that carried more importance in its futility than my written work can ever assume in its permanence. Now, as a poet, I feel especially inclined to believe that everyone, everyone has a story that deserves to be told. All of you here. However, some of you were more willing to share yours and that is how I decided to choose. Without further ado, I would like to introduce to you your substitute storyteller for the night, a young woman from the Beaumont School all the way in Rhode Island: Charley Adler.*

Charley, by her startled *"Me?"* expression, had clearly not been expecting this outcome. She smiled nervously at Ezra, who gave her a *"We can't get arrested now, so may as well make it as honest as possible"* kind of shrug in return. The audience began cheering, whistling, escorting her to the microphone stand at the front, perhaps out of tipsiness or merely fascination that Linneman had chosen someone so young and inexperienced in the realm of life to replace his own profound erudition. Much to Ezra's surprise, or maybe not so much, Charley proved to be an excellent raconteur. She had the audience constantly in stitches from both laughter and doleful empathy. Even better, she recounted the details to a T, smiling wryly at Ezra whenever this led to his embarrassment. Anyway, the bias was minimal. He wouldn't have told much differently if it'd been him up there, and he was glad it wasn't. When she'd finally reached the moment they'd walked into the bookstore, the audience applauded thunderously, giving her a standing ovation while she blushed and refused to take credit for anything. All Ezra wanted was to stay there forever and talk about words and life with people who knew a lot more about it than the impersonal, overhead-addicted teachers back at Beaumont.

Like all nights and adventures-of-a-lifetime, there was always an end. But perhaps, Linneman-style, it would be more appropriate to conclude with an ellipsis rather than a period. There was much hope for the two young protagonists. Charley (whose phone was now charged, GPS programmed with Beaumont as the end destination) opened the door for Ezra in a grand sweep. It was finally his turn to choose the music.

They made their way through the crowd, and back to the El Dorado. And as they approached it, a crow flew directly over their heads and landed on the hood and then looked at them. They stood some distance away and watched the crow watching them. Another crow flew directly overhead and landed beside it. The first crow squawked and then both flew away. They watched the crows disappear, looked at each other, and then got in the El Dorado. Only one way to go this time, with five bars and full battery.

TACOS IN THE OLD CITY
Rick Allen Wilson

No coverage, not even one bar, the battery was dead anyway. It was still daytime, but there was an overcast and the sky had a perfectly even dullness, so there was no way to tell what time of day it was, much less which direction was north or south or anything else for that matter. A two-lane blacktop road snaked up into the distance and disappeared into some trees, or a forest if you wanted to get technical about it. It also snaked down toward some lumpy hills and disappeared there as well. What sounded like a two-stroke chainsaw could be heard in the distance, but it was impossible to tell whether it was up in the forest or down in the lumpy hills. This had been happening more often lately. Two different ways to go, with a dead battery and no bars, and nobody left to blame.

His mom had been after him for weeks to have the gas gauge fixed, but her wisdom was lost on him. That cost money—and he had forgotten the damn charger for his phone. He could order one but that would take weeks, and, besides, money was something Joel did not have. He had recently lost his job at Harold's Ice Cream over near the ReEducation Center and hadn't the heart to tell her. Hadn't she been through enough during these years of governmental restructuring? Wouldn't it be better to tell her *after* he found some other job? He told himself something would turn up, and he just needed time to figure everything out.

In the meantime, his friend Megan had loaned him forty units so he could meet this kid from a place called New Valley in the Desert.

But now, he had run out of gas, and that creepy old guy seemed harmless enough when he offered Joel the ride. But, then, whoa, did that go wrong and quickly, too. When the old guy turned onto that other highway a few miles back, Joel knew—or believed, anyway—that he had to get out of the car immediately. So calling the guy a perv and bolting from the car seemed like a good idea at the time.

But here he was on this road in the middle of nowhere and he wasn't so sure if he was in the right place. As he assessed the problem, he concluded he was basically screwed. He thought of that poem from the Old History he had to memorize for ReEducation, the one by Robert Frost. As he stood on the blacktopped road, he rewrote it in his head:

Two roads diverged
In the middle of Effing Nowhere.
(Nowhere!
Yup! That's pretty much where I am!)
And long I stood
And looked up one
As far as I fucking could
to where it disappeared in the Hills
where the rich people obviously live—
with their manicured lawns,
their BMW's,
their garbage disposals,
and their burly fucking stra8t kids who play lacrosse
and still go to Ivys
and cradle their lacrosse sticks
like swords ready for battle
as they join the privileged ranks
of soldiers in this New World,

No Bars and a Dead Battery

who wear their white privilege
like letterman sweaters from the fifties
from Riverdale or Remmington High
or whatever the hell the best high school
is left in this country
which God forgot.

Whatever, he thought. It pissed him off that Kyle Stephens on the lacrosse team was so hot. *Why are the cocky jerks always so hot?*, he thought. And, truth be told, he was coming to see this kid of the Desert because he looked like Kyle Stephens. Well, Kyle Stephens minus the lacrosse stick. He looked both ways again, trying to decide which way to go.

That chainsaw was really starting to annoy him. He couldn't figure out where the hell it was coming from because it seemed to fill the sky above him. Was it in the hills in what he figured was the Freaky Rich People Forest or in the other-worldly-mystical world in the lumpy hills below that looked more like snowless death moguls? Whether it was the forest above or the lumpy hills below didn't matter a damn really. But it bothered him that he knew the chain-saw was a two-stroke. It reminded him of his father and that time they went to cut down a Christmas tree. That was the last Christmas before his dad left. And then the Revolution happened and they were all fucked anyway.

He decided the sound was probably coming from the weird hills below, so why not start walking for the Rich Kid Hills above? He finished his poem as he walked, staring intently at the trees ahead:

Oh, I kept the one
without the chainsaw
for *another* day!

And that has made all the difference!

Will make all the difference?

But wait. The chainsaw was coming from the upper hills after all. Whatever. He wasn't a poet and he knew it. Even though he had about twelve journals packed with all kinds of scrawlings, drawings, poems, stories, and etchings, and even though he went to the New World Poetry Festival back East when he was visiting his cousin, he knew poets had to write lots of poems about politics, nature, identity, the New World, gender, sexuality, war, and all that shit that basically bored him.

Joel was a bisexual. At least that's what he thought. He had only made out with one guy and hadn't so much as held a girl's hand. He was pretty happy calling himself a bisexual, though, when it came right down to it. It was kind of like just keeping his options open. He didn't want to limit his chances either way if the mood struck.

And as for being a poet, he couldn't imagine either Robert Frost or even Billy Freakin Genius Shakespeare made the kind of money needed to live next to some rich guy in The Hills with his BMW (which was in his poem now) and who was probably using the chainsaw right this minute to dismember his wife for not making pancakes all the same size or some other bullshit rich people in Rich Hills fight about.

Joel decided he couldn't be more than twenty minutes from the kid's house, and he was starting to let it in, slowly, that this kid who looked like Kyle was a *rich* kid. A rich kid from the rich hills. With a rich dad and a rich mom who can't make pancakes.

He imagined they were filthy rich. That meant the Kyle look alike was a filthy rich gay kid. Joel's pace slowed as he imagined what refined style a filthy rich gay kid might possibly have. The kid was probably a slave of fashion and style. He probably shopped away his loneliness with a platinum merchandise card. It had to be lonely up there, locked away in a rich kid's castle.

Joel continued up the hill, thinking about the kid as he walked. For starters, he should stop thinking of him as the kid and it was weird to keep thinking of him as Kyle. The kid had a name, didn't he? True, Dorian was a rich kid's name, but it was still a name, wasn't it? So he should stop thinking of him as Kyle or the kid. The kid—Dorian—said he was fifteen. And Joel was 17. That made Dorian younger, but it definitely did not make him a kid.

As Joel walked, he looked down at his shoes, which were dirty, faded black and weather-cracked white. With each step up the hill, he fantasized about shoes Dorian might have in his private shoe closet that was probably the size of what used to be Macy's in New York. And those antiquated and historic designers, many dead now: Michael Kors, Kenneth Cole, Cole Haan. Georgio Armani, Stefano Ricci, Adidas. Adidas? Joel thought it a solid brand, but hardly what a rich kid might wear. Under Armour, though. Everybody in the world wears Under Armor. Even the creepy child molester who gave him the ride probably had an Under Armor jacket. Or even UA shoes. Even hot rich gay kids named Dorian who looked like dreamy but jerky studs like Kyle Stephens probably had a vintage pair of Under Armor shoes.

Joel was getting closer to the top of the hill and could see it was not a forest after all, though a thick ring of trees that separated the houses from the wildness of the desert and its spires. To his left, he saw four dust devils, probably about half a mile away. To his right was a crow, worrying a discarded bag of food near a cactus.

Just then, the crow took off carrying the bag, but when it reached about fifty feet up, the food began spilling, drifting back to the ground like an infantry of small parachutes. Joel paused, knowing exactly how the crow felt. You try and you try, then get a bit of a break, and you even catch some air and get a little lift off and it seems like smooth sailing into the cottony clouds and baby blue skies, but then the physics of your whole damn life are just wrong and you end up being the bastard who just makes a mistake in this New World and your whole treasure trove of sweet and salty fun food just falls into the air behind you. It all disappears and you're just screwed again. Two roads, indeed.

He passed under an arch that read Welcome to New Valley. Joel told the sign it was very nice of it to welcome him and began a one-sided conversation with it in which he was pretending the sign could speak. He answered a question the sign posed, telling it, no, he would not be staying long; yes, he agreed, New Valley seemed like a lovely place to raise a family; no, he did not expect he'd be staying for dinner because his mother would want him home.

He told the sign that he sort of hoped Kyle Stephens would give him a ride home—at least back to the El Dorado. Not Kyle Stephens he added, correcting himself. The rich kid from the app who looked like Kyle Stephens. Dorian Something. He asked the sign if he knew where Dorian lived.

He looked down a street to his right and agreed with the sign. Yep, right down there is where I would live if I were a rich kid who looked like Kyle Stephens. He thanked the sign for its courtesy and the pleasure of its conversation, then sauntered on down the road looking for Dorian.

Sure enough. There it was, dead ahead. He recognized it from the pictures Dorian had on the app, which told a collage version of Dorian's life. Here was where he was on a tricycle. The tree was taller than in the picture, thicker in its trunk, but it was definitely the same tree.

Joel hadn't really thought through what he was going to do after he got here. Now that his phone was dead, he couldn't message Dorian. What if Dorian's mother or father answered the door? How

No Bars and a Dead Battery

was he supposed to introduce himself? *Hi, I'm a stranger, and I've never met your son, but could you tell him I'm here? Why? Because we met on a sex app. I'm bisexual and he's gay, and I'm here to shag him.*

No. He would have to think of something else.

Still not knowing what he was going to say, he walked right up to the front door and rang the bell. Thirty seconds later, Dorian opened the door and looked at Joel from head to toe. Then he simply told Joel he wasn't his type and shut the door. Joel was flabbergasted. He had prepared for several possible responses but that wasn't one of them. Now what was he supposed to do?

He stood looking at the other houses. Joel was grateful when the chainsaw suddenly stopped. He started to ring the doorbell again. But Dorian opened the door before Joel's finger touched the buzzer and asked what Joel was doing. Joel told him he was just ringing the bell, and Dorian said he should go home. Joel told him he'd very much like to do that, but, unfortunately, the El Dorado was broken down back near the highway, and his phone was dead. He asked Dorian if he could use a phone. Dorian said he wasn't allowed to talk to strangers or have anyone over when his parents weren't home. And, again, Dorian shut the door.

Joel stared at the door. *Son of a bitch*, he thought. Here, once again, two roads were diverging in a mysterious suburban wood. Or, rather, it's sort of like the roads were disappearing. Joel hadn't a clue what to do, but Joel liked talking to himself about himself. He often did so in the third person.

What kind of day do you think Joel will have today? he often thought to himself as he stared at himself in the mirror after his morning whiz. *Will Joel win a million dollars? Would Kyle Stephens at least come out as bi so the two of them can get married or at least go to the prom together?* What a stink that would create. He so wanted to do it.

Such were Joel's thoughts. Right now, though, he was just

thinking, *What the ef? What the effing ef? I don't suppose there's public transportation around here? A subway?* Just then, the door opened. A guy who seemed older—probably twenty-two, twenty-three—stood there with safety goggles just above his forehead, holding a chain saw. Dorian stood behind him.

The guy holding the chainsaw stared at Joel and said to Dorian that he thought he said there was no one at the door. Joel quickly spoke up and said he was no one. No one at all, and he was just leaving. The guy with the chainsaw told him not to go, then pulled his goggles over his eyes, turned on the chainsaw and revved it. Joel was sure he would pee his pants.

The guy stood assessing him, with one eyebrow raised, then suddenly turned off the chainsaw and doubled over laughing. He kept saying he was sorry, over and over, but then would be seized by another wave of laughter. He was trying to imitate somebody out of a chainsaw massacring movie, but he couldn't hold it. Dorian told him he was a moron and disappeared into the house.

The guy kept staring at Joel, and, finally, when his laugh had subsided enough, he asked if Joel wanted a beer. But he turned around and went further into the house before Joel could answer. At first Joel stammered, but then shrugged his shoulders. He muttered something about how, of course, Joel would like a beer, thanks. *And don't mind at all if Joel comes in for a bit. Judas H. Priest,* Joel thought, and walked into the house.

The guy was digging in the refrigerator as Joel got to the kitchen. He took two beers from the fridge, then, one by one, opened them by placing them on the lip of the counter and hitting down on the bottle, leaving the bottle's top spinning and falling to the floor. He picked up the beers. As he handed Joel one, he didn't let go as Joel wrapped his hand around the bottle. Instead, he moved his index finger so he was touching Joel's hand and left it there, staring at Joel.

No Bars and a Dead Battery

He winked at Joel, let go of the bottle, and took a long swig on his beer. He told Joel his name was Ace, and then pointed at Joel and told Joel his name was Joel. Joel agreed that it was and watched as Ace sauntered to the doorway, turned around, and lifted one forearm to rest on the doorframe, holding the beer in the other hand. He posed that way for a moment, then burst out laughing again, doubling over, saying he was too much. Too much, he kept repeating.

Then he told Joel he was glad he was there and that he had been waiting for him. Joel was confused but Ace said he was exactly the man for the job, sort of a Robin to his Batman, a Jimmy Olson to his Clark Kent, a Sundance to his Butch Cassidy, a Thelma to his Louise. Joel said he didn't know what the hell Ace was talking about. Ace shouted to Dorian telling him that he and Joel were going to take a walk through the neighborhood and stop over at Jack and Marilyn's. Dorian shouted that this was a totally stupid idea. Ace shouted back that Dorian should stop being a baby and asked if he needed a juice box. He winked at Joel again, gave a couple of clucks and a head nod, indicating that Joel should follow.

As they walked through the neighborhood, Ace pointed out where the Richmonds lived, the Sorrells, the Simpsons, and Mrs. Black who had been all alone since the uprising. Joel said that was really interesting and all, but what he really needed was some gas and a lift back to the El Dorado. In a breathy and mock-sexy voice, Ace said, if Joel would be his, forever, Ace would carry him to the El Dorado on his back. Joel stopped walking and asked if Ace was gay. Ace quickly explained that he didn't believe in the old definitions or systems of the Previous Order. Here in the New World, though there was much to mourn for in the society that was gone, you were now free, if you'd let yourself be, just to connect and let that connection be Truth. Ace told Joel he had the most truthful eyes of anyone he'd ever known. He also told him he'd be happy to drive him to the El Dorado. He just needed his help with something, if he didn't mind.

Just then, a crow landed in the street, maybe twenty feet from them. Ace put his hand on Joel's shoulder and smiled at the crow. Anthropomorphism, he said, is the notion that humans are the center of everything. How arrogant, he said. We raped the earth. We slaughtered the animals. And that was our downfall, he explained. But this crow, he believed, was his, sent from the Creator, reminding him, always, of the darkness in us all—to be mindful of it, to strive, always, to leave others better than you found them. He felt the crow was his, even, because it frequently appeared to him like this. And there was only one in the whole development. In all the years he had lived there, there was only this one. But just then, another crow flew up and landed near the first.

Both crows seemed to be looking right at them. Joel heard Ace whisper something that sounded like *Son of a biscuit!* Ace turned toward Joel and told him he was gold. No, better than gold. Ace called himself lucky that Dorian had trolled Joel on the InfoPathway. He thanked Joel for showing up. Joel asked what the fuck Ace was talking about. Ace smiled. He began singing *Buffalo Girls, Won't You Come Out Tonight?* as he did a meandering dance toward a house ahead of them.

Inside the house, Ace knelt in front of the old couple who were in their recliners watching *This is Your World*. Ace kissed each of them on the cheek. He asked how Jack's shingles were doing and wanted to know if Marilyn's arthritis was any better. He introduced Joel to them by his full name: Joel Markus Pinkham. Jack and Marilyn said they had heard so much about Joel, and they were so glad James had Joel to make the run with him. Joel asked who James was, and Marilyn pointed at Ace, saying James, of course, was right there. Ace winked at Joel, kissed Marilyn's hand, gave Jack a fake punch, and motioned Joel to follow him toward the kitchen.

In the kitchen, Joel wanted to know if Ace's name was James, and Ace said, yes, it was. Joel wanted to know why James had said it was Ace. Ace asked Joel if he was kidding, then said James was a boring name. He felt Joel would like him more if his name were more adventurous. Joel asked why that was important to Ace. Ace smiled, opened a door to the basement and asked Joel to follow him, please.

The basement looked like any other basement. A workbench with an industrial pendant light was on one wall. A small laundry room was off the main room. Ace said to make sure, always, they were not being followed, then said aloud to the empty room that they were there and nobody had better fudge with them. Joel was beginning to like this Ace/James character who said fudge. Ace told Joel he was about to show him something incredible. Joel asked if the basement was where Ace brought his victims after he chainsawed them to death. Ace said, no, he didn't like to transport his dismembered victims. Ace pulled the pendant light down and said James 237419, please open for me and guest 32149. A voice asked if that was Joel and Ace said yes. The voice said she was so looking forward to Joel being there. Ace reminded the voice that she was a computer and to back off. He had first dibbs. To one side of the workbench, a portion of the wall swung open. Joel asked himself wtf, and, again, Ace asked Joel to follow him.

Underneath the houses above them, a vast Safe House and Training Center had been constructed. Ace explained that Jack and Marilyn had been billionaires of the Old Order, but they escaped to this place in the Desert when they saw the experiment of Democracy crumbling, where the Training Center could be constructed and hidden among the populace and those previously known as the Middle Class. Indeed, there were a few houses on the streets above who did not know that 100 young migrants were living below. Some of the houses, though, were fake fronts, like speakeasies of the previous century, seeming to be middle class families but were a part of the new Underground. There were rooms upon rooms in the bunker. An education center, where the young were taught to find on the InfoPathway all they needed to escape, build, or survive. The children ranged from ages five to nineteen, Ace explained. They had escaped the Great Extermination after the rise of the New World Order. Joel was looking at a group of children doing fence-climbing drills. Ace asked if Joel had anything to say. Joel said he guessed Ace might not be a chainsaw murderer after all.

Ace said great pains had been taken by some of the Freedom Fighters to reunite five of these children on this evening's reunion mission with their parents in the Free Zone below the Wall. And, he said, all Joel had to do was help him because he was the man for the job.

Late that afternoon, Ace and the Mobility Team loaded the five children into the Cleaning Van, a van which seemed to transport laundry and linens in mass quantities. The children were well trained at hiding themselves and each other. If the Border Patrol stopped them, the van, at first glance, would like any transport van, providing a la carte cleaning services for all the Greater Valley. As they drove through the welcome arch into the desert beyond, Joel looked over his shoulder into the back of the van. Not one child was visible. The saw-toothed ridges of the great spires rose before them, and Joel knew they would be back at the El Dorado before nightfall.

The El Dorado was to the side of the Old Highway near Old Blue Lake. They put gas in it as the children played. It didn't start at first, but Ace knew a thing or two about carburetors. When they

No Bars and a Dead Battery

finished, Ace built a fire. He and Joel fed the children and then opened the van doors and put the children to bed in the van with the cool desert air soothing them. He and Joel made a pallet in front of the fire and talked into the night, their voices echoing back to them occasionally from across the lake. They told each other dreams they had which were lost and taken away by the New World Order. Ace had wanted to be an architect; Joel, an actor. Ace asked Joel about his mother, and Joel opened his heart to him. Joel asked what was up with the chainsaw thing. Ace said he had a little business. He cut firewood most days so some of the neighbors who weren't a part of the project would be annoyed by him and keep their distance. Joel said he didn't want to keep his distance. Ace put his arm around Joel and brought his head to his shoulder. He told him Dorian worked for Resistance Recruitment and had sought Joel out on the InfoPath. Stalking him, basically. And James/Ace said he liked Joel long before he met him, because of his poems, his writing, his stories. He told Joel the New World would need poets, storytellers to make people not give up. Joel said he wanted to give up, but Ace asked where they would be if some of the heroic poets had chucked it in. He told Joel about a great poet from almost two centuries earlier—a gay poet, but long before there were words like gay, or bi, or trans. But how comforting to know others had told their stories, even encoding them when they feared imprisonment or worse. Take one of Ace's favorites, for example, a dude called A.E. Housman. Ace stroked Joel's hair and spoke the following words slowly, deliberately, with the fire crackling in the background.

Others, I am not the first,

Have willed more mischief than they durst:

If in the breathless night I too

Shiver now, 'tis nothing new.

More than I, if truth were told,
Have stood and sweated hot and cold,
And through their reins in ice and fire
Fear contended with desire.

Agued once like me were they,
But I like them shall win my way
Lastly to the bed of mould
Where there's neither heat nor cold.

But from my grave across my brow
Plays no wind of healing now,
And fire and ice within me fight
Beneath the suffocating night.

Just before morning, Ace opened his eyes. Something he heard had awakened him, and he uickly sat upright. Joel was still asleep beside him. He looked to the East and heard a crow caw, another one answer, and the first one respond again, more urgent than before. Then Ace heard it—the sound of a Patrol car as it whirred along the blacktop in the distance. Ace shook Joel awake and told him they were coming. Ace shouted *yo* to the children, who were immediately in motion, packing the van and loading into the trunk of the El Dorado. In less than thirty seconds and before the Patrol could could come into view, the van seemed perfectly stacked, as if the children were never in it. Such was the precision with which they had been trained: Survive. Leave no trace. Give in to the next thing you must do, and do it well.

Ace told Joel to follow his lead. He shucked off his shoes, socks, shirt, underwear, and pants, and Joel disrobed as well. They quickly lay down again in front of the dead fire with Joel's head on Ace's

No Bars and a Dead Battery

shoulder, pretending to sleep as Ace told Joel the plan. When the car got near enough to see them, Ace sat upright and pretended to be waking up. He frantically grabbed his clothes, which were strewn on the ground around him. Joel did the same. Ace jumped in the van and shut the doors as the Patrol came speeding toward them. The Patrol car skidded to a halt, dust flying around it, and the Guard opened his door, aiming a rifle at Joel. Joel glanced toward the van, and the Patrol called to whoever was in the van to open up and come out with his hands up. Ace did as he was told.

Ace fastened his jeans and called good morning to the Patrol, but the Patrol ordered him out of the van and forced them both to lie face down on the ground. The Patrol searched the van, turning over piles of cleaned linens and packages of freshly laundered uniforms. He walked to the El Dorado, looked through its windows, then slowly walked back to Ace and Joel, telling them that he knew what was going on there. Ace feigned ignorance, asking the Patrol what he meant. The Patrol turned and shot two of the tires on the van, then walked around it to the other side and shot one more. He told the two on the ground they were disgusting. He then called them handsome, and so sexy, and laughed, getting back into his car. One tire, the Patrol laughed, and wished them luck with that. Then, he drove off, the car disappearing, finally, among the rust colored spires in the distance.

Ace and Joel finished getting dressed. They opened the trunk and gave the children some water. They carefully closed the trunk again and got in the car, with Ace at the wheel of the El Dorado as they headed to the border. The Wall stretched 100 miles each way and there was only the one Check Point to pass through. Joel asked Ace what would happen if the Patrol at the border opened the trunk when they got there. Ace shrugged and told him they would be killed. Then he playfully and dramatically said, but if in the breathless night I too shiver now, 'tis nothing new!

At the Check Point, the Patrol scanned their tattooed identity marks on their wrists, and asked if the day's visit to the Old Land was for business or pleasure. Ace replied that it was for educational purposes only. One guard was staring at the trunk. Ace volunteered to get out so the Patrol could search them and the car, but the head guard declined, waving them through.

It was eighty more miles to the Old City. Joel said his mother must be way worried. It wasn't like him not to call if he was staying out. Ace told him not to be a jerk and worry her and asked why Joel hadn't called already. Joel said he bloody well would if he weren't such an idiot and left his charger behind. Ace reached in his pocket and pulled out a charger. Joel plugged it in and sent her a text: *Sorry, I'm a moron. I crashed with a friend last night.* She wrote back that she loved him. Just to be safe and have fun.

When they arrived, The Villagers were going about their day: a huge crowd of inhabitants living off the land, carrying water, chopping wood, selling vegetables, exchanging goods. Ace opened the trunk and said to the children not to weep for him when he was gone. The youngest called him a moron. They piled out of the trunk, peering at the crowd. An attractive young woman approached them. Ace said yo to her. She asked who the drink of water was. Ace told her to calm down. Joel was his drink of water. He introduced Angela to Joel and Joel to Angela. He gave Angela the children's medical clearances, their identity papers, and they each had a small backpack of belongings on their backs. Angela told the kids to come with her. Three of them had parents waiting and two would be meeting them for the first time since they had been ripped from them as infants by the Redistricting Police. The youngest, a girl, lifted her hand in a high five to Ace, which Ace returned. She winked at him, gave him two clucks in her cheek, and then they all

No Bars and a Dead Battery

disappeared with Angela into the flowing crowd. Ace stared after them and his eyes welled up with tears. Joel asked him why he, himself, was there. Ace simply said he needed him. He wiped his eyes and again Joel thought he heard Joel mutter *Son of a biscuit!* Ace put his hands in his pockets, walked in a circle for a second, peered into the crowd again, and then looked at Joel. Ace said, well, there was only one thing to do when a run was complete. He walked into the crowd and Joel followed him, zigzagging across cobblestones and turning from street to street, finally up a small winding street to a small shop, where he asked for two tacos. He paid, and he and Joel ate them.

They made their way through the crowd, and back to the El Dorado. And as they approached it, a crow flew directly over their heads and landed on the hood and then looked at them. They stood some distance away and watched the crow watching them. Another crow flew directly overhead and landed beside it. The first crow squawked and then both flew away. They watched the crows disappear, looked at each other, and then got in the El Dorado. Only one way to go this time, with five bars and full battery.

RIVER FLOWING ON

Callie Zucker

No coverage, not even one bar, the battery was dead anyway. It was still daytime, but there was an overcast and the sky had a perfectly even dullness, so there was no way to tell what time of day it was, much less which direction was north or south or anything else for that matter. A two-lane blacktop road snaked up into the distance and disappeared into some trees, or a forest if you wanted to get technical about it. It also snaked down toward some lumpy hills and disappeared there as well. What sounded like a two-stroke chainsaw could be heard in the distance, but it was impossible to tell whether it was up in the forest or down in the lumpy hills. This had been happening more often lately. Two different ways to go, with a dead battery and no bars, and nobody left to blame.

Most of New Mexico felt like this; less a landscape than a canvas. When it got cloudy, the beige of the sand washed out grey and even the trees started to resemble stone. Santa Fe seemed almost an oasis with its ponderosas and spruces, dark lakes and bighorn sheep. The herd had nearly doubled in size since the evacuation of the area. I never did get used to seeing them, their thick curved horns the stuff of science fiction, not New Mexican ecosystems. New Mexico seemed as close as you could get on Earth to alien terrain, though.

I got back in the car and tossed the phone next to Vi's sleeping thigh. The hills seemed our best bet for reception, but I figured it best to keep north until we hit Colorado. It was hard to tell if either road would lead to reliable cell reception anyway. The forest promised more cover than the open hills, at least. I didn't let Vi have a say, although I'm sure she would've agreed with me in the end, after disagreeing for disagreement's sake.

We stopped in Raton, New Mexico, to gas up the El Dorado and get cigarettes. The front dash was a graveyard of cigarette butts; little circles of burned plastic polka would dot the car long after I cleaned out the ash and quit smoking. I hadn't taken good care of the car. It felt like an extension of my body; keeping it tuned up and clean felt wrong somehow, like a denial of the state of my own health.

It was the first gas station we'd seen in hours, and the attendant took our money through a slit in the clouded up glass partition. Gas was cheap in Raton. It was cheap throughout all of those states, those long winding shit stains of highways through desolate terrains. They all have their own eccentricities, their own special breeds of strange. Even the populated towns feel like ghost towns, big cities feel like nuclear test zones. Pedestrians move slowly, as if they've only recently sprung alive after being plastic their whole lives. The southwest feels like this to me; a nuclear wasteland filled with test-people. Even in the mountains, I think of Los Alamos, of a mushroom cloud above a wasted horizon. Of a sea of green glass in the desert. I think my body feels the radiation in the ground, and every irradiated atom in me tenses up and screams, tells me something's not quite right. After the accident, I looked at pictures of the victims of Nagasaki and Hiroshima, waffle patterns burnt into their flesh and charred limbs. I stroked my bandages and felt some sort of deranged historical oneness.

There was a hotel in Raton with a pattern of swastikas circling the top bricks. When we drove past, Vi pointed at it and scowled, opening her mouth to start on one of her spiels before I turned sharply into the gas station parking lot. My head ached in a crown of pain, and I couldn't bear to even give her the satisfaction of my attention.

She told me she didn't smoke Marlboros after I bought them. Camels were her brand, she told me, and the pack of Reds suddenly felt clumsy in my hand. She always had a knack for making me feel wrong without realizing it; like I was a massive idiot but she tolerated me anyway.

I could never commit to a brand myself, switching from Camel to Lucky Strike to Marlboro with abandon. I guess it made sense, because holding onto a brand felt an awful lot like holding onto a person, or a place, a sort of permanence that made me panic. Brandless, nameless, homeless in the sense that I could never stay in one place long enough to make it home for me.

But when I look back on that week we spent driving, I think Vi was a more static presence in my life than even myself. It never did make sense to me but somehow, by always changing, she managed to stay exactly the same in my eyes.

♦

there's a little girl playing make-believe on the banks of the urakami alone always alone. in today's make-believe she's the goddess of the waters and mud streaks her skinny ankles as she kneels down to pick up a rock from the shallows. it's slippery-wet and perfectly palm sized even a small indent where her thumb rests comfortably she thinks, maybe a dead man held it underwater for a long time and the stone reformed in his fist but she decides it is her rock now, a talisman of sorts and she holds it tight for this is where her powers lie the strength of the river and the tides. it's lucky i'm a nice goddess she thinks because i can flood cities with this rock i can make water dry up in an instant i own the rivers! she revises her title to queen of the waters. the river burbles. i did that! she yells to no one. i am your queen! she tells the river.

it's around eleven which means the girl should head back home soon but she

No Bars and a Dead Battery

doesn't like to be indoors long although outside the air feels off today, like it's heavier or dirty with invisible soot. grandma should be home but the girl knows sometimes grandma steps out for a quick walk with her manfriend at this time and won't be home for another tenfifteen minutes so the girl decides to stay out by the river a little longer just in case.

she sits on a dry rock with her feet in the cool water and slaps the surface with her feet. she makes the surface bend and her reflection fracture. it shakes violently with the force of her foot and comes to calm again, a full mirror view of her face and hair pulled back behind her ears. she makes a silly face and laughs loudly because no one is around to tell her not to. she squirms—she is bored. everything is still.

◆

We'd been living in a perpetual Cold War, waiting for the imminent bomb to hit. We pictured demolished cities, the Russian or North Korean or some other foreign government rejoicing in victory as America waved a burning white flag. We watched Lady Liberty crumble in our minds, we hid under our desks during drills and clasped our hands behind our necks.

My father always thought it would be Russia; he'd been raised on the original, home-grown Cold War fear. My mother never feared anything specifically, she only feared. She wore heavy lead vests over her clothes, internal Geiger counter in her head ticking ceaselessly. It got worse after I left home, their worry for me directed into the creation of a heavily stocked doomsday bunker. It was the last thread that kept their marriage together, probably. I pictured the two of them going to Sam's Club together and buying out the canned section, buying discount guns and stocking up on ammunition. They took out a second mortgage on the house to fund the creation of the bunker without my knowledge; the first time I came home to Martinez I found that they were living in the bunker already, a secondhand mattress lay sheetless on the floor, polyester blend blankets of greys and greens strewn haphazardly across the floor on summer nights too hot for coverings.

One particularly warm July night I tiptoed down into the bunker to grab the car keys and I found my mother asleep on the mattress, a light film of sweat on her brow, her chest barely rising with her soft and shallow breaths. In her sleep she didn't tremble or stutter; if she had nightmares it never showed. But she rarely slept. She'd stay up, listening to the radio and staring at the television at the same time. She waited, she waited, she waited.

But that night I found her asleep and I found her at peace. In my youth she'd always been a formidable presence, a woman of discipline. She'd felt enormous to me as a child, spread hand pinking my right cheek or my little boy ass. I'd always thought of her hardened grey eyes and my skin would start to sting, memory prickling my senses like it tends to do. But in the bunker, asleep, I realized just how tiny she was. I'm still not sure if the anxiety made her lose weight or if the sharp bones of her shoulders had always jutted out like that, but I hadn't felt frightened of bombs until I saw her face in repose. I saw the way it could be if the threat weren't always there, lingering like the smell of smoke.

And it was always there, the threat. Maybe I didn't feel it as strongly because I was so young, or because I knew so little of nuclear war or atomic bombs then. Even when I did feel the fear, in drills or in close-calls, in moments of sheer panic when an alert would flash on my phone or on the news: NUCLEAR MISSILE APPROACHING YOUR AREA. We'd become so accustomed to it that it felt like a permanent state of limbo. I stopped feeling like a bomb would ever come. Maybe the day I got too comfortable was the day it came.

No Bars and a Dead Battery

I guess what I'm trying to say is that for all we feared and prepared and hated, the foreigners we spat at and the guns that we bought and the bunkers we made, we never expected the bomb would be one of our own.

The first one, they said, was intentional. Southern California, around Needles, had been in lockdown for months at that point, the riots were only getting worse and the violence was out of control. Of course, I'll never really know what was happening in Needles at that point because I only know what I was told, and after the second bomb hit outside Los Angeles the truth became a word in the dictionary and nothing more. But they told us the anti-nuclear state created in Needles was a danger to the United States, that the leaders of the riots were leaking secrets to foreign governments and funded by various overseas corporations dedicated to the takedown of the American government. The first bomb, smaller but devastating still, decimated Needles and the residents. The exits were sealed off. No one could get out despite the thirty-minute warning.

They say there was a ring of still distinguishable bodies around the outskirts of the region. A fairy circle of death. Riot control, they said. Necessary evils, they said. Foreign threats, they said. Foreign had become a dirty word. Foreign was synonymous with danger. We feared the unknown so deeply that we didn't think to fear the known.

When Los Angeles got hit, they said it was an accident. They said it was a second strike on Needles gone astray. They said the epicenter was on the edge of South Central. Everyone else said it was no accident at all. I was in Koreatown at work when it hit; I remember thinking the flash was a kitchen explosion and then I woke up with my T-shirt seared into my chest, slivers of glass as big as toothpicks sticking up from my thigh. I couldn't hear a thing—I wouldn't be able to for a week. The walls of the restaurant were totaled, the remnants flaming beside me. Bodies were buried or burned beyond recognition. The new busboy, Ed, had taken over at the stove while I took the trash out. In the autopsy they would call his body "completely excoriated." But lying in the hospital three days later watching strangers vomit stringy black bile, I wondered if Ed wasn't the lucky one after all.

♦

light has always seemed just that without a weight or heft to accompany it but the heavy light that spreads this morning isn't like the light the girl has seen before not in fire or lightning or sunsets here is a light that hurts a light that takes her with it fourfive feet in the air it covers her eyes like an eyelid of white-purple and then she finds she's on the ground. the girl screams but she can't hear anything save the ringing in her ears and the white noise of what she swears is the blood rushing through her body searching for somewhere to go searching to escape herself.

she keeps her eyes shut tight while she breathes and she doesn't move until she can hear the wind again and the crashing of wood and brick and building from nearby. she opens an eye and finds she is still alone and her river sits glimmering in the midday sun. the sole of her foot that she splashed in the river is burned and her back is burned and she is burned but not in pain just thirsty, so thirsty, so thirsty.

she wants to cry and she wants her grandma but her throat aches dully and her sobs get caught on their way out her tongue a swelling snake trapping noise that seeks to escape so she breathes hard keeping track of the in-out in-out in-out while she starts to sit up. she feels very alone and very dizzy and she wonders who is safe and then she passes out to the noises of a burning city and its screams.

No Bars and a Dead Battery

◆

Vi had a bright red silk scarf wrapped around her head like a film star from the fifties throughout all of New Mexico. She had left the windows down from Santa Fe to Raton; the way the wind blew the scarf around her neck made her feel glamorous. I told her to roll them up when I saw the rainclouds.

Every time it rained I found it a miracle that it ran clear. If I closed my eyes during a storm the irradiated drops were black again, Mom gathering them up in bins and boiling them as if it'd help. She thought staying hydrated would save her, but the water swelled her stomach and her cells died fast and took her with them.

There was no rain, not yet, but I was still nervous. Vi was never nervous. She wasn't in Los Angeles then; she doesn't quite know. She'd only been down there the last few months of the year, helping pick up the pieces of a shattered city. I found her after the warnings came, at a bus stop waiting for a city line she didn't know wasn't coming. This time, I'd been prepared. The El Dorado contained the remnants of the shelter; it boasted a full gas tank ready for flight, enough iodine tablets to last me a lifetime, canned and dried fruits and vegetables. The building blocks for survival.

I'd been out of the hospital for a few weeks. I'd returned home to find my father's body next to my mother's on their bed. He'd shot himself beside her bloated body, the barely dried blood stains on the mattress suggesting it'd all happened not long before I'd been released. I wondered if I could've stopped it had I been there, but I knew it was no use wishing. It took me a bit to figure out what to do, but when the alerts started coming again I knew I couldn't stay in Los Angeles; I had to get out quick.

I picked Vi up on my way out of the city. I intended on dropping her once we hit the safe zone but she had something I desperately needed: a place to go. And so, Glenwood Springs became Eden in my mind.

Vi stayed quiet over Raton Pass, our only soundtrack the white noise of the car winding up through the mountain. She tapped her long nails on the middle console. The chipped red remnants of nail polish made her fingertips look bloody to me, and I waited for the crimson stain on the suede. I looked for blood everywhere now. Nearly all my shirts had specks of brown on them from the bloody noses I'd tried so hard to stop. We'd reach the border of Colorado soon and be one state closer to safety.

The first fat drops fell on the windshield and ran clear down the glass. I exhaled, thankful for a storm that felt safe. Of course, there was no such thing as a safe summer storm in the Southwest, and the tires on the El Dorado were dangerously lacking in tread. I pulled over at the top of Raton Pass. The rain hammered on the top of the car and I bristled as the tiny glass shards still embedded in my leg begin to shift. Every few months or so they stretch their bodies and cut into me again; I needed X-rays to even find them once and I couldn't bear to enter a hospital again. So instead I let the pieces scream throughout my body and I fall asleep fantasizing of morphine.

I envied the ease with which Vi was able to fall in and out of sleep, her arms loosely holding her knees into her chest. I wasn't quite an insomniac, but I was a light sleeper before the bomb and the dreams didn't help me stay asleep. I wouldn't call them nightmares, necessarily, but they weren't sweet dreams either. There was one dream where I was in the middle of my high school's auditorium, dipping a tea bag in an out of a Styrofoam cup listening to people read their own autopsy reports. Always someone I vaguely knew, a friend of a friend or an old coworker. When it came round to me I would wake up, like the dream was waiting for me to get my folder, my heart's weight, a list of the places where the glass ended up.

Then there were the dreams about the girl in Nagasaki. She was maybe six, seven. The dream was always in black and white, as if the 1940s happened that way. It was one of those dreams where I couldn't tell if I was watching her or if I was her—I didn't know which I preferred. In the dream, I felt the heat like my hand on a hot glass door; I could see it all so clearly but the pain was once-twice removed. Closed to me.

I crawled into the backseat to sleep in the fetal position, toes curled against the car door and the stained leather rubbing my cheek. I wondered what it'd take for just a few hours of dreamless sleep, just a few hours of darkness.

◆

when the girl comes to there are people beside her elbows and knees on the ground lapping up water from the river to soothe their burning throats and she watches them dizzily with her face screwed up like melpomene's mask. she whimpers for water and the woman closest to her glances at the girl with pity and guilt in her eyes and she stands nudging her companion to come with her but the other woman does not rise with this push but instead falls to the side and her hair spreads in the water like blackened tributaries from her head.

the girl has never seen a dead body and scoots away from this one in fear and the rocks scrape her raw hands. she leaves streaks of blood on the stones she moves over and clambers to the street dragging her leg behind her. she still wants to cry and she still wants her grandmother and she most of all wants to be queen of the river again and laughing and splashing along the banks.

on the street a woman she does not know picks her up and carries her with her. the girl pees in relief and the heat stings running down her legs and she begins to cry finally and the tears burn trails down her muddy face.

♦

When I woke up, the car was moving. Vi was driving with the windows closed, a rarity for her. I could tell she was unhappy because she was chewing the side of her mouth, her lips squeezed into a tight little O pushed towards the left side of her face. We hadn't been driving long, just barely past Pueblo and miles away from our destination. The phone was still dead on the passenger seat. I figured this was the source of her discontent; she'd been hoping to reach her brother in Glenwood Springs to ask about the safety of the roads up to his place. Once we got past Denver it'd be risky territory. The southernmost parts of Colorado were good and dried up but the further you got into the mountains the more the locals desperately clung to whatever water they had near them.

I knew Vi was frightened to pass through Denver and everything north of the city. She'd spent her childhood splashing in streams and waterfalls in that part of the state, before the land was purchased and the water went with it. She said now the cut banks were perpetually rusted with blood, that they never investigated the deaths of trespassers on owned water. Even driving through the wettest areas now would be a risk until we got to Glenwood Springs. Groups of water refugees were being robbed daily, hands bound and mouths gagged until their dry lips split and the only water left in their body leaked out in bloody foam. She said she couldn't imagine a worse way to die, but I remembered the blackened rain and my mother's waxy belly and I figured I'd rather dry up than drown.

Back in Algodones we'd sat on the banks of what was left of the Rio Grande there, digging little holes in the mud talking about the before, about how it'd been for us when we thought it was bad but didn't know the half of it. Vi had been less prepared than I had

No Bars and a Dead Battery

been; my parents' doomsday training, although seemingly silly, had almost prepared me for the worst. So when the worst did come, I came out the other end slightly better off than others. This meant I knew we'd have to stop in Denver whether Vi liked it or not, to gas up the car and charge the phone. There was no way we'd be able to get through the mountains without a full tank or a charged phone, so stopping in Denver was the only option. I told Vi this, and her mouth-chewing intensified. She must've known it was what I was going to say.

We didn't stop the car until Denver. It was only a couple hours, anyway, and I had to spend one of those convincing Vi to stop anyway. Union Station seemed our best bet—we'd heard that it'd been converted into a shelter of sorts. I hoped we'd be able to rest, charge the phone, and find somewhere to get gas there. The station had seen better days, as had everyone in it. Military blankets and blue tarps were draped over the seats, propped up with poles and chairs. It was clear the station was more of a hideout than a shelter now, and we found out from a couple in the corner that the relief aid had abandoned camp a few months ago for Calgary, leaving some canned food and water jugs along with blankets behind. I asked what was in Calgary—they said some sort of safety. It was better than here, it wasn't America.

That's when I saw her. The girl from my dream. No matter how many times I closed and opened my eyes and shook my head hard, it looked just like her. She was cleaner here, maybe a year older, but it was her. The same round stomach and cropped hair, the same shriveled foot, pocked with burns. She wasn't alone, but her mother had a hollowed look, one I recognized all too well from my own. Vi didn't want to bring them along. Didn't think there was room. But I knew they had to go.

I don't want to paint myself like a charitable type, like some sort of hero. I'm not a hero. I'm not a villain, either, but I've found that reality rarely sorts people into neat categories the way movies can. If we could boil it down to heroes and villains, well, I don't know why anyone would choose to be a hero when being a villain is so much easier. Anyway, I didn't do it for her. The girl, I mean. I did it for me. The dreams would never end if I didn't let her go instead.

The girl didn't really speak, but her mother and Vi fought all night. The mother figured Calgary was the best option, wanted to push clean through Colorado and Wyoming and Montana until they got into Canada safely. Vi disagreed, said Glenwood Springs was safe enough. I was inclined to agree with her, too, until we got the call.

Vi's brother was dead. He'd been dead for nearly a week, which is why we hadn't been able to reach him when the phone had still been alive. His wife, Vi's sister-in-law, was headed up to Calgary, too. She'd heard the same rumors, heard that they might find asylum in Canada, heard that there was clean water and a place to stay and a community to mourn with. I'd never seen Vi stay silent so long. She sat on the train bench the way she sat in the front seat, knees close and chin tucked in. She kept her sunglasses on but we all knew she was crying. She cried as if water were still free.

♦

in the hospital days later the girl holds her rock in her hand and whispers I am queen of the rivers, I am queen of the rivers to her roommate, a man of fifty with burns covering the left half of his body. Her grandmother has not been found.

she is dizzy all the time and her nurse changes every week as more people flood the hospitals with burns and wounds and radiation poisoning but they tell her she's going to be okay and everything will be okay and that it is all okay. she's not sure she believes them but she also has no choice and when the war is officially declared lost they stop telling her it's going to be okay as often and when

No Bars and a Dead Battery

the American soldiers come they stop saying it at all.

when she is released the rain still runs black, and the water still isn't safe to drink. when she is released she goes home with the wife of the man with the burns and she uses a cane. she sits by the river and does not put her feet in. she watches the water closely holding the stone tight in her hand, and notes how the river keeps on.

♦

Vi didn't want to leave me behind, even though I'd given her no reason to cling to me so hard. I guess it was the vague false comfort of familiarity that kept her so drawn to me. She'd been a person with a place to go before and now she too found herself unmoored like I'd been. Well, I was still unmoored too, but staying at Union Station until I could get to Calgary too felt like a kind of solid ground I hadn't felt in a long time. Vi would send word when they reached Canada, try and see if she could get me up there. I watched them as they left the station with the other groups of travelers heading north, the girl holding hands with both her mother and Vi.

They made their way through the crowd, and back to the El Dorado. And as they approached it, a crow flew directly over their heads and landed on the hood and then looked at them. They stood some distance away and watched the crow watching them. Another crow flew directly overhead and landed beside it. The first crow squawked and then both flew away. They watched the crows disappear, looked at each other, and then got in the El Dorado. Only one way to go this time, with five bars and full battery.

ABOUT THE AUTHORS

Deborah Boller was born in Los Angeles in 1949. Eight years later, her family moved to the Wind River Indian Reservation (culture shock, anyone?), where her father was enrolled with the Eastern Shoshones. She graduated from the University of Wyoming with a Master's Degree in English. She has taught domestically and overseas and worked in (too many) offices. Her story "Forgiveness" took fourth place in Writer's Digest Short Short Story Competition, and her story "Lessons" was shortlisted in Still Life, a collection of stories for the Rubery Book Award. She lives in Oakland, California, with her husband.

Colin Brezicki, retired teacher and theatre director, has written two novels—*A Case for Dr. Palindrome* and *All That Remains,* which were published by Michael Terence UK. His short fiction has won awards, and essays have appeared in *The Globe and Mail* (Canada) and *The Kappan* (US). He lives in Niagara-on-the-Lake, Ontario, and writes to stay sane. You can learn more about Colin at his website: colinbrezicki.com.

Shannen Camp lives in Utah and is the author of 13 published books. When she's not writing novels or playing video games, she's writing articles for SVG.com or working on her YouTube channel Persephone Plasmids. She keeps busy with her husband, baby girl, and miniature schnauzer named Hemingway.

Shelby Carleton loves writing, video games, and writing for and about video games. She looks forward to all the adventures to come with her best friend in the entire world, and a German Shepherd named Commander.

Savannah Cordova grew up in the San Francisco Bay Area and recently moved to London to pursue a career in publishing. She currently works for Reedsy, a platform that connects self-publishing authors with freelancers online. Savannah lives in a cozy flat with her partner and many books.

Helen Montague Foster, a retired psychiatrist, lives, writes, hikes, and canoes in Virginia with her husband, Thomas C. Foster. Her poems have appeared in JAMA, the Pharos, Rattle, Hektoen International, Tuck Magazine, and Big River Poetry Review.

Peter Gikandi has designed art for video games in Canada for, like, ever. He wrote and illustrated *Big Lizard, Hidden Spider* for iBooks, which some people like. He's working on a book about a little troll, her imaginary dog, and the Pope. Peter was born and raised in Kenya and now bounces around Asia with a plastic bonsai tree, a cat plushy, and a few geckos which come and go.

Dianne Gorveatt is a semi-retired technical writer. This is her first hackathon, and she thought it was great fun.

David Greenson grew up in Oakland, California, before it was hip, and then spent twenty-seven years in New York City, many of them living in an intentional community and working as a grassroots political organizer. He now lives in Asheville, North Carolina, in spite of his disinterest in beer, dogs, and hiking. He is studying to be an interfaith chaplain, and writes every day, although he's not sure yet to what purpose.

Julie Hall grew up on various Air Force bases across the U.S. and one in Japan. After retiring from the position of military brat she attended college, raised a child and had a career in computer programming in Las Vegas, Nevada. She has been published in the *Rio Review* and *The Jellyfish Review*. Julie currently resides in Austin, Texas with her partner, musician Christine Cochrane.

Hannah Jackson is a writer and artist from Newark, New Jersey. She is currently developing the final draft of her first full-length novel, but pauses every once in the while to challenge herself with short stories such as "Puppy Feet". Visit her online at hatchedbyhannah.com
Luke Kingsbury is a Minnesota native and a graduate of the University of Iowa.

Jon Krampner's short stories and flash fiction have appeared, or are about to appear, in Across the Margin, *Eunoia Review, Eclipse, Page & Spine* and *Collective Unrest*. He lives in Los Angeles and is sarcastic in three language. You can contact him at: bluewombat134@startmail.com

Juliana Lamy is a Haitian-American undergraduate student History & Literature in Massachusetts. She loves art in all of its forms, and she's particularly interested in how it speaks to which emotions take precedence for people.

Casey Lefante earned her MFA from the Creative Writing Workshop at the University of New Orleans. Her work has appeared in various journals and anthologies, including *Third Coast, Zone 3, Monday Nights*, and, most recently, *Mud Season Review*. She lives, writes, and teaches in New Orleans.

Tucker Lieberman is the author of *Painting Dragons: What Storytellers Need to Know About Writing Eunuch Villains*. His prose is in *Cerurove*, his photography is in *Barren*, and his poems are in *Neologism, Defenestration*, and *Snakeskin*. He and the science fiction writer Arturo Serrano live in Bogotá, Colombia.

Amr Mekki lives on the border of boredom and peace, where his works keep him fixed in unfulfillable longing for something the world does not manufacture. He is one of those unfortunate insomniacs who have found themselves too soon, and who have too much time on their hands as a result. When asked what he has done with his life, he prefers to say nothing.

Jonathan Moyer has been writing fiction and nonfiction since his childhood. This is his first fiction publication, and he is currently writing a fantasy young adult novel. In his spare time, Jonathan loves to read science-fiction and fantasy, cook, and play tabletop games. He also blogs at jonathanmoyerwrites.com. Currently, Jonathan lives and travels in Southeast Asia with his girlfriend and their German shepherd.

Syche Phillips lives in the San Francisco Bay Area, where she works at a professional theater company, and writes fiction, plays, and creative nonfiction. Her work has been published recently in *Burnt Pine Magazine* ("Trying," Pushcart Prize nomination), *Synaesthesia Magazine*, *Cease Cows*, and more. Her short plays, including "Swipe," "Tumble Dry Low," and "The Certain Bride," have been performed around the Bay. She lives two blocks from the beach with her husband and two young kids. You can learn more about Syche at her website: sychela.com

Andrea Poniers began writing fiction more than 20 years ago, in a class at a community college. Her short stories have been published in print and online, including *Mountain Gazette*, *Trivia: Feminist Voices*, and *Laura Journal: The Women's West in Short Fiction*. In 2018, her first novel won first place in the Rocky Mountain Fiction Writers' Colorado Gold Contest for unpublished manuscripts (mainstream category). Andrea moved to Boulder, Colorado, from Michigan in 1997.

Christopher Schiller. By day Christopher Schiller is an entertainment attorney focused on helping writers and filmmakers get films made. This gives him lots of ideas of what to write about in his regular column at ScriptMag.com on the business and legal aspects of filmmaking called Legally Speaking, It Depends. At night, of course he's working on writing his own scripts and stories hoping to someday find enough time to market them as vigorously as he does his clients' works. But you know what they say about the shoes of the cobbler...

Jeff Somers (www.jeffreysomers.com) began writing by court order as an attempt to steer his creative impulses away from engineering genetic grotesqueries. His feeble memory makes every day a joyous adventure of discovery and adventure even as it destroys personal relationships, and his weakness for adorable furry creatures leaves him with many cats. He has published nine novels, and over thirty short stories, including "Ringing the Changes," which was selected for inclusion in *Best American*

Mystery Stories 2006. He lives in Hoboken with his wife, The Duchess, and their cats. He considers pants optional.

Lorain Urban was a runner up in Kenyon Review's 2017 short fiction contest, a finalist in Indiana Review's 2017 1/2 K Contest and in Narrative's 2018 Winter Story Contest. She was also the recipient of Calyx Press's 2016 Margarita Donnelly Prize for Prose Writing. Her work has appeared in the *Kenyon Review*, *CALYX Journal*, *Tahoma Literary Review* and *Midwest Review*, which nominated her short story for a Pushcart. She made her first road trip from Ohio to California in the back seat of an aquamarine Pontiac Catalina.

Ansley Vreeland is currently a college freshman studying international relations in New York. She hopes to eventually become a UN ambassador while writing screenplays and novels on the side.

Rick Allen Wilson's plays and musicals have been produced in the U.S., Canada, and England, and his prose has appeared in *Screendoor Review* and *Primetime Cape Cod*. A dedicated advocate for LGBT youth, he is on the board of directors for Long Island Crisis Center, which is home to Pride for Youth, Long Island's oldest LGBT service organization. A Harvard Club distinguished educator, Rick teaches A.P. Literature and Composition, creative writing, and creative nonfiction at The Wheatley School in Old Westbury, New York, and makes his home on Long Island with his partner and their four dogs. (rickallenwilson.com)

Callie Zucker is an emerging writer currently pursuing a Creative Writing major at Colorado College. She splits her time between Colorado and California. Her work can be seen in Furrow magazine and Longlong journal, and is forthcoming in several other literary magazines.

CPSIA information can be obtained
at www.ICGtesting.com
Printed in the USA
FSHW021823280719
60479FS